I0838394

# SANCTUM

---

## BLACKWATER PACK #1

### HANNAH MCBRIDE

Copyright © 2020 by Hannah McBride

SANCTUM
Blackwater Pack Series, Book 1
Original Publication Date: August 2020



✿ Created with Vellum

*For Aria, the girl who inspired me to live my dreams.*
*…Can I keep you?*

# AUTHOR'S NOTE

This book is not intended for readers under the age of 17.

This book contains dark themes (including scenes with bullying, violence, and sexual assault) that may be mature or triggering for some readers.

Side note: if you're related to me … maybe don't read this? Or anything I publish? Please?

# SANCTUM

*Blackwater Pack #1*

By: Hannah McBride

# 1

My brain barely registered the hand between my shoulder blades a second before the shove sent me careening face-first into my open locker. I slapped a palm against the frame to brace myself before I ate a mouthful of rusty metal.

Gritting my teeth, I straightened myself and ignored the laughter behind me.

My leg jerked as a foot connected with the backpack between my feet, but it barely budged. I habitually stood on the shoulder straps when changing books at my locker for this very reason.

I had almost survived the eight-minute class change break without incident, which might have been a new record for me.

Now I only needed to keep that going for another two hours until school ended for the day. And then walk home without incident.

Yeah, I didn't like my odds either.

I was thinking of routes through the pack compound that would give me the best chances when the speakers overhead crackled and popped with an incoming announcement. Startled out of my thoughts, I whirled around and nearly slipped on the frayed nylon strap I was standing on.

The obnoxious noises of conversations around me died down almost at once. Eyes flickered up to the speakers that hung over chipped beige lockers, as if expecting them to sprout a screen for everyone to watch. Sneakers came to a stop with sharp squeaks that bounced off the plain beige cinder block walls. The teachers even came out of their classrooms to stand in the doorways.

Long Mesa only had one school for all grades, but even still, there weren't even a hundred people total in the building. The high school side of the small building had thirteen students and three teachers. The only time we all mixed was during class changes since there was one corridor that held all the lockers.

Usually if a message needed to be relayed to everyone, a messenger went from class to class. The announcement speakers were hardly ever used, so the break in normalcy stunned everyone into silence.

Several people near me gave each other quizzical looks, but they all turned to sneers and glares when they saw me watching.

With a soft sigh, I turned back to my locker and remembered that no amount of curiosity was worth unintentionally challenging a pack member who would be all-too-happy to slap me back into my bottom of the pack status.

Invisibility was my ally in my daily game of survival.

I kept my eyes down, taking out my chemistry book and shutting my locker. The metallic ringing of the door shutting caused several sets of eyes to fall to me again, and I flinched. The disgust and the annoyance were glaringly obvious in their stares. The exact same looks I had seen my entire life from the exact same people.

So much for trying to be invisible.

"Jesus, Skye," a scornful voice hissed.

I glanced up though a curtain of mahogany hair to see Lilly Peters, a girl three years younger than me, staring with open hostility. Her tiny nose wrinkled in disgust. "Be a little fucking louder, dumb bitch." With a loud huff, she spun away from me.

I bit the inside of my cheek to keep from replying—it wouldn't end well if I did. I had learned years ago that any response gave them more fuel. Hell, sometimes even my silence fed the flames of hate amongst my pack. There was no winning; there was only surviving.

I had managed to endure the first seven weeks of my senior year without too much trouble other than the usual being shoved into lockers, food dumped on me in the cafeteria, and random objects thrown in the path to literally trip me up. And considering even before that, I spent every day in our pack focusing on just getting through the day, I was doing a pretty decent job of it.

Most of the time.

Being an unofficial pack omega had a lot of drawbacks, the biggest of which was filling the role of pack punching-bag. Sometimes physical, always emotional.

"Attention, faculty and students," the static voice began, the tone grave and somber despite the accompanying high-pitched shriek as the speaker figured out how to work. Any type of mid-day announcement was an anomaly, and everyone seemed to tense as they realized this wasn't going to be a happy announcement. The air crackled with nervous energy.

"It is with deep regret we have just learned that our beloved Alpha, Alpha Warren, has passed."

A wave of stunned gasps rose up in the hallway, accompanied by a couple of screams and several loud sobs. The news was a shocking turn that even surprised me.

Alpha Warren had ruled the Long Mesa pack—*my* pack—for decades. He was actually *beloved* by very few and feared by most, but he was still our Alpha. Our leader. Losing him was a blow to the pack.

It was no secret he had been unwell lately, but the idea of such a formidable man and wolf dying was a foreign concept. He had been Alpha of the Long Mesa pack for nearly thirty years, taking over after his father had passed.

Several sets of eyes drifted over to me and the whispers started up again.

Alpha Warren had been my grandfather. Not that he ever accepted me as any sort of relation to him, which honestly was fine by me. He had disowned my mother before I was born, and he hadn't been in my life in any type of grandfather role ever.

I couldn't stop myself from letting my gaze land down the hall on my cousin, Bella.

The granddaughter he had doted on at every turn.

Her usually radiant mocha skin had gone positively ashen, her big green eyes wide with grief. Several people bowed their heads in her direction, giving their support and deference to the pack princess.

"Move."

A loud male voice snapped the command and people scattered to do his bidding as he stalked through the small crowd, shouldering teachers, and students away as he moved until he was by Bella.

Arms reached out and surrounded her as she was pulled against her boyfriend and future mate, Cassian. His large hand covered the back of her head, pulling her head to his broad chest. Her fingers curled into the cotton of his t-shirt, fisting around the material as a keening sob whined out of her throat.

Bella was younger than me by eighteen months, but even if the age gap didn't separate us, there was no way we would ever be allowed to play together or hang out.

She was now the granddaughter of the former Alpha, daughter of the current Alpha, and potential mate to the future Alpha.

I was the daughter of the pack traitor.

We didn't mix.

Cassian was one of the largest shifters in the school, standing well over six feet. He had classic All-American good looks with blue eyes and short blond hair. I could see why other females liked to throw themselves at him, despite his almost taken status. He was strong, aggressive, and dominant.

And he was the person who lived to make my life a living hell.

Even as he comforted Bella, his eyes moved down the hall, finding me with perfect accuracy and laser intensity. He smoothed a hand down Bella's back as he smiled cruelly at me. After a beat, Bella pulled away and whispered something to him, drawing his attention back to her and off of me.

Cassian nodded and kissed her cheek quickly, releasing her from his grip. He watched her walk away and turn the corner before looking back at me. With deliberate slowness, he reached down and adjusted himself in his jeans. Everyone was still whispering about the Alpha and missed his little show, but it didn't matter.

That crude gesture was only meant for me.

I shuddered and turned away quickly, pulse racing and fear churning in my gut. I took a second to settle my racing heart, knowing that heightened shifter senses would catch my panic and draw attention like a heat seeking missile on a volcano.

"Classes are canceled for the remainder of the week to allow a proper mourning period," the announcement continued. "Classes will resume as normal next week." There was a short pop as the announcement ended, and everyone seemed to hesitate. Then movement exploded at once as students slammed lockers and started for the exit.

Not even the death of the pack Alpha could stop teenage shifters from the allure of an impromptu five-day-weekend.

I spun the dial on my locker to shove my chem book back inside since I wouldn't be needing it now. Even after I had deposited the book, I kept my head in my locker, rooting around to kill time until the halls emptied. It was easier to sneak out of the school unnoticed when the halls were empty of people.

I had just closed the door when a massive shoulder body checked me into the locker. I didn't have time to brace my hands this time before my full face hit the metal. The taste of copper flooded my mouth, and I instinctively licked my lips, not surprised when I tasted blood there.

My wolf surged to life inside of me so fast it made me dizzy. My blood popped and fizzed with anger, my wolf pawing at my insides for release.

I squeezed my eyes shut, trying to reason with the animal that lived inside of me.

The temptation to shift was strong, the temptation to fight even stronger. I could feel my own wolf rippling at the surface.

I sucked in a sharp breath through my teeth, trying to control the violent reaction of a beast I shared a body with.

While most shifters had a balanced harmony with their wolf, mine always seemed elusive and temperamental. She roared to the foreground when she wanted on occasion, but mostly laid dormant. The act of shifting on command was a struggle for me, so I rarely did it unless mandated by the seasonal pack runs. Even then I was the last one who forced her wolf into this shift, and I was usually exhausted from the fight before the run even began.

My wolf and I didn't get along. All I knew was she chose shitty times to try and assert herself. Like now. My mother told me it was due to my omega status—the stronger the position in the pack, the stronger the shifter bond, supposedly.

I wasn't the strongest in the pack, something my pack mates loved to remind me of all too frequently.

Lately, though, she seemed a little more inclined to surface, which only caused me to panic. The last thing I needed was to shift suddenly when I was cornered. It would be an automatic challenge to whatever wolf I reacted to.

Judging by the scent of the person behind me, shifting right now would be a death sentence.

The hall was almost completely empty now except for the press of a body crowding behind me. Hands came up on either side of my head, caging me in. I pulled in a deep breath, trying not to panic as I was blocked from all sides. All my muscles tensed, bracing for whatever was about to happen next.

"Skye, Skye, Skye," he whispered softly, his tone light and menacing all at once. I felt my hair move as he dropped his head to bury it in my neck, inhaling deeply. "For such a dirty little whore, you smell amazing."

Snickers and chuckles rose up from behind me. I didn't have to look to know it was Cassian at my back, flanked by his best friends and betas, Marc, and Preston. I could picture the matching looks of lusting disgust that always reflected on their beautiful, cruel faces.

The Unholy Trinity is what the other wolves called them, mostly joking and adopting the 'boys will be boys' narrative that gave them a pass to do whatever they wanted to whoever they chose.

I tried to slow my breathing, urging my wolf to calm as she struggled to the surface.

*Fight. Hurt. Kill.*

Her demands pressed against every cell of my being and I glanced down, horrified, as my hands started to shake with the urge to shift. Now was not the time for her to decide to be a suicidal badass.

If I shifted, these three would tear me apart. Literally. And no one would stop them.

It was no secret that Cassian was third in line to be the next pack Alpha. It was why he was promised to be mated to my cousin. Females couldn't be alphas, and Cassian had proven over the years to be the most dominant, if not sadistic, male in our generation.

*Second in line*, I reminded myself.

With the death of Alpha Warren, Cassian was now one Alpha away from ruling the Long Mesa pack. He already ruled our school, and even in the compound we lived in. Most of the wolves gave him and his friends a wide berth; they were vicious and volatile.

If I gave him any reason to attack, he would. There would be no reprisal or punishment for hurting, or hell, even killing me. I was an omega—completely expendable to the pack, even if I was a female in a world where female shifters were a dying commodity.

Preston came around Cassian's right side, leaning his shoulder against the bank of lockers. His gray eyes locked with mine until I forced myself to look down, to submit.

His hand lifted, a finger tracing the curve of my cheek before his hand came around my throat. He barely applied any pressure, but the threat was there.

Preston Loomis was the batshit to Cassian's crazy. There was something deeply disturbed about this guy, and it terrified me to the core. He was literally capable of losing it at any given moment.

He punched someone unconscious during lunch last year for chewing too loudly.

"Soon, Skye. So soon," he reminded me with a wicked smile. His hand moved to my hair, curling a lock in his fist. He rested his head against the lockers, his dark hair falling over one eye.

Marc laughed behind his friends, bouncing on his feet as he watched the exchange with a slightly unhinged look of his own.

The problem with Marc is he was all brawn and no brain. Simple math definitely eluded him, but he was the biggest of the three. His neck was the size of my thigh, his fists as big as my head.

Preston hummed under his breath, the back of his hand intentionally brushing against my chest as he released my hair. "Soon you'll be ours," he murmured. "I can't fucking wait."

Cassian laughed, his breath hot against my neck. "If the new Alpha has any say, we may not have to wait much longer." His hands dropped from the lockers and circled my waist, pulling me flush against him.

My blood turned to ice, freezing my body, as I felt the hard ridge of his erection pressing against the small of my back as he rubbed against me. One hand slid under my shirt, cupping my breast. Preston's eyes tracked his assault with an excited gleam.

*No. No. No.*

My wolf was roaring inside of me now, and for the first time in a long time, I didn't want to control her.

I *wouldn't* control her.

I would pick death over whatever hell these boys had in store for me.

"Cass!" The shrill, pointed voice of my cousin had Cassian dropping his hands from my waist and taking a step back from me. Preston slid off the locker, falling into step behind him. Marc rounded out the group, his dark eyes raking up and down my body until I wrapped my arms around my torso with a shiver.

I glanced down the hall, torn between gratitude and fear at Bella's appearance in the hall. Her arms were crossed under her chest, her green eyes void of all emotion as she only looked at Cassian.

"Hey, sweetheart," Cassian greeted, as if nothing were wrong. Probably because to him, nothing was.

Bella wasn't his mate yet. He didn't owe her his allegiance despite being promised to her, plus she was almost two years younger than he was. But something told me even after their mate bond was secured and they were adults, I would still be seeing Cassian and his friends regularly.

My stomach cramped painfully at the thought.

"My father wants us at the house. He's planning to name his council before sunset," she informed him, arching a perfect brow. Her gaze slowly slid to me, her lip curling up slightly as she regarded me coolly. "He wants you and your mother at the house at seven."

Her father, my uncle, would most certainly be the new Alpha, barring any challenges. But no one would challenge him. Linden Markham had been groomed to be the next Alpha for the last eighteen years. He had spent nearly two decades making sure the pack knew who was boss.

There was no question in the pack who was in charge now that Alpha Warren was dead. His son would take over the Long Mesa pack.

There weren't enough prayers in the world to save any of us now.

I watched Cassian, Preston, and Marc walk down the hall and out the door with Bella, leaving me alone in the hallway. None of them spared the omega another glance. I wasn't worth the effort.

A shiver skittered down my spine as I realized my uncle being Alpha might be far worse for me than my grandfather. Grandfather had treated my mother and I with apathetic indifference, barely acknowledging our existence.

But it was no secret Uncle Linden despised my mother, and by extension, me. Being hated by the new Alpha was the worst thing that could happen to any wolf—let alone an omega.

I waited several more minutes before heading out in the hot New Mexico sunlight. My feet started moving on muscle memory towards the house, every step drawing me closer to the Alpha who now controlled my fate.

## 2

My mom once told me years ago that it wasn't always like this. That once upon a time, she was my grandfather's golden girl. Adalynne Markham was Warren Markham's oldest child, and it was no secret my grandfather adored her. Honestly, she was loved and adored by the entire pack.

Female shifters were rare, and Adalynne had been the first Markham daughter born in several generations. She wasn't just a female, she was a *Markham* female. Which meant whoever my grandfather chose as her mate would help forge a strong alliance for the Long Mesa pack.

Females weren't just daughters and life bringers in the shifter world; they were currency. The ultimate bargaining chip for power in the shifter world where males outnumbered females three-to-one and birth rates were at an all-time low. A female, especially one with the pedigree of the Markham line, was almost priceless.

When she was a few years older than me, an alliance was planned between our pack and the Stone Valley pack of Arizona. The alliance would strengthen the borders between our packs. My mother was to marry the second son of their Alpha. It was to be the perfect marriage of two strong packs, giving both sides the most territory in the southern part of the continent. The guy my mom was engaged to was going to eventually be the Alpha of the Long Mesa pack with my uncle poised to be his beta.

That all changed when, at the mandatory physical a week prior to the wedding, the doctor discovered my mother was pregnant.

The alliance exploded into a war, and my mother, refusing to name my father, went from Alpha's prized possession to omega in a matter of hours. My grandfather had banished her to the omega section of the compound— a corner piece of land with a single, crumbling house that flooded anytime a storm rolled in from the desert. He never spoke to her again, turning all his focus to grooming his son, my mother's bitter younger brother, into being the future Alpha.

Uncle Linden had always resented my mother for the love their father gave her growing up. While my grandfather never spoke to Mom again, my uncle was happy to remind her of how far she had fallen as frequently and as vindictively as he could. He even took her best friend as his mate, forcing Zara to sever all ties with my mother after the mating ceremony was complete.

My mother's downfall was the greatest stain on the Markham line. Our family had been Alphas of the Long Mesa pack for over one hundred and sixty-five years. After my mother's indiscretion, no less than eleven wolves challenged my grandfather for Alpha. He defeated every one of them, but it left the pack fractured for years.

Even now, there were still those who hated the

Markham rule of the pack. While my grandfather and uncle proved to be formidable opponents, my mother was an omega and completely at their mercy. And grievances against the untouchable males in our line were settled with my mom.

Looking back, I didn't see how bad it was through the eyes of a child. It wasn't until I was ten and came home to my mother sobbing, bloody and broken and naked on her bed, that I realized exactly how low being an omega in the pack was.

The omega house stopped being my home that day, and I finally noticed it for the prison it truly was. My only saving grace was my place in the pack wouldn't be official until I reached the age of majority—eighteen.

But that day was only a few months away now.

I wound around the final turn of the dirt road that led to the omega house. The dust storms hadn't been kind to it. No repairs were ever done unless the omegas themselves did them, which wasn't often. Omegas focused on survival, not homemaking.

The two-story house had four steps leading up to the weather beaten front door, one of which was missing a board. Part of the porch ceiling had rotted away, leaving a gaping hole to the cloudless blue sky above. The windows were grimy, and the once white house was now a muddy tan. All the sinks inside it leaked, constantly dripping. The floors creaked and groaned, and the wallpaper was peeling in chunks.

It was as broken and run down as the shifters that lived inside it.

There were four omegas, counting me, and we all lived together.

My mother and I lived in the smallest bedroom, tucked back in the far corner of the house. The room barely fit the double bed we shared and a dresser, but it had a large window that looked out to the mountains in the distance and a tiny private en-suite bathroom attached.

Maisie and Shane were the other two omegas who lived with us.

I had barely made it to the first step when the front door swung open, and a large male shifter came stumbling out. His gaze dropped to me, his smile leering as he finished zipping his pants. I stepped back off the step, moving to let him pass as I bit the inside of my cheek.

"Hey there, Skye-baby," he greeted. Allan Loomis, Preston's father, was a common face around the omega house. I used to wonder if his mate ever guessed how often he was over here, but then one day I saw Norma Loomis going into the male omega's bedroom.

She and her husband were both at the omega house at least once a week.

My stomach churned, twisting into a knot that left me nauseous as Allan stopped in front of me. He glanced back at the house, winking at me as if we were old friends. It made my skin crawl. I wanted to bleach every part of me his eyes lingered on.

"Your momma's upstairs, but you might want to give her a minute. She needs to clean up a bit." He laughed loudly, hooking his thumbs in his jeans. He hadn't bothered with a shirt today. He reeked of sweat and sex. A combination of smells that constantly lingered in the house, no matter how many surfaces I wiped down or windows I opened.

Granted, shifters had enhanced smelling along with several other fun bonuses like a faster healing rate and sharper eyesight, but I was almost positive a regular human could smell this stench from a mile away.

I fought the urge to curl my hands into fists, keeping

them loose by my sides even as his eyes kept inspecting every inch of me, lingering in places that made me cringe. It was easy to see where Preston got his cruel streak from.

I skirted around him, almost making it to the top step when his heavy hand landed firmly on my shoulder.

"Tell your mom I'll see her later, will ya?" He squeezed my shoulder, hard enough to bruise, for a beat before letting go and continuing on his way as if nothing were wrong. He even fucking hummed under his breath as he walked.

*Kill.*

I pressed a hand to my chest, rubbing hard against my sternum. As if that would keep my wolf calm. Her temper seemed to be flaring more and more frequently.

I hated it. My emotions were already fragmented and jagged, exposed nerves being stomped on daily. The last thing I needed was a psycho wolf adding to the chaos in my head.

I closed the door behind me as I went in, the silence around me speaking volumes. I glanced around the open foyer, my gaze landing on Maisie, the other female omega. She was curled up on the sunken end of the couch in the living room. A worn book was held in her shaking fingers, her eyes squeezed shut. I didn't have to wonder why— Allan seemed to always have this effect on her. Usually it was her he came to see. It had only been in the last few weeks his attention turned to my mother.

Maisie was only a few years older than me, but the bruises under her eyes from worry and no sleep seemed to age her a decade. She was too thin, her clothes always hanging off her.

We were all on the malnourished side of skinny for that matter.

Maisie had come to the Long Mesa pack a year earlier from a pack in Central America. It was surprising that she was sent to the omega house, but then I learned the doctor in our pack determined she was sterile and incapable of bearing a child. Therefore, she was useless to the pack as a traditional mate, and since my mother and Shane were the only omegas in the pack, she was sent to the omega house.

It was a cruel twist of fate that she escaped an abusive mate in her last pack and ended up seeking sanctuary in hell. She never had a choice to leave once she stepped inside the walls of the compound.

Not that it would have mattered if they found out she could bear a child, because shifters seldom had more than one child. She would have been married off to whichever male offered my grandfather the highest price. Either way, she was completely screwed in every sense.

Several males offered my grandfather to take her as their mate, but my grandfather thought she would be a better addition servicing the pack as a whole.

The two years before Maisie came, my mother was the only female in the omega house. I'm still not sure how she survived, even with the ability shifters had to heal faster than regular humans. The pack definitely preferred to have at least two available omega females.

"Mais," I started softly, taking a step in her direction.

She whimpered, the book slipping from her fingers and she curled her arms around her knees. She started rocking as deep sobs ripped from her throat.

"Fuck," I muttered, dropping my backpack and crossing the old floorboards to kneel in front of her. I tentatively rested a hand on her ankle. She jumped a mile, a keening wail slipping through her clenched teeth.

"Hey, Maisie," I cajoled gently, stroking the exposed

skin of her ankle with my thumb, trying to calm her. "It's okay. He's gone. I promise."

Her eyes opened, luminous and wet. A tear spilled down her tan skin. "Gone?" She hiccupped the word, her accent thicker the more emotional she got. "*Ya no está aquí?*"

"Yeah, he's gone," I replied softly.

She gasped, reaching down to clutch my hand. Her jagged nails dug into my skin. "Your mother."

I swallowed around the growing lump in my throat. My eyes lifted to the water damaged ceiling. "I know."

She looked around the room and I could see her pulse fluttering at her throat. Her eyes turned to me. "He said ... Alpha Warren? He is dead?"

I nodded slowly, standing up. "Yeah." I wiped my palms on my worn jeans.

I didn't think it was possible for eyes to get any bigger. "Your uncle ... He is to be Alpha." She stumbled over the words, her entire frame shuddering.

I nodded again. The lump got bigger as the fear swelled in my chest.

"*Dios Mío.*"

"I need to talk to my mom," I said, stepping back and heading for the stairs. I glanced back at Maisie as I went. She was curled in a ball, crying silently, her eyes staring unseeingly at the wall.

I made it to the landing and headed down the hallway to our bedroom, avoiding the broken floorboard that was ready to give any minute.

The air on the second floor was always hotter, stickier. The house had no air conditioning, so all the heat collected throughout the day and lingered on the second floor. I paused at the threshold of our room, not sure what I would find when I pushed the door open. Curling my hands into fists, I nudged the cracked door fully open with my shoulder.

The smell of Allan was stronger in here, sharp and pungent despite the open window. I started breathing through my mouth before I gagged. Looking around, I could hear the shower running in the bathroom.

My gaze dropped to the bed. The sheets had been stripped from, thrown in a careless ball in the corner beside the dresser. With a sigh, I went to the closet and lifted out a different set of sheets from the top shelf. I was just stretching the fitted sheet across the mattress when the shower turned off, and I was tucking in the flat sheet when the door opened.

My mother emerged in a threadbare towel amongst a cloud of steam. I could see her skin was pink from the temperature of the water. Fresh bruises marked her arms and legs, adding to the road map of scars that she had spent the last seventeen years acquiring. She winced as she stepped into the room before seeing me. Once she did, she quickly schooled her features and even offered me a small smile.

Years and a hard life hadn't dulled the beauty of Adalynne Markham. Her dark blond hair hung halfway down her back. Her frame was still thin, but still had feminine curves that even the edge of starvation couldn't diminish. She had the same green eyes I did.

Markham green was what the pack called them. A vibrant shade of emerald that looked as supernatural as we were.

She paused in the room, clutching her towel a bit tighter to her chest. "You're home."

I nodded quickly, pulling the quilt over the bed. I straightened and eyed her critically, trying to see any other signs of damage. "Are you okay?"

"Fine," she answered sharply, her voice tight. She turned to pull jeans and a shirt out of a drawer, and I saw the range of scars from her neck down her legs.

But it was the omega brand on her shoulder blade that always caught my attention. The puckered pink scar on her shoulder was nearly two decades old, the silhouette of the mesa with a ring around it branding her as part of the Long Mesa pack and her omega status. All the omegas bore the same mark.

I could feel my own shoulder ache, already anticipating the branding iron I knew would be my eighteenth birthday gift from the pack.

*Soon, Skye.*

That stupid reminder whispered against my ear, oily and insidious. Two words nearly brought me to my knees. As a child, my birthdays were somewhat happy days. The omegas at the house banded together to make me feel special in their own ways. Homemade gifts and singing filled the day, making me feel somewhat normal for a few hours.

I was the only child to ever live in the omega house— omegas weren't declared until they reached the age of majority dictated by Pack Law, which was at eighteen. My mother's screw up and my bastard status was all it took for me to get a permanent residence inside the omega house, despite being an infant in a world where females were a rarity.

Maybe with a different pack, a different Alpha, I might have climbed out of the omega status eventually. I might have even been adopted by another couple who wanted a baby of their own. Upon my birth, my grandparents and uncle had made sure the entire pack knew I was just as damaged as my mother. Hell, maybe even more so since she never told anyone who my father was. All anyone knew was that he wasn't part of the Long Mesa pack. So not only was I a bastard, but I was the bastard of an outsider and a pack betrayer.

The more birthdays that ticked by, the less the cause for celebration. The omegas were my family, my pack, but they knew what my eighteenth birthday would bring. My last birthday, only my mother acknowledged the day with a quiet "Happy birthday".

That was fine by me. I was happy to forget the day, too.

"I take it you heard about Alpha Warren," my mother said softly, ignoring my question. She never referred to him as my grandfather or her father. Always Alpha Warren.

"Yeah," I said slowly, sitting on the bed. I tucked my legs under me and looked away as she pulled on her clothes. "Bella said her father wants us at the main house tonight. At seven."

She stiffened and then sighed deeply, toweling off her wet hair. "I know. Allan told—" Her gaze dropped to me and I could see the worry there, stark and consuming. "Skye ... Maybe you should stay here. I'll go and speak with Linden alone."

"No way," I shot back sharply. No way in hell was I letting her go in there to face her psychotic brother solo.

She moved gingerly to the bed and sank down beside me, reaching out to clasp my hands in hers. "Honey, there have been talks, rumors." She hesitated, biting her lower lip between two rows of even, white teeth. Her small, button nose wrinkled with worry, and it struck me again how beautiful my mother was.

Whatever she was about to say was bad. She was practically vibrating with nervous energy. I steeled myself for the killing blow.

"There's talk that Linden will remove the age of majority law for omegas."

All the air rushed from my lungs. I wasn't prepared for that.

Not that.

Anything but *that*.

I scrambled to form a response as my mind raced. "But the council has to agree ..."

Her eyes slid shut, a single tear escaping as she shook her head. I heard her breath hitch on a cry. "Linden will announce his own council. He won't wait to make sure they're in place. The sooner he and the council are finalized, the less likely a challenge will be issued. The men he chooses are ones who agree with him. *His* friends. Ones who frequent the omega house."

Men like Allan Loomis, she meant. Men who had no issues treating omegas like nothing more than whores.

That was the entire purpose of the omega house—a brothel for the wolves of Long Mesa. A place where anything went. Where upper pack members could act out their most twisted fantasies without anyone to stop them.

Omegas were nothing. Less than nothing. We received whatever scraps of food and clothing the rest of the pack didn't want, which meant often going to bed hungry or swallowing down stale and expired food. All of the clothes I had were ones not even the local donation center could use. Even my bras and underwear were second hand. The only things we received brand new were generic bars of soap, bottles of shampoo, and laundry detergent.

Because no one liked a whore that actually smelled like a whore.

Her hands tightened against mine. "Maybe if I talk to Linden—"

I shook my head slowly. "It won't make a difference." I

remembered then what Cassian told me in the hall. He said they might not have to wait much longer. He knew. They all knew.

All that needed to happen was for my grandfather to die so there would be no one standing in the way of Linden Markham.

**3**

———————

THE ALPHA HOUSE WAS IN THE HEART OF THE COMPOUND. It was a simple clay brick structure, slightly larger than the other adobe style homes around it. Two stories high, the Alpha family lived there. The Alpha's council convened there. The surrounding homes were smaller versions, housing the pack betas and upper pack members. Mid and lower pack members shared communal housing a few streets over, near the school.

This was the house my mother grew up in. The house that was supposed to be where she got married and raised a family.

Now she was forced to ring the bell and wait for someone to answer to grant her access.

Long Mesa was a moderately sized compound and pack, and was surrounded by a ten-foot-high concrete fence. There was a single access road that was guarded at all times.

It was home to the two hundred and forty-three wolves of the pack and included the school, a grocery store, a doctor's office, and a gas station. Mostly it was land. Acres upon acres of land that butted up against the Cerrowa Mesa. Plenty of space for a pack of wolves to roam and live.

According to local lore from the towns fringing the area, the compound was a cult.

I wasn't entirely sure that they were wrong.

It was important that normals—humans—not know of us. Wolves kept to themselves, only interacting with the outside world when absolutely necessary. As an omega, I had never left the compound and probably never would.

The front door swung open, revealing a beautiful shifter with dark skin, soft brown eyes, and long dark hair gathered into a low ponytail. She wore a black dress and a large heirloom diamond ring on her left hand.

"Hello, Zara." My mother greeted her former best friend quietly.

Zara smiled gently, first at my mother, then at me. "Hi, Addie," she greeted gently, glancing over her shoulder to make sure her husband wasn't within earshot before meeting my mother's gaze. Her lips turned into a frown. "It's not good."

My mother frowned and took a sharp breath in, leaning forward a bit. "Is there any chance?"

Zara's lips pressed together in a thin line. "I don't know. Linden doesn't say much to me. You know how—"

"Zara? Who's at the door?" My uncle appeared behind her. His cold green eyes assessing us both as he settled his hands on his mate's shoulders. Zara winced as his hold tightened, but she didn't say a word of protest.

"Why didn't you tell me my sister and her ... offspring were here?" His tone sounded casual enough, but there was no mistaking the dark undercurrent of his words. Or the way his knuckles were turning white from the grip he had on his wife.

"We just arrived, Linden," my mother said, her eyes downcast. A grimace flashed across her face for a second, the skin around her lips pulling taut.

"Come in," he invited, stepping back and pulling Zara with him. She stumbled a bit, but he held her tightly and she didn't fall.

My mother and I crossed the threshold, first her and then me. I had been inside this house one other time, right before my grandmother had passed away. My grandfather and uncle had been away at the annual pack Summit meeting in Utah, and grandmother requested my mother come and bring me.

I sat there, five years old, as she told my mother I never should have existed. That I was an abomination to the Long Mesa pack. And perhaps, if my mother ridded the pack of my existence, a daily reminder of Mom's betrayal, my grandfather would remove her from the omega house.

My mom swept me up into her arms and stormed out the door. She shook the entire walk home, barely able to control her rage. She handed me off to another omega as soon as the house was in sight and immediately shifted, her wolf snarling as she changed. She tore away from the house at a dead run and didn't return until the next day.

Three weeks later, my grandmother died of a sudden heart attack. Ironic that the woman my mom called heartless was killed by that very organ.

The main level of the house was mostly open, boasting a massive kitchen with dual built-in refrigerators and two sets of double ovens. The granite countertops gleamed under the recessed lights. Trays of food were laid out on the island in the center. Beyond that was a large seating area with roughly seven shifters, including Bella, Cassian, and Allan and Norma. I recognized Cassian's father, Patrick, sitting in a leather recliner. A large stone fireplace loomed as the focal point—fairly useless in New Mexico, but it helped with the rustic opulence of the house. Several large leather couches and chairs were around the room, shifters lounging casually on them.

I knew all of the shifters in this room, and every fiber of my being wanted to run away. Most of them frequented the omega house on a regular basis. All of them were cruel and heartless. Cassian's mother might have been sitting in this room if his father hadn't killed her a few years earlier.

Apparently, his dinner wasn't ready one night he came home early and he lost it. But she had already provided him a child and couldn't have another, so there were no real repercussions for her death.

He had been one of the males who made an offer for Maisie to be his mate when she arrived.

After quickly glancing around the room, I dropped my gaze, reminding myself to be the picture of a submissive wolf. The last thing my mother or I needed was to challenge a room full of dominant, sadistic shifters.

Linden whispered something in Zara's ear and she stiffened, her breath catching. Her eyes flashed up to meet Bella.

"Come with me, Bella," she commanded in a shaky voice. Her husband's hands dropped from her shoulders. She couldn't help but roll her shoulders slightly, trying to ease the ache from his hold.

Bella frowned, setting down the coffee cup she was drinking from. She had changed from her clothes at school earlier, now wearing a black dress with a bell skirt. Her dark hair was curled around her slim shoulders. "I thought we were discussing pack matters." Her gaze slid to her father.

He smiled indulgently. "Go with your mother, Bella."

Her jaw dropped. "But Daddy—"

"Now." The word came out final and firm. An Alpha command. Every wolf in the room shifted, deferring to the Alpha.

With a sigh, Bella got to her feet and stalked past us, following her mother out of the room without sparing a glance at us.

Linden waited until Bella and Zara had left the room before walking past my mother and I to claim the wing-back armchair in front of the fireplace. We weren't offered a seat, and he seemed content to watch us, a darkly amused smile pulling at his lips.

It was a waiting game. He knew my mother couldn't speak unless spoken to. The longer we stood there, the more anxious we both became. This was a power play, plain and simple. I could feel my wolf stirring in my chest, anxious and angry. She didn't like this any more than I did.

"How are you, sister?" Linden asked nonchalantly, as if asking about the weather.

My mother's head lifted, but she kept her eyes down in deference. "I'm well."

Smiling, Linden leaned forward. "You seemed to be walking with a limp. Are you injured? Should I call the doctor?"

Allan laughed behind him, which set off a series of giggles and snorts amongst the shifters in the room. Cassian grinned broadly, his gaze never leaving me.

"I'm fine," she whispered. I could feel the humiliation rolling off of her in waves. Of the shifters now facing us, I knew at least six of them had been to see her personally at the house.

"Very well," Linden agreed. "I asked you here because we are considering making some changes to the omega house."

My mother looked to me before dropping her gaze

again. "May my daughter be excused? She is not yet an omega and doesn't need to be concerned with the details of such things."

He chuckled darkly in response and I already knew what he was going to say before he spoke. "No. This directly involves her." He got to his feet, pacing to the window. "My council and I have been talking about removing the rule regarding the age of majority for omegas."

"No!" The word flew out of my mother's mouth, sharp and desperate.

And completely out of turn.

It only took seconds for Linden to cross the room, grabbing her by the throat and forcing her to her knees. "No?" he mocked, enraged. "I am the Alpha. You do not tell me, no, whore."

She gasped for air and something in me started to fracture. She was only protecting me. Now all I wanted—and my wolf wanted—was to protect her.

*Hurt. Kill. Hurt. Kill. Hurt. Kill.*

The words chanted in my head so loud I almost missed what my uncle said next.

"We're not removing the age law," he hissed, finally releasing her with a shove. She fell down to her hands, gasping for air and coughing loudly, gagging as she tried to suck in air. I caught the damp spots of wood beneath her as tears fell.

"Thank you," she whispered, broken but relieved. Her shoulders trembled as Linden circled her, his boots thumping against the hardwood and coming dangerously close to crushing her fingers.

"As you know," he continued easily, as if he hadn't just almost killed her, "we seem to be having an issue with the younger wolves. Seems the teens can't quite seem to get a grasp on their emotions. Adolescence is a volatile time. Hormones running wild. Young wolves make stupid, foolish choices. You of all people know this, Adalynne."

Linden crossed to the other side of the room. "I've spoken at length with Cassian and several other teens and, with my council, I believe we have worked out a solution to help channel their baser impulses." He went back to his chair, crossing his ankle over a knee, looking every bit the king on the throne.

"Instead of removing the age of majority, we're lowering it to sixteen. This also means that wolves can begin utilizing the omega house at the age of sixteen." His gaze landed firmly on me. "And omegas will now be defined as such any time after their sixteenth birthday."

A sob tore from my mother's throat and she physically collapsed against the floor, pressing her forehead to the gleaming wood. Everything stopped and sped up at the same time for me, the floor falling from beneath me as Cassian grinned at me, his eyes glittering with awful promises of what the future held.

Linden steepled his fingers, blinking once before settling his cold gaze on me. "Starting tomorrow, Skye is officially an omega and will fulfill her obligations as such to the pack."

# 4

---

We didn't speak the entire walk home. Neither of us knew what to say out loud, so we stayed locked in our own turbulent thoughts. I could feel my mother's fear radiating off of her in waves. I felt the same way—furious, frustrated, and absolutely fucking terrified.

I felt Cassian's eyes on me the entire way home. Felt the promise that lurked in his gaze as he watched me leave, knowing he would likely see me in the morning.

A new omega was typically branded and broken in by the Alpha. Even my uncle wasn't depraved enough to do the deed, but I knew beyond a shadow of a doubt he happily handed the task off to Cassian. His eyes told me as much as we left, sparkling blue pools of joy. Like a kid on Christmas morning.

The worst part, I remembered once upon a time actually liking Cassian. I remembered the boy who snuck me pieces of his lunch in kindergarten when I came in with a piece of bread and an apple that was this side of rotting. He was the kid who gave me my first pack of fruit snacks. I had no idea such sugary, gummy goodness existed.

We were innocent and naive. Not tainted by the problems of our pack and our parents. We sat by each other in class and at lunch for almost the entire year. He always played with me on the playground.

Cassian was my friend until the last day of school when, at kindergarten graduation, his parents saw their precious son sitting next to the bastard. I'll never forget the look on Patrick Clarke's face as he yanked Cassian up by the arm hard enough to dislocate the boy's shoulder. As Cassian screamed, his father slapped him and told him to stay away from the "whore's daughter".

The next time I saw Cassian, he led the crusade of taunts against me. By the time high school rolled around, the boy who shared his lunches with me was gone and a vicious bully had taken over. He made it his mission in life to break me.

And now he finally would.

The second the house came into view, a cold sweat broke out on my forehead. My hands clenched into fists, my heart slamming against my ribs. Blood roared in my ears, and, for once, I wanted to shift. My wolf and I felt the same fear, the same rage. Instead of fighting her as I had all day, I almost surrendered to her demands.

I wanted the feeling of my bones shattering and reforming, my fingers curving into claws. I craved the ability to sprint as far away from this house as I could. All I wanted was to run. To fight. To destroy something the way my insides were breaking apart.

The way I knew tomorrow my body would be violated and ripped apart.

A strong shudder rippled down my spine. Picking up my pace, I jogged the last few steps to the house. I threw open the door, and froze, completely horrified by the sight in front of me.

I had seen a lot in the omega house and heard even more. And while there were whispers of this being done, seeing it was beyond anything my mind could have ever imagined. Worse than any nightmare that snaked into my head.

Maisie was on the floor, on her hands and knees, naked and sobbing as a large, muddy brown wolf snarled and snapped, backing her into a corner.

I had heard rumors that this sometimes happened—that pack members would shift to use omegas in human form, or order omegas to shift to take their wolf in human form. It was an abomination and the most humiliating thing for any shifter.

But seeing it firsthand? Seeing Maisie violated in the absolute worst way possible—sweet, quiet Maisie—was too much.

The snarl tore from my throat even as I heard my mother scream my name. My wolf surged to the front, and I let the shift happen. My body was hurtling through the air, slamming into the brown wolf. I was vaguely aware of my mother pulling Maisie away as the brown wolf rounded on me, growling low in his throat.

My nose caught the scent of blood, and I didn't have to see Maisie to know it was coming from her. Once shifted, our wolves were bigger than normal wolves. Human bodies weren't meant to withstand that type of brutality. He could have killed her.

The brown wolf lunged and I feinted to the right, dropping my shoulder so low it was almost to the floor. I reacted on pure instinct, letting my wolf dictate our movements for the first time ever. His jaws snapped by my ear and my head twisted, my teeth locking onto his throat. The taste of blood, warm and hot, filled my mouth and trickled down my throat.

A low whine vibrated through him and his legs slipped out from under him as he tried to submit, his wolf knowing I'd gone for a killing blow. I felt my jaw lock tighter and jerked my head away, ripping out a large chunk of his throat as my mother shouted at me again.

The entire fight was over within seconds, but I was breathing hard, trembling with adrenaline as if I had just gone ten rounds with an upper pack member.

My wolf was happy, sated. She had come out on top.

We weren't the omega in this fight.

The brown wolf lay at my feet, motionless and lifeless. His blood seeped across the floorboards, staining the white fur of my paws.

I blinked over at my mother and Maisie. My mother seemed stunned, but there was a sad resignation in her eyes. She didn't blame me for what I'd done. If she had entered first, it might have been her covered in blood.

Maisie was gone. She simply stared at the brown wolf, not blinking and eyes vacant. Blood ran down her back and sides, deep gouges from the wolf's claws. The blood was pooling around her, but she didn't move.

I caught my reflection in the hall mirror. Crimson stained the front of my white coat, my muzzle practically black it was so saturated. My mother had the same snow-white fur that I did, but while she was pure white, I had a single black star on my forehead. Most Markham wolves were white or gray—another signature of our line along with our green eyes. None of them had any black. The patch of onyx fur on my forehead was simply another way to tell I was different.

Long Mesa had no black wolves. White, gray, brown, and red. But none were black. The mark on my head was yet another mark against me.

"Skye." My mother's voice was firm. I swung my head

around to see her standing now, Maisie still unmoving at her feet.

"Skye," she started again, her tone low and controlled, "you need to shift back. Now."

My wolf whined against the order, but I forced myself to take control, shifting back to my human body. I blinked hard and looked up at my mother once the shift back was complete, crouched and naked on the floor, blood slick on my skin. I had changed so fast that there hadn't been time to shed my clothes, so they exploded at the seams when my wolf form tore through them.

Mom exhaled a shaky breath, looking from the dead wolf to me. "Go upstairs. You need to get cleaned off."

I looked down at the wolf, the realization that I had killed a member of the pack sinking in. Not only had I killed a fellow wolf, but now I could see the wolf in question was Dane Loomis, Preston's older half-brother and Allan's oldest son.

Fuck.

I had killed a council member's son.

"Skye!" My mom snapped. "Shower. Now."

My mouth opened but no sound came out. I looked at Maisie. "But—"

Footsteps thudded on the stairs and the male omega, Shane, came downstairs. His eyes widened, so big I would probably find it funny if the situation weren't so grave. His eyes moved to me. "Shit, Skye. What did you do?"

"He was hurting Maisie," I tried to explain weakly, standing up. God, blood was all over me. I could feel it matting the ends of my hair, drying on my skin.

"Christ." He ran a hand over his jaw and looked at my mom. "What do we do?"

"Skye needs to go take a shower," she said, her eyes still on me. "We'll clean this up."

"We?" Shane echoed weakly.

"We," she replied. Maybe it was residual from when she used to be higher up in the pack, but the omegas deferred to her. My mother was the alpha of the omega house, and ignoring her wasn't something they would, or could, do.

She looked at me again, her face softening slightly. "Go clean up, honey. Hurry."

I took the stairs two at a time until I hit the bathroom. I didn't wait for the water to heat up, a process that usually took several minutes on a good day. I stepped into the cold spray, letting the water start to wash away the blood. I kept my eyes shut tight, scouring my nails across my face. I could feel the blood caking under my nails as I tried to clean my face.

I shampooed my hair no less than three times, standing under the spray long after the water ran from pink to clear. The water went from scalding back to frigid as I emptied the tank of all hot water. Finally, I twisted the knobs. They squeaked in protest, the pipes rattling on the other side of the chipped tile as the water turned off.

I was still shaking and it took several tries to secure the towel with a knot around my chest. Stepping to the small mirror over the sink, I barely recognized the girl standing in front of it. My already brown hair was practically black from the water, my green eyes were huge on my face. My usual tanned complexion was pale. I bit my lower lip between my teeth, worrying the skin until I tasted my own blood.

All I wanted was to crawl into bed and forget today happened.

I had just finished brushing through my wet tangles when the bathroom door opened and my mom appeared. She set a pair of jeans and a black shirt on the counter before closing the door and leaning against it, her eyes blazing with intensity.

"I need you to listen to me," she said quietly, so softly I had to strain to hear her. "We're leaving."

My heart thudded in my chest, my breath catching.

"Get dressed. Be as quiet as possible."

"Mom, what the hell is going on?" I whispered, already reaching for my underwear.

"I already packed a bag for you. We need to get to the other side of the compound in the next ten minutes. Hurry."

I started pulling on my jeans, the heavy material sticking to my damp legs. I struggled to pull them on. "We can't leave. The wall, the guards——"

She held up a hand, cutting me off. Moving forward, she framed my face in her hands, touching her forehead to mine. "Trust me, baby. We have to go now if we're getting out, and we have to leave tonight. Before they find the body ... before *tomorrow*."

Before I became an omega.

That was assuming the pack let me live for killing another member.

I nodded and stepped back before pulling my shirt over my head. If we ran, we might make it across the mile and a half to the other side of the compound, but even that would be pushing it. I started braiding my hair quickly as my mom opened the door. She glanced around, lifting a backpack before handing me my school one.

Judging by the weight, it no longer contained the textbooks I brought home from school hours earlier.

I went to the nightstand and grabbed the book I had been reading, shoving it into the front pocket before I pulled the pack onto my shoulders. I held my breath as she eased the door open, looking around the hallway. She reached back, threading our fingers and tugging me behind her.

I pulled her to a stop outside the door. "What about Maisie and Shane?"

Her mouth flattened. "I wish they could come with us, but there isn't time."

"But Mom—"

She pressed a shaking hand to my lips. "Skye, you are my priority. Now be as quiet as possible. Maisie and Shane can't know we're leaving. It's safer for them to be in the dark if Linden asks questions."

Years spent in the omega house had its benefits. We knew every floorboard that creaked, every nail that protested under our weight. Moving swiftly, we avoided them, going down the staircase and heading for the back exit in the kitchen. The concrete stairs leading out to the backyard had long since crumbled so we jumped the two feet to the ground. Without speaking, we broke into a dead sprint.

My heart pounded, muscles burning as I worked them harder than ever before. We raced across the hard dirt, keeping to the shadows, avoiding the glare of the floodlights stationed around the compound. Everything was quiet and muted, the air hummed with the sounds of cicadas. The swollen full moon hung low in the sky, casting a soft silver light across the ground at our feet.

After nearly ten minutes of running, being sure to stay off the roads and paths of the compound, we came to a set of boulders and rocks near the western gate entrance. Staying downwind of the wolves on patrol, my mother pulled me down into a crouch.

"Come on," she murmured under her breath, her eyes sweeping the area. A few agonizing seconds later, headlights turned around the bend of the road leading to the compound. The car stopped several yards in front of the gate and the driver got out.

Zara.

"*Run*," my mom ordered, pulling me with her. We circled around behind the rocks, running silently across the ground to the back of the SUV. She lifted the hatch, only allowing us a small amount of room to slip into the empty back.

The SUV reeked. Something strong and floral that almost made me sneeze as my mom covered us with a blanket. She gingerly pulled the hatch closed, locking it. I held my breath, waiting for the guards to notice, but Zara had them under control.

"Alpha Linden didn't mention you would be leaving the compound tonight," the first guard argued.

"My husband," she snapped, her voice firm and level, "is planning the funeral of his father. I'm heading into town to pick up a few things I thought might comfort him and our daughter. And last time I checked, I was the Alpha's mate. Don't forget who you're speaking to."

I could practically feel both guards submitting.

"Yes, ma'am," the second voice whispered, contrite. "May we do anything to assist you?"

"Get out of my way," she retorted coldly, turning back to the car. Her feet crunched across the gravel of the road and she got in the car, slamming the door. The perfumed scent was even stronger now. She must have bathed in the most potent fragrance she could find, but it definitely did the trick—no way would they be able to scent us under the haze of that stench.

A minute later, we were driving through the gates of the compound for the first time in my life. I held my breath until I was dizzy, and my mom reminded me to breathe.

"You two okay?" Zara called over her shoulder, maneuvering a turn that had us both sliding into the left side of the car.

"Is anyone following us?" Mom asked, her voice muffled under the flannel blanket.

"No," Zara answered. I heard the engine rev as she stepped on the gas. She took another sharp turn, drove for a few minutes and then stopped the car.

Mom threw the blanket off us as Zara got out to open the hatch. Once we climbed out, I realized we were standing in a parking lot. There were four cars on the lot and two light posts, only one of which wasn't working. The yellow light cast a sickly pallor across our skin.

Mom threw her arms around Zara. "Come with us."

Zara hugged her back for a moment before shaking her head and pulling away. "I can't leave Bella. You remember what I told you? Where you're going?"

Mom nodded, reaching for me and pulling me under her arm.

"How did you know?" I asked in a rush, my mind still reeling that I was outside the compound for the first time in my life. "How did you know what happened?"

Zara sighed. "I came by to see how your mother was after meeting with Linden. I saw Maisie and ... Your mom explained what happened. We agreed the safest thing for both of you is to get you out of the compound. This was our only shot, while Linden was still meeting with the council and planning the funeral." She looked at me, reaching up to cradle my cheek in her hand. "I'm so sorry, Skye. I'm sorry for so much."

I looked from my mom to my aunt. "So, what happens now?" I looked around the dark parking lot, expecting to see headlights piercing the dark as my uncle came after us.

Zara glanced at her watch. "I need to go before Linden realizes what happened. Here." She pressed a set of keys and a rolled wad of cash into my mom's hands. "This is all I could get without Linden noticing. The car is clean—I bought it a few years ago in case I needed to grab Bella and get out. It can't be traced. The cash should be enough to get you to Washington."

"I'll pay you back," my mom promised, tucking the money into her pocket.

Zara waved her off. "No, you won't. You're my best friend, Addie. I can't believe how long you stayed. It never should have gone this far. Linden is out of control." Her gaze shot to me, her mouth fixed in a grim line. "I can't believe he's doing this. The Long Mesa pack is falling apart. There's so much more going on you don't know about."

"Then come with us," Mom urged, grabbing her hand.

"Bella won't leave her father, and I can't leave her any more than you could leave Skye." She pulled a phone from her pocket, handing it to my mom. "The only number programmed in here is my sister's. When you get to her pack in Washington, Zoe will let me know. If you run into trouble, she can help. She's expecting you in a couple of days. If you stick to the back roads, you should make it in about two days. There are a few motels on the way you can stay at. Use the cash. There are wigs in the trunk of the car you can use for disguises."

*Disguises?*

The realization that we really were using the getaway meant for her and my cousin was sinking in. She was worried enough about my uncle to feel the need to go off the grid and hide their appearances to escape him.

Mom took the phone, looking at it with uncertainty. "I don't want to start a pack war. Zoe is taking a big risk helping us."

"Zoe loves you, and she hates Linden. She says the best

thing she ever did was leave and marry into another pack. She says their Alpha, Gabriel, is a good man. He'll protect you." Zara smirked. "Besides, I think he hates Linden more than Zoe does. Apparently they had a major disagreement years ago."

"I remember," Mom said softly. "They were teens. Linden was furious for months but wouldn't say what had happened."

"Gabriel will protect you," Zara assured her. "Blackwater is a large pack, one of the biggest in the country. And we both know that Linden is in no position to launch a pack war. Truthfully, if things don't start turning around soon, I don't know how much longer the pack will last. We're losing members and gaining too many loners that don't want to follow the rules. Pack members aren't being held accountable—what happened tonight to Maisie is proof of that."

Jesus, *Maisie*.

"Mom, we left Maisie. And Shane!" Panic twisted in my gut all over. We left the other omegas completely unprotected.

Mom sighed, stroking my hair. "I told you we couldn't get everyone out and save you," she said.

I recoiled. My life wasn't any more important than theirs. I opened my mouth to argue, but Mom stopped me.

Her gaze caught mine and held. "You are my daughter, Skye. I never should have let it go this far with Linden. I should have figured out another way to get you away from that pack a long time ago."

"You need to get on the road. Linden will know you're gone soon. You need to be firmly inside Blackwater territory before he catches up. He can't touch you once you're there." Zara moved back towards her car.

"I love you, Z," my mom said, reaching out for one last hug.

"I love you, too, Addie," Zara whispered, hugging her tightly. She let go and looked at me for a second before drawing me into her arms.

"You did the right thing tonight, Skye," she told me quietly, her hands smoothing across my back. "You're stronger than you know. Long Mesa was never the pack for you. You're going to find your place. Promise me you'll take care of your mother."

"I promise," I swore, looking over her shoulder at my mom. I hesitated for a second and looked at Zara. "You need to get Bella away from Cassian. He's ... he's a monster."

Zara clenched her jaw and looked away. "I'm well aware of what Cassian is. But Bella thinks it's an honor to wed the future Alpha. She's so consumed with what her father wants and expects ... I've tried. She won't listen to me."

I hugged Zara once more, wishing there were a way she could come with us.

She let me go and got into her car, turning it around and heading back towards the compound.

Mom walked over and wrapped her arms around me. "Ready to go?"

"Absolutely."

**5**

———

I was completely mesmerized by the scenery as we drove. Watching the landscape change from brown and dirt to green and lush was a crazy dichotomy. The further north we got, the cooler the air became and the more vivid the colors grew. By the time we crossed into the Washington state limits, I felt like a little kid. Every mile brought new wonders. My current favorite was the mountains looming in the distance, their snowy white peaks hiding amongst clouds.

Mom hummed along to a song on the radio I had never heard, her fingers drumming on the steering wheel. Her blonde hair was pulled in a ponytail and bounced as she bobbed her head to the beat. She had smiled and laughed more the closer we drove to Washington.

I was loving our road trip. If it were up to me, we would never make it to Blackwater and just drive around seeing all the places I never knew existed.

"Are we staying in another motel tonight?" I asked, hoping the answer was yes. The first motel we came to, my mom had sighed and apologized to me as soon as we

44

opened the door. I wasn't sure why she was apologizing—I launched myself at one of the two beds with a laugh.

My entire life I had shared a tiny bed with her. For the first time, I had my own bed to sprawl out in.

"No," she replied. "I called Zoe when you were in the bathroom at the diner. We should be in Blackwater territory in the next half hour or so. She's coming to meet us at the border to introduce us to Gabriel."

I twisted my hands together in my lap, picking at a fraying hole in my jeans. "You think they'll let us stay?"

She glanced over at me, reaching over to place a hand over mine and squeezing. "Yeah, baby. Gabriel is a good man from what Zara and Zoe say."

I took a deep breath, steeling myself to ask the question that had been plaguing me since we left New Mexico. "Do you think we'll be omegas here, too?"

She paused. "I don't know."

I swallowed and nodded, looking out the window.

"Hey." She waited until I turned back to look at her. "Skye, what happened in Long Mesa. You need to understand that I won't let that happen here. I wouldn't bring you to another pack to let you be turned into a ..."

"Whore?" I supplied softly after she had trailed off.

Her jaw clenched. "Yeah."

"I don't blame you for what happened," I told her gently. "It wasn't your fault, Mom."

She blinked, tears sliding down her cheeks. "Actually, sweetheart, that was all on me. I never should have stayed. I should have taken you and left. Shit, I should have left when I was still pregnant with you. I'll never forgive myself for letting you grow up the way you did. Seeing the things you did ..." Her hands clenched hard around the steering wheel. "That's on me. I'm so sorry I failed you. I should have tried harder."

"You didn't fail me. You got me out."

"Not soon enough," she said bitterly.

"Why did you stay?" I had always wondered why, but never asked her. I would always tell myself there was no other option, but I knew pack members sometimes left. Some, like Zoe, married into a new pack. Others left for different reasons. Rarely was a pack member forbidden from leaving.

"After … After I moved into the omega house, I was constantly guarded. I think they knew I would try to run, and that would defeat the goal of punishing me. Keeping me present in the pack showed that no one was above their laws."

"They're assholes," I muttered.

A smirk twisted her lips and disappeared just as fast as she slid into another memory. "Then after you were born, I was constantly afraid they would take you from me if I stepped out of line."

She sighed again, her shoulders slumping as she took the ramp to get off the highway. "Even still, I actually tried once to get us out. Right after we saw your grandmother. Do you remember that?"

"Hard to forget when your grandmother tells your mom she should kill you," I replied tersely. "Even if I was only five."

"Stupid, old bitch," Mom muttered, stopping at a red light. "I shifted and took off."

"I remember. You didn't come back until the next day." I frowned, remembering how worried I was. That was the only night we had ever spent apart.

"I knew there was a hole in the northern corner of the fence. A grate for drainage." She smiled wryly, her mind caught on a memory. "I used it a few times when I was a teenager. Zara, Zoe and I would leave and go into town. Go dancing."

"And get knocked up?" I teased.

She sighed, and for a second, I regretted my offhanded comment. "Yeah. That, too." She paused and then shook her shoulders. "Anyway, I realized after seeing my grandmother that you had no shot in the Long Mesa pack. I knew I earned my omega status. I betrayed the pack, and I could own up to my mistakes. But, usually, there are ways for an omega to work their way up in the pack ranks. I knew you would never be allowed to be part of the higher ranks of the pack, but assumed that as you got older, you would be able to establish your own place in the hierarchy. Especially since you're a female."

I snorted. "Yeah. That was never gonna happen."

She nodded. "Which I realized after talking to that old shrew. They would always keep you down. And even if you got pregnant in the omega house, odds are they would take your child or sentence it to the exact same fate. So, I decided to get you out. I was trying to figure it out, watching the guard shifts at night when Linden caught me."

I sucked in a sharp breath.

"He told me in no uncertain terms that you and I were pack property. If they ever caught me trying to escape— with or without you—that the guards had orders to shoot you on sight or rip you apart. Whichever they wanted. The next day, the drain was filled with cement and closed off for good. It's part of the reason why the eastern part of the compound floods when there's a storm."

She looked at me again briefly. "I wasn't going to risk your life. I knew we had at least a decade to figure something else out. I was working with Zara on a plan to get you out before you turned eighteen."

"Get us out, you mean," I corrected.

"No, honey. Just you. I didn't think I could get us both out. Besides, all that has ever mattered is keeping you safe."

I growled. "And leave yourself to that psycho? To those assholes? Great freaking plan, Mom."

"Hey!" She snapped, her green eyes flashed with irritation. "You don't get to judge. I was doing everything I could to keep you alive."

"What about my father?" I demanded.

Her eyes flashed with warning. "We aren't discussing your father." Her knuckles turned white on the steering wheel.

*Shocker.*

"We never discuss my father," I snapped back. I should have stopped then. I knew I should stop, but this had been on my mind for seventeen years. "Why didn't you go to him for help?"

Her teeth clenched together. "It wasn't possible."

"And now? Why don't we go to him for help?" I pressed.

"It's still not an option." Her nostrils flared and she kept her eyes glued to the road in front. "Drop the subject, Skye. It's not open for debate."

"Why? Why not?" I kept pushing.

"He doesn't even know you exist!" She finally yelled. The silence that followed filled the car like a physical being.

"He doesn't know I *exist?*" I parroted back hollowly.

She shut her eyes briefly, huffing. "No. And believe me when I say it's for the best. Long Mesa is nothing compared to the world your father came from. It was … something that could never happen. I was an idiot to even think it could work. That night was a stupid moment of weakness from a silly girl who thought she knew love could conquer all."

"A stupid moment of weakness," I repeated softly, turning to stare out the windshield. "So, I was just the result of your stupid moment of weakness?"

"Yes," she replied vehemently. "You were the only good thing that came out of that night. The only good thing in my entire life. I would endure a million more stupid moments of weakness if it meant I got to be your mother. I might regret a lot of things where your father was concerned, but you need to really hear this, Skye: I have never for a *second* regretted having you."

I blinked back tears, not realizing how much I needed to hear that. The raw emotion in her voice created a fissure in my heart. I knew she loved me. I had always known that.

"Do I hate that I pulled you into this twisted world? Absolutely. But I will never, ever be sorry that I had you. That I was able to raise you. I'm just so damn sorry that you've had to endure all you have these last seventeen years." She swiped at her eyes with her fingers. "You're my world, baby girl. I love you."

I sniffled and glanced at her. "I love you more."

A small smile played on her lips as she turned the car down a side road. "I love you most."

She took another turn onto a dirt road and drove a few minutes more before she stopped the car. I looked up to find a woman and a man standing several feet away beside a gray sedan in the middle of the clearing in front of us. They straightened as they saw us.

"We're here," Mom said, turning off the engine and giving me an encouraging look.

*Here goes nothing.*

Stepping out of the car and into the lush woods of Washington was mind blowing. My senses were immediately assaulted by new sounds and scents. I felt my wolf perk up. She wanted to explore this new landscape, wanted the feel of the soft earth under her paws. It was so different from the arid, dry place we had left behind. It was still mid-September, but here was a chaotic world of colors, cool breezes, and waning sunlight.

I closed the door and met Mom's gaze across the roof of the car. She smiled, her eyes full of hope. Taking a deep breath, I walked around the front of the car with her, falling into step slightly behind her to approach the man and woman ahead of us.

The woman's face broke into a beautiful smile as we approached, her teeth bright white against her dark skin. She looked fit and strong, her head high and shoulders set back. There was a striking confidence to her I couldn't help but be drawn to even dressed in jeans and a flowing blouse. "Welcome, friends," she greeted. She seemed to hesitate for a second, but then reached forward with a laugh to hug my mother.

"It's good to see you, Zo," my mom said, hugging her tightly.

Zoe pulled back and glanced at me. Her hazel eyes ran up and down me as she shook her head slowly. "My God, is this Skye?"

Mom turned and smiled at me. The pride in her gaze made something flutter in my chest. "Yes. A little different from the last time you saw her, huh?"

Zoe's eyes sparkled as she lifted her brows. "The last time I saw her, she was naked and dipping her crackers in desert sand before eating them."

Mom's head dropped back and she laughed loudly. "I forgot she used to do that."

"I used to eat ... sand?" I blinked, stunned. That didn't sound appetizing at all.

Zoe winked. "It was a phase. Didn't last long." She reached her hand back to the man with her. His green eyes were shining as he watched her. He laced their fingers before raising her hand to kiss the tips of her fingers. "This is Michael, my mate. He's part of the Blackwater council and one of Gabriel's betas."

Immediately I dropped my eyes and shifted back a few steps to show deference. Years of constantly submitting had been drilled into my head. My shoulders hunched, and I tried to seem as non-threatening as possible. I felt my mother mimic my motions beside me.

"Oh, hey, no," Michael said quickly, stepping forward. He reached out and touched my mom's shoulder. "You don't have to do that. This isn't a test. You're friends of Zoe's, so you're friends of mine. Please."

We both looked at each other, unsure, and then at the man before us. He smiled kindly. "Zoe told me a bit about your old pack."

Mom's back went ramrod straight and she visibly swallowed hard before glancing at Zoe, trying to figure out exactly what he knew. What Zoe knew or what Zara had told him. "I ... I don't know what to say."

"You don't have to say anything," he answered. "Gabe will have questions. Zara told Zoe a little of what was going on a few days ago. She called right after you two got on the road."

Mom went still. "A few days ago?" Her gaze zeroed in on Zoe. "You haven't talked to her since?"

Zoe shook her head with a sigh. "No. To be honest, I'm a little worried. I called the house since she wasn't answering her cell phone, but Linden said she was busy." Her bitter tone left little unclear about how she felt about her brother-in-law.

"But you couldn't speak to her?" Mom asked carefully.

Zoe nodded once. "He said Zara was busy planning the memorial for Warren and she would be indisposed for a while before he hung up. Asshole."

Michael wrapped an arm around her shoulders, pressing his lips to her temple. "We'll figure out what's going on."

"Damn it," Mom hissed under her breath. "I knew we shouldn't have left her."

"We could go back," I offered quietly, my stomach twisting violently at the thought of crawling back to the compound. But I would for Zara. She had risked everything to help us.

"No!" Zoe and my mom shouted the word at the same time. They both looked horrified at the suggestion. Even Michael was frowning.

"Your uncle asked if I had seen you or your mother," Zoe told us seriously. "He knows you're missing. If he asked me that means he probably knows Zara and I helped you."

Mom drew in a deep breath. "This is exactly why I wanted her to come with us."

Zoe gave her a sad smile. "You know my big sister. She never would have left Bella behind, and Bella thinks her father can do no wrong."

"Gabriel and the council are working on a solution," Michael informed us. "Zoe still has a few friends in the Long Mesa pack we can reach out to."

"It's not the pack you remember, Zoe," Mom told her, her jaw set in a hard line. "It's so much worse than Zara probably told you."

"Zara hasn't told me much," Zoe admitted. "Linden frequently monitored her calls."

"That doesn't surprise me. My little brother is nothing if not completely paranoid. He's been running Long Mesa the last few years even while Warren was still technically the Alpha. His father didn't bother controlling him. Truthfully, I don't think he could. I half expected Linden to challenge him any day." Mom shook her head, her ponytail swishing over a shoulder. She absently reached up and twisted the ends around her fingers.

"We should get going," Michael said. He pulled a set of keys from his pocket. "We'll leave your car here. I'll have some of the pack members bring it back to our house later on this evening. Gabriel and Mallory are expecting us for lunch. She's cooked enough for an army."

I tried not to tense but failed miserably. Michael caught it and gave me another open smile. "Don't worry. Mallory is always looking for an excuse to throw a party, but Gabriel convinced her to keep it low key. It'll just be the six of us today."

Telling myself to relax and breathe was a lot easier than actually putting the words into practice. Again, Michael caught my hesitance.

"Skye, you're safe. You and your mom are safe now. Trust us, please." His gray eyes studied me, imploring me to trust him.

Zoe smiled at her husband, looking at him as if he had just climbed into the sky and plucked out the moon just for her. She turned that smile on me and held out a hand. "Let's go home, honey."

Taking a deep breath, I stepped forward and took her hand.

## 6

Whatever I expected the Blackwater Alpha house to look like, this wasn't it.

The drive to the house took a little over fifteen minutes, up a winding road. The car climbed higher and higher, thick trees lining the way. The Alpha home sat atop the mountain surrounded by woods, and I could see a small town set below. It was like the residence and people who lived within the walls were standing sentry over the people below.

The building itself was a sprawling log cabin, three stories high with large windows and smoke curling out of the stone chimney above. It was beautifully rustic. The wraparound porch had several seating areas that looked comfortable and inviting. It was a stunning home that made the one my mom grew up in look tiny in comparison.

We barely made it to the stairs leading up before the double front doors were pulled open. A tall woman with dark hair curled into glossy brown waves beamed a smile down at us. She was dressed in jeans with a red flannel shirt and a pair of socks with dancing sloths, no shoes. Her brown eyes were sparkling in the fall sunlight as she watched us approach.

"Welcome to Blackwater," she greeted kindly, coming down the stairs to meet us, stepping onto the grass with her socks. She extended a hand to Mom, clasping it firmly. "I'm Mallory Holt."

"Mallory is our Alpha's mate," Zoe supplied, taking Mom's place to hug Mallory.

Mallory returned the hug but waved her comment off. "Please. All that means is that I have to make sure Gabe behaves himself."

"But you do it so well, babe."

*Gabriel*, I realized, forgetting to look at the ground and instead taking him in with wide eyes.

We all looked up to see a man leaning against the door frame, one muscular shoulder propped against the wood. He looked completely at ease in a black t-shirt and jeans and ... also no shoes. His light brown hair looked like he had been running his hands through it all day. The stark domesticity of it was jarring. I was used to an Alpha who insisted his mate be seen and not heard. Zara was mostly just pretty decoration for Linden and a big screw you to my mother.

This man screamed Alpha, but he also gave an air of safety and kindness. The way he watched his mate was beautiful. He looked at her like she hung the moon and the stars just for him.

Mom elbowed my side, and I quickly ducked my head the way she did in deference, waiting for the Alpha to acknowledge us.

Gabriel cleared his throat. "Thank you, but that isn't necessary."

Mom and I exchanged wary glances before lifting our heads.

Gabriel looked down at his mate. "One of your timers went off before I came out here."

Mallory froze and gave him a suspicious look. "And you left it alone, right?"

He flashed her a sheepish grin. "You shouldn't have made my favorite cookies if you didn't want me to touch them."

She shook her head and climbed back up the stairs. "You would think that with the children at school I would get a bit of a break from chasing people out my kitchen."

Gabriel pushed off the door frame and hooked his fingers in Mallory's belt loops, tugging her against him as he smiled down at her. "You love me."

Her eyes narrowed playfully. "Sometimes." She pushed away and walked back into the house, motioning for us to follow. "Come on in. You must be starving from your trip. We prepared lunch. We can talk while we eat."

Gabriel smiled as we all came up the stairs. He clasped Michael's hand firmly. "I hope you're all hungry."

Michael and my mom followed Gabriel into the house, but I paused, still in shock. Gabriel and Mallory were nothing like what I expected. In Long Mesa, the only time I saw Linden touch Zara was with force, like at the night we escaped. Most of the male shifters in the pack treated women as though they were beneath them. Only a few female shifters were part of upper pack members, and they were just as cruel as the males.

"They're bonded," Zoe said softly, pausing beside me.

I looked back at her. "What?"

"Gabriel and Mallory." She inclined her head towards the house. "They're true mates. I don't think there are any true mates left in Long Mesa now."

"What are true mates?" The term sounded completely foreign.

"They're soulmates, essentially. Their wolves are bonded. It's a deeper, even sacred connection that's more than just being mated or married. True, bonded mates are a rare blessing. Once wolves bond, the connection between them ..."

Zoe sighed, rubbing the back of her neck with a wry grin. "It's hard to explain. There's an added layer of awareness. They can sense each other's emotions, even across long distances. In wolf form, they can eventually learn to communicate with each other. It also slows the human side of the aging process and increases fertility. It's why they have four children instead of the usual one or two most shifters can conceive."

That sounded like something out of a novel. "So you're saying that they're telepathic immortals who have lots of babies?"

Zoe considered that with a laugh. "I guess that's one way to put it."

"How did they know they were bonded?" I asked, curious about the whole thing.

"They grew up together and were always inseparable, as Mallory tells it. They played together as kids, went to school together, dated, got married ... There's no obvious predictor of what pairs will bond. It's a connection that just happens, and, once it does, it's undeniable. One day, when they were in wolf form, the bond snapped into place. Like the final piece of a puzzle."

"And it just happened? No warning?"

Zoe nodded, a soft smile ghosting across her lips. "A mate bond is a strange thing. Most pairs don't find it. We have couples in the pack that the bond snapped into place after they had been married for a decade. Usually the bond seems to happen in pairs in their late twenties or thirties. Occasionally when they're older than that, though."

"Wow," I whispered, wondering why I had never heard of such a thing.

Zoe gave me a soft look. "My parents were true mates. It's the only reason why we can figure they had two daughters."

"They died, though, right?" I asked hesitantly. Mom had told me a few stories of her life with Zara and Zoe before she was banished.

Her smile slipped a bit. "Yeah. They were killed in a car accident outside of the compound. I was eighteen, Zara was nineteen. It was a year before your mom ..."

*Got pregnant,* I filled in silently.

"Anyway," she said, breathing deeply and shaking away the memories, "I had already met Michael the summer before, and we planned to get married. I begged Zara to come up here with me, but she didn't want to leave her pack. She didn't want to leave your mom. Then when your mom found out she was pregnant, Zara got sucked into everything between the packs and married to Linden before Michael and I could get her out."

"I'm sorry," I told her honestly.

"Thank you," she replied, wrapping an arm around my shoulders. "I did get to come back a few times and visit for the first few years. We used to try and sneak things to you and your mom, but the guards always seemed to find them. Eventually your grandfather and uncle decided we were no longer welcome in the pack."

"But you like it here?"

She nodded enthusiastically. "I love it here. Blackwater is my home. A lot of that is because of Gabe and Mallory. They're amazing friends, and a terrific Alpha pair."

I smiled, unable to stop the chuckle. "They seem happy."

Zoe reached over and stroked my hair. "They *are* happy."

"Are you and Michael...?" I trailed off, not sure if it was appropriate to ask.

Zoe nodded, grinning. "Our bond actually snapped into place last year. We were all out on a pack run, and it just happened. Like being struck by lightning. Suddenly I was hyper aware of him. I could feel his emotions as if they were mine. I'll never forget it."

"Are there a lot of true mates here?"

She shrugged her shoulders. "In the pack we have about a couple dozen bonded mates. Considering the pack here is a bit over six hundred—"

My jaw dropped. "Six *hundred?*" I sputtered.

Zoe nodded. "We're definitely one of the bigger packs in the US." She motioned to the town below us. "It's why we have an actual town. We're our own community. Inside the pack territory we have zones that are watched by betas and deltas on the council, but ultimately, when it comes down to it, Gabriel is our Alpha. Michael is one of the betas and keeps an eye on the center of the town proper where we live and work."

"It sounds too good to be true," I admitted, crossing my arms over my chest as a breeze blew cold air across us and sent a wave of multicolored leaves fluttering across the front yard.

Zoe smiled at me sadly. "I know. I felt the same way when I came here from Long Mesa. Everything here is different. It isn't perfect by a long shot, but it's definitely better." She reached over and plucked a burnt orange leaf from my hair, arching her brows. "At least we have more than one color as the seasons change."

I was still laughing as we walked inside to join the others. Maybe this would work. Maybe this could be home.

☾

"I NEED you to know that you're both welcome in the Blackwater pack for as long as you like," Gabriel started after we had finished eating. He pushed his plate back and glanced from my mom to me.

Mom nodded, ducking her head as she pushed food around on her plate before setting her fork down. "Thank you, Alpha."

"Gabe," he corrected with a wry half-smile.

Mallory smiled at him, then mom. "We understand there is a time for formal titles, but a meal amongst friends isn't it."

I forced myself to sip my water slowly, making sure I left some food on my plate. Mallory had piled it high with food—roasted meat, cheesy potatoes, veggies, and corn-bread. I had quickly learned after the first meal mom and I ate outside of the compound that I needed to pace myself. I had eaten so much, amazed by the texture and taste of food that was hot and not expired, that I threw it all up less than an hour later. Neither of us were used to rich foods, or any kind of food really that wasn't prepackaged.

Our bodies were trying to get used to a more normal caloric intake on a regular basis.

"That being said," Gabriel continued, "we do have some questions about the Long Mesa pack."

"You mean about Linden," Mom murmured. She raised her water glass to her lips and took a sip.

Gabriel exchanged a rueful smile with his wife before

60

nodding. "Yes. Should we be concerned he'll come after you?"

Mom seemed to consider the question for a moment before answering. "I honestly don't know. Long Mesa doesn't have the resources you do. And to come after a couple of omegas doesn't necessarily make sense."

"But?" he prompted, resting an elbow casually on the arm of his chair. His blue eyes didn't miss a thing as he studied her.

"My brother hates me. Hates us. He's driven by that hate, and by rage and paranoia. And I know you and he have a past." She lifted her eyes and met the Alpha's stare head on. "I don't know what he'll do."

A muscle ticked in Gabriel's jaw and I held my breath, waiting to see what he would do. Maybe he would decide we weren't worth the trouble and send us packing.

"Did Linden ever tell you what happened when we were younger?" Gabe asked.

Mom shook her head.

"I caught him slapping a young shifter who was serving us at a dinner during the Summit one year," Gabe said frankly. "She jumped when he grabbed her inappropriately and spilled some water on him. He struck her before I could stop him."

I winced. That sounded about right.

A brief smile drifted across Gabriel's mouth as he spoke. "I forced him to apologize to her."

"In front of all of the Alphas?" Mom asked, amazed.

He nodded. "And then the Council leveled a fine against the Long Mesa pack. You father was livid, but your brother was humiliated."

We were all quiet as that sunk in. I wished I could have seen that firsthand.

"Everyone in Blackwater contributes in some way,"

Gabriel finally said. "Michael and Zoe have said you can stay with them until you're on your feet and find your place amongst the pack, but there is no rush."

He looked at me. "The school year is a few weeks in session, but you should be able to catch up easily. What grade are you in?"

I cleared my throat. "I'm a senior."

He nodded again. "How are your grades?"

"Good," I replied. Truthfully, my grades were awesome. Without friends or a social life, all I had were books to read, both for homework and ones that I got from the school library.

"Straight A's," my mom added with a smile. "Skye's always been a straight A student. She'll have no problem picking up here, I'm sure. She could start school as soon as we're settled."

"Actually," Zoe said, leaning forward, "the school here only covers elementary classes through grade eight. All the high schoolers attend a different school."

"A different school?" I echoed, curious.

"Granite Peak Academy. It's in Montana," Mallory explained. "The school was established as a way to help the upcoming pack generations begin to network. Several generations ago, they found that children raised solely on their own pack lands were more volatile and territorial as adults. Blood lines were getting too ... familial since pack members only mated to other pack members. The academy has been in operation for nearly thirty years and packs have been thriving as a result."

"We have twenty-two Blackwater pack members at the academy this year," Gabriel added "including our two oldest children, Remington and Katherine. The academy had students from twelve packs in the northern part of the continent, from Alaska to Maine, and several Canadian packs."

"Twelve packs?" My mother asked, astonished.

"Roughly two hundred and fifty students annually," Michael chimed in. "Each pack sends several members to teach and supervise the teens. A good amount of students return home and continue their education at local colleges and universities."

"College?" I whispered the word that had seemed like an impossible dream for my entire life. Occasionally Long Mesa teens graduated and attended online classes, but we were told that it was best to keep to the pack and only interact with humans when absolutely necessary.

Zoe smiled at me. "Yes. College. Part of the purpose of the academy is to help teens learn how to become one with their wolf, to control their impulses, so you can interact with the world as a whole."

"We have quite a few pack members who work in nearby cities," Mallory told me.

"How is something like that even funded? Doesn't the school have to be registered with the state?" My mom's brow furrowed as she tried to figure out the logistics.

"All the packs have an equal stake. Each pack puts money into the school to aid with upkeep and such. And we're just like every other private school on paper ... we just happen to only select students from the same twelve cities around the world." Zoe winked.

Gabriel pointed to Michael. "The original part of the school was purchased a long time ago. It was roughly thirty acres and butted up onto the Granite Peak national park. Michael here helped us acquire the surrounding four hundred acres about five years ago. We expanded the dorms, added new facilities and a few computer labs."

Mallory cleared her throat, taking a drink of her iced

tea. "Originally the school started with forty-two students and five faculty. As the school grew, packs in the area began to thrive. We would love to eventually be able to offer the option to all packs to send their children. Expand the campus or even open a second school."

"But I would have to go to Montana?" I looked at my mom. Leaving her wasn't something I ever considered. We had just gotten free, and now we were splitting up.

"You come back for holiday breaks," Mallory promised. "And you can call and video chat your mom as much as you like outside of classes."

"I don't have a phone," I murmured.

Gabriel smiled. "We can give you one, provided your mom agrees you can have it."

I looked at my mom. I could see the indecision on her face. She wanted me to stay with her, but she wanted me to go and start living like an actual teenager. She met my eyes across the table, her gaze watery as she blinked away tears.

"I think this would be good for you, honey," she said quietly.

"Are you sure?" The idea of leaving her sucked, but I also couldn't ignore the hope that surged at the idea of eventually going to college.

Pressing her lips together, she nodded.

I looked at all the adults around the room before agreeing. "Okay."

## 7

THREE DAYS, TWO SHOPPING TRIPS, AND ONE AIRPLANE later, I was getting into a car in Montana on my way to Granite Peak Academy. I had called mom after the plane landed to tell her I had arrived and promised to call again when I got settled in at the school. Both of us had been fighting tears for days. Now that I was actually in Montana, I wanted my mom in a way I never had before.

I felt like I was going to get sick as the car pulled away from the curb. The driver, who held up a sign with my name near baggage claim—strange to think I was a girl who now had luggage—had introduced herself as Amanda. She was one of the teachers at the school and a member of the Blackwater pack. Since there were no classes on Saturday, she had offered to come and collect me from the airport.

I sank into the leather seat as she pulled onto the highway. Montana was so flat compared to Washington. Similar to New Mexico except for the massive mountain range looming in the distance, the cooler temperature, and it had a more muted version of the fall colors in Washington. I was glad for the coat Zoe insisted I bring.

Amanda hummed under her breath. "Looks like winter might start early." She tucked a lock of blonde hair behind her ear and then adjusted the red rims of her glasses. Her lips were painted a bright red to match. With her pale skin, dark jeans, and a leather jacket, the style seemed effortless and chic. I wished I could pull off anything like that.

I looked out at the gray skies. "Snow?"

She grinned at me and nodded. "I always love the first snow. There's something supremely magical about it. We always cancel classes for the first snow. The packs usually go out together for a run to celebrate."

I tried not to show my unease at a pack run. The last few days, my wolf had gone back to her silent self. Mom had gone out with Zoe on a run the other night, letting her wolf get to know the smells and sights of our new home. They offered me to come and I declined, but not because I didn't want to. I couldn't get my wolf to come out and shift.

Finicky bitch.

"How long have you taught at the school?" I asked, trying to change the subject.

"About five years now. My mate and I both teach. Ricky teaches math. I teach English. You're a senior, right?"

I nodded.

She beamed at me. "Fabulous. You'll be in my senior English class."

I had always loved English, especially when we had assigned novels to read. Escaping into a world of fiction was one of my few salvations at the compound.

"Mallory said you came from a pack in New Mexico?"

I swallowed hard before nodding. "Yeah. We just transferred to Blackwater last week."

Amanda snorted. "Bet you're loving this cold weather, huh? You came from the land of warmth and sun and now you're basically moving to the arctic tundra. Spring here is nice, though."

"It's different," I agreed as I forced myself to smile around the words.

Gabriel and Mallory suggested that for the time being we not mention the Long Mesa pack specifically. Mom had eventually explained everything to Gabriel and Mallory, including exactly why we left.

Mallory had cried. Gabriel had snapped the phone in his hands like it was made of toothpicks. Michael and Zoe looked physically ill. All of them swore they would let us stay in Blackwater for as long as we wanted, and Gabriel promised Zoe he would find Zara.

"You'll definitely get seasons here," she agreed. "Maybe a little too much of winter, but it is gorgeous when everything is sparkly and white."

"It sounds amazing." I looked around as the scenery passed by in a blur. There weren't many cars on the road at all. Nothing like in Washington. "How long does it take to get to the school?"

"A little over two hours, but we'll be on the academy grounds in about an hour."

"Alpha Gabriel said that you guys just bought a bunch of extra land a few years ago."

A teasing smile played on her lips. "Alpha Gabriel? Clearly your last pack was super formal."

"Oh. I ... Um—"

Amanda burst out laughing. "I'm kidding. Seriously. But we do just call him Gabriel. The only time anyone uses his formal title is if they're at the Summit, an official pack meeting or trying to kiss his ass."

My jaw dropped.

She glanced at me and waved a hand. "Gabe's my cousin. I'm not being disrespectful to our fearless leader. But it's hard to think of him as anything but an older brother most of the time."

We drove several miles in silence, the radio playing an unfamiliar song in the background. I snorted softly to myself; almost all songs were unfamiliar to me. At one point we had a radio that got one station, but it broke when I was nine. There had never been a replacement. Occasionally I would hear music at school playing from phones or portable speakers, but I didn't usually hang around long enough to catch any lyrics.

"Are you nervous?" Amanda asked suddenly. "I mean, starting a new school, leaving your friends ..." She trailed off and slapped a hand over her ruby lips. "Shit, I'm making it worse, aren't I? Also, sorry. I shouldn't curse around a student."

I couldn't help but laugh at her rambling. "It's fine. Cursing doesn't bother me." I shrugged, tugging at the hem of my long-sleeved shirt, curling my hands inside the sleeves and tugging them down over my knuckles. "I didn't really have many friends."

She stared at me for a beat before turning her eyes to the road. "A girl as pretty as you? I bet you had boys lining up at your door."

I was glad she was focused on the road so she didn't see the jolt that physically rocked my body. I shuddered, remembering every time Cassian, Preston or Marc touched me. Every time they managed to corner me.

If I had stayed in Long Mesa, I would have had boys lined up at my door, but for all the wrong reasons.

"Hey, you OK?" Amanda reached over and touched me. "Jesus, you're shaking!" Her wide blue eyes looked back and forth from me to the road. "Are you carsick? Do you need me to pull over?"

"No, no," I stammered, trying to calm my racing heart. My wolf stirred within me, sensing the impending wave of panic rising in me. I kept reminding myself I was half a continent away from my former pack. My former life.

"You're scaring the shit out of me here, Skye," Amanda pressed. "I can pull over—"

"Seriously, I'm okay. I swear." I met her eyes and forced a smile on my lips. "I promise. Just a minor panic attack."

"Was it something I said?" Amanda looked completely horrified at the thought she did something wrong.

"No. It just ... happens. Sorry if I freaked you out." I ducked my head. God, I was a total basket case. I considered asking her to turn the car around and take me back to the airport. How the hell was I going to survive a world of new people asking me completely normal questions without losing it?

But I couldn't do that.

The last three days, my mom had smiled and laughed more than I remembered in my entire life. Her bruises were almost completely faded, and she was planning on starting to work at the café Zoe owned in town. She was happy, and she deserved time to simply be by herself.

It was only a few months until Thanksgiving break when I would see her.

I could last two months.

"Well, we are now officially on academy grounds," Amanda said. She waved a hand in front of us with an exaggerated flourish. "All this? Academy grounds. There's a perimeter fence around all of the property so you'll know where you can and can't run. It's one of the reasons we expanded—more wolves meant more of a chance at being caught. About ten years ago a farmer reported seeing a massive wolf on his property. A bunch of other farmers, worried about their cattle, decided to hunt the wolf down."

"Oh, God." My eyes went wide. "Did they catch the wolf?"

"Nah," she said. She glanced over and winked at me. "We're smarter and faster than that."

Another forty minutes of driving and we pulled up to an impressive gate, flanked by two stone and wood guard houses. The sun was starting to set in the mountains in the distance. A shifter stepped out of one of the guard houses and approached the car.

Amanda rolled the window down with a smile. "Hey, Paul."

"Amanda," he greeted with a nod. He looked past her to me and smiled. "This must be our new student."

"This is Skye Parker," Amanda explained, glancing at me.

Gabriel had suggested we use a name other than Markham for my mother and me. When we couldn't figure one out, Zoe mentioned that Mallory's maiden name had been Parker, and we adopted it, both happy to be free of the Markham name. Parker was a common enough name that no one would think twice.

"Welcome to Granite Peak," Paul said with a grin. "The whole school has been buzzing about your arrival since yesterday."

A tendril of dread crept up my spine. So much for staying under the radar.

"We don't get a lot of new students, plus the vast majority are male," Amanda explained. She rolled her eyes at me. "I'm afraid you're going to be a bit of novelty around here for a while, especially with the boys."

"Awesome," I muttered under my breath, smiling grimly.

Amanda pulled through the gates, pointing to different buildings as we circled around to the parking lot of the left side. In the fading light, I could make out some tall buildings, lights twinkling in them, showing someone was home.

I took a deep breath and got out of the car after Amanda parked. I met her at the back of the car, pulling out my suitcase and backpack when she opened the trunk.

She pointed to a building down a well-used path from the parking lot. "That's the female dorm. You're going to be in room two-ten on the second floor. The first floor has a communal kitchen that's stocked with drinks and snacks. It also has a game room and a big communal living space. You're welcome to use it, but lights out are midnight on Friday and Saturday, ten on school nights. There's also a dorm monitor on the first floor. If you need anything, go to the monitor's room."

I nodded to show I was paying attention as I wheeled my suitcase down the path to the dorm she had indicated.

Amanda fell into step with me. "They have you rooming with Larkin. Since there's fewer females here, the dorm is smaller and there are less rooms, which means some of the girls have to room together. Larkin's part of Blackwater. She's a year younger and an absolute sweetheart. I think you'll really like her."

Amanda paused at the entrance to the dorm. "Do you want me to walk you up to your room? Are you hungry? The cafeteria is probably closed, but I can—"

"I think I'm good," I said quickly.

"You're sure?" Amanda pressed. "You remember your room?"

"Two-ten. Second floor."

"OK." She let out a long breath and snapped her

fingers. "Class schedule! Larkin said she would take you to the main office tomorrow so you can get your schedule. She'll give you the whole tour. I'm sure, at some point, you'll meet your other pack mates. They're really curious about you."

Fan-freaking-tastic.

So tomorrow I would get the tour and then be a new exhibit for a group of teenage wolves to study. Wolves that were now part of my pack.

I swallowed hard.

"I got this," I told her, praying I would find some of the confidence I hinted at in my tone.

"Okay. Right." Amanda stepped back. "This is me leaving and not hovering. At all."

I laughed and picked up my suitcase by the handle to walk up the steps to the dorm. I opened one of the glass doors and turned to see Amanda still standing there. She gave me a big smile and a wave.

Laughing, I waved back and walked inside the dorm.

The large foyer was open, with a bank of elevators to the left and a set of double oak doors on the right. The plaque hung beside the doors said, "Dorm Monitor". There was a hall leading to the back and I could hear music and loud laughter coming from it.

I hurried to the elevators, not exactly wanting to meet anyone right now. I wanted to get to my room and get settled in. Maybe I would even manage to fall asleep before my roommate came up from hanging out. I didn't think I was in the right state of mind to handle any more questions. I needed to decompress.

I got into the elevator and pressed the number two, waiting as the doors slid shut. Looking around I saw several posters in the small box with different activities going on over the next few months. I was still reading the one about intramural archery when the doors slid open.

Stepping into the hallway, I was grateful to see there wasn't anyone about. I hurried down the hall, stopping when I got to two-ten.

"Here goes nothing," I whispered with a sigh. I slid the key into the lock and turned, pushing the door open. My gaze immediately fell to the girl sitting across the room at a desk. She spun in her seat as soon as she saw me, a bright smile on her face.

"Hey," the brunette grinned, getting up from her desk. She held out a hand, the glitter purple polish of her nails catching in the light. "I'm Larkin Dawes. I guess you're my new roomie?" She was dressed in cotton yoga pants and a blue tank top, her dark hair pulled into a messy bun.

"Um, yeah. Hey. I'm Skye. Parker," I added, remembering my new last name as I looked around the room. I didn't know what I had expected, but it wasn't this. I dropped my backpack on top of my suitcase as I closed the door.

The room was large with two full beds tucked into opposite corners with nightstands that had matching lamps. There was a desk at the foot of each and two closets on either side of the room. Everything was symmetrical except the large flat screen hung over one desk. One half of the room was obviously well lived in. There were pictures on one nightstand and framed black and white photos of landscapes on the wall.

"I like taking pictures," Larkin supplied, noting me studying the photos.

I took a step towards them. A beach scene hung next to snow-covered mountains. Beneath them, a lush forest was juxtaposed beside a barren desert.

"They're beautiful," I told her softly, wondering how far she had traveled to take each picture.

Larkin blushed, the apples of her cheeks turning a pretty shade of pink. "Thanks." She scuffed the toe of her converse sneakers into the area rug in the middle of the floor. "It's a hobby."

"You've traveled to these places?" I asked, glancing back at her.

She nodded, excited. "Yeah. My parents like to travel, too. We pick a new place to go each summer during break." She pointed to the desert. "We went to Death Valley in California two summers ago. Last year we went to the coast in Texas. The forest is back home in Blackwater." She smiled wistfully, letting her index finger trace one of the trees.

She touched the last image. "The mountains are from here. I took this last year before Christmas break when we had a blizzard."

"So, it snows here a lot?" I asked, moving to the window. I couldn't see much in the dark.

She laughed. "In Montana? Oh, yeah."

I touched the window, feeling the cold seep into my fingertips. "I've never seen snow in person."

"Wait—seriously? Never? Where did you grow up?"

"New Mexico," I said quietly. I turned and smiled sheepishly. "I've actually never been outside of New Mexico until last week."

Larkin's jaw dropped, her mouth forming a perfect 'o' of surprise. Her brown eyes sparkled. "Seriously? Not even on vacation?"

I tried to shrug it off. "We didn't go on vacations."

"Wow," she murmured. "Your parents never—"

"Just my mom," I cut in quickly. "It's just ... us."

"Oh. Shit, sorry," she apologized. Sadness flooded her

eyes, and I knew she assumed the worst—dead father. I considered correcting her but didn't want to open *that* can of worms my first time meeting her.

Or ever, really.

"Well, it snows here. A lot," Larkin said with a mischievous grin. "You'll love it. There's nothing like running in the snow. Your wolf is going to seriously flip her shit."

"I guess we'll find out," I replied with what I hoped was an encouraging smile. Who knew what the hell my wolf liked?

I looked back at my bags. "I guess I should unpack."

She clapped her hands together. "I can totally help! You look about the same size as me—we can probably share clothes!"

"Share clothes?" I frowned. Was that a common thing? A good thing? She seemed excited about it, but at the omega house, sharing clothes was a necessity. It definitely wasn't something that we were happy about.

"Yeah!" Larkin was still smiling. She glanced at me, and her expression fell. "I mean, only if you want to. We don't have to or anything. Some of the other girls do ... It's like a sister thing. Not that we're sisters. Or even friends. But we can be! If you want. Since we're living together it might be weird if we hated each other." She covered her face with her hands, peeking at me from between her fingers. "I'm acting like a complete idiot."

I cocked my head to the side, amused at her rambling. She reminded me a bit of Maisie. Or who Maisie might have been if she had never been completely broken.

"We can be friends," I said slowly. I'd never had a friend. It might be nice. Larkin definitely seemed nice. I looked her in the eyes and tried to smile. I held her gaze for a long beat.

Larkin let out a long breath, breaking my eye contact

and looking down with a small, nervous laugh. "Damn. Wow. Are you sure you're on the right floor?"

I felt my smile slipping. I tried to remember exactly what Amanda had said. "I think so. Floor two, room two-ten, right?"

Larkin nodded, looking up quickly and smiling again. She shrugged a shoulder. "You just don't seem like one of us by that stare you've got." She winked at me.

"One of us?" I repeated, confused.

She nodded with a chuckle. "Yeah, an omega. This is an omega floor."

## 8

I was going to throw up. Actually throw up all over the plush area rug with little white daisies in the middle of the dorm. Panic flared violently inside me and I felt my wolf stir, pushing against my mind. She whined, sensing danger.

Wanting to fight.

This had to be the biggest fucking joke of my life. A mistake. No way in hell did I escape Long Mesa to be shoved right back into the same situation.

*This is the omega floor.*

Her words rang in my head like a freaking marching band parading through, jarring and loud and impossible to ignore.

Larkin looked at me, her face worried and then ... ashamed?

She shuffled back, hands clasped in front of her. She fixed her eyes firmly on the floor. "I'm sorry. I'm sure it's a mistake. You don't have to stay here. I mean, of course you're not an omega. Obviously." She swallowed, still not meeting my gaze. "I can sleep downstairs in one of the couches, or bunk with another omega tonight so you can have the room."

Wait—*what?*

I blinked, my panic attack loosening its stranglehold on me as I processed her words. It took a second for them to fully penetrate the fog of my mind, but when they did, I was stunned. "What are you talking about?" I flinched, my tone raspy and harsh. Larkin visibly shrunk.

From me.

"I'll go. It's fine." She hurried to sidestep around me, fully intending to cede ground to me. She was all but running to the door. She didn't have to be in wolf form for me to see her tail firmly tucked between her legs.

Thinking fast, I blocked the door.

Larkin yelped and skittered backwards, nearly falling. She tripped over her feet in an effort to put maximum distance between us.

"Wait, stop!" I cried, holding up my hands. "Please, please stop. I didn't mean ... It's not. Shit. I'm so sorry. This is on me. Please don't leave."

Larkin looked up, her chest heaving. Her big brown eyes were wide, scared. Freaking terrified. My heart ached. I knew that look so well. Too well. The idea that I made her look like that had my stomach roiling all over again.

I ran a shaking hand over my face. "I didn't mean to freak. It was a ... reflex."

"Reflex?" Larkin echoed softly, licking her lips. "I don't understand." Her body was still tense, poised to run.

I squeezed my eyes shut for a second, trying to figure out the most tactful way around this. How much could I tell her that made my reaction understandable without getting into the entire mess that was my life story?

"You said this is an omega floor," I started slowly, measuring my words carefully. I leaned against the door, trying to put more space between us to show I wasn't a threat to her.

That I wasn't a threat. That was fucking ironic as hell.

"I don't have anything against omegas," I said quickly when she frowned. "In my old pack ... I was an omega."

She cocked her head, eyes narrowed. "No way."

"Yeah," I said, looking away. "And there being an omega ... was a bad thing. A really, really ... bad thing." My jaw clenched, teeth grinding together.

Her expression softened as she sat down on the corner of her bed. "You mean, like, you were bullied or something?"

"Yeah," I whispered, swallowing hard. Now I was the one unable to meet her gaze. "Or something."

"Wow," Larkin replied. "I mean, I've heard of that happening, but ..." She crossed her legs and leaned her elbows on her thigh, resting her chin in her hands. "It's not like that here, Skye. I mean, some of the omegas get picked on or whatever, and sometimes it's pretty nasty, but nothing really bad. The teachers and the alphas step in before it can get too far."

"That's good." Unable to support my weight anymore, I slid down the door and sat on the floor, hugging my knees to my chest.

"Sierra—you'll meet her, she's part of the Blackwater pack," Larkin explained with an eye roll, "she made me do her history paper last year. I guess I could have said no, but she made it hard to. But then Remy found out and went off on her. Sierra apologized."

"Remy?" I asked.

Larkin nodded. "Remy's our campus alpha here. He's Gabriel and Mallory's oldest. Since we're not in Blackwater, Remy's technically in charge."

I frowned. "Is he one of the teachers?"

She laughed loudly, throwing her head back. "Oh, no. Remy's a senior. He's in line to be Alpha after his father."

My heart sank.

Remy was this pack's version of Cassian.

Larkin leaned back, watching me curiously. "How much do you know about the school?"

I shrugged, glad we were moving past the omega issue. "They told me the school is about thirty years old, there's twelve packs that run it, there's like two hundred and some students."

Larkin rolled her eyes. "Leave it to the adults to just talk about the numbers." She stood up and walked to a mini fridge by her desk. She reached in and pulled out a can of cola. "Want one?"

"Sure." I accept the can she offered, cradling the cold aluminum in my hands for a beat before opening it.

She sat back down in her desk chair, straddling it backwards as she took a long drink. "Okay, so there are twelve packs. Each pack has ten to twenty-five students in it, depending on the pack."

"Blackwater has twenty-two, right?"

"Twenty-three, counting you," she corrected with a grin that made a dimple appear. "Each pack has an alpha. Not a full alpha, but someone who is likely to take over as alpha for their generation. It's usually pretty clear cut, like us. Everyone in our generation knows Remy will take over after his dad."

"What about the teachers? Shouldn't they be in charge?"

"They are when it comes to school and stuff like that. None of the teachers are alphas or even betas. When GPA first started, they tried having alphas and betas as teachers, but it basically turned into a giant pissing contest, so they decided that unranked pack members made the best instructors." Larkin waved a hand. "The teachers do just that—they teach. Some of the security guards at the gate are betas and deltas, but there's always a campus alpha who handles all pack issues. Remy is ours, and he also happens to be one who is going to eventually be an actual Alpha."

I nodded slowly. "Okay, so what keeps the alphas from—"

"—starting their own pissing match?" Larkin grinned. "For starters, no more than two of the alphas have classes together. They all rotate so they aren't in the same class. They also have individual housing."

"They aren't in the dorms?" That sounded freaking amazing. I cracked the top of my soda and took a long pull, loving the combination of sugar, caffeine, and bubbles.

"Each pack has their own cabin around the lake. The alphas stay there. Sometimes their beta lives with them. Depends on the pack. Rhodes is one of our betas and since he's best friends with Remy, he stays at the Blackwater cabin. The cabin is also where we have pack meetings. Like tomorrow. Remy called a pack meeting so everyone could meet you."

I groaned with a long sigh. "Fabulous. Sounds awesome."

Larkin chuckled. "I swear it's not that bad. Our pack is pretty close. We don't have a lot of the in-fighting and stuff other packs deal with."

"In-fighting?"

"You know," Larkin replied, waving a hand, "betas who think they can be alphas, alphas who are too busy trying to get laid than watch out for their pack mates." She rolled her eyes. "Remy keeps everyone in check, but he's a good guy."

I stretched out my legs, crossing them at the ankles in front of me. "You said this is an omega floor—so only omegas are here?"

She took another drink. "Yeah. This is the female omega floor. The other dorm has a male omega floor. Guys in one dorm, girls in the other. It's like they think we're like horny teenagers or something and we need to be separated."

I couldn't help but laugh at that, but I was slightly glad to know this was a girls' only dorm. It gave me a layer of protection.

"Betas all have a smaller dorm on the other side of campus. That's coed, but there's like special key cards to get onto each floor so the guys can't go onto the girls' floor and vice versa."

"I'm sure that's a foolproof plan."

She laughed again. "Exactly. Half of the alpha cabins double as party pads. For the most part, the teachers and advisors leave us alone. Hell, we all know half the reason this school exists is to play matchmaker."

"Matchmaker?" I asked.

Larkin stood, tossing her now empty can into the recycling bin. "Oh yeah. It's the best place to spot potential marriage alliances. You'll see. Some of the girls around here treat it like a season of *The Bachelor*."

"*The Bachelor?*"

Larkin frowned, confused. "Yeah. The TV show? Brainless bimbos throw themselves at a hot guy, hoping that while he's dating the other umpteen chicks that he'll fall madly in love with them?"

She tapped a finger on her jaw. "But I guess here it's more like *The Bachelorette* since it's multiple guys trying to impress one girl."

I was still confused.

She cocked her head at me. "You still don't know what I'm talking about?"

I shrugged. "I never really watched TV."

Her jaw dropped. "Not even Netflix?"

I made a face. "What's that?"

With a gasp, Larkin pressed a hand to her chest before falling backwards onto her bed. "Dear Lord."

I got off the floor, setting my drink down on the empty desk. "Sorry?"

She propped herself up on her elbows, looking at me sternly. "Tomorrow we're starting with *Stranger Things*." She motioned to the TV. "We'll binge watch in here after the pack meeting."

"Binge watch?" I echoed. It was like she was speaking a different language.

Closing her eyes, she sniffled, pretending to wipe her eyes. "You poor, sweet child. I promise I'll make it better for you."

A laugh burst from me, catching me by surprise. The smile that stretched my lips felt oddly natural. "Okay. Tomorrow you can make it better."

"We should get to bed," Larkin admitted, glancing at the clock. "Remy wants us at the cabin before breakfast so you can meet everyone before you meet the rest of the school."

I groaned again. "I'm guessing there's no way to avoid this, huh?"

Larkin grinned at me, her eyes sparkling. "You probably won't be saying that tomorrow when you see Remy." She arched a brow. "There's a reason the females all act like bitches in heat around the alphas, especially Remy. He's definitely hot."

Now I arched a brow. "Does someone have a thing for her alpha?"

Blushing, Larkin looked away. "No. His beta, however, is another story."

I smirked. "Rhodes, right?"

"Ugh. Yes," she cried, throwing herself back and covering her face with a pillow.

"Have you told him?"

"No!" she said quickly, eyes huge. "Rhodes is … he's been one of my best friends since we were little. We live next door to each other back home, but he sees me as, like, a little sister or something else that's completely unromantic."

I bit my lower lip. "Are you sure he doesn't like you back?"

"I'm sure," she said firmly as she looked at me with pleading eyes. "Please don't tell him."

"Your secret's safe with me," I swore. Something warmed in my chest.

I was a girl who was keeping someone's secret. Someone who might be a friend. It was a fascinatingly wondrous feeling.

☪

LARKIN and I were the first ones to the Blackwater cabin the next morning. Apparently, Remy had asked her to bring me early before the others arrived so he could speak with me privately.

My stomach clenched and churned the entire walk to the cabin, our warm breath fogging into the crisp fall air as the sun started to rise in the east. By the time we reached the cabin, my hands were shaking. I couldn't appreciate the clean A-frame of the wood cabin, the curl of smoke coming from the white stone chimney, and the open porch.

My gaze was firmly fixed on the boy leaning against

the railing post in a pair of ripped black jeans and a black t-shirt stretched across his wide chest. His head lifted as we approached, golden eyes assessing us. He ran a hand through long dark hair as we reached the steps, his forearm flexing and showing off a tattoo I couldn't quite make out.

"Ladies," he greeted with a smirk. His eyes fell to Larkin and he winked. "Hey Lark. How's it going?"

"Good," she stammered, looking from me to him.

I forced my shoulders back and head high, shoving my hands into the pockets of my own jeans to hide the trembling. It was hard not to let my past experiences with alpha teenagers color this meeting. They couldn't all be as cruel and sadistic as Cassian.

"It's Skye, right?" he asked slowly, coming down the steps slowly. His black boots thumped hard against the wooden planks. He stopped in front of me and smiled suddenly. The smile transformed his face from brooding to boyish in seconds.

I stepped back on instinct. He was a good five inches taller than my five-six height, and my brain was already sizing up all of the ways he could overpower me.

His gaze flickered to Larkin for a second before coming back to me. He extended a hand. "I'm Rhodes."

Wait—this was *Rhodes*? The guy Larkin liked? He wasn't the alpha. He was the beta, and, according to Larkin, the alpha's best friend.

I realized he was still standing there with his hand out while I was processing the situation. An awkward stretch of time passed and as I was starting to recover, he dropped his hand and looked at Larkin.

"Is she okay?" he whispered loudly, eyes dancing.

"Yeah," Larkin said quickly, nudging my shoulder. She smiled at me encouragingly. "You're good, right?"

I shook my head, trying to focus. "Yeah. Sorry." I

attempted a weak smile at Rhodes. "I didn't sleep that great."

He rolled his eyes and nodded. "I bet. And now you have some asshole telling you that you have to wake up at this ungodly hour and entertain the pack with stories of your life."

"That's alpha asshole to you," a warm voice said above us, clearly amused.

I looked up to see another guy had stepped outside onto the porch. He was dressed in jeans, brown boots, and a red flannel shirt open over a plain white tee that stretched across a wall of muscle on his chest and torso. He held a steaming mug in one hand. His warm brown eyes were the color of melted chocolate, his hair had the same shade of brown, but I saw golden highlights as the sun caught it. It was shorter and styled in messy spikes, like he had been running his hands through it or just woken up. He was wider and slightly taller than Rhodes.

My breath caught as my wolf woke up. I braced for her usually violent reaction, but instead she settled after a moment of curiosity. Almost like she was content.

Rhodes snorted at the newcomer. "You wish, dude."

The new guy leaned against the railing; his gaze intense on me as he studied me. "You must be Skye."

My entire life, I had always dropped my eyes in submission out of a need to survive. My mom taught me early that holding the gaze of a pack member could quickly be viewed as a challenge, especially with an Alpha and upper pack members. A lifetime of training had me constantly averting my gaze to survive.

But it was always an act until this moment.

Submission for wolves wasn't just about strength, but about respect. And something about this guy demanded respect.

The longer he stared at me, the more I felt my wolf moving inside me. She was just as conflicted as me, torn between wanting to take in every detail of him and yield in deference. I wanted to look away, but there was something hypnotic about his gaze that I couldn't break.

His dark eyes narrowed for a second, still locked unblinking on me. Slowly, a smile spread across his handsome face. "I'm Remy."

## 9

------------

REMY SHUT THE DOOR BEHIND US, CLOSING US INTO THE small office off of the kitchen. There was a large oak desk in the center of the room and a set of French doors matching the ones we had just come through against the far wall, leading outside to what looked like a deck. I didn't have time to truly appreciate the large picture window with the bench seat under it or the wall of full bookshelves behind the desk.

I turned slowly to him, studying him as he studied me. He leaned back against the glass doors.

"I thought we should talk before everyone got here," he started, his voice warm and calm.

I liked the sound of it way more than I should. It was strangely soothing my frayed nerves that had been buzzing since he said he wanted to speak to me alone.

"Okay," I replied softly, waiting for him to continue. I expected to feel more nervous about him closing us into this room away from everyone else, but the panic never welled up. Probably because I knew Larkin and Rhodes were in the other room.

At least, that's what I told myself.

"My dad called," he said slowly, moving around me to sit on the bench near the window. "Do you want to sit down?" He motioned to the armchair across from him.

I crossed my arms over my chest and shook my head. "I'm good." No sense getting too comfortable. I wanted this over with.

He nodded, not offended in the least. "Okay. Like I said, my dad called. He explained about how you left your old pack."

My blood turned to ice in my veins, my teeth grinding together as my jaw clenched. "What did he say?"

Remy frowned, his brow furrowed as he looked at me. "That you and your mom escaped from your last pack. You haven't had the easiest time. He asked me to look out for you."

I shifted on my feet, suddenly embarrassed and frustrated. "I can take care of myself."

A smile ghosted across his lips. "I'm sure you can." He stood up and gave me a knowing look. "He told me about your former pack. About you being an omega." His eyes stayed locked on me, not moving in any direction as he studied me with startling severity.

My hands curled into fists and I could feel every single pounding beat of my heart. I felt heat suffusing my cheeks. My breath came out in ragged pants born of fear and frustration. "Right. So that's what this is about? Me being an omega?"

He cocked his head to one side, his expression giving nothing away as he waited for me. His eyes slid down the column of my throat, catching the pulse racing there as my anxiety spiked. He missed nothing.

I scoffed, shaking as I took another step away from him. "Forget it. I'll leave."

His eyes narrowed. "What—"

I held up a hand, cutting him off. "I get it. Larkin explained how things work here. You're the alpha of the pack on campus so what you say goes. I didn't escape *that* pack," I spat the word, "to come here and be a whore for this pack. No fucking thank you."

I barely caught his eyes going wide as I spun to leave. I was too busy mentally ripping myself apart.

How stupid was I to trust these people? Was mom going through the exact same thing back in Washington? I needed to get to her now. Maybe I could get Amanda to drive me—

"Stop!" The command came out hard and firm. I had no choice but to obey.

I hated myself for freezing where I stood, mid-stride, hand on the doorknob. The instinct to obey an alpha— okay, *this* alpha—couldn't be ignored, no matter how pissed off I was.

"Jesus *Christ*," he hissed softly. "That's not ... That's not what I meant at all."

Taking a shuddering breath, I turned around and was stunned to see the complete horror on his face. He had no idea what I was talking about. Humiliation flooded me.

Oh, God. What had I done?

The horror etched into his strong features was quickly eclipsed by enough rage that I stepped back.

He exhaled hard and seemed to release the anger in the same breath, his new expression softer and open.

He held up his hands, eyes still on my face as he sensed I was about to lose it. There was a beautiful sadness in his eyes as he realized what I was talking about. "Skye, I didn't ... My dad said they forced you to be an omega without giving you a chance to find your own rank in your pack. He didn't mention anything about ..." He let out another long breath, and I had the distinct impression he was trying to control himself once more.

I squeezed my eyes shut, wanting the floor to open and swallow me whole. "Can we just forget I said anything? I'm sorry—I shouldn't have insulted you. Shit." I scrubbed my hands over my face as I felt the hot sting of tears prick the backs of my eyes.

"Hey," he said. I heard him move towards me and then warm hands were circling my wrists, tugging my hands down gently.

I opened my eyes to see Remy standing in front of me. I had to tilt my head back to look into his eyes, but the kindness I saw there was more than worth it. His thumbs rubbed gentle circles on the insides of my wrists. The small act helped center me and settle my nerves.

"It's fine," he said softly, patiently. "Nothing like that will happen here. Ever. You're safe here, Skye. I just wanted to let you know that, as far as we're concerned, you decide your place in the Blackwater pack. What you were before doesn't define you now. I thought you should know that before everyone else showed up."

I nodded quickly. I blinked furiously but a single tear still escaped, sliding down one cheek slowly.

His eyes followed the path of the tear, his teeth catching his lower lip between his teeth as he seemed to internally struggle with something. "Skye, if you need anything, you can come to me, okay? If you want to talk—"

I stepped back, grateful he let me break his hold. "I don't. I just wanted to move on." No way was I going to open up to this guy about the shitshow of Long Mesa. I didn't want to look back down that road. I wanted to start living.

His dark eyes studied me, seeing way too much for my liking. "All right. But the offer stands."

I sniffed and wiped my cheek with the back of a trembling hand. "Thanks. But I'm good."

"Okay," he relented. He jerked a chin towards the door. "Sounds like everyone's about here. You need a minute?"

I shook my head quickly. "No. Let's do this."

He moved around me and opened one of the doors, waiting for me to leave first before closing the door and following me into the open great room.

"There you are," an annoyed redhead said from the couch. Larkin sat beside her, Rhodes next to Larkin. More than a dozen other teenage shifters were seated on couches, chairs and on the floor around them.

We had breezed past this room when we went to his study, but I could see now there was a lot of seating and the floor plan was open to the kitchen to allow for people to gather.

The redhead stood and walked over to us. She peered up at me with a frown. Her eyes cut to Remy, narrowed. "What did you say to her? She looks upset."

Remy rolled his eyes to the ceiling and sighed.

"Nothing," I answered quickly. "He was actually really ... nice." I was surprised to know I meant it. Remy had actually been more than nice.

"See? I was nice," he retorted, a corner of his mouth hooking up into a grin.

The girl still didn't seem impressed. She looked at me again. "He might be ten months older, but I can kick his ass, Alpha or not, he's still my brother."

"Brother?" I repeated, looking back and forth between them. They had the same brown eyes and full lips, but that was absolutely where the similarities ended.

She smiled broadly at me. "I'm Katy. The better Holt."

Remy rolled his eyes again, throwing his head back with a groan. "Are you done yet?"

She clicked her tongue against her teeth. "Depends. Are you done making us wake up early on a freaking Sunday?"

"Sit down, Kit-Kat," Rhodes called. He dropped his head onto Larkin's shoulder, eyes closed as he pretended to nap. I caught the blush rising in Larkin's cheeks while Rhodes seemed completely oblivious to the effect he was having.

"The sooner Remy gets this meeting going, the sooner we can go eat," Rhodes muttered.

With a sigh, Katy moved back to the couch and sat down. She arched a brow at Remy, prompting him to continue.

Remy snorted and glanced around the room before frowning. "Where's Sierra? Ainsley?"

A petite girl with elfin features tossed a mane of shiny dark hair over her shoulders. "She said she'll be here. She had a ... late night." She finished with a smirk as three girls around her giggled. The four of them were the only other females in the room.

Rhodes opened his eyes, all teasing gone. He looked annoyed. "Want me to go find her?"

Remy was shaking his head as the front door opened and a stunning blonde sauntered into the room. Her makeup was perfect, her clothes obviously expensive, hair curled into loose waves, and she was wearing heels.

Unless she knew of a paved path out to the alpha house that I hadn't seen, she had just walked across campus in a pair of stilettos.

"Nice of you to join us, Sierra," Remy said dryly, his warm eyes now cold and hard. "Are we keeping you?"

She actually glanced at her watch for a beat and then lifted her head, a seductive smile on her glossy lips. Her blue eyes ran up and down the length of Remy, and I saw Katy glower at her.

"I always have time for you, Rem," Sierra said sweetly. She crossed the room to the girl who commented on her late night. The girl stood and sat on the floor so Sierra could sit. She perched on the armchair and crossed her legs as she leaned back, looking every inch a queen on her throne.

Standing next to Remy, I could hear the low growl rumble from his throat, expressing his displeasure. A muscle ticked in his clenched jaw.

My left hand raised in his direction, as if to touch him. Like I could comfort him.

With a sharp breath, I shoved my hands into the pockets of my jeans. I rocked back on my heels, wondering if I should sit or stand.

"Okay, we'll keep this quick," Remy started. Immediately he had everyone's attention, even Sierra, I noted with an inward smirk.

He gestured to me. "This is Skye. She and her mom just joined the Blackwater pack, and she'll be in the senior class. I trust I can count on you all to help her transition to Granite Peak smoothly. If you can help out or show her the ropes, make sure you do. Go ahead and introduce yourselves."

The shifters went around the room, giving their names and grades. Of the twenty-three of us, eight were seniors including Remy, Rhodes, and Sierra.

I was just praying there wouldn't be a pop quiz on everyone's names at the end of the meeting.

After Katy finished out the name game, Remy turned to me. "Anything you wanted to add?"

I forced a smile on my lips, knowing it looked unnatural. "Nice to meet you all."

Remy nodded. "You can sit down, if you want."

Larkin and Katy immediately scooted apart so I could sit between them, and I was grateful I didn't have to go sit on the floor by myself. I noticed that Larkin moved over but made sure she wasn't touching Rhodes.

Interesting.

Once seated, I fixed my attention back on Remy, who looked around the room expectantly.

"Any other pack business we need to be aware of? Any issues?" he asked, opening up the floor.

"You mean other than the Norwood pack being dicks?" A male wolf snorted derisively; he was sitting next to a guy who looked identical to him.

Sierra rolled her eyes and huffed. "You're so sensitive, Kyle. Grow a pair and grow up."

Kyle and his twin glared at her with flashing eyes. "Maybe if you didn't act like a bitch in heat every time their alpha was around, you would see all the shit they start."

Sierra leaned forward, her blue eyes practically glowing. "Maybe you—"

"Enough!" Remy boomed and they both shut up.

Katy leaned over to me. "The Norwood pack hates us, and the feeling is mutual. Well, hates us except for Sierra, but that's because she's been banging their alpha for the last month."

Sierra bristled, clearly hearing Katy. "I spent most of the summer with the Norwood pack. Trace and I have been together since last year."

"You mean since Remy shot you down for the last time?" Katy said sweetly, arching a brow. "You had to find a new alpha to sink your claws into?"

"I said, *enough*," Remy repeated, glaring at both Sierra and Katy until each looked at the ground.

"Sorry," Katy muttered, sounding anything but. She folded her arms over her chest, sinking down into the couch.

Remy looked at Kyle. "Has something new happened?"

Kyle shifted, not happy but clearly willing to let the issue die. He traced the edges of one of the hardwood planks he sat on. "No, nothing." His gaze flickered up and I caught him looking at ... Larkin. Her cheeks were tomato red and she looked like she wanted to crawl under the couch.

Remy looked from Kyle to Larkin and then finally to Rhodes. They seemed to have an entire conversation without speaking before Rhodes finally nodded. I noticed him casually rest an arm along the back of the couch. The movement shifted Larkin towards him.

"Anything else?"

Silence reigned in the room.

"Okay," Remy said. "We're done. Let's go eat."

**10**

"ARE YOU GONNA FINISH THAT?" RHODES DIDN'T WAIT FOR me to reply before reaching across the table and swiping the last piece of bacon from my plate, popping it in his mouth. He had already finished his own plate of breakfast and part of Larkin's.

I arched a brow at him. "Help yourself, by all means."

"Thanks," he grinned wolfishly at me and winked.

"You're such a pig," Katy muttered with a grimace. She slapped the back of his hand as he reached for her bacon. "Try it again and I'll take your paw off."

Rhodes retracted his hand as if she was brandishing a knife. His wide eyes went to me and then Larkin before fixing on Katy. "That hurts, Kit-Kat."

"And stop calling me 'Kit-Kat' while you're at it," she continued with a glare that had no heat behind it.

"You love it," Rhodes teased. He rested a head on her shoulder. "And you love me."

Katy shoved him off her shoulder. "You wish."

He winced. "That hurts."

She grinned at him, sucking the last of her orange juice through a straw. "Truth always does."

With a loud sigh, Rhodes looked across the table to Larkin and me. "So, ladies, what's the plan for today?"

Larkin blushed adorably, fidgeting in her seat. I caught Katy's eye and she rolled her eyes with a soft smile. Clearly, she could see Larkin was deeply infatuated with the pack beta, but he seemed completely oblivious.

"Well," Lark started slowly, tucking her hair behind her ear, "Skye needs to get her class schedule and finish unpacking, then we're marathoning *Stranger Things*. She's never seen it."

Katy blinked. "How the hell have you never seen it?"

"We didn't have ..." I glanced at Larkin for help.

"Netflix," she supplied.

"Netflix," I finished with a shrug.

Katy looked appalled. "That's tragic."

"I'm in," Rhodes announced, raising a hand.

"Put your damn hand down," Katy snapped. "You weren't invited."

"Wasn't invited where?" Remy asked, sitting down on the other side of Rhodes. After the pack meeting broke up and we had all headed to the cafeteria for breakfast, Remy had said he needed to meet with a couple of the pack teachers.

Remy looked expectantly from Rhodes to me. His tray was loaded with food—bacon, sausage, eggs, toast, pancakes, and hash browns in addition to milk, juice, and coffee. Considering Rhodes put away almost the same amount of food, I supposed it was normal for guys to eat that much.

At Long Mesa, I hadn't been permitted to eat with the other students, which was fine by me. Any chance I had to avoid my classmates, the better.

"Rhodes thinks he can worm his way into our *Stranger Things* girl-time day," Katy replied.

Rhodes's jaw dropped. "What the fuck? You weren't invited either."

Katy barely spared him a glance. "*Girl-time*, Rhodes. I have a vagina and therefore a standing invite." She flipped her red hair over her shoulder. "Do *you* have a vagina?"

His eyes were sparkling as he opened his mouth to reply.

Katy held up a hand quickly. "And no, spending copious amounts of time *inside* one doesn't qualify."

He closed his mouth with an audible snap and looked at Remy. "Can you control your sister?"

Remy looked from his best friend to sister and then back to his food. "You're on your own, buddy."

"Dude," Rhodes pressed, "what about bro code?"

"Nothing compared to the blood between siblings," Katy retorted smugly.

Watching them bicker was fascinating. Remy didn't seem phased at all by the way they were sniping at each other, and despite some of the barbs having some sharp points, there was an undeniably comfortable vibe between Rhodes and Katy that kept me from thinking they were actually mad at each other. The way Remy smiled indulgently at them made me think he knew they were just trying to get a rise out of each other as well.

"Right, Skye?" Rhodes demanded.

I blinked and realized the four of them were staring at me. Clearly, I missed the question. "Sorry, I missed that. What?"

Rhodes tsked lightly, wagging a finger at me. "You gotta pay attention, Skywalker."

I frowned. "What?"

"Skywalk—don't tell me you haven't seen *Star Wars*

either." Rhodes threw up his hands, exasperated. "It's only the greatest film trilogy ever made."

Katy frowned, propping an elbow on the table and resting her chin in her hand. "Which trilogy? Episodes four through six? One through three? Or the newest?"

Rhodes looked disgusted. "I thought we agreed to never speak of the complete fuckup that was episodes one through three."

Larkin cleared her throat and leaned towards me. "I've never seen them, either."

Rhodes' head whipped around, his long brown hair flying in his eyes. He shoved it back impatiently. "Are you kidding me? How the hell did I not know that?"

Remy groaned beside him. "I told you not to tell him that, Lark."

Larkin shrugged, holding her hands up in surrender. "Sorry?"

Rhodes slammed a fist down on the table. I caught my cup of water before it spilled. "This is a travesty. That's it—I'm vetoing the *Stranger Things* marathon and we're watching *Star Wars*." He fixed Katy with a stare. "Episodes four through six."

Now I was confused. "Wouldn't you need to watch episodes one through three first?"

Rhodes pinched the bridge of his nose, closing his eyes as he took a deep breath. "No, Skye, we don't."

"Technically episodes four through six came out decades before episodes one through three," Remy explained to me. He held up a hand when Rhodes started to protest. "But Rhodes doesn't acknowledge episodes one through three because they're shit."

"Oh," I said slowly, still not getting it entirely.

"Trust me," Remy said with a knowing grin, "just let him have this if you want him to shut up."

Larkin giggled beside me and I cracked a smile at him. It felt good to laugh with my pack.

"I'm not spending the day watching movies that didn't even know what CGI was," Katy announced. "You guys can go watch your oldies—"

"*Classics*," Rhodes growled.

"Whatever. We'll watch something else." Katy smiled at Larkin and me.

"But Skye and Larkin haven't seen it," he argued.

"And God willing, they never will!" Katy snapped back.

Rhodes was just ramping up for another argument when a body dropped into the empty chair beside me, startling me. I spun on my chair to stare at the newcomer, only to see him staring back at me with a lazy smile.

He was gorgeous with dark skin and onyx eyes. His teeth were brilliantly white, his lips smiling wide. He was clearly muscular and, judging by the look in his eyes, used to getting his way.

A beta, at least.

"You must be the new girl I've been hearing about," he said, his voice rough and playful.

I caught Remy, Rhodes, and Katy all stiffen across from me.

"Aren't you sitting with the wrong pack, Trace?" Rhodes asked, his normally warm voice icy enough to send chills down my spine.

I moved back and felt a tremble. Larkin was literally shaking next to me. I could see her eyes transfixed on the half-eaten tray of food in front of her as she shook. She was fucking terrified of this new guy.

Remy was frowning as he watched Larkin. His gaze slid back to Trace and narrowed.

I turned, feeling my wolf stirring in me. We seemed to

agree on one thing—protecting Larkin from whatever this threat was.

"I just came over to say hello, Katherine," Trace snapped. He looked back at me, his dark eyes assessing as they raked over me.

I met his heated gaze and, for once in my life, I didn't flinch back. I didn't look away. I lifted my chin a notch. His eyes widened a fraction. I had surprised him, and judging by his growing smile, he was enjoying the challenge.

The air crackled around us, charged with energy. I could hear conversations dying off at tables around us as people turned to watch us.

I swallowed hard and Trace tracked the movement, sensing my unease, but thinking he was the reason for it.

He wasn't.

I just wasn't crazy about everyone looking at me. I was aware enough to still feel Larkin shuddering beside me, and that was all the fuel I needed to keep the staring contest going.

"Stop." Remy finally snapped, getting to his feet.

Trace and I blinked and turned to him at the same moment. Now I swallowed again, but for a whole other reason.

Remy was furious, his brown eyes hard and unyielding. All his muscles were coiled, ready to attack. He looked like an avenging angel coming down to smite the guy next to me.

Beside him, Rhodes and Katy were perched on the edge of their seats, ready to stand united with him.

Trace slowly got to his feet beside me. "Relax, Rem. No disrespect meant."

"This is over," Remy spat. "Go back to your own pack and stay away from mine."

Trace smirked at him. "I'll stay away, but you might

want to tell your pack to stay away from me. I mean, that was your bitch who woke up in my bed this morning, right? Not sure why you let Sierra go. The things that girl can do—"

"Do I look fucking interested?" Remy asked coldly, ice dripping from his words. "Sierra can do whatever she wants with whoever she wants. She's made it quite clear she's not staying with the Blackwater pack. She's all yours."

Trace shrugged, pushing in his chair. "We'll see. She's fun to play with, but not exactly mate material."

"Still not sure why you're telling me this," Remy replied coldly, crossing his arms over his massive chest.

Trace took a step back, still grinning. "Gotta keep my options open, ya know?" His gaze slid behind me. "Larkin, I almost missed you over there. How've you been?"

Now I stood up, Rhodes and Katy getting to their feet as well. I folded my arms over my chest, glaring. A shiver tripped up my spine, my wolf begging to come out because of course *now* would be the time she wanted to make an appearance.

I was starting to think she only wanted to play when there was a chance of ripping someone's throat out.

Trace blinked slowly and looked at me, blocking Larkin. He nodded once, lips pressing together as his smile faded. "Nice to meet you, new girl. I'm sure I'll be seeing you around soon."

**11**

———————

No one seemed to really care about eating after the run-in with Trace. We picked at our food, trying to make small talk before Rhodes eventually decided we should go back to the cabin for a binge watch of something yet to be determined. In the meantime, I had to go pick up my schedule and finish unpacking. Katy offered to come with us, and we cleaned up our trays while Remy and Rhodes talked quietly, saying they would meet us later.

I liked Katy, but I had been hoping to get Larkin alone to see what was going on. I made a mental note to ask her when we were alone in our room.

As we left the cafeteria, I caught Sierra sliding onto Trace's lap and wondered if she knew she was as temporary as Trace made her out to seem. Or maybe he told her one thing and everyone something else.

Cassian used to do that all the time with Bella.

I'd lost track of how many corners I had turned to see him all over some other girl from our pack. I would see him with Bella almost immediately afterward, ever the doting boyfriend. He would make comments to me, touch me in some way that made me want to bathe in bleach, and then go right back to Bella. Hell, sometimes Bella would even walk in on him tormenting me and they would walk off together, hand in freaking hand.

Granted, Bella was younger than he was by almost two years, but still. It was disturbing how easily he could go from predator to prince.

I never understood how he could do that. Maybe because he didn't have a soul.

The entire time at Long Mesa, I never had anyone to stand up for me. Mom would try to shield me as much as possible, but at the end of the day, she couldn't protect me, especially when I was at school.

Rationally I knew Remy was the alpha here at school for my new pack, so if anyone was going to defend Larkin, it should be him. But I was tired of watching assholes like Cassian and Trace do whatever they wanted simply because they were born genetically superior.

Trace wasn't touching Larkin again if I had any say in the matter.

"So, who exactly was that guy?" I asked as we made our way down the hall, forcing myself not to react when Larkin flinched. I knew what she probably wanted was for us to forget the whole thing happened, but I needed more info.

Katy snorted, her brown boots clicking down the polished marble tiles and echoing off a row of large, shiny blue lockers. "That was Trace Valois, heir apparent to the Norwood pack and overall dickhead extraordinaire."

"The Norwood pack was the ones you guys mentioned this morning, right?" I asked, thinking back to when one of the twins had brought them up.

Katy nodded. "Yeah. Norwood and Blackwater don't

mix well." She scoffed. "Well, unless you're Sierra, then you mix well with everything and everyone."

Something Trace said still wasn't sitting right with me. "Trace mentioned something about Sierra and Remy?"

Katy stopped cold, and I worried for a second she might be ready to vomit. "No. No *fucking* way. Sierra chased Remy for years, ever since we were little. Bitch wouldn't take no for an answer. She had the nerve to show up in Remy's bed last year, naked, after the Spring Formal. Rem basically threatened to throw her out of the school and her family out of the pack if she tried anything like that again. The next week she was glued to Trace, saying how they were going to be mates, and she was done with Blackwater after she graduated."

"So, in the meantime, she's still part of our pack?" I frowned. That didn't seem right.

Katy nudged me with her shoulder as we resumed walking. "Look at you calling it *our* pack," she teased.

I tried to back pedal. "I didn't mean—"

"No, no," Katy cut me off, "I'm happy you see us as yours. You're right—it is *our* pack, and unfortunately, until Sierra turns eighteen and reaches the age of majority, she's in the pack unless her parents decide to leave."

"Do you think they will?"

I had almost forgotten Larkin was walking with us until she spoke up. "No. I've met her parents. They're really nice and love Blackwater."

"They are amazing. They do a lot of work outside of Blackwater, working with other packs and helping keep the treaties in place. They're basically Blackwater pack ambassadors," Katy admitted. "Who knows how the hell the birthed a creature like Sierra."

Katy paused in front of a door and waved an arm at it with a flourish. "Behold, the office!" She pushed open the door, introducing me to the woman at the front desk who printed out my schedule.

The whole process only took a few minutes. We started to head for the cabin when Larkin mentioned she left something in our room and we changed course for the dorm.

Katy reached over and plucked the schedule from my hands. "Let's see what you've got. Pre-calc, English, social studies, earth science ... Looks like you're in most of my classes." She squinted at the schedule. "You took an extra English lit elective? Intentionally?"

I shrugged as we walked outside into the bright fall sunlight. "I like to read."

"You and Remy have that in common," she muttered. "Pack studies and intro to shifters." She passed the paper back to me. "At least you'll be with Larkin and I most of the day."

I glanced at Larkin. "I thought you were a junior?"

"Larkin's a genius," Katy teased with a wink. "She'll be graduating with us in the spring."

Larkin ducked her head. "I like school."

"She finished all the math courses here when she was a freshman," Katy continued. "She's had to take online college courses the last couple years. Statistics and shit like that."

Larkin shrugged, a half-smile on her lips. "Math makes sense. I like numbers."

"Numbers I get," I admitted, "but when they start throwing letters into the mix, it gets confusing."

"Every letter has a numerical value. It's a puzzle to figure out what it is," Larkin replied firmly.

Katy linked her arm through Larkin's and smiled at her. "You are such a nerd."

The campus was coming alive as we walked. Groups of

teens were hanging out on the lawn, enjoying the sun burning off the last of the cold morning airing. Ten or so had a pickup game of soccer going. I recognized a couple faces from the meeting this morning. A few lone shifters were reading in different spots around the area.

We made it back to our room, and I stopped short when I came inside and saw three large boxes sitting on my bed that hadn't been there before.

"Oooh!" Katy squealed, brushing past me to look at the boxes. "What'd you get?"

"I don't know," I replied, confused. I looked at Larkin, who had joined Katy.

Larkin held up the smallest of the three. "They all have your name on them."

"Can we open them?" Katy asked.

"Sure," I answered, watching as she ripped open the top of the cardboard box. A piece of paper fluttered to the ground.

Larkin picked it up. "There's a note for you." She passed me the paper.

I unfolded it, tears suddenly pricking the backs of my eyes as I read the feminine script.

*Consider this our way of making up for all the Christmases and birthdays we missed.*

*-Zoe & Michael*

"This is gorgeous!" Katy exclaimed. I looked up to see her lifting a crimson red dress with capped sleeves and a flared skirt. She held it against her front and smiled at me. "You realize I plan to borrow this, right?"

I laughed, tucking the paper into my pocket. "Whatever you want."

The boxes were all filled with things I remembered looking at when Zoe and my mom took me shopping. Things I knew were too expensive or too silly to bother with trying on or buying. The trip had been strictly utilitarian—jeans, basic shirts, a coat, a pair of sneakers and some new underwear.

In the new boxes, Zoe had also included several sets of lacy, girly underwear that I actually kind of loved. They definitely weren't the hand-me-downs from Long Mesa or even the new, plain cotton ones I had bought with her and my mother. The fact that Zoe footed the bill for both shopping trips still felt wrong to me, but Mom only had a little cash leftover from what Zara had given us. Mom finally made Zoe agree it was only a loan until she found a job and could pay her back.

Katy opened my closet door and started hanging things up. After a beat, she turned back to me. "You realize all of your clothes have tags on them, right?"

I nodded slowly. "Yeah. They're all new. Mom and I left our old pack and we didn't really have time to pack much."

Katy frowned. "My mom gave me a few basics about you before you came here. She mentioned you and your mom left a really bad pack."

I nodded again, glancing at Larkin, who offered an encouraging smile as she settled onto her own bed. She pulled her pillow onto her lap, hugging it to her chest.

Katy hung up the red dress. "Do you want to talk about it?"

I flinched.

*No.*

No way did I want to talk about it. Now or ever.

"You don't have to, or anything," Katy continued, her tone light as she kept putting my things away like a personal assistant. "I just want you to know that if you want to, or need to, talk, I'm here."

"Me, too," Larkin added.

Katy glanced back at me. "Zero judgment. Whatever you say stays here."

I let out a shaky laugh. "Thanks. I'm not used to having friends or people to talk to."

"You do now," Katy announced, hanging up the last shirt. She closed the closet door and leaned against it, her red hair hanging in loose waves around her shoulders. "You're part of our pack now. And besides, I like you. I think you'll be good for the pack. Lord knows we could use some members who are actually loyal."

Larkin sighed. "It's only Sierra and Ainsley who want to leave."

Katy grimaced and sat down at the foot of Larkin's bed. She leaned back against the wall, resting her hands on her stomach. "I don't know. Sierra's been talking to some of the younger girls. It's like she's playing some sort of matchmaking pimp for the Norwood pack."

I sat on my own bed, curling my legs up. "What's the deal with the Norwood pack?"

"It's so stupid and so freaking misogynistic," Katy muttered, rolling her brown eyes to the ceiling. "Basically, it goes back to when my parents were at school here. The now-Alpha of the Norwood pack decided that my mom should be his mate. When they all graduated, he challenged my dad for her."

My eyes rounded. "But aren't your parents true mates, or something?"

"They are *now*, but then they were teenagers and my mom's parents had a lot of money. My grandfather handles investments for the majority of our pack. The Norwood pack was hoping that by challenging my dad for her, she would marry into their pack and bring all her family's money with her." Katy snorted. "Anyway, my dad kicked his ass *and* got the girl. It caused a big rift between the two packs."

"Wow." That was absolutely crazy. It was strange to think that anyone wouldn't see how perfect Gabriel and Mallory were for each other.

"Exactly. It's so stupid and so archaic that males can still challenge mate rights." Katy made a face. "Like women are still property that can be traded around."

Larkin hummed in agreement. "It's always been that way."

"Hopefully not for much longer," Katy replied. "My dad is hoping to bring the issue to the Alphas at the Summit meeting next year."

I loved the spring Summit meeting. It was an annual event that happened each spring where all the pack Alphas in North America came together to discuss shifter issues, treaties, and pack boundaries. Alphas and those expected to become Alphas one day were required to attend.

Which meant I got two weeks every year free from thinking about my grandfather, uncle, and Cassian.

Larkin leaned forward. "Do you think they'll actually remove the law?"

Katy sighed. "I hope so. Our pack and the Brooks Ridge pack have been pushing hard for it, and a lot of local packs seem on board. Between the challenge law and the fact that arranged matings are still technically legal, it's like living in the dark ages. And girls are the ones getting the shit end of it."

She didn't have to tell me that.

"The Brooks Ridge pack?" I asked, unsure of who they were.

Katy grinned. "Yeah. They're out on a pack run this weekend, so you'll meet them later. The Blackwater and

Brooks Ridge packs have been allies for almost a century. They're based out of northern Alaska."

Larkin nudged Katy with her toe. "And you're particularly fond of them."

Katy looked at me. "My girlfriend, Maren, is part of the Brooks Ridge pack."

I blinked, somewhat shocked. "Girlfriend?"

In Long Mesa, and most surrounding packs, same sex female pairings were forbidden. With pack numbers dwindling, all females who weren't omegas were expected to mate and breed. It was considered their duty to our race and sole purpose for existing.

Katy stiffened, her eyes flaring. She arched a brow with deadly elegance. "Yes, my *girlfriend*. Is that a problem?" She focused her eyes on me. Even Larkin looked bothered by my surprise.

I held up my hands slowly. "No problem at all. It's just ... my old pack, it was forbidden."

Katy relaxed but huffed, still eyeing me. "So, you're from a southern pack?"

I tensed, wondering if I had given too much away.

"Most northern packs don't have an issue with gay shifters," she explained. "It's the southern packs that had made it a crime to be yourself and love who you love."

I nodded slowly. "Yeah. In my pack, being a lesbian shifter would get you killed. If you were lucky."

"If you were *lucky*?" Larkin repeated, horrified.

Jaw clenched, I looked out the window. "If the pack found out a female was with another female, the females were forced into a mating bond with a male of the Alpha's choosing. They weren't given a choice. Females are meant to breed, according to them."

"Fuckers," Katy swore, getting off the bed and starting

to pace. "That's disgusting. These women were raped by their mate so they would have a kid?"

Swallowing hard, I nodded. I only knew of two females who had ever been forced into mating bonds for being gay, probably because all the other women had been forced to hide who they truly were. Neither story ended well.

"Did you tell my dad this?" Katy demanded. "This is exactly the shit that everyone needs to hear about at the Summit."

I hesitated for a second. "We told your dad everything that happened at our old pack."

"Good." Katy gave a firm nod. "Thank God you and your mom got out of there."

*You have no idea.*

I cocked my head to the side, not entirely sure what I was seeing on the television. "What the hell?"

Katy, Rhodes, and Remy burst out laughing. Larkin shushed us.

"No, seriously," I said, sitting up and staring at the screen. I pointed at the TV. "What is that thing?"

"It's a werewolf," Larkin huffed, reaching for the popcorn.

My jaw dropped and I made a face. "Are you *kidding* me? It looks like an overgrown dog."

Rhodes was still cracking up. He looked up from his spot on the floor, leaning against Larkin's legs. "Face it, baby girl, you're the only one who can watch this shit with a straight face."

Larkin grumbled under her breath and fixed him with a glare. "It's a love story, Rhodes. I guess you wouldn't understand that."

Rhodes raised his brows. "Love, I get. Pick a position and we can make love happen."

Remy snorted while Larkin blushed as she quickly looked away.

I was still transfixed on the screen. "Is that seriously what they think we are?"

"I don't think there was much thinking involved in the world of sparkly vampires and overgrown doggies," Katy snarked.

I had followed the first movie okay. Vampire, girl who falls down a lot, creepy bloodsucker watching her sleep, psycho vampires and a trip to the hospital where the glittery one professed his love. Fine. Whatever.

But we were not even halfway into the sequel, and the scrawny kid from the first movie with the bad wig was now a large, not at all anatomically correct, wolf.

Katy and Rhodes were content to make fun of the movies. Remy was in an armchair near the fireplace reading. Larkin seemed completely invested, complete with wistful sighs.

I pushed up from my spot on the couch between Larkin and Katy. "I can't. I'm sorry, Larkin, but I can't watch this anymore."

Larkin's face fell. "We can watch something else."

Katy's jaw dropped. "Don't you want to know who she picks?"

"I really don't," I said helplessly. I gestured to Remy. "He has the right idea."

Remy glanced up. "You're welcome to pick a book out of the study—"

"-Library," Rhodes corrected quickly. He gave me a serious look. "Please don't tell me you're another bookworm. I thought you were cool, Skywalker."

I shrugged. "Sorry. Total bookworm."

Rhodes groaned, dropping his head back onto Larkin's lap and nearly upending the popcorn bowl.

Remy stood up, setting his book on the side table beside the chair. "Ignore Rhodes. He wouldn't know entertainment if it slapped him in the head."

Rhodes smirked. "I know entertainment, but it's a different kind of movie."

Katy shoved him with her foot. "Don't be gross."

Rhodes turned and blinked innocently at her. "I was talking about *Star Wars*." He arched a brow. "What were *you* thinking of?"

"Behave, you two," Remy replied lightly, walking by and kicking the beta's foot. He nodded at me, motioning to the study where we had our first conversation. I followed him into the room, this time filled with less terror and more curiosity as I let myself really look at the rows of books.

"So, you like reading?" he asked, standing back and watching as I looked through the shelves.

"I really do," I admitted. I hesitated for a beat. "In my last pack, there wasn't much to do except read. It was an escape, I guess." It seemed more than a little embarrassing to tell him reading was how I learned about almost everything about the world.

"I get that," he agreed, not bringing up my old pack, for which I was grateful. "Growing up in Blackwater, I was always surrounded by people. Books became a way for me to escape, too."

I turned, surprised. "But you're going to be the Alpha one day, right?"

He frowned, brows raising. "And that means I can't like reading?" He sighed dramatically, shoving his hands into his pockets. "If that's a rule, I guess I'm going to have to tell my pack I'm not interested in being Alpha."

"Maybe Sierra can be Alpha," I teased back before I could stop myself.

Remy rolled his eyes with a laugh. "That's a great plan. Katy can be her beta."

I couldn't help the giggle that came out of me, the sound foreign and not unpleasant. "I think I would pay to see that."

He smirked, sitting on the arm of the couch by the window. "Right? You think she's bad with Rhodes ... She would kill Sierra."

I picked a book off the shelf. "Katy told me that Sierra ... That she wants to leave Blackwater."

"Is that all she told you?" Remy folded his arms over his wide chest. My eyes dropped to his arms and the way the sleeves of his white shirt stretched around the large muscles.

I blinked, shaking my head. "She mentioned Sierra pulled some crap with you last year."

He growled softly under his breath. "Yeah."

"I'm sorry," I said suddenly.

He waved it off with a sigh. "It's fine. I knew Katy would tell you. She hates Sierra."

I swallowed, pressing my lips together. "No, I mean I'm sorry Sierra did that to you. It was wrong. No one should touch another person without their consent."

He stared at me, a muscle in his jaw jumping. I could see the questions he wanted to ask, but he was too good a guy to push me.

"Your collection is amazing," I said, changing the subject back to books as fast as I could. I held up the one that caught my attention.

"Feel free to borrow it. It's one of my favorites," he said, not missing a beat.

I let out a shaky breath and nodded, hugging the book to my chest. "Thanks."

"Anytime." He flashed me a wide smile that made my chest tighten.

It had been ages since I felt anything but terrified of guys my own age. Hell, of males period. It felt nice to be able to talk to a guy and not be worried about when the attack or the insults would come.

The fact that he was absolutely gorgeous didn't hurt either.

"Do you have everything you need for classes tomorrow?" he asked suddenly after a moment of silence.

I nodded and leaned back against the bookshelf. "Yeah. Katy and Larkin took me to get my schedule. Looks like I'm with most of you guys for classes." I smiled then. "Katy told me that you're also taking the English Lit elective?"

He nodded with a grin. "You'll like it. We just started *The Great Gatsby*."

"I love that book!" I blushed, realizing I sounded like a nerd.

"So, you've already read it?"

"Yeah. A few summers ago. For fun."

He seemed impressed. "Then I know who to ask for help with the term paper for it."

"Sure," I replied, loving the feeling that someone might need my help for something.

"Did Katy or Larkin tell you that the pack run is the weekend after next?"

*Shit.*

My stomach clenched. Just for fun I reached out, trying to see what my wolf thought about the idea of a run.

I was met with complete silence.

"What's wrong?" Remy asked, not missing a damn thing.

I clutched the book tighter, ducking my head. I wished

I had left my hair down instead of braiding it so I could hide behind it now.

"Skye?" he pressed, standing up.

I cleared my throat and sighed. "You're gonna figure it out eventually anyway," I murmured absently.

"Figure what out?"

"I have a problem with shifting," I admitted, the humiliation pooling low in my gut.

He looked confused. "A problem? What kind of problem?"

"The kind where I can't do it," I replied tersely. "My wolf is really freaking temperamental. The only time I can really shift is when I'm really mad or ..."

"Or?" he prompted, dark eyes fixed on me.

"Or really scared," I finished quietly, looking at the floor. Dust motes danced through the slats of sunlight from the window and French doors.

"Skye, look at me," he ordered gently.

My eyes flickered up to his, expecting to see pity or annoyance. Instead they were understanding.

The kindness made my breath hitch.

"The biggest reason this school exists is to help us get in sync with our wolves so we can be stronger members of our pack. You're not the first person to need help with that."

I scuffed the toe of my sneaker into the hardwood floor. "It's stupid, though."

*I'm stupid.*

"It's not stupid, and neither are you," he corrected, saying exactly what I needed to hear.

"Okay, but I still can't shift and go with you guys unless you're planning to scare the hell out of me or really piss me off," I said with a huff.

"I'd kind of like to avoid doing either," Remy suggested wryly. "I think you need to see Elias."

"Elias?"

"Elias Samuels. He's from a pack in Maine originally, but he lives at the school now. He's one of the oldest shifters alive," Remy explained. "He's the guy to go to if your wolf is giving you issues. He spent his life studying shifters and packs across the globe."

"Elias Samuels," I repeated, unsure.

Remy shrugged. "What have you got to lose?"

I was still nodding when the door opened, and Rhodes and Katy tumbled through. They glared at each other before looking at Remy and starting to speak.

"I think we should—"

"Can we—"

Remy held up a hand and they went silent. I tried not to smile.

"Katy?" he prompted, looking at his sister who turned to Rhodes and stuck out her tongue before speaking.

"We were thinking we should do a bonfire cookout tonight. The pack can come, and we can all hang out. It'll give Skye a chance to get to know the others."

Rhodes grumbled under his breath, sounding something like it was his idea.

Katy glared at him. "It wasn't *your* idea. You said the five of us. I said the whole pack."

Rhodes snorted. "You're just hoping the Brooks Ridge pack crashes so you can see Maren."

Remy shrugged his broad shoulders and looked at me. "What do you think, Skye?"

I wasn't used to offering my opinion. Usually, my opinion was the last thing on anyone's mind, but I could see Remy extending the olive branch. He knew I was nervous and was letting me have a say.

"Yeah," I finally agreed. "It sounds kinda fun."

"All right," Remy said with a grin. "Cookout it is. But we need to make a grocery store run into town. We don't have enough for everyone here."

"Let's all go," Katy said quickly. "Skye hasn't been into town yet."

"Town?" I echoed, uneasy. As in around other people? I had never been around people other than shifters, and while I knew what a grocery store was, I was never allowed inside of one.

"It's not that exciting," Rhodes drawled. "It's a few boutiques, the grocery store, a hardware store, and a diner. We go a couple times a month to get supplies for the cabin."

"How do we get there?"

"I have a truck out back," Remy explained.

☪

REMY'S TRUCK turned out to be a massive SUV that easily fit the five of us. Rhodes had turned off the TV and plucked Larkin off the couch, carrying her out to the SUV and setting her down in the backseat. He slid in beside her and Katy got in on her other side, leaving me to the front seat with Remy driving.

Like with Amanda, I was fascinated watching the views while we drove. This time, the night wasn't pressing in around. The sun shone high and clear in a cloudless blue sky as far as I could see. The outside world blurred around us as Remy sped down the road.

It took almost thirty minutes to pull into the small, sleepy town. Rhodes was right—there was a strip of small shops and the other places Rhodes had mentioned. There wasn't even a stoplight in the town.

Remy parked in the front and we all got out of the car. Katy and Rhodes led the way in, bickering about what we were going to eat. Larkin followed, still trying—and failing—to play peacemaker.

I hesitated at the entrance, the doors sliding open to wait for me.

Remy came up beside me. "You good?"

"I've never ..." God, why was I so embarrassed about this? "I've never actually been inside a grocery store."

His eyebrows flew up, his jaw dropping before he could hide his surprise. "What?"

I scuffed the toe of my sneaker against the cement. "Omegas didn't go shopping for groceries. We were given whatever was left over from the pack. Besides, we didn't have our own money, so no need to shop."

His jaw clenched, a muscle thrumming to life like it had its own heartbeat. He looked away from me, and I got the distinct impression he was yet again trying to reign in his reaction.

"I know," I said, forcing a chuckle. "It's ridiculous, right?" Shaking out my shoulders, I started to walk inside when I felt his hand catch mine.

"It's not ridiculous," he said softly when I turned to look at him. "You have every right to feel however you want to feel, Skye."

I nodded, taking a big breath. I smiled at him. "I feel hungry. So, show me what's so good about this grocery store thing?"

Chuckling, Remy nodded and walked inside with me.

We caught up to the others, who were rolling a large cart, already filled with different kinds of meats and bread. There were several large bags of chips, and Katy and Rhodes seemed to be arguing over condiments.

Larkin sighed loudly. "Just get ketchup *and* barbecue sauce, guys."

"Skye!" Rhodes turned to me.

I jumped, busy looking at the vibrantly colored fruits and vegetables in huge bins.

"Ketchup or barbecue sauce?" Rhodes looked at me expectantly.

I shrugged. "Larkin said get both."

"But what's your preference?" he pressed, holding a container of each in his hands. He acted like they were on a scale as he balanced them.

"I guess ... ketchup?" I'd tried ketchup with my french fries at the diner and liked it. I'd never had barbecue.

Rhodes smirked triumphantly at Katy and tossed a container into the basket. "Told you."

With a growl, Katy grabbed the other container and dropped it into the basket, too. "We're getting both." She pivoted on her heel and started walking down the aisle. "We need drinks!"

Twenty minutes later, we had a car loaded full of food and drinks, and a bunch of other random things Katy grabbed like shampoo and nail polish.

Remy hadn't complained once, just smiling at his friends as they ran around the store grabbing stuff. He paid for it all when we checked out, and my eyes went wide at the price of the final bill.

The ride back took another thirty minutes but was strangely quiet as only Katy and Larkin talked much, occasionally dragging Remy and me into it. I glanced back and saw Rhodes was asleep, his head on Larkin's shoulder.

By the time we parked back at the Blackwater cabin, several of our pack mates had gotten the word that there would be a bonfire. A few broke off to help unload the car while three others kept piling sticks and logs high into the center of the small field behind the cabin.

Rhodes, now fully awake, bounded out of the car, pulling Larkin with him. He then opened my door and tugged me out.

Glancing around at his pack mates, he raised his arms and yelled, "Let's party!"

# 13



Rhodes wasn't kidding when he said it was a party.

Word had gotten out and shifters from other packs had slowly trickled in, mingling with our pack until I lost count of how many people joined in. What started out as me sitting around a campfire with Katy and Larkin was now an inferno. The bonfire's flames licked towards the skies, bright against the dark of the night.

Several speakers had been hastily set up and music pulsed a heavy beat from them that throbbed in my bones. A few people had started dancing near a copse of trees, hidden in shadows. Which, considering the noises I heard coming from that area when I walked past, was probably for the best.

Drinks were set up on the back deck, and somehow bottles of alcohol had joined the two-liter bottles of soda we had bought at the grocery store. The identical twins, Kyle and Konnor, manned the grill. Some didn't wait for them, opting to shove their hotdogs or marshmallows on to sticks and hold it over the bonfire.

Rhodes and Remy were surrounded by several females,

smiling and talking easily. Katy was currently talking to a bunch of people on the deck.

And I was sitting on a log by the fire with Larkin sticking close to my side.

"You don't have to stay with me," I told her, somewhat embarrassed that she felt the need to babysit me even if I was secretly glad she was by my side.

I knew there had been parties in Long Mesa, but I had never been invited and honestly never wanted to go.

Even though I barely knew my new pack, this was nice. Overwhelming, but nice.

Larkin smiled brightly and nudged my shoulder with hers. "I don't mind. Besides, if I stay with you, I can ignore *that*." She jerked her head in the direction of Rhodes, who had just put his arm around a brunette with an impressive … smile.

I made a face. "Have you told Rhodes you like him?"

Her face went pale. "No. No way."

I frowned. "Why not?"

She took a deep drink of her soda. "Because he's … *Rhodes*. And I'm just me."

I glanced up at Rhodes. He caught my eye and smiled with a wink before turning back to the brunette. A loud squeal had me jerking my head to see a blonde launch herself into Remy's arms.

I gave Larkin my full attention, ignoring the boys and their fanbase. "What does that even mean?"

Larkin reached down, tracing a design in the dirt by our feet. "Rhodes is one of the most popular guys here. He'll be with someone like her, not the omega who can barely talk around him without turning bright red."

"I thought you said you guys grew up together and are friends? Besides, he didn't seem to have a problem cuddling up to you in the car today."

Again, her cheeks flamed. "That was … he didn't …"

"You don't give yourself enough credit," I replied, hating to see her not seeing how truly awesome she was. "And Rhodes is always touching you or finding a way to include you."

She glanced up. "I'm fine with who I am, don't get me wrong. But I'm also not stupid enough to think Rhodes is anything but a giant flirt. Trust me." She glanced over at Rhodes, her eyes dimming slightly. "See?"

I looked over to see Rhodes and the brunette full on making out now. My heart hurt for her.

"So, tell me what to expect tomorrow," I started, trying to change the subject.

But Larkin was still looking at Rhodes, her expression growing sadder by the second. "I'm going to get another drink. Want anything?" She got to her feet quickly.

"I'm good. Do you want me to come with you?"

She shook her head, already moving away. I looked back to see Rhodes pulling the brunette up the stairs of the deck, towards the house. I sighed deeply as Larkin stood frozen in place as she watched them enter the house from her position at the foot of the stairs.

"As a rule, girls as pretty as you shouldn't be frowning like that."

I was startled at the voice above me. My surprise turned to unease as a guy my own age with curly blond hair and blue eyes sat down in the seat Larkin had just vacated.

I shifted further to the right when his leg brushed mine.

He smiled broadly at me. "I'm Caleb. You're Skye, right?"

I nodded slowly, not speaking. My eyes flickered over him quickly, taking in the wide expanse of shoulders and the way his shirt stretched across the muscles of his arms and chest. His hair was carefully styled, and his eyes danced as he watched me, but I got the feeling I wasn't in on the joke.

Or maybe I *was* the joke.

"Welcome to GPA," he said. His eyes raked over me, not leering but definitely assessing and sizing me up.

"Thanks," I replied carefully. Something about him had me on edge and I could feel my wolf stir in my chest, waking up to take notice.

"So, what has you frowning, pretty girl?" he asked, with what I think was supposed to be a flirty wink. "It's a party and there's at least a dozen guys who would jump at the chance to get to know you."

I glanced around us, looking for Larkin but she was still getting a drink and now talking to someone. "Did you need something?"

His brows rose. "Wow. Testy much?"

I wasn't before, but I was now. My jaw clenched.

He nudged me with a shoulder, and I almost shoved him off his seat.

"I just wanted to say hi," he explained, still grinning. But something had shifted in his smile. It was less congenial and definitely more calculating. "You have to know that someone like you is going to make waves here."

"Someone like me?" I echoed scornfully, arching a brow.

"Most of us have grown up together. It's been over a year since we had someone new transfer into GPA, and he definitely wasn't as gorgeous as you are." His eyes moved across me in a way that had my hackles raising.

I looked away, staring at the fire. "Not interested."

"I get it. You're keeping your options open," he said with a nod I caught in my peripheral vision. "Truthfully,

I'm not looking for anything serious either. But we could definitely have some fun."

I took a deep breath, trying to control the rage that simmered in me.

His hand landed on my shoulder and his voice dropped as he whispered in my ear, "Why don't we get out of here?" *Now* he was leering.

And I was sick of being the new piece of meat at school.

"Why don't you take your hand off of me before I break it off?" I countered, turning to look him fully in the eye. "When a girl says she isn't interested, it usually means she isn't interested."

He removed his hand slowly, raising them both innocently. "Chill. I thought we were just getting to know each other."

"And now we're done," I finished firmly, my heart racing. I jerked my chin. "Get lost."

He stood slowly, still smiling. "Feisty. I like that in a girl."

I stood as well, not wanting to give him any advantage even though he still was several inches taller.

"And I like guys who can actually take a hint," I retorted coolly.

His smile slipped slightly. "I'll see you around, Skye." He stepped over the log we had been sitting on and I watched until he blended into the darkness around the trees.

"Are you okay?" Larkin came up behind me, touching my arm. I turned to see her wide eyed, staring in the direction Caleb had left.

"Fine," I muttered. "That guy was a total ass."

"He didn't do anything, right?" she pressed, looking at me.

"Other than annoy me? No." I snorted and rolled my neck, working out the tension.

"That's Caleb, the beta for the Norwood pack."

I grimaced. "So, he's friends with Trace? Explains a lot. I guess dickhead is a pack trait."

Larkin bit her lower lip nervously. "You shouldn't make them angry."

My eyes narrowed. "What's going on, Larkin? I saw you earlier when Trace was at breakfast. You looked like you were going to crawl under the freaking table."

She looked away, shifting her weight on her feet. "I don't know what you're talking about."

My brows lifted. "Jesus, even right now, you're shaking because I mentioned him. What's going on?"

"The Blackwater and Norwood packs have always had this rivalry, like Katy said. It's better to just stay away from all of them."

"I get that," I replied, not letting the issue slide, "but you seemed terrified of him."

Larkin looked at me and I was stunned to see tears gathering in her eyes.

"Can you just leave it?" she whispered. "Please?"

Without thinking, I reached out and pulled her into my arms. Other than my mom, and occasionally Maisie, I hadn't been hugged. The sensation was still new, but the compulsion to do it was strong.

Larkin's arms came around behind me, hugging me tightly as her body shook.

"I'm here if you need me," I told her quietly. It felt strangely right to say those words I had only ever before told my mom.

"Thanks," Larkin replied, wiping her eyes and forcing a smile as she pulled away. "I promise I'll tell you if I need to talk about it."

"I'm going to hold you to that," I warned, seeing Katy approach from the corner of my eye.

"Ugh," she groaned, throwing her arms around our shoulders as soon as she was in range. "That makes me nauseous. I mean, can they be more obvious?" She waved a hand in the direction of Remy.

He was near the bonfire now, the flame making his brown hair reddish gold. In addition to the huggy blonde from before, he was surrounded by four other females. It was pretty telling that in a world where females had their pick, they were all picking the same guy.

And I couldn't really blame them.

Katy wrinkled her nose. "So gross. It's the same at every damn party."

Larkin shrugged, taking a drink from her cup. "He's a good guy. And he's cute."

"Did you really just call my brother *cute*?" Katy deadpanned.

Larkin chuckled. "I hate to break it to you, but your brother's gorgeous. And I don't know why you're surprised —it's been this way since we were kids. Girls always flocked to Remy and Rhodes."

Katy rolled her eyes. "Rhodes is a man-whore. We all know that. At least my brother is more selective."

I caught Larkin flinching out of the corner of my eye.

"But still. Remy is my *brother*. I don't want to see this." Katy groaned and turned away from them. "I miss the days of Sasha."

I frowned as Larkin outright laughed. Her head tipped back, her glossy dark locks gleaming from the firelight.

"Careful what you wish for," Larkin teased, wagging a finger.

"At least when he was with Sasha, she kept all the bitches away," Katy groused.

"You *hated* Sasha," Larkin reminded her. She looked at me and stage-whispered, "Sasha was Remy's girlfriend for most of last year. She's from a pack in Maine and graduated in the spring. She and Katy hated each other."

"Sasha was a Level One Bitch," Katy confirmed. "And I'm so freaking thankful to all the baby angels and wolf puppies in the world that Remy dumped her ass, but at least she kept the harem away from him. They don't even care about him, just the fact that he's going to be Alpha."

"And he's hot," Larkin added, winking at me. I cracked a smile, happy to see her joking again.

"Can we stop talking about how hot my brother is?" Katy whined with a shudder. "I just want—" She stopped mid-sentence, her jaw dropping open a second before she squealed like a little kid and took off running.

With wide eyes, I watched as she ran towards the trees, dropping to her knees as a gray wolf emerged. The wolf nuzzled into her side.

"That's Maren," Larkin said, smiling. "Katy's girlfriend."

"The one from another pack?" I asked, watching as several other wolves came from the trees.

Larkin nodded. "Looks like they all just got back from their pack run."

Pack run.

My stomach flipped nervously, remembering the Blackwater pack was scheduled for their run in only a few weeks. Other than when Caleb had shown up, I hadn't felt my wolf in days. I reached out now, trying to see if she was there but was met with silence.

Maybe I would try to track down Elias sooner rather than later, like Remy suggested earlier.

I watched as Remy separated from his groupies and approached the wolves, stopping in front of the massive brown one that towered over the rest of the pack. He cocked his head to one side, studying the wolf.

"We figured you guys would be back hours ago," Remy said with a smile.

The wolf gave a low whine, shaking out his fur.

Remy chuckled. "There's extra clothes upstairs if you guys want to change here."

The wolf turned his head and gave a low bark before leading the other wolves across the yard and up the deck where Kyle opened the door for them.

☪

THE BROOKS RIDGE pack liked to party as much as the rest of the student body at GPA.

The dozen or so wolves that joined the gathering all had drinks in their hands, and a new level of energy seemed infused when they joined the group. The music had definitely gotten louder. I could feel the bass thumping in my chest.

Maren had emerged from the house first and made a beeline for Katy. Where Katy was fair and had red hair, Maren had tan skin and dark hair and eyes and was several inches shorter.

The massive brown wolf, who I now knew was Dante, the alpha of the Brooks Ridge pack at GPA, was currently talking with Remy and Rhodes, who had come outside with the pack after they had changed clothes. I had no idea where his brunette conquest had gone.

There was a new brunette with them now, between Remy and a taller guy with a million tattoos that Katy called Ryder. I wasn't entirely sure if the brunette was with Dante or Ryder, to be honest, but she was the only female standing around them. Anytime a new female approached the group of guys, her glare sent them scurrying away.

I couldn't blame females for approaching—the four of them were easily the hottest guys at the party by a landslide.

And I meant that in a completely objective way.

I looked up as Katy came over, Maren's hand tucked inside of hers.

"Mare, this is Skye," Katy introduced. "Skye, this is my girlfriend, Maren. I demand you two be friends."

Maren laughed and shook her head. She extended her free hand to me. "Nice to meet you, Skye."

"Same," I replied with a tentative smile.

Maren grinned at Larkin, reaching over to hug the omega with her free arm. "Hey, Lark."

Larkin returned the hug and my chest relaxed. Something in me was super protective of Larkin and seeing her at ease with Maren made me happy.

"How was the run?" Larkin asked.

"Would have been better if Ryder didn't decide to take a shortcut through the mountain pass that was closed off due to a rockslide," a new voice said wryly. I glanced up to see the brunette that had been with the guys now standing with us.

She was my height, with intelligent hazel eyes and long, dark hair.

Her face split into a wide smile and she held out a hand. "I'm Tate."

"Skye," I replied, taking her hand in mine.

Her eyes rolled. "Oh, I know. You've caused quite the stir around here. Like these guys have never met a new shifter or something."

Katy smirked. "Right? I'm taking bets on the first guy to ask her out."

Larkin's lips pressed into a thin line. "Caleb was already here earlier."

Tate glowered and Katy looked around quickly, her dark eyes scanning the party.

"He left," I said when I realized she was looking for him.

"He's such a dick," Tate muttered, running a hand through her hair. "I can't believe he had the nerve to show up to a Blackwater party."

"He came by himself," Larkin added, still nibbling her lower lip.

"That's something," Katy replied with a frown. "But Trace came by our table at breakfast and tried to start something."

Maren snorted into her cup. "I bet Remy and Rhodes shut that down quick."

"Actually, Skye did," Katy said smugly, lifting her cup slightly in my direction. "She basically told him to fuck off. It was pretty epic."

"Good for you," Tate said with a grin. "That guy needs to be taken down a notch or twenty." She took a drink of her own drink and looked past me, her gaze narrowing.

"For fuck's sake," she muttered with a huff. She stormed off in the direction of the guys. A petite newcomer was currently stroking the arm of an unimpressed Dante. We all watched Tate walk up and physically insert herself between the two of them until the girl stepped back and slunk away with her tail tucked firmly between her short legs.

Tate whirled to look at Dante, but Ryder settled his arms around her waist and pulled her back against him. Rhodes said something that made them all laugh. Even Tate relaxed, and Dante reached up to touch her cheek.

My confusion must have read on my face because

Maren leaned over and explained, "They're all three together."

I nodded slowly, watching Tate smile at both boys. With the decline of female shifters, seeing two guys sharing a female wasn't unusual, but in Long Mesa, it was usually an order by the Alpha or decided by the males, not a choice the female made.

Tate definitely didn't look coerced to be with both of them.

I was still studying them curiously when Remy's eyes lifted to mine. Across the fire, his eyes glowed molten gold. His lips curved into a half smile as he nodded to me before turning back to his friends.

Sucking in a sharp breath, I focused back on the conversation between Katy, Larkin, and Maren.

Yeah, I could definitely see why girls couldn't stay away.

**14**

―――――――

THE PARTY HAD GONE ON UNTIL THE EARLY HOURS OF THE morning, but Larkin and I left shortly before midnight. She was tired, and I was exhausted from all the new people I had met, and I desperately wanted to decompress. It only took seconds for me to fall asleep, but in those few seconds I realized I hadn't talked to my mom in over twenty-four hours, which was a definite first. After mentally vowing to call her after my first day of school, I fell into a hard sleep and only woke up once Larkin's alarm went off.

We both showered in the omega floor bathroom, and I tried to ignore the curious stares as I left the steam of the room wrapped in a big towel. We hurried and changed to get down to breakfast. I opted to braid my wet hair instead of drying it but regretted that decision the second I stepped out of the dorm and into the brisk September morning.

Larkin and I grabbed our breakfast from the buffet line, my stomach growling as I smelled all the foods. I mimicked Larkin's choices, grabbing a bright green fruit

137

that smelled amazing, but I wasn't entirely sure what it was.

Remy, Rhodes, and Katy joined us, each looking more exhausted than the other. No one spoke as we started eating, the cafeteria slowly filling up with students.

Again, I felt their eyes on me, studying and assessing. Thankfully I hadn't seen Trace or Caleb make an appearance yet.

Glancing up, I saw Katy smile a second before a dark blur in a red shirt launched at her. My fork clattered against my plate, and I watched in shock as Katy caught her with a laugh, pressing her lips to the human missile.

Maren laughed, breaking their kiss to settle on Katy's lap and then pressed her lips to her girlfriend's neck. Katy let out a decidedly feminine giggle, squirming on her seat.

"No PDAs where we eat," Remy said, keeping his eyes on his tray. He stabbed a fork in the general direction of his sister. "*Your* rule."

Katy leaned back as Maren settled on her lap, looping an arm across her shoulders and stealing a bite of waffle from Katy's plate.

"I've barely seen her in three days, Rem," Katy whined.

He shrugged. "You saw her last night. Besides, you made the rule."

"When you were fourteen and realized what french kissing was," Katy retorted. She rolled her eyes. "If I had to see you try to tonsil fuck another girl, I was going to stab myself."

Rhodes smirked at Remy. "I remember those days. You and ... Gina DeVrys! That was her name. The senior from the Quebec pack."

Remy sighed, shaking his head. I thought he would tell them both to shut up, but instead he looked at them with a wicked gleam in his eye. "I learned a lot freshman year."

Rhodes laughed, Katy grimaced, and I tried to ignore the ugly feeling worming inside me.

"Ew. Sick." Katy shuddered.

I looked up as Tate, Dante and Ryder joined us, pulling over the table beside ours. Rhodes and Larkin stood up so they could drag the table flush to ours before settling in. Dante leaned down, whispering something to Tate who smiled and nodded. Dante and Ryder headed off towards the buffet line while Tate sat down by Larkin.

"So, Skye," Tate started, her dark eyes like chips of warm amber gleaming at me, "ready for your first day at GPA?"

I shrugged a shoulder. "I guess."

"She has English with us first," Katy added, spearing a bite of waffle and then feeding another bite to Maren.

"Oh, good" Tate said with a grin. "Dante does, too."

"Am I the only one not in this class?" Rhodes groused, shoving an entire slice of bacon in his mouth and chewing.

"Ryder isn't." Tate shrugged. She propped an elbow on the table and rested her chin in her palm. She gave a sniff of entitlement, clearly teasing them. "I guess you two weren't good enough to make honors English."

Rhodes snorted. "It's English. I don't see why honors is so different. Ryder and me could absolutely handle it."

"Ryder and I," Katy corrected with an eye roll.

Rhodes frowned. "What about you and Ryder?"

"And this is exactly why you need to be in a different class." Katy huffed a laugh as Dante and Ryder brought their trays over. Dante carried two trays, one of which he set in front of Tate before going around to the other side of the table and sitting down.

"How's the move been?" Dante asked me from his seat

beside Remy. Both of them watched me for an answer and I shifted in my seat under their stares. Two alpha stares was a bit disconcerting.

"It's been fine," I finally answered, going back to my scrambled eggs. There was melted cheese mixed into them and I barely wanted to take the time it took to chew. It was like my body was trying to inhale as much food as I could before I was inevitably sent back to minimal meals and crappy food.

Dante's eyes slid to Remy. "I heard Trace made an appearance over here yesterday."

Remy tensed, the corners of his mouth tightening. "Just being Trace."

Dante looked at me. "And I heard you put him in his place."

I flushed, not sure how to answer.

"It was pretty fucking amazing," Rhodes admitted with a grin.

Ryder groaned and leaned back in his seat as Tate reached over and finished his last piece of sausage. "Jesus, I wish you had that on film. I would watch it over and over, man." He pointed to me. "You're my hero, Skye."

I ducked my head. "I didn't do anything."

Katy snorted. "You stared down an alpha dickhead. Take the credit, babe."

I rolled my eyes and caught Larkin studying her food intently. Shit. Something was definitely going on there. Anytime Trace was mentioned, she all but froze in place. I wanted to give her the space she asked for, but something was seriously not right.

My stomach clenched and I set down my fork, appetite gone. That checked out look in her eyes reminded me way too much of the last time I had seen Maisie.

Instantly I felt like the biggest bitch. While I had been

bonding with my new pack mates, watching movies and playing with clothes, what the hell had Maisie been enduring without me or my mom there?

All the things I hadn't thought of in the last several days seemed to catch up to me all at once.

I had killed another shifter. Not just any shifter, but Preston's brother. Had his body been found yet? Was my uncle on his way to Blackwater to come after us? Or maybe he would just show up here instead. Jesus, or maybe he would send Cassian and Preston.

I could feel my thoughts starting to spiral when Remy cleared his throat. I looked up into his chocolate brown eyes. For a second, it was just us, and I felt the full weight of his alpha stare as it anchored me to the present. Slowly, the panic receded to a manageable level.

"Skye?" he prompted, and I realized everyone was studying me, waiting for me to answer a question I never heard.

"You good?" he asked, keeping his tone light, but I could see the concern in his eyes.

I nodded stiffly. "Yeah, I'm great."

"You sure?" Katy pressed.

I scrambled for a plausible excuse. "Just nervous about today. I hope I can get caught up quick."

Katy waved a hand dismissively. "Please, you'll be fine. And we'll all help you if you need it."

A bell rang over our heads and I jumped at the sudden noise. Chair scraped against the tile floors as students started to get up.

"Warning bell," Larkin explained, reaching down to grab her backpack. "We have ten minutes until first period."

Butterflies took off in my stomach as nerves started to settle in. GPA was definitely bigger than the school I had attended in Long Mesa, but at least here, no one knew me.

*Yet.*

I still wasn't sure if that was a good thing or a bad thing.

Everyone finished their breakfasts and quickly put their dirty trays away before gathering their bags. We all headed for our English class, except for Ryder and Rhodes who headed for a different class across the hall from us.

Half the class was full already and every single student turned to look at us when we walked in.

No, they looked at me.

Dante, Tate, Maren and Katy all split off to sit towards the back while I hesitated under the weight of the stares from the shifters in front of me.

A gentle hand settled against my lower back, the heat of it radiating through my shirt.

"Come on," Remy murmured quietly, his voice pitched low so only I could hear it. My tummy flipped at his deep timbre, and I resisted the urge to lean back into his touch. "Sit with us."

His hand on my back, he guided me to an empty seat behind Maren before sitting down in the seat next to me.

I slid onto the plastic, shivering at the contrast between the cold plastic and his warm hand.

My thoughts were still churning, but as I looked at Remy, he was methodically pulling his books from his own backpack, completely unaffected.

Giving myself a mental shake, I pulled out my own notebook as Amanda entered the room. She smiled at me from the front of the board, giving me a friendly wink before turning to start writing on it.

A few other students entered, including Trace, Caleb, and Sierra at the last minute. They all sat on the complete opposite side of the room, and I could feel the fire spitting from Sierra's eyes.

Squaring my shoulders, I kept my eyes forward, trying to give my new teacher my complete attention.

I wasn't interested in getting into any pack drama ever again.

☾

BY THE LAST period of the day, I was exhausted. GPA was more academic than Long Mesa, and I would need to study to catch up. But academics aside, I was over the stares and the whispers anytime I walked by.

Thankfully, no one really approached me. A few people said hi, but I always seemed to have someone with me to run interference. I hoped the new girl status would wear off soon. I wasn't crazy about the idea of another school where I was stared at, even if it was for a completely different reason.

Larkin and Ryder had just finished Earth Science with me and walked me to my last class—English Lit. No one I knew had this class with me except Remy, and as I stepped into the doorway, I could see he wasn't there.

Keeping my head down, I hurried down a row towards the back of the class, sliding into an empty seat in the back corner.

Several students turned to look at me, and I kept my head down as the whispers started.

Taking out a fresh notebook, I was rooting for a pen when I heard footsteps approach.

Thinking it was Remy, I looked up with a relieved sigh, but found a guy I had seen in a couple other classes smiling at me.

"Hey," he said brightly, with an easy smile that showed off twin dimples. "Skye, right? I'm Andy."

He seemed harmless enough—average height and build, dirty blonde hair cut short and bright blue eyes. His hands were shoved in the pockets of his jeans and I got the distinct impression he was ... nervous.

"Hey," I said slowly, my fingers closing in around the pen at the bottom of my bag.

Andy glanced back, probably at his friends, who were openly gawking, before looking sheepishly back at me.

"How do you like GPA so far?"

"It's fine," I answered slowly, wondering where this was going.

He nodded enthusiastically. "Good, good. That's good." He glanced down at his shoes for a second. "I think we're in some of the same classes."

"Yeah, I think so," I agreed cautiously, leaning back in my seat.

His cheeks flushed and he rubbed the back of his neck. "Right. I mean, you were there so ... of course you probably noticed. Not that you noticed me, I mean. Classes aren't that big. It's good, you know? Keeps student to teacher ratios low, which improves test scores and ... stuff."

I cocked my head to one side, trying not to smile as he rambled on.

He was definitely nervous.

"Anyway," he said brightly, and so suddenly it made me blink, "I just wanted to offer to show you around, if you want. Or not. But maybe we could grab dinner or something? If you want. Totally up to you."

My eyes went wide as he stammered on.

"But your pack is probably showing you around," he went on, shaking his head with chagrin. "Blackwater is a big pack."

I nodded slowly, unable to keep my lips from curving into a small smile.

"Or we could just hang out. I'm from the Salt Lake Pack. From Maine? It's a small pack. Not like … yours. Or maybe you came from a small pack? And now you're in one that's … big."

Definitely rambling.

Andy cleared his throat. "Fall Fest starts next week. Maybe we could go to the kickoff bonfire together?"

Wait -what? Was he asking me out?

His eyes went huge and wide. "Not like a date. Unless you wanted a date, but as, like, friends. Not that we're friends, but we could be. If you want."

I started to open my mouth when I was saved, yet again.

"Hey, Andy." Remy clapped a hand on the smaller boy's shoulder and tossed him a grin.

He eased past Andy and sank into the seat beside me, tossing me an easygoing smile. "Thanks for saving me a seat."

Andy coughed and stepped back. "Um, hey, Remy. I didn't know ... I mean, I didn't ... " He looked wildly around the room, his Adam's apple working as he stammered. "I need to make sure I have everything for class."

Andy turned and nearly crashed into the desk behind him as he scrambled to get away.

Remy chuckled under his breath, plucking a pencil from behind his ear.

"What the heck just happened?" I was still stunned.

"I think Andy was asking you out," he replied, eyes grinning as he looked at me. "You didn't seem like you knew what to do, but if you're interested, I can have him come back."

"No, thank you," I said quickly.

Remy chuckled, shaking his head. "I was kidding, Skye."

I looked over to see Andy looking at me. He blushed and quickly looked busy as he dug through his backpack for something.

"What's Fall Fest?" I asked, leaning forward on my desk.

"It's basically GPA's version of homecoming week," he explained.

I gave him a blank stare.

"In normal school, they have this week of school spirit shit followed by a big football game, and then there's a dance at the end."

"Oh," I replied slowly. At least I knew what football was. Cassian and his friends used to play pickup games, mostly as a way to literally throw their weight around and hurt other wolves.

"Each day has a theme next week," he went on, his eyes rolling to the ceiling. He pushed the sleeves of his Henley up, and I swear I tried not to linger on the way the muscles of his forearms corded and shifted.

I *swear* I tried.

And failed.

Miserably.

They were forearms. What was there to stare at in a *forearm*?

And yet, I couldn't stop from watching the way the muscles and tendons shifted and pulled his skin.

Swallowing, I forced myself to look him in the eyes, grateful he didn't seem to notice me ogling his freaking *arm*. "Themes?"

"One day is pajama day, one day is pack color day ... I think there's a calendar." He shrugged. "Katy's really into it."

"And you're not?"

"I'm game for anything that helps unify the packs," he admitted, tapping the eraser of his pencil against his desk. "Kids have fun with it, but it isn't mandatory to participate. You don't have to do it."

I ducked my head. "Kind of sounds fun."

"It can be, I guess. Anyway, GPA ends the whole thing with a dance on Friday night."

"No football game?"

He laughed. "No. They tried that once. It nearly turned into a pack brawl. They try to limit competitive sports between packs."

"Alphas can't handle losing?" I teased.

He smirked. "Definitely not." He leaned forward, eyes sparkling. "Don't let anyone know I told you, but alphas are the most insecure assholes in the world when it comes to competition."

I couldn't help the smile that curved on my lips. "I don't think anyone could call you insecure, Remy. Or an asshole."

His smile softened. He looked genuinely surprised by my compliment. "Thanks, Skye."

We sat that way for several beats, leaning towards each other, smiling at each other, before I blinked and pulled back.

Was I flirting? Was that a thing I did now?

"So, there's a dance?" I looked down at my desk.

He nodded. If he sensed the weirdness between us, he didn't let it show. "We dance, we party. It's fun. And then the next week is the pack run."

I froze, reminded again about the damn pack run.

The teacher walked into the room, a small man with dark hair and glasses who slammed the door a bit louder than necessary.

"Room three-oh-one," Remy whispered.

My head swung to his direction and I arched a brow. "What?"

"Elias Samuels," he said gently, quietly. "Talk to him about the issues you're having with your wolf. It's important you be part of the pack on your first run with us. See what Elias says."

I swallowed around a lump in my throat, nervous as hell.

**15**

———

THE SMELL OF DUSTY BOOKS TICKLED MY NOSE AS I PUSHED open the cracked door to room three-oh-one. I poked my head in, looking around with wide eyes at the overloaded bookshelves and stacks of books and papers all over the floor. The sign on the door read: Dr. Elias Samuels, Ph.D.

"Hello?" I called out softly, not wanting to intrude but desperately wanting access to the room to run my fingers across the leather spines. Books of every color and size filled the small space.

"Back here," a muffled voice called, somewhere behind the stacks.

Easing the door fully open, I slipped inside before closing it behind me. I carefully made my way through the makeshift path left in the floor. I wound around behind the first set of bookcases and the room opened into a small circle with a desk and chair, a small armchair, and several stacks of loose books.

The man bent over a book at the desk didn't look up as I came in, his white hair shockingly bright against his dark skin. He held a magnifying glass over the text, lips moving silently as he read.

"Yes? Can I help you?" he asked, not looking up.

I cleared my throat. "I was told to come here."

Amusement threaded his tone. "And now you have. Were you told to do anything else upon arriving?"

I laughed softly, my shoulders relaxing. "Right. I was told to see Elias Samuels. Are you Dr. Samuels?"

"Sometimes," he answered cryptically. He set the magnifying glass on top of the open book and looked up at me with knowing gray eyes as he lowered himself into the desk chair. "You must be the new Blackwater pack member. Skye Parker, isn't it?"

"Sometimes," I replied, the left side of my mouth hooking up.

He arched his brows. "Touché." He leaned back in his chair, folding his weathered hands across his stomach. "Please, call me Elias. And how can I help you today?"

"My alpha ... Remy, told me to see you. I've been having issues with shifting," I admitted quietly, embarrassed.

"What kinds of issues?" he asked, cocking his head to one side.

"The kind where she only wants to come out and play if I'm super angry or terrified out of my mind. I can't shift whenever I want the way everyone else can."

He held up a hand, wagging a finger. "First, stop comparing yourself to everyone else. Everyone had their own issues with their wolf. Anyone who says they didn't is lying." He rubbed his jaw. "The bond between a human and their wolf is a sacred thing, and no two bonds are alike. Some start shifting as pups, some don't shift until puberty, and some struggle through adulthood, never getting the shift to happen more than a few times."

I snorted and rolled my eyes. "Great. So, it's going to always be like this?"

"No, I didn't say that," Elias replied. He motioned to the armchair in front of him. "Why don't you sit down?"

I moved across the small space and dropped into the armchair.

"Now," he started, leaning his forearms on the desk, "you say your wolf comes out when you're scared or angry?"

I nodded.

"When your emotions are extremely volatile," he surmised. "You just joined the Blackwater pack? Where were you before?"

I shifted on the cushion. "A southern pack."

His brows raised again. "Can you be more specific?"

I gritted my teeth. "New Mexico."

He hummed under his breath, the lines around his eyes deepening as he studied me. "Only five packs in New Mexico. Klarendon, Long Mesa, Small Top, Desert Sands, and Flatrock. Flatrock and Small Top have a dying population and no wolves younger than thirty. I don't think Flatrock even has a female left in their pack. Desert Sands and Klarendon are small packs with less than a dozen members each. That leaves us with Long Mesa?"

My breath caught in my chest, my heartbeat wild and erratic.

Elias nodded once. "I can see why you left. Long Mesa doesn't have the best reputation. Once it was a great pack, one of the strongest in the southwest. The last several Alphas have slowly driven it into the ground."

I snorted. "Yeah. That sounds about right."

His eyes sharpened on me. "But what about you? Why did you leave?"

I tried to choose my words carefully. "Like you said, it's not the best pack."

"And?"

"And what?" I countered defensively. "My mom wanted something better for us."

He sighed sadly. "I'm an old man, Skye. I've lived longer than most, and I've met more wolves than you can imagine. I've devoted my life to studying our kind, and that means traveling across the world to interview and observe them."

I waited for him to continue, taking a deep breath.

"I remember being young and meeting a beautiful young wolf out in the desert of New Mexico. She brought me into her pack and I spent weeks with them, learning their ways and customs." He didn't blink as he looked at me. "Considering you look almost exactly like her with dark hair, I'm guessing she was your grandmother or great-grandmother. And then there are your eyes. Anyone from the south knows those eyes."

My hands curled into fists. My muscles tensed, bracing to run if I needed.

"Which would mean your last name is Markham, not Parker," he continued calmly, as if he wasn't completely dismantling my cover story piece by piece. "And if that's true, that would also make you the bastard daughter of Adalynne Markham, the wolf who started a war in the south."

I jumped to my feet. "You don't know anything—"

He held up a hand. "I'm not judging, my dear. I'm just saying I know. And knowing what I know about the aftermath of the war, and the rumors of Long Mesa, I can hazard a guess why your wolf is dormant."

I was torn between walking out of the room and

wanting to know more. Curiosity won, and I sat back down. "Why?"

"I need you to answer a few questions for me first," Elias replied. "And I need total honesty. Nothing goes beyond this room. You have my word. My ability to help you will depend on having all the facts, but I can also see why you would want your privacy."

Reluctantly, I nodded as dread coiled in my stomach.

"You are Skye *Markham*?"

"Yes."

"Your mother was an omega of the Long Mesa pack?"

"Yes."

"You lived with her at the omega house?"

I swallowed. "Yes."

"Omegas are still treated as community property in the Long Mesa pack?"

"I guess," I replied bitterly.

His eyes narrowed. "I doubt much has changed in the several decades since I was there. Omegas were used as grunt labor, little more than janitors and servants. You're telling me life has improved since then?"

"No, I'm telling you it got worse," I snapped, my temper flaring. "Omegas aren't maids or janitors, they're ... whores. Pack members come to the house and do whatever they want, whenever they want. *However* they want."

Elias was utterly silent for a moment. "My, God," he whispered. His eyes went to mine. "And you were forced to live as such? Since you were a child?"

"Omegas weren't declared until they were at least the age of majority—eighteen," I clarified through clenched teeth. "The night my mother and I left, they had just decided to lower the age to sixteen, which would have made me a full omega. I was told the next day I would start ... *serving* my pack." I spat the last words, stomach churning violently.

"So, you were never abused, but you knew it was imminent?" Elias asked gently.

I looked away, heat flaming across my cheeks. "I didn't say I was never ... The boy next in line to be Alpha was in my grade. He and his friends ... They never ... I mean they didn't force me to ... *you know*, but ... There was other stuff."

Elias lowered his head. "And how did that make you feel?"

My head snapped up. "How did it make me feel?" I demanded, my body flushing with anger. "You mean, did I like it?"

"No, not at all. Let me clarify: how did this make your *wolf* feel?"

"Sometimes furious. I would start to shake, wanting to change at first. But mostly she stayed silent and quiet the longer it went on. Lately, though, it got worse."

Elias nodded solemnly. "She was likely protecting you."

"Protecting me?" I scoffed. "By letting them—"

"If you had shifted," he cut in gently, "what would have happened?"

"I would have killed them," I hissed. I knew it in my heart. Just like I had killed Dane, I would have killed Cassian.

"Exactly. And in that situation, killing one or all of those boys, what would have then happened?"

I paused, thinking it through. "My uncle and his friends would have killed me. And my mother."

"Could you have taken them all on?"

I shook my head, defeated. "No."

"But by staying quiet and dormant, your wolf had given you both the best chance at survival," Elias explained. "She knew taking on multiple wolves would only lead to your death. She knew any form of aggression on her part would have had catastrophic results for you both."

"I killed a wolf the night we left," I admitted. "He was raping one of the other omegas, and they had just told me I would be an omega the next day, and I lost it. I shifted and had my teeth around his throat in seconds."

"You killed his human form?"

"He was shifted when he was ..." I trailed off, swallowing back bile at the memory.

Elias looked stunned and then horrified. He went ashen. "That's sacrilege, an abomination. For a wolf to attack a human and... "

"It was kind of common around Long Mesa," I whispered, tucking a stray lock of hair behind my ear.

"Does your new Alpha know this?" Elias asked, his voice tight.

I nodded. "My mom and I told Gabriel everything when we came to Blackwater."

"Good," Elias said. "Gabriel is a good alpha. He won't let this pass without consequence. He'll likely bring it to the Alpha Council at the Summit for a formal inquest."

"That's good. I guess." I couldn't see Linden or Cassian changing things in Long Mesa because the Council said they had to.

He looked at me. "This explains a lot about why you have issues shifting. Not only did your wolf bury herself to protect you, but she likely didn't trust her pack mates. A pack is meant to thrive together, to trust and love. You grew up surrounded by mistrust and fear. An Alpha should be a source of comfort and safety while yours was the center of your anxiety."

"So now what? I just have an emotionally damaged wolf to live with?" I rolled my eyes.

"Spend time with your new pack. Make friends. Let your wolf sense she can trust these new people. For now, if you feel the need to shift, don't fight the urge. She's let you take control for the last seventeen years, trusting you to keep both of you alive. It's time for you to trust her."

"Trust her?" I repeated skeptically.

"Yes. Spend some time by yourself outside. Try to reach her, let her take over. I don't think your issue is that your wolf wants to be dormant, but that she's done it for so long, she doesn't know how to stop, except when you experience extreme emotional distress. You need to spend some time reassuring her that you're both safe."

I flopped back into the chair. "All this because of a freaking genetic anomaly. Normals have it so much easier."

"Genetic anomaly?" Elias repeated, amused and confused. "You think being a shifter is a result of a genetic anomaly? Like you're a superhero or something? A mutant?"

"Isn't it? I've taken the science courses—shifters have an extra chromosome that causes the shift. It's science. So, yeah. Kind of like a mutant."

Elias snorted and got off his chair. "Your generation is all about science and proof. There has to be a scientific reason for everything." He moved to a stack of books, shifting three off the top and grabbing the fourth. It was a small, black leather volume with an embossed star and wolf on the front.

He held up the book. "So much has been thrown into the science of being a shifter, that the true story has been lost."

"True story? Isn't that an oxymoron?" I arched a brow with a smile.

He glared at me, exasperated. "Young people think you know it all."

"What's to know?"

He settled back in his chair, opening the book to the first page. "History, little one. History is what there is to know. Did you know where the first wolves originated from? Or how they came to be?"

I stared blankly for a second. "It was a genetic anomaly. Evolution at its finest. Or worst, depending on how you look at it."

"Two words often used to try to explain the unexplainable," Elias muttered. "The first shifters came from the Old World."

"The Old World?" I repeated, frowning.

"Before there were countries and boundaries. What is technically now divided into Russia and eastern Europe. When people lived life instead of watching television shows about it."

"Okay," I said slowly, crossing my legs and sensing this was going to be a longer conversation, but I was admittedly curious.

"Her name was Namina, and she was the most beautiful girl in her village. She was loved by two men, the son of the Grand Prince and the bastard of a drunkard. One who wanted to control her and one who wanted to love her." He looked at the book before him, turning the page.

"What happened?" I licked my lips, trying to see the faded, handwritten words from my side of the desk.

"What always happens," Elias said softly. "Men went to war. The reasons are always different, but the outcome is always the same. The Prince's son believed he had a right to Namina, but Namina only loved the bastard. They planned to run away, when the Prince's son summoned a *Roma* from a nearby traveling group."

"*Roma?*" I asked.

He smiled. "A gypsy woman. He made the woman place a curse on the bastard, turning him into a beast known to terrorize the villages. Clearly Namina could not wed a wild dog. A wolf."

"So, what happened?"

"The devotion between the bastard, now a wolf, and Namina never wavered. Eventually the Prince's son grew bored of Namina, seeing a prettier girl in a neighboring village."

"But he had already turned the bastard into a wolf," I realized. "So, they could still never be together."

Elias turned a page. "As legend tells it, Namina's mother was a descendant of the Romani tribe herself. Upon seeing her daughter's distress, she wove a spell to ensure her daughter's happiness. The magic was too strong to turn the bastard back to a man, but it allowed him the ability to shift at will from wolf to man."

"And they lived happily ever after?" I teased, not wanting to admit that the story was kind of sweet and kind of awesome.

Elias's face darkened as he turned the page. "No. The greed of man knows no bounds. When the Grand Prince discovered what had been done, he rounded up all the Romani he could find. He saw the potential for an army of wolf-men. Imagine the battles he could win. He would be able to conquer the world with such an army at his behest."

"And then what?" I was more invested in this story than I wanted to admit.

"He forced the Romani to turn hundreds of soldiers, and then dozens of women so he could breed his own army."

"That's awful," I whispered.

"Namina and her wolf knew they couldn't let the Grand Prince continue his plans, so they worked with the turned army and overthrew the Grand Prince. In a single, bloody night, they killed the Grand Prince and his entire family. The burned the village to the ground and escaped into the night, forming the first shifter pack deep in the Ural Mountains."

"And Namina and the shifter?"

"They became the first Alpha pair," Elias turned a page. "They had several children, all who carried the shifter genetic anomaly, as you call it. The pack eventually grew too big for the area and they began splintering off, moving across the world as they sought new territories to claim."

"But now the shifter rate is declining. Why is that?"

Elias inclined his head to the side. "In some regions more than others, yes. Especially in the south. There's no clear-cut explanation for why, but it's something I have devoted my life to studying. It could be as simple as it is for human women—stress plays a large part in infertility. Southern packs have started to die out, and thus the stress on females to bear children is greater."

"But there's still less females than males."

"It's always been that way. Fewer females were created than males. Males were to be the army and females simply the vessels to make more soldiers. The Grand Prince didn't know the toll a single birth would place on a female. He came from a time when women gave birth to child after child after child."

"Lovely," I muttered.

"It also may have something to do with your genetic anomaly," he continued with a shrug. "Males already have an altered chromosome, so it's easier to manipulate another whereas females have double chromosomes.

Perhaps thus making it more complicated for them to change two. The truth is, we don't really know. There's no clear-cut reason why in vitro fertilization doesn't work for female shifters either. It works for humans and it works for animals, but a hybrid of the two can't seem to accept a foreign embryo."

I studied him for a second. "But you have a theory about that?"

He smiled serenely and closed the book. My eyes again caught on the star and the wolf mark on the cover.

"Perhaps the reason is in how we were created. The Romani believed there had to be a balance in nature. The Chinese call it yin and yang. Perhaps in creating what was never meant to be, nature found a way to control the shifter population on its own."

"But you're saying that shifters were basically created from magic?" I asked, flicking my eyes up to him.

He smiled distantly. "My dear, isn't everything magic in some way?"

**16**

———

The giant brown eyes of the wolf in front of me was starting to get annoying.

I sighed. "I'm trying, Larkin."

The gray wolf cocked her head to one side, tongue lolling out, her dark eyes still imploring.

"Focus, Skye," Katy urged behind me, and not for the first time. I grit my teeth and bit back a reply.

It had been several days since I met with Elias, and while I had settled into GPA and mostly caught up on my classes, operation "Get In Touch With Your Wolf" was still a no-go.

I had tried sitting on my own, under a tree, trying to commune with my wolf. A few times I had felt her stir, but mostly she didn't seem to care about bonding.

Last night I had finally told Larkin why I disappeared after dinner every night, and she offered to come with me. Her logic was that Elias was right—we needed to bond with the pack, and what better way than in wolf form?

That was about the time Katy walked in and announced she would help. She had offered to pull in the rest of the pack, but I quickly shot down that idea. As much as I was enjoying getting to know my new pack, I didn't want that much attention on me.

Or to be known as the girl who couldn't shift.

Which led to the three of us sneaking towards the far end of the campus to work on my shifting. Larkin had shifted first, easily, while Katy stayed in human form to coach me.

It definitely wasn't going great.

I was sitting, wrapped in a damn towel, on the ground, pretty sure my butt was going to freeze off before my wolf appeared. I had a change of clothes nearby but shifting was usually a job best done naked unless you had ample spare clothes.

Since I wasn't quite ready to go commando in front of my new friends, I had opted for the towel.

"This is useless," I announced, throwing up my hands.

Katy sighed, running a hand through her long red hair. It gleamed in the light of the setting sun. "It's not useless. You just need to try harder."

"I *am* trying," I growled, frustrated and annoyed.

Larkin whined in her throat a second before she shifted back, the naked girl crouched in front of me. She reached for the spare towel to her right, pulling it around herself.

"Okay, let's try something different," Larkin started calmly as she tucked the end of the towel inside. "When you shifted last, what were you thinking of?"

*Rage. Murder. Hate.*

Probably not emotions I should recreate.

"I tried that," I muttered. And I had, by myself. I tried to remember the way I felt that night, the fear and hatred. I got as far as my hands trembling before the feeling faded.

"OK." Her cheeks puffed out as she let out a breath. "Do you remember the first time you shifted?"

I blinked, thinking back. I had been young, barely eleven. On average, wolves shifted when they reached puberty. My shift had come earlier than most others.

I smiled to myself, remembering how proud I felt. I could do something that no one else my age could. I walked the halls of my school knowing I had something they didn't. Even if I didn't share it with them, I knew. It was a private little secret I had all to myself. For the first time, I didn't feel alone when I stepped into the school.

I had spent weeks talking to my wolf like she was an imaginary friend who existed in my head. She had been my best friend.

Quietly, like the sun slipping behind the mountains, I felt her stir.

I felt her move, stretching like she had just woken up from a long nap.

"Hold on to that," Larkin whispered softly, edging back away from me.

She didn't have to tell me that. Now that she was awake, I could feel my wolf. The more she woke, the stronger I felt.

The stronger *we* felt.

Taking a deep breath, I closed my eyes and surrendered to her.

There was a moment where nothing happened, and then I felt it. I felt my bones begin to crack and snap and knit back together. I felt the tickle as fur brushed against human skin for a second.

When my eyes opened, the world was sharper, clearer. I could hear everything from the wind in the leaves to the bird sitting in them whistling. I could hear the tandem heartbeats of Larkin and Katy.

And the *smells*.

I hadn't shifted since Long Mesa, and this was a whole

new world. Soft earth, mossy grass, and fresh air. The clean scent of water clung to the breeze that tickled my nose.

"You did it!" Larkin exclaimed, clapping her hands. She caught her towel from slipping down at the last second.

"Damn," Katy said with a low whistle.

I swung my head to look at her and she gasped, pressing a hand to her chest.

"Holy shit," she breathed.

I cocked my head to the side, curious.

She shook her head. "It's unreal. You're like the exact opposite of Remy." She knelt in front of me, reaching out slowly to touch the black star on my head. "He's got a totally black coat, except for a white star."

"You're right," Larkin breathed, leaning towards me.

That was all well and good, but my wolf whined, the sound low in my throat. She wanted to run, and I wanted to let her.

Larkin and Katy exchanged smiles and then Larkin shifted. A second later, Katy shed her clothes and shifted, her russet brown wolf shaking out the effects of the change.

With a yip, Larkin lunged at me, nipping playfully at my heels.

*Pack.*

My wolf hummed the word in my head, and I completely agreed. I turned and nipped back at Larkin, who rolled onto her back. Katy growled and then batted a paw at me. I barked in return, letting my wolf bond with her pack.

Our pack.

A sense of complete rightness settled deep in my bones. For the first time in my entire life, I was home.

After that, we ran several miles, stopping a few times to

play, but mostly just enjoying running together. It wasn't until almost an hour later that we returned to the trees where our clothes were.

I shifted back easily, relieved that I still felt my wolf as part of me even now that I was back to human form. She was there, a quiet hum in the background chaos of my life. The thread tethering us together wasn't that strong yet, but at least now I knew she was there.

I had a start to bonding with her.

Picking up my clothes, I quickly dressed. The sounds of Larkin and Katy pulling on their clothes was the only sounds of the night. I could see the distant lights of GPA and knew we had to get back, but something in me hesitated.

Katy and Larkin finished dressing and looked at me with identical smiles.

I took a step towards them and stopped, finally dropping to the ground and sitting.

"What's up?" Katy asked, cocking her head.

Sensing my mood, Larkin sat, too. After a beat, Katy joined us.

I laced my fingers together in my lap, staring at them. "Long Mesa."

"Huh?" Katy frowned, not getting what I was saying.

I cleared my throat. "Long Mesa. That's the pack I ... escaped from."

Larkin's dark eyes softened, and she reached out, covering my hands with hers and squeezing.

"Escaped from?" Katy echoed, worry lines creasing her porcelain face.

I nodded slowly, licking my lips. "My mom was the daughter of the alpha and was supposed to marry the son of a rival pack. It would have been a treaty of sorts. Except she got pregnant ... with me."

I let out a shaky breath, tucking my long hair behind my ears. "Her father was so furious, he cast her out as an omega."

Katy winced. "That sucks, girl."

"There's more," Larkin said slowly. "When we first met and I said you lived on an omega floor, you almost lost it."

"Yeah," I whispered, sniffing. I wiped at my nose. "Omegas weren't treated that great in Long Mesa. They *aren't* treated that great, I mean."

Katy bit her full lower lip. "I've heard stories about omegas being forced to clean houses and shit. Like being submissive means you're less of a person or something. I never thought it was true."

My eyes slid shut and I ducked my chin to my chest. "God, I wish that had been it."

Neither of them spoke, letting me gather myself for a minute.

"Upper pack members could do whatever they wanted to omegas. No rules. Anything went. They were kept in a house together. The omega house. Kind of like a twisted shifter brothel. It's where I grew up."

They both gasped audibly.

"Jesus, Skye," Katy whispered, her hand covering her mouth.

Larkin's eyes filled with tears. "Wait. So, your mom—"

I nodded quickly, wiping my eyes. When had I started crying?

"Skye," Larkin said quietly, "were you ..."

"The night we left, my uncle, our Alpha, had just made me an omega and basically told me that I had to start ..." I trailed off, unable to speak around the lump in my throat. My chest ached from swallowing back sobs.

Katy buried her face in her hands.

"Growing up, I was always the bastard," I kept going.

"Ever since I was a little kid ... I never had any friends. Being the daughter of an omega, and basically knowing I would one day be an omega ... School was hell. The guy who will be Alpha after my uncle, Cassian, and his friends ..." I shuddered.

Larkin scooted around to sit next to me, wrapping her arms tightly around my trembling shoulders.

"There were no rules," I whispered, broken and hurting. "They would corner me, threaten me ... *touch* me. I couldn't fight back. I couldn't say no."

Katy looked up at me with teary eyes, her expression fierce. "But you got out, Skye. You survived."

"My grandfather died, and my uncle became Alpha. He called my mom and me to his house where he told me that the next day, I would be an omega. When we came home, another omega, Maisie, was ... She was being raped by a pack member. She was crying and bleeding and ... I lost it."

My hands curled into fists, nails biting into my palms until I scented blood.

"I shifted and killed him. I didn't think about it. I just did it."

"Good," Katy hissed, her eyes bright. "Fucking *good*."

I blanched. "Katy, I *killed* a member of my pack."

"No," she corrected with a grim face, "you killed a rapist hurting an innocent woman. Those people weren't your pack. That isn't a pack."

"She's right," Larkin told me gently, her hand smoothing down my back. "That's *not* a pack."

"Thank fuck you got out," Katy said, shaking her head.

I closed my eyes and leaned into Larkin.

Katy moved around to sit on my other side, her arms coming around me, too,

All the tears I never cried for years came rushing out.

Aching sobs ripped from my chest as I finally let myself acknowledge the well of emotions I had held back for over a decade.

I pulled my knees up, crying harder, but feeling anchored at the same time by the arms around me. By the friends holding me together as I split apart.

"We got you," Katy said, her arms tightening around me.

"We're your pack now," Larkin promised, leaning her head against mine, "and we aren't letting you go."

**17**

———

THE PHONE IN MY HAND ONLY RANG FOR A SECOND BEFORE my mom answered, her face filling the screen of the video chat. Her grin was infectious, and I found myself smiling back at her.

"Hey, baby," she greeted. Her eyes moved around, trying to see behind me. "Where's your roommate?"

"Taking a shower," I answered, settling against the pillows at the headboard of my bed. We had gotten back from our impromptu run and all gone to hit the showers, but I was the first out. I'd decided to call Mom as soon as I got back to my room.

"How's school?" she asked. Her body moved and I could tell she was sitting down, getting comfortable, too.

"Pretty good."

"Any issues catching up in your classes?"

I shook my head. "No. I think I'll be fine."

Her voice lowered. "And how are things with the new pack?"

I bit down on my lower lip. "Really good, actually."

Her brows rose quickly, but a small, hopeful smile bloomed on her lips. "Really?"

"Yeah, really." I gave a quick nod. "I actually just went on a run with Larkin and Katy."

Her hand covered her mouth. "You shifted?"

I was still as amazed by it as her. "Yeah. It took some time, but I got it."

"How do you feel?" she pressed, eyes wide.

"Good," I answered honestly. I absently toyed with the wet ends of my hair with the hand not holding the phone. "Mom ... I really like it here."

Her eyes closed for a second and she let out a long breath. "That's great, baby. I'm so glad. I've been worried ... We haven't been apart you entire life, so ..."

"Don't worry," I assured her. "I'm good."

She nodded.

"How's everything in Blackwater?"

I watched as she nibbled her lower lip, obviously thinking about something.

"Mom?" I prompted, narrowing my eyes.

"It's probably nothing," she started, keeping her voice intentionally light. "A shifter has gone missing from the pack."

"Missing?" I repeated. I blinked. What did she mean *'missing'*?

"We're not sure exactly what happened. She wasn't very active in the pack. A lone wolf who showed up a few weeks before we did. She lived on the fringes of town and kept to herself. Gabriel isn't sure if she's missing or just decided to leave."

"That seems kind of weird." Now that I had found Blackwater, I couldn't imagine leaving. I had seen the worst a pack had to offer, and I was pretty sure that I was now seeing the best.

Mom pressed her lips together. "It is. Gabriel sent out a search party, but they couldn't get much of a scent. And there's no way of telling when she might have left since she was rarely seen around town. The last time anyone saw her was over a week ago at the café."

"The café where you're working? Zoe's?"

She nodded again. "Yeah. Zoe actually has me managing some shifts for her. She and Michael just found out she's expecting."

My eyes went wide, and I grinned. "That's amazing!"

She giggled a little and smiled back. "It is. I'll be handling the restaurant more now. When she goes on maternity leave, I'll take over until she's ready to come back."

"And you like it?"

"I really do. I even got us a two-bedroom apartment in the heart of town," she said. The pride in her voice was tangible and nearly brought me to tears. "It's a few blocks from the café, and it isn't much, but it's ours."

I swallowed around the lump of emotion in my throat. "I'm sure it's perfect. I can't wait to see it."

Our own place. An actual home. Something in my chest swelled to near bursting.

"Only a couple of weeks until you're back for Thanksgiving," she chirped happily. "I should have everything set up by then. Zoe and Michael are turning the room I was using into a nursery and offered me the bedroom furniture set at a great discount. The pack has been really supportive. We went on a pack run the other night."

"How was it?"

A dreamy smile slipped across her face. "I forgot how much fun running with a pack could be," she admitted. "I missed it, and I'm glad you're finding your place in the pack."

"Yeah, I guess I am," I replied softly.

She sat up straighter, her green eyes glittering. "So? Any cute boys?"

I groaned and leaned against the wall. "*Mom.*"

She laughed and shrugged. "Come on. You've been there, what? Five days now? I'm sure someone has caught your eye."

The image of Remy ghosted into my mind before I could censor it. I'm not sure what changed in my expression, but Mom immediately latched onto it.

"Tell me!" she demanded, sounding more like Katy or Larkin than my mother.

"It's nothing," I said quickly, feeling my cheeks heat.

"Your lips say nothing, but your blush says *something,*" she teased. "Who is it?"

I was still trying to figure out what to tell her, if anything, when the door opened, and Larkin came in.

"Larkin!" I called loudly, grateful for the reprieve.

Larkin froze in the doorway, eyes wide. "Hey. You okay?"

"Talking to my mom," I told her, waving the phone. I flipped it around so they could see each other.

Larkin smiled easily. "Hi, Ms. Parker!' She gave a small wave, dropping her wet towel on the floor. "Nice to meet you. Skye's told me a lot about you."

"Hello, Larkin," Mom greeted warmly. "She's told me a lot about you, too. Thanks for being such a good friend to my girl."

I cringed, but Larkin, sweet as ever, waved her off with a smile.

"She's pretty awesome to have around." Larkin met my eyes over the phone as she said it.

I rolled my eyes to keep the real emotion I was feeling at bay.

I wasn't going to cry again tonight.

Again.

I turned the phone back around. "We need to finish up some homework."

"Sure," she drawled, rolling her eyes. "Don't think you're off the hook, Skye. I'll get the truth out of you eventually about this mystery guy."

"Yeah, yeah. I'll talk to you soon, okay? Love you."

Her expression softened. "I love you, too, baby. Bye."

"Bye."

I hung up and dropped the phone on my bed, falling backwards. I covered my face with a pillow.

"Mystery guy, huh?" Larkin teased.

I moved the pillow to glare at her. "Don't start."

She shrugged innocently, backing away with her hands raised. Her eyes glittered mischievously. "Do I know this guy?"

"Shut up, Larkin," I groaned, covering my face again.

She hummed under her breath but dropped the subject. I could hear her sit at her desk, her pen scratching across the paper as she worked on an assignment.

After a few minutes, I sat up and tossed my pillow aside, reaching for my own homework and trying to push the lingering thoughts of our alpha from my mind.

REMY WASN'T at breakfast the next morning.

He also wasn't in English class or our English Lit elective. I asked Rhodes, and he said Remy was handling something for his dad related to pack business. Neither he nor Katy seemed concerned, so I didn't give it a second thought.

At least not until I headed to see Elias after school

ended and saw Remy walking out of the office. He was dressed in a black t-shirt, dark jeans, and black boots, his hair messy as if he'd been running his hands through it a lot.

He was distracted, eyes down in thought as he walked towards me.

"Remy?"

His head snapped up, eyes dark and unfocused. He blinked and his attention zeroed in on me.

He smiled, but I could see the effort behind it.

"Hey, Skye." He glanced around. "Did you need me for something?"

I motioned to the door behind him. "I wanted to talk to Elias, actually."

"Oh, right." He nodded and stepped around me. "I'll let you get to it, then."

I turned as he walked by me, uneasy. "Remy, are you okay?"

He glanced back at me. Another forced smile. "Yeah. I'm fine. Just distracted."

"Rhodes said you were handling some pack business?" I asked slowly, not wanting to overstep.

His expression went carefully neutral. "Yeah. Looking into a couple things for my dad. No big deal."

"I shifted last night," I blurted suddenly, the compulsion to keep talking to him strong.

His brows rose and a genuine smile curved on his full lips. "Really? Skye, that's awesome."

I blushed, scuffing a toe on the tiles. "Katy and Larkin helped. Elias gave me some good advice about bonding with the pack."

"Can I do anything to help?" he offered. His expression was so open and honest, I wanted to say yes.

I almost said yes.

"I'm good," I replied finally. "I just thought I would ask Elias about a couple of other things."

"Okay," he agreed easily, shoving his hands into the pockets of his jeans with enough force to push the waistband down, exposing a flat stretch of tanned skin between the hem of his shirt and top of his jeans.

I tried not to look, but it was hard to miss the way part of the muscle curved and dipped, disappearing under the band of his jeans.

Clearing my throat, I looked up and took a step towards Elias' office. I pointed a finger in that direction. "I should go."

"Yeah. Let me know if you need anything." He turned back to leave.

"That goes both ways, you know," I called to his back. "If I can help ..." I trailed off, letting it go with a one-shouldered shrug.

I wasn't used to being on either end of the help line. Getting and offering it seemed like a foreign concept I could happily get used to.

Not that a guy like him probably needed help from someone like me.

The corners of his mouth hitched up. "Thanks. If I can steal your Lit notes, that would be a big help."

"Want me to bring them by when I'm done here?" The offer again tumbled from my lips before I could second-guess it.

Was I actually inviting myself over to his cabin?

*The pack cabin*, I reminded myself. Where the whole pack was welcome.

This wasn't weird at all.

He gave me a grateful nod. "That would be awesome. Thanks."

"I'll see you later." Jesus, when did my voice get that

breathy? For that matter, when did the air leave the hallway?

Another genuine grin and he winked at me. "Later."

I waited until he was around the corner before leaning against the wall and letting my head drop hard against it. Who the hell was I turning into?

The door to Elias' office opened and his head popped out, his white hair on end. His dark eyes settled on me, wide and curious. He pulled off the glasses he wore, wiping them on his shirt.

"Miss Markham? Did you knock?"

Only my head against the freaking wall.

"Yeah," I lied easily, pushing off the wall. "Do you have a second?"

He glanced down at his watch. "Several, in fact." He opened the door and waved me in. "Come in, come in."

I followed him through the maze of stacks to his desk, taking the seat across from him again.

Elias sat down, gathering some papers and moving them to the side before bracing his forearms on the beat-up desk. "How can I help you?"

I dropped my eyes, pressing my lips together, suddenly embarrassed.

"I did it," I started quietly, my eyes lifting. "I shifted."

A smile broke across his weathered face, a single dimple appearing in his left cheek. "That's wonderful! How did it feel?"

"Really good," I admitted. "I tried doing it on my own, but it happened last night. Katy and Larkin were with me, helping me."

His snowy brows raised. "And how did your wolf react to your pack mates?"

"Calm. She had fun, I think. We ran for a while."

"And now? Can you sense her?"

I narrowed my eyes in thought. "Yeah. She's definitely there, but it feels kind of ... muffled?"

He nodded sagely, leaning back in his chair. It creaked in protest. "That's to be expected. The more you let her out, the more you bond with her and your pack, the stronger and clearer your bond will be."

"I hoped it was something like that." Relief swept through me that I was finally on the right path.

"You must keep practicing," he encouraged. "Now that you've established a link, you mustn't let her slip away from you again."

I crossed my legs, leaning back. "It's almost like when I first shifted—the bond, I mean."

"The first shifts can be a very volatile time for a young wolf. Lots of hormones and emotions ... It's hard to keep them in check. I suspect it was even more of a challenge for you since you had to always be on guard."

"I told Katy and Larkin everything that happened. About Long Mesa?" I bit my lower lip.

He looked surprised. "That's a fairly big step towards trusting your pack."

"They were both really understanding about it," I said, picking at the hem of my blue shirt. "Supportive, I guess is the best word."

"I've known both girls since they were children. I would expect nothing less. The Blackwater pack has a very strong reputation in the shifter community. You and your mother couldn't have picked a better pack to seek sanctuary in." He gave me a kind look. "Gabriel is a great Alpha, and his son will likely surpass all of our expectations."

"He was in here earlier, right?" I frowned, remembering how off Remy had seemed in the hallway.

Elias sighed. "He was. As a young alpha, much is expected of him. I offer guidance when I can."

"But he's okay, right?"

Elias smiled fleetingly. "I would not betray your confidence, nor would I betray his."

I flushed, feeling like a total idiot. "Of course. I'm sorry. I didn't mean—"

His head cocked to the side. "You care for him."

I coughed, choking on air for a second. "He's a nice guy. He's been really ... welcoming."

*Welcoming?*

I mentally face-palmed.

He chuckled softly. "Yes, he's definitely one of the more hospitable alphas we have on campus."

I let out a long breath. "Anyway, I just wanted to give you an update on my shifting and to say thank you."

"It was truly my pleasure, my dear," he responded. "Hopefully I will get to see your wolf amongst us one day."

I snorted, remembering what Katy had said last night. "Apparently, I'm just like Remy, except backwards."

His eyes narrowed carefully, and he leaned forward slightly. "How so?"

I waved a hand. "He's all black with a white star and my coat is all white with a black star. Weird, right?"

He gave a curious hum under his breath. "Long Mesa packs don't have any black coats in their lines. Black is a northern and European color."

I blinked slowly. "Um, okay."

"It's definitely curious," he said, mostly to himself.

"A lot of wolves have similar coats and markings," I said with what I'm sure was a confused look. I shrugged. "It doesn't mean anything."

His gaze drifted to the corner of his desk where the book with the wolf and the star on the cover sat. "Markings used to mean a great deal in the old world. It was a way to distinguish from an early age what a pup might become. The role he or she would play in pack dynamics."

Laughter bubbled out of me. "Seriously?"

His smile was faint. "Maybe it is a bit of an old wives' tale."

"More like my mom has a pure white coat and my dad had some black markings in him somewhere."

"You don't know who your father is?"

I shook my head. "No. My mom has never said."

"You've asked?"

I gave him an incredulous look. I was a seventeen-year-old girl. Of course I had asked who my father was on more than one occasion. Mom shot me down every single time.

"She won't tell me. She's only said that we were better off in Long Mesa than with him."

A troubled look crossed his face. "She believed you were safer in your former pack than with your birth father?"

I sighed. "I've tried to get her to tell me about him. Anything about him. She either gets really angry or shuts down. I barely mention it anymore. Besides, my mom is enough. And it's not like word of what she did didn't spread like wildfire throughout the shifter community," I pointed out. "If my father wanted me or her, don't you think he would have heard about the war in the south over what she did? Wouldn't he have come looking for her?"

"Perhaps," he allowed. He folded his hands over his stomach and studied me. "Would you be willing to tell me if your mother ever divulges the truth?"

I raised my eyebrows. "Um, sure? But can I ask why?"

"I told you I've spent my life dedicated to studying shifters and pack dynamics," he reminded me, waiting for me to nod. "I'm curious as to what would pose a bigger threat to you than your uncle and your former pack."

Also something I had wondered. Anytime I realized that Long Mesa was the good option, I got nauseous.

"If she ever tells me, I'll let you know."

Elias still seemed troubled. "Female shifters are becoming rarer in our society. It's perplexing why she would hide you away to be an omega."

He seemed to still be thinking aloud to himself, but it didn't stop my anger from igniting. "She didn't *hide* me away. She tried to leave with me when I was little, and my uncle threatened to kill both of us. She got me out before they could ... *They* made me an omega."

Elias startled as I all but growled the last sentence. He looked instantly apologetic. "Forgive me, Skye. I meant nothing by it. I've spent the last decade trying to increase the population and carelessly let my thoughts wander."

I was still tense, my hands curled around the armrests of the cushioned chair I sat in.

He held up his hands, trying to appear non-threatening. "Shifter population is rapidly declining, and it's due to the fact that fewer and fewer females are being born, and those who are born, are only able to bear one, perhaps two, children if at all."

I frowned, thinking back to what Zoe said. "I thought true mates could have more children."

He nodded quickly. "Yes, but the odds of finding a true mate are decreasing with the fertility rate. It's been nearly a year since a true bonded pair found one another in the United States. Some packs haven't had a child born into them in over a decade."

My eyes narrowed. "That's how it was in Long Mesa. There hadn't been a baby born in nearly a year when we left."

"But in packs like Blackwater, there are numerous pups. Women become pregnant frequently, and even the odds of a true mate bond are more apt to happen." He seemed genuinely excited. "I've been working on a hypothesis for this for the better part of the last three years."

"And?" I waited for his explanation.

He hesitated with a sigh. "It's a very rough theory, you see. Untested and untried."

I huffed out a breath. "OK. It's not being published in any shifter medical journals next month, I get it."

He smiled at my sarcasm. "It's the Alpha female."

"Alphas can't be female," I said after a heavy beat of silence, for the first time wondering if Elias was all there. "The Alpha is always male."

His hand settled on the book on the corner of his desk. The wolf and star book. "It wasn't always so. True mates, especially the true mate of an alpha, are meant to live in a different sort of harmony than other bonded mates."

"You're losing me."

"It's like sound waves. True bonded mates operate on a higher frequency than a basic bond. A forced bond operates on the lowest frequency."

"Like a radio station?" I was barely following his train of thought.

Elias stood up suddenly, coming around behind his chair and resting his hands on the back. "Precisely."

If this guy hadn't given me sound advice about tackling my inner wolf, I would seriously be considering recommending he be evaluated.

Magic and radio stations.

Right.

"If you look back in pack history, instances where the alpha of the pack is in a true bond with his mate, pack fertility rates rise." He waved a hand. "Compare your old pack and your new pack. Blackwater is filled with children. Its Alpha female has birthed four children. There are talks of expanding the town because of the rise in population."

My brow furrowed. That was news to me. Blackwater definitely had the highest population at GPA, and, being in the town a few times before I left, I had seen a lot of children. The entire vibe of Blackwater was so vastly different from Long Mesa that I didn't think about it too much.

His eyes were bright. "You're seeing my point, aren't you?"

"It's definitely a theory," I conceded.

"I need to keep working on my research." Elias moved back to his chair, reaching for his stack of papers again. "But I believe there is a direct link between fertility amongst pack females and the Alpha's pair."

*Huh.*

I stood up. "Well, I'll let you get back to your research." Elias was already reading a paper when I left his office.

I still wasn't sure if he was crazy ... or onto something.

**18**

———

My eyes went wide as yet another girl walked by in a thin tank top and barely-there lace shorts. Apparently, Pajama Day was some sort of code for lingerie.

Katy snorted when she followed my gaze. "Yeah, that's always a thing. We should've warned you."

Almost a week had flown by since I had first shifted. A week of bonding with my pack.

Okay, mostly I was bonding with Katy and Larkin, practicing shifting, and catching up in all of my new classes. I had settled into a routine at Granite Peak that felt refreshingly normal. The beginning of the week had ushered in Fall Fest, and it was fascinating to see the school buzzing with excitement.

The students, and faculty, were all very involved in participating.

The week had kicked off with Pack Color Day on Monday, Clash Day on Tuesday, and my personal favorite, Rainbow Day, where students wore as many colors as possible. The insane creations some people came up with were hysterical.

I had resisted all of Katy and Larkin's urges to join in, not sure how I felt about the different themes, but I finally caved on Pajama Day, but I was glad I opted for a casual pair of red and black flannel bottoms with a black t-shirt instead of a skimpy, lacy outfit that most of the girls were prancing around in.

As was true in the shifter world, girls here were outnumbered easily three to one by guys, ensuring a lot of male attention went to the girls who opted to show more skin. That didn't bother me, but I had finally started to not be seen as the shiny new girl at school, and I was more than happy to keep as many eyes off me as possible.

I watched the girl in the matching pink lace outfit turn a corner down the hall, noting no less than a dozen pairs of hungry eyes on her.

I shrugged as I turned my attention back to my friends. "She looks cute, though."

Katy arched a brow. "Why, Skye," she started in a slow, southern drawl, "are you coming to play on my side of the fence?"

Larkin giggled behind me as she shut her locker, also dressed in a pair of flannel bottoms, but with a matching long sleeved top. It was baby blue with flowers and bunnies and was one hundred percent Larkin.

I smirked at the redhead with a wink. "You wish."

Katy nodded solemnly. "I do."

"You have a girlfriend," I reminded her.

Katy shrugged. "Maren thinks you're hot, too. We can share."

Larkin outright laughed, and I flushed. She was kidding ... right?

Katy threw back her head and laughed. "Face it, Skye, you're pretty fucking hot. Even if I'm positive my mom has those same jammies." She winked at me and turned, heading down the hall in her set of silk forest green pjs.

I glanced at Larkin who grinned at me. Rolling my eyes, I put some of my books into my locker, getting out my English Lit book.

"Ladies!" Rhodes greeted, coming up behind us and throwing an arm across Larkin's shoulders.

I couldn't help but laugh every time I saw him coming. He had worn a bright yellow footed onesie today. He stood out like crazy when he walked ... anywhere, really. What was even more disturbing was Ryder has opted to wear a matching one in hot pink. The sight of the tall shifter with a ton of tattoos coming at me in a pink onesie during breakfast made me choke on my orange juice.

I closed my locker and noticed Remy had come over with Rhodes, but he was dressed in a pair of jeans and a white shirt. With the exception of Pack Color Day, he hadn't seemed to care about joining in the daily dress challenges.

"Hey, Remy," Larkin greeted. She shrugged Rhodes' arm off and barely spared him a glance. "Hey."

My eyes met Remy's, and I winced at Larkin's brush off.

Ever since Rhodes had announced he was taking a girl from one of the Canadian packs to the dance at lunch at the beginning of the week, Larkin had given him the cold shoulder. Breakfast the last two days had been seriously awkward. The worst part was Rhodes truly didn't seem to get why Larkin was brushing him off.

Which made Larkin even more frustrated.

"I need to get to class," Larkin told me with a thin smile.

I saw Remy frown out of the corner of my eye. Clearly, he noticed something was going on with his friends.

"Okay," I said. "I'll meet you later? Same spot?"

"What spot?" Rhodes asked curiously. "I want to come to the spot."

The spot was the copse of trees on the edge of the property that Katy and Larkin and I had been using to work on my shifting.

"You can't," Larkin said sharply.

Rhodes blinked and took a step back. "Why not?"

"Girl time," I said quickly, flashing him a weak smile.

Rhodes grinned unabashedly at me. "You know I love girl time."

I scrambled for another excuse. "Larkin and Katy have been helping me catch up on my classes and stuff."

"Yeah," Remy said suddenly, snapping his fingers. "Katy mentioned you guys have put together some kind of study group."

I smiled at him, grateful for the assist. The secretive smile he returned made my stomach flip in the best way possible.

In the last week I had gotten closer to Katy and Larkin, but I had also gotten to see more sides of Remy. From him settling a fight between younger shifters from different packs to the way he was almost revered around GPA. There were other alphas on campus, but even they seemed to seek out Remy when they needed help.

I still wasn't sure why he had seemed so bothered coming out of Elias' office, and even this past weekend when we were all hanging out at the cabin with a few others from the pack, Remy stayed in his study with the doors closed most of the time.

Katy and Rhodes both said it happened from time to time, but I could sense both of them were a little concerned.

"Exactly. Studying," Larkin said. She flashed a smile at

Rhodes that was anything but genuine. "We all know that's the last thing on your mind."

Rhodes was still frowning at Larkin as she turned and walked away down the hallway. After she disappeared from sight, he turned and looked at us. "Am I missing something?"

I wasn't sure what to say until Remy grinned at his friend and clapped a hand on his shoulder. "All the time, man."

Rolling his eyes, Rhodes shrugged off Remy's hand with a huff. "Whatever. I'll catch you guys later."

Remy and I started walking towards English Lit. It was definitely my favorite class, and when I was actually being honest with myself, a lot of it was because of the alpha walking next to me.

We slid into our usual seats in the back row, and I glanced up to see Andy hurrying down the aisle.

My eyes went wide when he tripped over a backpack on the floor and almost went flying before stopping in front of my desk. Remy leaned back with an amused smile, but I could see him glance at me, checking to make sure I was good.

A herd of butterflies took flight in my tummy.

It felt nice to have someone care.

Who was I kidding? It felt nice to know *Remy* cared.

It was getting harder and harder to hide the fact that I had my first crush from Mom when she called.

"Hey, Remy," Andy said with a nod, making sure to greet the alpha first. Then he turned to me and gave me a soft smile. "Hi, Skye."

"Hey, Andy. How's it going?" Remy replied nonchalantly.

The smaller shifter shrugged. "Not bad. Hey! I heard you're going to the dance with Natalie! Good for you."

Remy stiffened slightly beside me before nodding. "Yeah, she's cool."

All the blood in my body drained from my head, pooling like ice water in my gut.

He had a date? When had this happened?

It wasn't like we were best friends or anything—definitely not anything—but wouldn't he have mentioned taking someone to the dance tomorrow night? Or wouldn't Katy have mentioned it?

Then again … why did I care?

I was still trying to sort out my emotions on this when I looked up and realized Remy and Andy were staring at me.

Shit. I had missed whatever they said.

"I'm sorry," I apologized with a sheepish shrug, desperate to downplay the roiling emotions in my heart. "What was that?"

Andy cleared his throat with a blush. "I asked if, um, you might want to come to the dance tomorrow? With me?"

My eyes went wide and the pen I held slipped from my fingers. "Go to the dance? With you?"

He nodded slowly, and I could see him bracing himself for rejection.

I glanced at Remy, who sat there with a completely neutral expression, staring at the front of the classroom like he hadn't heard a single word.

"Sure," I answered slowly as I looked back at Andy. I bit down on my lower lip hard, not sure if I was giving the right answer or not.

Andy's eyes went wide, an incredulous grin breaking out. "Really? O-okay, wow! That's awesome."

I heard Remy snort lightly under his breath, but he was

still a block of concrete when I checked him from the corner of my eye.

"So, do you want me to pick you up at your dorm?" Andy pressed. He gave me a big smile. "I can escort you in, my lady."

Remy stifled a barely disguised laugh, morphing it into a cough at the last second.

"Actually, how about if we meet there?" I countered weakly, trying to ignore the awkwardness. "I'm not sure if Larkin is going with anyone, and I don't want to make her go in solo."

Andy bobbed his head, understanding. "I get it. I'll bring some of my friends. Maybe she'll hit it off with one of them."

"Sounds great," I replied, not sure if Larkin was good that I had basically just wrangled her into a date, too. Several guys had asked, but she said no to each of them. I think she had been secretly hoping Rhodes would ask her.

"I'll see you tomorrow," Andy said quickly. After a beat, he suddenly reached down and gave me an awkward, but fast, side hug. I barely had time to react and process what was happening before he was heading back to his seat across the room.

We still had a few minutes before class started, and this was usually my favorite time. Remy and I would chat about anything—books we were reading or had read. He would sometimes tell me about growing up in Blackwater or hilarious stories about the pack.

But right now he was still impersonating a statue. The sudden, stark silence hanging heavily between us felt awkward and off. Even my wolf wasn't happy about it.

As my shifting abilities had grown, so had my bond with her. Most times I knew exactly how she felt.

And right now? She felt annoyed and frustrated.

*Me, too, girl.*

Unable to take the weird silence, I finally asked, "Are you okay?"

Remy's head turned and he fixed those beautiful brown eyes on me. "Of course."

"Oh. All right," I murmured, looking away.

Remy cleared his throat. "Andy's a good guy," he said, somewhat begrudgingly. "You two will have fun together."

Then why did it sound like he was chewing broken glass to get those words out?

"Thanks." My words were soft. "And you'll have fun with Natalie."

Of course he would.

The shifter from Quebec was in our grade, lithe and willowy with pale blonde hair that looked like a silk curtain. From everything I had seen she was as kind as she was beautiful.

They would make a striking couple.

My heart clenched painfully.

"Yeah," he replied absently. "Natalie's a great girl."

"Yeah," I echoed.

Thankfully the teacher came in and started class, but we didn't look at each other or speak to each other again for the rest of class.

And that made me even more sad for a reason I couldn't quite put my finger on.

Or *wouldn't* put my finger on.

**19**

———

THE GIRL IN FRONT OF THE MIRROR LOOKED LIKE ME, BUT there was no way she was me.

Katy and Larkin stood behind me in the mirror, matching grins on their faces as they high-fived each other. They had spent the last hour putting me together for the dance.

Larkin had called in Katy for help when I said I was planning to go to the dance in my usual jeans and t-shirt.

Who knew there was a dress code for a school dance?

But I couldn't deny that the dress looked stunning, and it made me feel pretty for the first time in my life.

My hand fluttered to my throat, landing on the exposed column delicately. Had my neck always been this long? Did I have some latent giraffe shifter gene lurking in my DNA?

"This is *me*?" I whispered, afraid to speak too loudly in case the image in front of me shattered.

"I tried to tell you how hot you are." Katy smirked at me in the mirror.

I couldn't even blush. The girl in the mirror was beautiful.

The red dress had tiny beads that caught in the light. It had a built-in shelf bra and lifted my breasts, making them appear fuller and higher against the deep V-neck. The dress stopped just below my knees, the skirt flaring gently around me as I walked. The halter straps were tied behind my neck, the waist cinched tight to show the feminine way my hips flared out from my narrow waist.

But the face is where I started to think the girl looking back wasn't me.

My dark hair had been pulled up and away from my face. Katy had painstakingly pinned it into place, shoving bobby pin after bobby pin into the thick tresses to create a casually sophisticated updo. Then she turned her focus to makeup, using light eyeshadow but using a thick black winged liner, going light with blush, and finishing with a lip oil that tasted like mint and made my lips shine.

My green eyes were bright with excitement and a smile played at my lips.

I looked ... *happy*.

I turned and hugged my friends together, crushing them both to me.

"Thank you," I whispered.

"Watch the hair," Katy griped, easing back with a grin. She reached up to toss her curled red ends, glancing in the mirror to make sure they were still in place.

Larkin rolled her eyes, looking every bit a princess in a soft pink silk dress that fell to her ankles. Her dark hair was swept to the side, half up and half down. Her cheeks had a beautiful pink flush, and her lips were soft and pink.

Katy looked us both over. Of the three of us, she had definitely gone the most glam. Her glittery black gown fell to her ankles but had a slit on one side nearly up to her hip.

Her lips were a vibrant, cherry red and her winged liner was sharp enough to cut.

She planted her hands on her hips and gave a sharp nod. "Okay, girls, I have to meet Maren, but I'll see you both there. Save me a dance."

Turning, she looked at me with pursed lips, her dimples flashing. "You, have fun with Andy." She turned to Larkin and sighed after a second. "I can go kick his ass."

Larkin squared her shoulders. "Nope. I'm not even saying his name tonight. I'm going to hang out with Skye for a bit and then dance. Maybe with a couple different guys. Andy said he was bringing friends."

"*That* is a great plan," Katy grinned. She looked at me, both of us vowing to keep an eye on Larkin when we could in that glance.

Katy left to meet Maren, and I left with Larkin a few minutes later. We almost made it down the steps of the dorm when I stumbled in my new heels.

Larkin caught me with a laugh. "Take your time," she admonished.

"Easy for you to say," I grumbled, watching as she moved effortlessly in a pair of nude heels. "I feel like a baby horse."

"But a really pretty baby horse," Larkin confirmed as we walked down the pathway to the main building. There was a steady stream of students heading into the building, and music became louder as we walked inside.

The dance was held in the large cafeteria, but most of the tables had been removed and the entire room transformed. Fake trees and leaves, a riot of fall colors, hugged the walls. Twinkling lights hung in strands from the ceiling, giving the effect of stars glittering above us.

Across the room was a drink station and a few tables with food. Several tables from the cafeteria stayed up but had burnt orange tablecloths spread across them, mason jars filled with leaves and twinkling lights tucked into them.

I stopped as we walked in, freezing the flow of traffic as I gaped, taking it all in.

"Pretty amazing, right?"

I turned to see Andy standing to my left with several males I recognized as his friends. A few were in classes with me, but right now they were all looking at Larkin with awe.

"You look nice," I told Andy with a smile. He was cute in a gray suit with a pale blue shirt. His hair had been slicked to the side, making him look even more innocent and boyish than usual.

"You look gorgeous," he breathed, his eyes moving across me, taking it all in. There wasn't a leer in his or even his friends' gazes. They were simply happy to be standing with us, which was unexpectedly nice.

I turned to Larkin and caught her staring across the room. Rhodes was standing behind a table, a hand on the chair of a blonde he was leaning down to talk to. She threw her head back and laughed, licking her lips as she met his gaze.

*Dammit, Rhodes.*

I reached out to touch Larkin, but she was already stepping past me to one of Andy's friends.

"Ian, right?"

The brunette with glasses gulped and nodded. "Yup."

Larkin turned a beautiful smile on him and extended a hand. "Dance with me?"

"Sh-sure," he stammered, taking her hand and letting her pull him onto the dancefloor where several other couples were moving to an upbeat song.

"Do you want to dance, Skye?" Andy offered.

I saw Remy and Natalie come in the other entrance then, moving towards Rhodes and his dates. Natalie looked stunning in a gold dress, contrasting against Remy's black pants and black shirt, his sleeves rolled up his forearms.

I forced myself to focus on Andy.

*My* date.

And his request, which was something I hadn't considered when he asked me to the dance.

I gave him a sheepish smile, embarrassed. "I don't really know how to dance."

Relief exploded across his face. "Me neither. Want to sit down and talk?"

I nodded, clocking Larkin dancing with Ian. A few steps over, Tate was dancing with Ryder. Maren, Katy, and Dante had joined Rhodes and Remy.

For the first time since coming to GPA, I felt out of place. Unsure if I walked over, I would be welcomed.

I let Andy take me over to a table on the edge of the dancefloor, sitting down with him and his friends. I knew Andy was a senior, but his friends were juniors named Luke and Isaac. They were from a small seaside town in Maine and loved everything computer programming related. Half the time I didn't understand a word they spoke, but it was fun to watch Andy and his friends joke and tease.

At one point, Larkin came over and switched dance partners, taking Isaac to dance with her. Several dances later, she returned him to the table and took Luke. Two dances later, Luke returned red-faced and panting, but sans Larkin.

"Where's Larkin?" I asked, looking around.

"Bathroom," Luke gasped out, reaching for his drink and draining the water in it in a single swallow. "I need more." He gestured to the drink table and started for it, Ian and Isaac got up to go with him.

I looked at Andy and watched him fidget on his seat.

"Are you all right?" I asked curiously, somewhat amused.

He blushed and pushed his chair back. "Do you mind if I go to the bathroom, really quick?"

I held in a laugh. "Go right ahead."

His chair scraped back in his haste to head to the exit that led to the bathrooms down the main hall.

I lifted my glass of punch and chuckled into it. I didn't see Andy and I dating as a thing, but he was a nice guy, and I could always use a new friend.

"What's so funny?" Remy dropped down into the now empty seat beside me.

I almost choked, setting my cup down.

"Hey." I looked around. "Where's your ... Natalie?"

A smile twitched on his lips and he pointed across the room where Natalie was dancing with someone.

My eyes went big. "Oh, my God. I'm sorry."

Remy laughed, the sound warming my body. "No, it's fine. I only brought Natalie to help her out of a sticky situation."

My face must have expressed my confusion.

"The guy she was dating last year is apparently having a hard time letting go and was bugging her about the dance," he explained. "She asked me to be her date to get him to back off. Anyway, he decided not to come tonight, so she's doing her own thing."

"So, you two aren't together?" The words came out way more hopeful than I would have liked.

He turned and looked at me, his smile slowly fading. He shook his head. "No," he said softly. "We're just friends. I was just helping her out."

"Oh." The word came out as a tiny breath.

He cleared his throat. "How's Andy?"

"Good," I answered quickly. "He's a really great guy."

Remy's smile froze for a beat. "That's awesome. I'm happy for you. You two look good together."

"No, no!" I said, my words tripping over each other as they tumbled out. "We're just friends. Andy's a great guy, but I don't see us being ... more than friends, you know?"

He nodded slowly, his eyes not leaving my face. He leaned in towards me and I caught the addicting scent of pine, woods, and soap.

"Dance with me."

It wasn't exactly a request, and before I thought better of it, I stood up. I watched, mesmerized, as he reached out, lacing his fingers through mine. I stared at our hands as he led me out onto the dancefloor, the music shifting from a fast song to a slower one.

His hand was almost twice the size of mine, engulfing mine in his. I could feel rough calluses on his fingers, the strength of his fingers as they flexed once around mine.

My breath caught, trapped in my throat when he turned and pulled me to him, lifting one of my hands, still caught in his, to his chest while his other hand settled low on my back, his thumb tracing the curve of my side. It seemed completely natural to lift my arm around his neck, shifting us closer.

I could have sworn I heard him sniff my hair as he dropped his head closer to mine.

"I've never done this," I admitted softly, praying that wouldn't matter. "Danced, I mean."

His lips curved into a perfect smile. "It's fine. Just hold on to me."

My fingers brushed the soft hair at the base of his skull, and I had the urge to bury my fingers in the thick locks as his thumb swept in a slow stroke across my hip, tugging me an inch closer.

He was warm, hard and firm in all the right places. I

could feel the muscles wrapped around his body. I felt the devastatingly masculine power in his touch. That massive hand cradling my hip could inflict serious damage if he wanted to.

And, for the first time in my life, I wasn't afraid of how that kind of power could be used against me.

I trusted Remy.

I sucked in a sharp breath, the realization that not only did I trust him, but I was starting to really like him, sinking in. For years I had resigned myself to a certain kind of existence, never considering an alternative.

Hope fluttered in my chest at the thought that Remy might be that alternative.

The hand he held against his chest tightened around mine, his index finger pressed to the pulse point inside the delicate skin of my wrist. "You okay? I can feel your heart racing," he murmured, warm breath tickling the shell of my ear.

I pulled back to look him in the eyes, stunned by the conflicted desire in his molten brown depths. His eyes dropped to my lips unconsciously.

I felt myself lean in towards him, my heart reaching for something I had never experienced.

The song we were dancing to had faded into nothing, and the next song came crashing through the speakers as the people around me let out a loud cheer.

I jumped, startled back into the present.

"I'm sorry," I whispered, dropping my arm and stepping back. "I need ... I need to go to the bathroom," I finished lamely.

Disappointment flashed briefly on his face, but he nodded with a reluctant smile and let me go. "I'll catch up with you later."

Nodding, I turned and fled the dancefloor, cursing myself the entire time.

Emotion turned in my stomach as I pushed open the doors of the cafeteria and stumbled into the hall.

Face on fire, I put my head down and headed down the empty hall for the bathroom. I reached for the door, but it swung open before I could touch it.

I jumped back, surprised. "Sorry," I apologized reflexively as I focused on the person in front of me.

I looked up and froze, my nose wrinkling in confusion. "Trace?"

The Norwood alpha grinned at me as the door swung shut behind him. He glanced around the hallway before settling on me.

"Skye," he greeted, his voice warm and oily. "You look amazing." His gaze lingered on the deep cut of my dress.

"This is the girls' bathroom," I said, ignoring his leer. I looked pointedly at the sign next to the door he had just walked through.

He smirked. "I was wondering why it was so clean. Guess I shouldn't have been drinking before the party."

Rolling my eyes, I stepped around him. "Whatever."

I entered the bathroom, glad he didn't say anything else, and went to the sink. I turned on the cold water, splashing the icy liquid over my face and the back of my neck.

I felt like a total idiot.

There was no way anything could ever happen with Remy. He was the golden boy of GPA. He didn't even know my real last name. And the thought of telling him all about the Long Mesa pack had me ready to throw up.

I braced my hands on the edges of the sink, dropping my head as I took several deep, calming breaths.

The pounding of my heart had finally started to settle, and I was thinking about going back to the dance and saying goodnight to Andy when I heard something moving behind me.

I turned, looking at the row of half open stall doors.

I heard another sound and something that sounded like a low whimper. Like an animal in pain.

Pushing open the stall doors, it was the third one that I saw someone on the other side. She was curled in front of the toilet, her pink dress torn down her back, scratches up and down it.

I fell to my knees with a gasp. "Oh, my God. Are you okay?"

The girl turned and my blood ran cold. Everything went quiet except for the blood roaring in my ears.

Larkin looked up at me, her lower lip split, a fresh bruise starting on her cheek. Her dress had been torn and pulled down ...

We both stared at each other for a long minute, trying to process.

My head turned slowly to the door.

*Trace.*

I got to my feet slowly, a low growl already rumbling in my chest as my fists clenched. My wolf roared to the surface, furious and out for blood.

I was going to kill him.

## 20

———————

MY BODY SHOOK WITH BARELY CONTAINED RAGE. I COULD feel my control slipping. All I wanted was to go after Trace.

I knew whatever happened in here, he was the cause. And Larkin was ...

My gaze went back to her, my heart cracking open, raw and exposed, as she cried. Hands and knees on the tile of the girls' bathroom floor, trembling like a broken flower.

The look in her eyes, the position she was in ... I had seen this before. So many times.

In Long Mesa I almost expected it. But here? And with this girl, it was like a sucker punch to the solar plexus.

I started to turn when I felt her hand on my ankle, barely touching me.

"No," she begged. "Please, no."

I knelt again, thinking maybe she didn't realize who I was. The thought that she might be afraid of me made me want to scream or cry.

*Kill*, my wolf whispered in my head. I could feel the ripple of fur under my skin as my wolf nearly forced me to shift right then.

I shoved her back, focusing my attention on Larkin.

"Larkin," I started gently, wanting to touch her, but knowing touch might be the last thing she wanted this second.

God *damn*, I knew that all too well.

"Please don't go," she choked out on a sob.

I pulled her into my arms then, letting her sob against me while my thoughts whirled. I looked at the door, hoping and worrying someone would find us.

After several long moments, Larkin moved, trying to push herself up. I helped her stand, bending to grab a shoe she was missing that had slid under the partition to the next stall. I slipped it onto her foot, and she hobbled to the sink, my arm around her waist for support.

She whimpered at the sight in the mirror.

"How can I help?" I begged quietly. "I can grab a teacher—"

"No," she said sharply, sucking in a shaking breath.

"Lark," I whispered, touching her tangled hair and blinking back tears.

We both jumped at the bathroom door swinging open.

"There you two are," Katy said with a laugh as she came in. The second she really saw Larkin, her eyes flared wide, her mouth dropping open in horror.

"What the hell happened?" she gasped, crossing the bathroom to stand in front of Larkin. She looked up at me, demanding answers.

"Trace." I spat his name, the word leaving a vile taste in my mouth.

Katy's jaw locked, her eyes going hard. "I'll get Remy. He'll kick that dick's ass once and for all."

"No!" Larkin's shrill cry stopped us both.

"Larkin, we need to tell somebody," I urged. I looked at Katy for back up.

"Please, guys," Larkin begged. "Help me get back to my room. I don't want anyone to see me like this."

Reluctantly, Katy and I helped Larkin get her arms back into her dress, thankful her bra hadn't been torn away during whatever happened. The zipper was destroyed, so I held the back of the dress together while Katy checked to make sure the hall was still empty.

We kept to the wall, heading out the side exit instead of going back through the dance. We stayed in the shadows of the grounds until we were able to slip into the girls' dorm. Thankfully everyone was still at the dance, and we made it to the room without anyone seeing us.

As soon as the door was shut and locked, Larkin started tearing at her dress, hands shaking. Fabric ripped as she shoved the dress off her body.

"Larkin, let us help," I started, moving towards her.

"No!" she shrieked, whirling as the dress pooled around her feet.

Standing there in her bra and panties, we could see the bruises on her arms and thighs. Around her wrists, the bruises looked like fingerprints.

I swallowed down a wave of bile.

"Okay, honey," Katy said soothingly. "What can we do?"

"I told him to stop!" she yelled, her voice cracking. Her eyes were wild and scared as they darted around the room. ""I tried to get away, but he wouldn't ... *stop*. I couldn't ... I swear, I tried!"

"I know," I replied, heartbroken. "Larkin, I *know*."

Larkin looked at me through tear-filled eyes, her knees giving out as she collapsed. Katy and I immediately surrounded her, kneeling by her sides.

"Larkin, we need to know ..." Katy sucked in a hard

breath. "We need to know how ... far this went. Do we need to call a doctor?"

The omega flushed. "He didn't ... I mean, he grabbed me and ... ripped my dress. But he didn't, *you know*."

I released a breath I hadn't known I was holding.

"I can still smell him on me," Larkin gasped, sobs ripping from her throat. She rubbed her hands across her arms, face crumpling. "Will it ever go away?"

God, I wanted to say yes. But if I closed my eyes, I still knew exactly what Cassian, Preston, and Marc smelled like. I still knew the smells that always lingered in the omega house.

My hands started to shake, and I knew I was rapidly losing control of my wolf. She wanted out and wanted out *now*.

"What can we do?" Katy asked, smoothing Larkin's hair out of her eyes.

"I need to shower," Larkin said, shaking her head. She looked at me and shivered. "Skye, are you okay?"

I gritted my teeth and nodded. "Fine."

Katy sucked in a sharp breath. "You're shaking like a fucking leaf."

A light dawned in Larkin's eyes. "You need to shift."

"I need to help *you*," I bit out, trying to shove my wolf back down.

Katy frowned. "No, you're almost out of control. Even your teeth are starting to change."

I ran my tongue across my teeth, hissing when I felt the sharpening of my canines.

"Go," Larkin urged softly, swallowing hard.

"Run it off," Katy ordered, helping Larkin to her feet. "I'll get Larkin showered and changed. When you're back, we'll figure out what to do." She looked at Larkin grimly. "But we need to tell somebody."

After a heavy pause, Larkin nodded sadly. "Okay."

Fuck. I knew I wasn't in any position to say no. Larkin needed me, and I needed to get myself under control.

Moving fast, I pulled my dress off and kicked my heels off into a corner. I jerked open a drawer and pulled on a shirt and yoga pants before shoving my feet into my sneakers.

"I'll be right back," I promised Larkin, my voice unsteady as I got up.

They both gave me teary nods as I unlocked the door to our room and headed into the hallway. I took the steps instead of waiting for the elevator, my feet slapping against the cement of the stairs.

I was practically vibrating as I hit the stone steps to the front of the dorm. I raced down them. I caught a couple of people giving me strange looks and then a wide berth as I stormed past.

I headed for the northern part of the campus, my wolf whining in my chest. I stumbled as a full body shudder ripped down my spine.

"Soon, girl," I swore, trying to let her know we were going to shift. I was so furious, I needed to channel it somewhere. Running for miles might start to help me calm down.

I started jogging and then outright running down the path, heading towards the western lake and the alpha cabins. The moon hung low and swollen in the sky, the silvery light showing the way.

I could see distant lights from the alpha cabins and knew I was close. As soon as I made it to the tree line, I would shed my clothes and shift.

"Skye? Hey, Skye!"

I growled loudly as footsteps approached. Rhodes came running up and slid to a stop on the wet leaves as he saw me. He was still dressed in his clothes from the dance.

"Shit," he whispered, his dark eyes growing round. "What's wrong? What happened?"

My wolf lunged at the cage of bone and muscle around my heart, demanding her freedom. My mind kept replaying Larkin's words, her broken words and sobs.

*"I tried to get away, but he wouldn't ... stop."*

Rhodes's eyes went wide, and he stepped back, his gaze flickering to my hands. "Skye, you're shaking and scaring the shit out of me. What's going on?"

I curled my hands into fists, feeling my claws sharpening and piercing my skin.

*"I can still smell him on me. Will it ever go away?"*

"Skye!" Rhodes snapped, his beta voice almost as commanding as Remy's, but I didn't care.

I glanced up at him. "Larkin," I ground out through chattering teeth.

His eyes went wide, and he looked around like Larkin would pop out of the shadows. Turning to me, expression thunderous, he demanded, "What happened to Larkin? Is she okay?"

"I ... I can't," I ground out. The base of my skull throbbed from the effort of holding back my wolf. "I have to—"

Rhodes ran a hand over his jaw, tossing his long dark hair out of his wild eyes. "Dammit, Skye, is she okay?"

"She's safe," I answered with a groan. My gut clenched so hard I almost folded over. "She's with Katy. In the dorm."

Rhodes took a step back. "I'm going to get Remy."

I nodded, not really caring and barely waiting until his back was turned before ripping off my shirt. I heard it tear with the force of my actions. I yanked off my shoes and pants next. They had barely hit the wet ground before I was shifting.

There was a certain pleasure-pain that came from shifting. Like cracking your knuckles or stretching a tight muscle. I relished the feeling as my fur sprouted across my body, my bones shattering and knitting back together. The whole shift took a few seconds, but each one felt like beautiful agony.

I shook out my coat and lifted my head with a deep, mournful howl. It echoed against the mountains, and I heard several others join the cry somewhere in the distance.

I let my wolf take over, and she lunged forward, tearing through the woods as fast as she could. She ran across grass and rocks, up hills and back down, heading deeper into the woods and pushing towards the forest.

The air was colder now, my breaths coming out in hard pants and puffs of steamy air.

I drove myself harder as thoughts of Larkin pushed in. I couldn't escape the way she had trembled, and the way the tears fell down her pale cheeks.

That look of complete heartbreak in her eyes haunted me.

It was like looking in a mirror.

I could remember every time Cassian put his hands on me. Every time Preston and Marc closed in around me. The sound of their laughter, their fingers clawing at me, touching me.

With a loud growl I pushed myself harder, shaking my head as I tried to dislodge the memories. The muscles trembled with adrenaline as I pushed myself to a high speed, the dark forest blurring.

I darted around a tree.

*We may not have to wait much longer.*

I snarled as I scrambled up an embankment.

*Skye is officially an omega.*

I stumbled over a root, collapsing to the ground. My heart was thudding in my body, blood roaring in my ears as I panted. I rolled to my side, limbs laid out as my chest heaved. I whimpered, wanting to cry. I whined low, a cry from my soul.

I wasn't sure how long I lay there under the trees, the moonlight my blanket. It felt like an eternity of minutes. Long after my breathing evened out and my skin cooled.

The snap of a twig had me lurching to my feet. My head swung around and I made out the shape of a human coming through the trees. A breeze brought his scent to my sensitive nose.

Remy.

He paused several feet from me, hands loose at his sides. His expression was alert and he was still in his dark clothes from the dance, but he had thrown a coat on over his outfit.

"Hey." He pitched his voice soft and calm as he approached, hands held in front of him to show he wasn't a threat.

I cocked my head, not sure what he wanted. If I shifted back now, I would be naked, my clothes a good two or three miles away. And even if I shifted to talk to him, I had no idea what I would say. Or whose story I would tell—mine or Larkin's.

"Rhodes came and got me. He went to check on Larkin. I came to see if you were okay." He hesitated. "Skye, what the hell's going on?"

I pawed anxiously at the ground when he mentioned Larkin, another whine scratching up my throat.

"Look, I'm not sure what's going on, but I can tell you're upset from here," he said softly, moving slowly closer. "Rhodes said something happened to Larkin? But he wasn't sure ..."

With a low keening cry, I backed up. He didn't stop moving forward and I forced myself to be still until he knelt in front of me, his dark eyes looking deeply into mine.

"Easy," he admonished, warm eyes worried.

With a huff, I dropped to the ground, resting my jaw on my front legs.

Remy seemed to hesitate for a second before reaching out and stroking my head. I let out a long breath, my eyes closing as I accepted the comfort. My wolf and I both relaxed against his touch.

"So strange," he murmured, his large hand stroking against my muzzle.

I opened my eyes.

"Katy was right," he said, looking at me with confusion. "Our coats are opposites." He traced the black star in the center of my head. His hand smoothed across my head, moving across my neck and down my back.

After several moments of being touched, I felt my heart rate slowing and my body relaxing as the adrenaline rush crashed. If he kept this up, I was going to fall asleep. The way his hands moved across me was soothing, grounding me again.

"Are you ready to head back yet? We need to talk about whatever happened," Remy said gently. "I don't want to call a pack meeting until I know exactly what happened with you and Larkin."

I couldn't help the whimper that escaped me, and I was shocked—and a little horrified—when I nuzzled his hand, not ready to head back ... or for him to stop touching me.

With a smile, he stroked my head again. "I'll shift and

we can run back to the cabin. Rhodes is having Larkin and Katy meet us there."

Stretching, I raised up onto all fours. I shook out my fur, eyes fixed as he moved back and toed off his boots. His jacket went next and then his shirt.

I swallowed, hard, locking my jaw to keep from panting.

His muscles were perfect—thick and defined. The muscles of his arms and back worked as he folded his clothes and set them under a tree. I could make out the shadow of a crescent moon tattoo on his shoulder blade. His hands dropped to the button of his pants and my eyes fixed on the thin trail of dark hair leading from his abs and disappearing under the waistband.

He coughed and I looked up, startled, to see him trying not to smile.

I turned around immediately, cursing myself inwardly and trying not to imagine what was under the pants I could hear him pulling off. There was a familiar series of cracks and pops as he shifted, his bones and joints reforming.

I turned to see him shaking out his coat and was stunned. Katy really was right.

Remy's wolf was a good several inches taller and longer than mine, but his coat was midnight black except for a small white star in the center of his forehead.

He finished shaking out his coat, arching his neck to howl up at the night sky. I felt the instinctive urge to join him, my own howl harmonizing with his in an eerie ballad.

Remy turned to look at me and our eyes met.

The ground shifted, shook beneath me so hard I wondered if Montana was prone to earthquakes. The sounds of the night died all at once, everything going deafeningly silent. The moon shone brighter, bolder, leaving no shadow to escape to. Everything in my world was rotating, spinning on its axis until I thought I would fall over.

All at once, something in me centered, and a peace I couldn't explain fell over me as I stared into his dark eyes.

*Mate.*

---

## 21

*MATE.*

My heart stuttered over the word even as I took several steps forward, my feet moving without any direction from me.

No, not me.

My wolf.

She was practically vibrating with pleasure as she tried to draw us closer. Every single part of her wanted nothing more than to run up to her mate.

*Our* mate.

Remy.

Taking control, I forced my legs to be still, staring across the space to where Remy was just as immobile as I was.

His chest heaved up and down, his large head cocked at a curious angle.

He was just as confused ... and intrigued.

It was like an invisible tether connected us and, through that tether, I could get a vague, fleeting sense of his emotions. Emotions that were strangely similar to my own. With it was a deep sense of longing and wanting, and I wasn't entirely sure who the emotions were coming from.

I flinched as my wolf rioted in my chest, not happy that I was keeping her from her mate. The force of her will nearly sent me running straight to Remy. I was barely holding on to control of my wolf form. If she kept pushing, I didn't know if I could hold us back.

In human form I was in charge, but for the last week, I had been practicing ceding power to her when we were shifted. Even if I got her to give me enough control to shift us back to human form, I would be completely naked with a several mile trek ahead of us.

That definitely wasn't an option.

Remy took the decision out of my hands, crossing the distance between us and not stopping until we were nearly nose-to-nose. He stood in front of me, and I could see the thick muscles of his shoulders trembling as he clearly fought the same urges I did, his wolf struggling to take control and run to me.

But he didn't touch me.

I got the sense he was trying to let me make the first move, and however I responded would be what he took his cues from.

A chaotic riot of emotions ripped through me, and in the midst of that storm, my wolf took the decision out of my hands, not waiting for me to use human rationale to figure out the right move. She stepped forward, dropping her head and nuzzling his neck under his chin.

It was an intimate gesture, one that most wolves, especially an alpha, wouldn't permit. The throat was our Achilles heel. Giving another wolf access to that part of your body was the ultimate trust fall.

And Remy never hesitated.

Like pieces of a puzzle fitting together, Remy rested his

massive head against my neck, and I felt something in him —in *us*—settle. That peace I felt when the mating bond snapped into place seconds ago was back, but even more potent. I leaned into him, letting myself fall into that sanctum.

I would sort out the emotional collateral later when I was back in human form.

But for now, this was what I needed after such a tumultuous night. Hell, after everything I had been through in my life. The sense of serenity coursing through me was a drug I needed. I had never felt this calm or ... safe.

*You're safe.*

I heard Remy's voice echo softly in a far part of my consciousness.

After several minutes of standing there, Remy nudged my shoulder and pulled back. There was an obvious reluctance in his gaze, but also a resigned determination. The look of a leader who was trying to deal with his own wants and the needs of his pack.

We needed to go.

Whatever was happening now between us would have to be tabled until we sorted out what was happening with Larkin.

As soon as I remembered Larkin, I whimpered low in my throat.

Remy rubbed his head against mine, huffing out a low breath. He looked up, his brown eyes huge and dark against his black fur, the white star on his head illuminated by the moonlight.

He turned and took off into the trees, me right behind him. He was fast, and I guessed he would have probably been a lot faster on his own, but he slowed his pace to match mine so I could keep up. We moved swiftly through the trees, across the soft earth until the light of the cabin flickered in the distance.

Remy turned his speed up a notch when the cabin came into view, and I pushed myself to a higher gear to match his stride.

We made it into the yard and Remy stopped suddenly by a tree.

My feet slid against the wet grass as I came to a stop beside him, my shoulder bumping him.

He looked down at the base of the tree, nudging a pile of clothes with his nose.

I immediately recognized them as my clothes.

He gave me an imploring look, basically telling me to change, before he turned and headed for the deck. He disappeared into the shadows against the wall.

My wolf whined, not happy her mate was out of sight.

*Larkin*, I reminded her.

A second later I was shifting back into human form, crouched low on the ground. I scrambled into my clothes behind the tree quickly, the cold night prickling across my exposed flesh.

I had just finished pulling on my shirt when I glanced up.

Remy waited for me at the top of the stairs, his frame large and imposing against the lights on the deck. I knew that in the darkness I was mostly a shapeless form, but the intimacy of the moment made me pause. A flush worked up my neck, heating my cheeks.

My heart stuttered a staccato beat in my chest. I stepped around the tree and crossed the yard, walking up the stairs until I stood at the step below Remy. My insides trembled the whole walk over, and I could only pray he didn't sense my anxiety as I approached.

He looked down at me, a softness in his expression I had never seen before as his eyes moved over my face.

The pounding in my chest increased to a level I knew he must have heard, my breath catching.

Remy was gorgeous, there was no denying that. From his broad shoulders to his square jaw, he exuded male confidence. It was something I had appreciated for the last week and a half since I met him. The wind caught his dark hair, tousling it slightly. His mouth was a map of sensuous curves I wanted to explore, and I was still staring at it when he opened his mouth to speak.

A loud crash from inside had both of us jerking and running for the back door. Remy wrenched it open, and we tumbled through it.

"Calm down!" Katy snapped at a clearly furious Rhodes. A coffee mug was in pieces on the other side of the room. Rhodes was glaring at Katy, a deep growl rumbling in his chest as his body shook with rage.

Larkin was huddled on one side of the couch, her hair still damp from her shower. Her split lip looked raw and harsh against her pale skin. She was staring with wild eyes at Rhodes and Katy, tears suspended in her lashes like pieces of crystal waiting to fall and shatter on her cheeks.

I stepped around Remy and went to her, sitting beside her as Remy went between his beta and his sister.

I sank onto the couch beside Larkin, careful not to touch her when all I wanted was to hug her.

She blinked up at me, registering I was next to her. "Are you okay?"

A sad smile drifted across my lips. "Isn't that my line?"

"I'm all right," she murmured. Her eyes flickered to Rhodes and she jumped as he slammed his fist down on the kitchen counter.

"Fucking *look* at her, Remy," he growled. He raked his

fingers through his black hair, pulled hard at the ends. "Trace is going to fucking pay."

"You need to calm down," Remy said quietly, his deep tone leaving no room for argument as he stared hard at Rhodes.

Rhodes' chest heaved and he opened his mouth to start talking, but I beat him to it.

"You're scaring her," I told him softly, a hint of a warning in my voice.

The angrier Rhodes grew, the more Larkin tried to melt into the couch. Her body was trembling with fear and stress and God knew what else. She had been through enough tonight, and I wouldn't have him scaring her, too.

Eyes wide, Rhodes took a couple steps towards Larkin who visibly tensed. She braced her heels on the edge of the sofa and pushed her back deeper into the cushions.

I got to my feet between them, blocking her from his view and him from hers. "Back off," I ordered. I knew Rhodes wouldn't hurt Larkin, but I also knew right now Larkin felt extremely exposed and vulnerable. She needed space and calm, not Rhodes losing his shit.

"I'm not going to hurt her," he said to me, exasperated. He looked around me, his face going solemn. "Lark—"

"Leave it," Katy snapped, stepping around him to help me in shielding Larkin. She folded her arms across her waist, glaring at him.

"Everyone settle down," Remy ordered, coming around to stand between all of us. His gaze flickered to Rhodes. "Give her some space, man. Back off."

With a growl, Rhodes turned and threw himself into one of the armchairs opposite the sofa. He didn't say anything else, but the expression on his face spoke volumes.

Remy sighed and looked at us, his eyes lingering on me. "Sit down." He reached out and touched my wrist, the act was supposed to be comforting but it felt like I had been touched by a live wire. The sudden jolt had me reeling back.

I gasped and pulled away sharply, ignoring the look Katy shot me when I sat down next to Larkin. Katy finally sat down on my other side.

Remy took a step backwards and moved to the other armchair across from Larkin's seat, sitting on the edge. He clasped his hands between his legs, leaning forward to look at Larkin.

"Larkin, please look at me," he started gently, waiting until her eyes found him. I saw him wince at the cut on her lip before he schooled his features.

"Do you need me to get the nurse?" he asked first. "We can have her come here to check you out."

She shook her head slowly. "I'm okay."

"Can you tell me what happened?"

Her eyes flickered to Rhodes for a brief second before going back to Remy.

Remy glanced over at his best friend, who looked like he was still ready to get up and beat the shit out of Trace at any given minute.

"Do you want Rhodes to leave?" Remy continued, trying to be as understanding as possible. The fact that he was trying to help Larkin, an omega, did funny things to my heart.

Rhodes growled. "The fuck you think I'm—"

Remy held up a hand for silence, shooting a warning glare at the beta.

"He can stay," Larkin whispered. She shrugged and looked away, her shoulders slumping in defeat. "It doesn't really matter."

"I need you to tell me exactly what happened." Remy's tone was endearingly patient and kind, his eyes soft as he waited on Larkin. "Whatever happened, we're on your side."

Larkin looked at me, and I gave her an encouraging smile.

She kept her eyes down as she spoke, her voice barely audible.

"I had to go to the bathroom. I left the dance and went into the hall. I had just opened the door when someone pushed me from behind."

I reached out tentatively, finding her hand and giving it a gentle squeeze. Immediately Larkin squeezed back, clinging to me like a lifeline.

"It was Trace," she whispered in a shaking voice. "He locked the door behind us. He told me ..." She swallowed and sniffled, wiping hard at her nose. My fingers turned white in her death grip. "He told me he saw me dancing ... and he knew I was trying to make him jealous."

Shame colored her voice as her cheeks turned red and a tear slipped out of her eye.

Remy and Rhodes both looked like blocks of concrete, barely moving as Larkin spoke. But I could feel their rage simmering, dangerously close to boiling over.

"He kissed me, and I tried to push him off, but then he hit me." She raised shaking fingers to touch her lips. "He tore my dress and ..." She flinched, pushing deeper into the couch. "He ... *touched* me." She whispered the last words so quietly, I barely caught them.

My eyes slid shut and I forced myself to be still, even though with every word she spoke, I knew exactly what she meant. Exactly what she felt then and now.

The embarrassment, the shame, the guilt.

How completely dirty I felt when unwanted hands had touched me.

Even now, all I wanted was a shower to wash away the memories.

"I swear I tried to make him stop," she said quickly, her tone pleading for them to understand. "I didn't want this."

"Of course you didn't," Remy said, his voice surprisingly calm even though I knew he was furious. A muscle in his jaw ticked as he clenched his teeth, grinding them together. His hands were curled into rock-hard fists. "You didn't do anything wrong."

"He kept grabbing at me, kissing me. I thought he was going to ... Then he let me go all of the sudden." She glanced at me, sudden gratitude splashed across her pale face. "I think he heard you coming."

Remy's eyes went wide, and I heard the growl rumble deep in his chest as his dark eyes flashed. "Did he touch you?"

I shook my head quickly. "No. I couldn't figure out why he was coming out of the girls' bathroom. But he left pretty quickly." My expression darkened. "I guess he wanted to get as far away from Larkin as possible before I saw her."

Larkin nodded. "Skye found me, and then Katy came in looking for us. They helped me get back to the dorms."

After a beat, Katy cleared her throat. She leaned around me, giving Larkin a pointed look. "Tell him."

My head swung to look at Larkin. She fidgeted, pulling the sleeves of her hoodie down around her fists.

"Trace has been making comments to me for a while now," she admitted. "He's cornered me a couple of times, made me uncomfortable ... But he never took it this far."

"Why didn't you say anything?" Rhodes demanded harshly. "We would have protected you!"

"It doesn't matter that she didn't say anything then,"

Katy ground out through clenched teeth. "All that matters is she's saying something *now*."

Rhodes grimaced. "I'm just saying maybe this could have been avoided if she had said something sooner."

Katy glared at him. "Way to blame the victim, Rhodes," she clipped out.

His jaw dropped, all the color draining from his face. "That's not what I meant!"

"Sure is what it sounded like."

Rhodes looked at Larkin, his gaze imploring. "I never meant you deserved this. I just can't believe this was happening and you didn't tell us. Or tell *me*."

Larkin blinked owlishly at him a second before looking away. "Why? It's not like you care."

Rhodes got to his feet. "What does *that* mean? You're one of my best friends, Lark. You're practically a little sister—"

I winced at his choice of words.

Remy got up, cutting him off. "None of that matters now. Larkin had every right to handle this how she wanted." He sent her a slightly injured look. "But I do wish you would've trusted us enough to tell us what was happening. Or trusted me, at least. I can't protect you if I don't know what's going on."

Larkin squirmed, more tears falling. My heart ached for her.

"She was probably embarrassed," I said quietly.

Remy looked at me. "But it wasn't her fault. She did nothing wrong."

Suddenly it didn't feel like we were still talking about Larkin.

I shrugged helplessly. "It doesn't change how your mind can twist things around."

His eyes slid shut and he ducked his head, breathing

deeply for a minute. He looked back at Larkin. "We need to report this."

Her eyes went pitifully wide. "No. I just want to forget this ever happened. Besides—it's his word against mine."

"But I saw him leaving," I reminded her. "I can tell the teachers what I saw."

"You saw him leaving," Larkin pushed, shaking her head. "He'll just say I asked him to meet me there. It will be his word against mine, and there's no proof."

"Look at your face," Katy said, eyes flashing. "Hell, you have bruises all over you!"

"What?" Rhodes looked alarmed, his dark eyes moving over Larkin as if he could see through her clothes to her injuries.

"I just want to forget this happened," Larkin said woodenly. "Please don't make me."

"No one's going to make you do anything," Remy assured her. He came and knelt in front of her on the floor. "But are you sure? We all believe you. Others will, too."

"And others won't," she said stubbornly. "Things are already tense with the Norwood pack—"

"Whatever is happening between the packs doesn't change what happened to you," Remy said firmly. "We're not going to sit on this just to keep from causing waves. Everyone would go to bat for you, Larkin. You're part of Blackwater. We all have your back *no matter what*."

"Thank you," she whispered, genuinely grateful for his support. She wiped her eyes. "But I still would rather not report it."

A muscle in Remy's jaw ticked. "Okay. But I'm going to talk to Trace."

"No—"

Remy shook his head. "I can't let this go. He hurt a

member of *my* pack. You don't have to report him to the school, but I won't let him touch you again. "

I shivered at how dark his tone was.

"But—"

"I'm sorry, Larkin," he told her kindly, but firmly. "It's my decision as the alpha on campus for our pack. I can't just let this go. Not when it risks your safety and the safety of other pack members. I'll handle it as discreetly as I can, but it *will* be handled."

Her lower lip trembled but she finally nodded, and then looked at Katy and me. "Can we go, please?"

I looked at Remy, who gave a reluctant nod. I didn't envy his position at all. He looked miserable and angry all at once. The urge to hug him was strong as I got up beside Larkin and Katy, but I forced myself not to.

"Lark," Rhodes called when we almost made it to the door, his voice tortured.

Larkin turned.

Rhodes sighed, looking helpless. "I'm here if you need me."

She nodded and followed Katy outside. I hesitated in the doorway, my eyes finding Remy's again.

My wolf protested, my chest aching as she struggled with my decision to leave our mate behind.

Squaring my shoulders, I followed the girls into the night, closing the door on Remy.

**22**

———

LARKIN CLOSED THE DOOR BEHIND US AS WE WALKED BACK into our room and immediately went to her bed, climbing up on it and laying on her side. She drew her legs up almost to her chin, looking at us with big brown eyes full of pain. Katy climbed onto my bed and I joined her, both of us leaning against the wall to watch Larkin.

"I'm all right," Larkin whispered with a small sniffle.

"Sure you are," Katy agreed. She got off my bed and walked to Larkin's, unfolding a blanket from the bottom and tucking it around Larkin's frame before returning.

"Thanks."

"Do you want to talk about it?" I asked. "I mean, trust me, I understand if you don't."

Larkin sighed, her fingers curling around the edge of the blanket. "I just feel so stupid."

"Don't do that," Katy begged, shaking her head. "Don't blame yourself for what he did. Girls always blame themselves for being victimized. You did nothing wrong."

"Maybe if I had said something sooner—"

"Katy's right," I agreed firmly, cutting her off from

trying to shoulder any blame. "I don't care if you told us or a teacher or even Remy a month ago. You did absolutely nothing wrong. Trace is the one who did this."

"Yeah, but it's my word against his," Larkin whispered, tucking the blanket around her neck. "They can't do anything."

"Remy will figure something out," Katy promised. "He won't let this go, and he won't let anything else happen to you."

Larkin nodded. "Yeah. But he seemed a little ... off tonight."

"Off?" The word came out strangled, and I coughed to cover it.

Katy frowned. "Yeah, he seemed distracted." She looked at me. "Did anything happen after he came to find you?"

I shrugged, but I couldn't meet their gazes. "No. I don't think so."

Larkin's brown eyes blinked at me. "You've been acting weird, too. I mean, you practically jumped out of your skin when Remy touched you."

Katy looked at me, her dark eyes narrowed. Her jaw dropped after a second of inspecting me. "Did you hook up with my brother?"

"What?" I yelped, eyes wide. "No! Definitely not."

"You like him?" Katy pressed.

"No, I don't like him," I retorted, but it sounded weak to me. Even as I said it, the words tasted bad in my mouth, and I got the distinct impression my wolf was annoyed with me for answering like that.

"It's because of me, isn't it?" Larkin said with a watery sigh. Katy and I turned to see she was crying again.

My heart twisted. "Lark—"

"What happened to me is making you think of what

happened to you all over, isn't it?" Larkin went on. The tip of her nose was bright red against the white of the blanket. "It's why you took off like that and had to shift. I'm bringing back all those shitty memories of when you lived with your old pack."

"Lark, this is not on you," I whispered, running a hand through my dark hair. I got off the bed and walked to the window, staring out at the darkness. "Something *did* happen tonight. With Remy. I'm trying to sort it out."

"What happened?" Katy asked suspiciously.

I leaned against the wall and sighed. "He found me in the woods and it was ... nice. He calmed me down. But when he shifted—"

I couldn't seem to find the words I wanted to say. It was so surreal. If it wasn't for the fact that my wolf was still mentally raging against me for leaving Remy at the cabin, I would probably have thought that I had dreamed what happened in the clearing.

Because there was just no way that we were ...

"And then what?" Larkin pressed.

I took a deep breath. "I don't know. It was weird. He looked at me and it was like there was an earthquake or something. And then I could hear his thoughts, and this one word kept chanting in my head."

"*Mate*," Larkin whispered. I turned at the awe in her voice.

I swallowed. "Yeah."

"Holy fucking shit." Katy covered her mouth with her hands, her eyes huge. "You two *bonded?*"

I flinched, my defenses immediately going up. "It just happened. One minute he was Remy and the next minute he was ... more than just Remy. I didn't ask for this, okay?"

Katy started to laugh. "Well of course you didn't ask for it—that's not how true mate bonds work. It simply *is*.

You guys are so young for this to happen! That's just crazy that the first time your wolves saw each other—"

"What does it feel like?" Larkin pressed, cutting her off as she sat up. Her eyes were bright again, curious.

I shrugged, hands splayed wide. "I don't know, it's like—"

"If this is the part where you tell me you're hot for my brother, I need to exit the conversation," Katy warned.

I felt my cheeks heat and I ducked my head, letting my hair cover my face. "Of course I don't."

*Lie.*

"So, you don't think he's hot?" Larkin asked.

I groaned, my mind bringing up the image of him pulling off his shirt in the clearing. "I didn't say *that*."

"Ew!' Katy grimaced, waving her hands around frantically. "Can we stop talking about how hot my brother is or isn't?"

I flipped my hair back in exasperation. "You brought it up!"

"And now I'm *un*bringing it up!'

"That isn't a word!"

"Hey!" Larkin called sharply, snapping her fingers. "Focus."

With a huff, Katy folded her arms over her chest. "Fine. But can we please make it a rule of the friend zone that we not discuss any sexual curricular activities you and Remy engage in?"

I growled. "Who the hell said I wanted anything to do with Remy? I didn't ask for this anymore than I asked for having green eyes. It just happened. And now I need to figure out what to do about it!"

"Hold on. Do you not *want* to be bonded?" Larkin picked her words carefully.

"Of course not!" I retorted, but then I hesitated. "I

mean, I don't think so? It's not like I have a choice. I can't *un*-bond."

"That's not true," Larkin said, causing Katy and I to both stare at her.

"I can break this thing?" I asked, moving to sit on Larkin's bed. Even as I spoke the words, considering their weight, my wolf pitched a fit.

Katy scooted to the edge of my bed. "True mate bonds are rare. Why would anyone want to break that?"

"Maybe because the people in the bond don't know each other and didn't sign up for a life sentence at the age of seventeen?" I answered, giving her a pointed look. "Remy didn't ask for this either, Katy. It's not like your parents who were together for years before their bond snapped into place. I've only known Remy for a couple of *weeks*."

"That's why other couples have found a way to break the bond," Larkin said. "Or so I've been told. When we went on vacation to the beach a few years ago, the shifter who ran the hotel we stayed at told me that his sister had just broken her true mate bond."

"How?" I demanded.

Larkin glanced at Katy and then me. "Apparently the bond is broken if one of you cheats on the other? I think that's how it works. Like, if you or Remy have sex with someone else, it destroys the bond. The sister of the hotel owner found out she was true bonded to an omega in their pack, and she didn't want it. So, she slept with his brother and it severed the bond."

Katy gave me an odd look. "You're gorgeous, but I'm not sleeping with you, Skye."

"Gee, thanks, Katy." I rolled my eyes so hard I thought I sprained a socket. I looked at Larkin. "So, if Remy or I have sex with someone else ... that's it?"

Larkin shrugged. "That's what the guy told me. I guess some people feel the same way you do—that the bond takes away their choice."

"But a true mate bond is a sacred, incredible thing," Katy argued. "I don't want to drink the Kool-Aid, but I've seen my parents and other couples in Blackwater who are true mates. Most people would be crazy not to want that."

I closed my eyes briefly. "I get that, I do. But I've spent my entire life having decisions made for me. When do I get to live my own life?"

"Would being with Remy be that awful?" Katy asked quietly, and I got the distinct impression I was on the verge of offending her.

"It's not about *Remy*," I replied, frustrated. "It's about having a choice. I would think you would be all about a girl's right to choose."

"And I am," Katy answered quickly. "But the true mate bond isn't something that comes along every day."

Larkin nodded in agreement. "She's right, Skye. You don't want to make a knee-jerk reaction that could affect the rest of your lives."

I all but growled at them. "I'm not making *any* reactions right now, okay? I'm trying to figure out all of my options."

Katy held up a hand. "All I'm saying is, talk to Remy before you decide anything. Odds are he's feeling just as confused as you are."

Larkin reached over and threaded her fingers with mine. "If this whole thing hadn't happened, how would you feel about Remy?"

"He scares me," I admitted.

Katy tensed. "Scares you?"

I reached over with my free hand and held hers, making sure I was looking at her in the eye. "I've never known someone like your brother. I've never known someone could be an alpha, and a protector, and a friend. It scares me because he's incredible and I'm ... me. I'm so damaged in so many ways, and he's ... amazing." My heart sank with each word. "How could he want to be with someone like *me*?"

Katy's eyes filled with tears. "I really need you to listen to me, Skye, okay?"

I nodded, pressing my lips together.

"You are incredible," she hissed. Her fingers squeezed mine hard. "You're a fighter. You have so much compassion. You've survived hell. If anyone deserves a happy ending, it's you. And you're right—my brother is pretty freaking amazing. He deserves someone as strong and beautiful as you."

She paused and glared at both Larkin and me. "If either of you tell him I said that, I'll burn your bras on the front lawn."

We both laughed. The tightness eased in my chest as we giggled together.

"I mean it," Katy continued. "You've only been here a couple of weeks, but you fit in perfectly with us. I know you see this bond as something else you don't have a say in, but you also didn't have a say in joining the Blackwater pack and look how well that turned out."

"You didn't have a choice in your roommate and look how that turned out." Larkin flashed me a cheesy grin.

I laughed again, feeling tears prick hotly against the backs of my eyes.

"Talk to Remy," Katy said gently. She gave me a small smile, both dimples flashing.

Larkin nodded, squeezing the hand she still held. "I agree."

"Okay," I agreed. "I'll go see him tomorrow."

Katy arched a brow at me and Larkin frowned.

"I *won't* go see him tomorrow?" I was confused.

"Sweetie," Katy said with a patronizing sigh, "do you honestly think either of you are going to get any sleep until you sort this out?"

I glanced at Larkin. "I don't want to leave you after everything that's happened."

Katy let me go and sank further into Larkin's bed, laying her head in the omega's lap. "I'll hang out until you get back."

"But—"

"It will give me something else to focus on," Larkin said solemnly, her large brown eyes innocently hopeful.

My jaw dropped and Katy started giggling, clapping her hands with glee.

"Oh, the emotional manipulation is *strong* with this one," Katy declared.

"You suck," I retorted.

Larkin shrugged and gave me a sweet smile. "Don't stay out too late. We'll want to hear all about it before you go to sleep."

Rolling my eyes, I got off the bed and headed for the door. "I hate you both."

"You love us," Katy replied in a singsong tone.

I smiled as I closed the door because I really did.

THE WALK to the alpha cabin usually took less than ten minutes. Between my pacing and detours, it took me nearly twenty minutes. The last three of which, I had been standing at the foot of the stairs leading to the front door.

I could see the lights from the TV flickering against the fragmented glass of the front door, so someone was definitely awake. Probably Remy, if he felt half as confused as I did.

"Okay," I told myself quietly, "you're just going to walk up there and figure this out, Skye."

Four more minutes ticked by. Four torturous minutes where I contemplated everything from running back to the dorm to finding a trucker to flag down and get me the hell out of Montana.

"Screw it," I whispered, squaring my shoulders. I jogged up the steps and crossed the porch. I rapped my knuckles against the glass and waited.

And waited.

It took forever before the door opened. Rhodes had barely cracked it before I pushed him aside and made my way through. I stopped short once I came in.

Remy was sitting on the sofa, the controller for a game in his hands. It slipped out of his grasp when he saw it was me, landing with a thunk on the rug.

"Skye. Hey." He stood up slowly, wiping his palms against his jeans.

"Is Larkin okay?" Rhodes demanded, touching my arm. "Did something happen?"

I blinked and looked at him, remembering he was in the room, too. "What? No, Larkin's fine. She's with Katy. I, um, need to talk to Remy."

Rhodes looked back and forth between us. After a beat, he reached for the denim jacket hanging by the front door and shrugged it on. "I'm just gonna go anywhere that isn't here." He hurried back out the door, slamming it behind him.

I turned back to Remy and we stared at each other for a long beat. I quickly cut him off when he opened his mouth to speak.

"Can I start?" If I didn't get this out now, before I lost my nerve, I never would. "I mean, please?"

Remy nodded slowly, his warm dark eyes sliding over me. He reached for the remote and turned off the television.

I walked around him and started pacing in front of the lit fireplace. The heat did nothing to seep into the sudden cold that weighed down my bones.

"I've never been alone," I finally blurted out, still pacing. "Growing up I was always in the omega house, and it was never empty. Hell, I even shared a bed with my mom until I started going to school here."

I hesitated and made a face. "Which you probably didn't need to know."

He smiled softly and sat down on the edge of the couch, his hands clasped loosely between his knees.

"My life before Blackwater sucked. It was literally hell. And there was never a break. It's why I like to read so much—it's an escape."

"You mentioned that."

God, had his voice always sounded that warm? That husky? That ... Dammit, I was getting off track.

I blinked. "I did? Right. I did." I gave a quick nod. "I mean, I know technically I'm rooming with Larkin, but for the first time in my life, I can just be *me*. Not the omega or the bastard or the ... whatever. I'm just me."

My pacing slowed and I let out a long breath. "I know you can't control this anymore than I can. You didn't ask for it. I'm just ..." I sighed, trailing off as I stopped pacing altogether.

"Scared that you're just being attached to yet another person who can control you?" He finished my thought perfectly. "That once again you don't get a say in your own life?"

My eyes went wide. "I thought Zoe told me you would only be able to read my thoughts in wolf form."

He laughed and shook his head, eyes smiling. "That's true. This is just me being able to guess where your head is since I've gotten to know you. It's not a big leap."

"Oh."

Remy stood up. "Skye, I don't know exactly what you went through at your last pack. Obviously, I have some ideas, but I don't really know."

"I'm not ready to talk about that," I whispered, all my defenses shoring up. I wrapped my arms around my waist, hugging myself.

"And I'm not asking you to," he assured me, coming to a stop less than a foot in front of me. "A mate bond means that we're meant to be together. But that doesn't mean that we *have* to be together."

"Larkin told me that there's a way to break the bond."

Remy froze, his expression smoothing as he schooled his reaction. His body went eerily still. "Is that what you want?"

I hesitated and looked at him, looked into those warm chocolate brown eyes and knew.

"No. I don't want that at all." Admitting it felt like a relief and like I was freefalling off a cliff all at once.

He shifted towards me. "This is all new to me, too, Skye."

A sobering thought crossed my mind. The one that had been plaguing me since the woods. "Do *you* want this, Remy?"

The corner of his mouth hitched up for a second as he looked at me. Slowly, he raised a hand, tracing the curve of my jaw. I shivered, remembering the feel of his hands stroking when I was a wolf.

This was so much better.

He inched even closer. His breath, minty and warm, fanned over my face. His eyes tracked the movements of his fingers hungrily.

"Yeah," he answered roughly, thickly. "I want this. I want you." He dipped his head and covered my mouth with his.

## 23

As far as first kisses went, I was pretty sure this was one for the record books. Obviously, I didn't have anything to compare it to, but this was one of the most incredible moments of my life.

Fire ignited in me the second Remy's lips touched mine, soft but demanding all at once. His hands settled on my hips, pulling me closer. The smell of him from earlier in the evening, pine and soap and something that was entirely Remy, filled my senses.

I was going to combust in the most exquisite ways.

His large hands almost spanned my waist, his fingers flexing against the soft material of my yoga pants. His tongue teased the seam of my lips until I opened my mouth on a gasp, letting him in.

I groaned as his tongue stroked mine, one hand sliding from my waist up my spine.

My hands had been clenched into fists on his chest, the fabric of his t-shirt bunched in my grip. I relaxed my hold now, letting my hands slide over the hard muscle and up around his neck, pressing my chest flush against his.

Now Remy groaned, changing the angle of his head to deepen the kiss.

Flames licked through my blood, and I was sure I was going to combust any second.

I was one hundred percent okay with death by kissing.

His other hand lifted to cradle my jaw, holding my head exactly where he wanted me for the best access to devour me. He shuffled backwards, tugging me with him until we were falling weightless for a second.

Remy landed on the couch, pulling me down with him. I fell against his chest, straddling his lap without breaking the kiss. His hands returned to my hips, pulling me down against him.

I rolled my hips on instinct as liquid heat pool low in my belly, my body knowing what to do even if my brain didn't.

His low groan, almost sounding pained, made my wolf sing. I could feel the evidence of his arousal pressing more and more insistently at my center. The fact that I could cause such a visceral reaction made me feel powerful; it was a total head rush to have this alpha male underneath me and coming undone.

Another roll of my hips had me gasping and breaking the kiss, my head dropping back in ecstasy. My hands dropped to the hard muscles of his shoulders, my nails digging in as I grew lightheaded.

Remy's mouth moved across my jaw and down my neck, nipping at the pulse point he found and then soothing it with his tongue and lips. His fingertips traced the exposed skin between my pants and my top that had ridden up. The heat of his skin on mine made me shiver with anticipation of more.

"Skye," he whispered against my neck, lifting his hips to meet my center.

My hand fisted in his soft hair, much the way I wanted to do when we were dancing only hours earlier. With a growl, I lifted his head before slamming my lips back onto his with bruising force.

He met every one of my movements with equal fervor, stroke for stroke, touch for touch.

A strange, foreign sensation started building between my legs. The way my body was reacting was all new to me, but wholly addictive. I craved that feeling, grinding my hips down against his.

"Shit," Remy moaned. He pulled his lips away from me and tightened his hands on my hips, stopping my movements instead of pulling me closer like I wanted.

I frowned and tried to push myself against him again, desperate for the fiction between our bodies as I chased a high I never knew existed.

He sucked in a sharp breath, fingers digging into my sides. "Skye, wait. Stop."

Breathing hard, I opened my eyes and looked into his. My chest heaved in time with his as we struggled to catch our breath. His eyes were dark with lust and ... uncertainty?

"Wait," he repeated softly, his hands relaxing on my hips as he realized he had my full attention.

*Wait?*

My wolf and I both whined the word internally. I almost whimpered out loud, frustrated as the insistent pulse between my legs throbbed.

What the hell did he mean, *wait?*

A thumb stroked the skin above my hip and nearly had me rocking against him again. "We need to slow down and talk about this."

It was like a bucket of ice water had been thrown on my head.

I scrambled off his lap and across the room in seconds, putting as much distance between us as possible. Humiliation and shame rushed through me, a levee breaking in my soul as I realized what I had almost done. I moved so fast I stumbled and almost went down in a blind panic.

My first kiss with Remy, and I practically mounted him like a bitch in heat.

I felt every bit the whore Cassian had always called me.

"I'm sorry," I gasped out, shaking my head as disgust washed over me. "I'm so sorry. I didn't mean—"

"Whoa, Skye, stop," Remy ordered gently. He got off the couch, adjusting his jeans with a wince. He caught my gaze with a rueful smile.

Heat bloomed across my cheeks as I looked away.

"Hey, come on," he implored, coming to a stop in front of me. His hand reached up to touch my face, but I shied away, more than a little embarrassed. "Shit. Skye, I didn't mean—"

"It's my fault," I interrupted quickly. I just wanted this over so I could get out of here and lick my wounds in peace. "I came here, and I shouldn't have ... I can go."

"No!" he said sharply as he grabbed my wrist. His touch was infinitely gentle.

I looked up, stunned when I saw his fierce expression.

"Don't go," he added softly. "Please, don't go." He ran his other hand through his hair. It was a mess from my fingers tangling in it.

I shifted my weight from one foot to the other, trying to ignore my stinging pride and the wolf currently raising hell in my chest. She wasn't sure why we weren't naked already.

He took a deep breath. "This bond between us ... I don't want to hurry and mess this up. I know things at your last pack weren't good. I don't want to do anything tonight you might regret later."

"Oh," I replied simply. As my embarrassment eased, I was actually kind of relieved one of us had kept their head. If Remy hadn't stopped us, I wasn't entirely sure I would have.

My wolf huffed, annoyed, as she calmed down.

Yeah. I definitely wouldn't have stopped.

The rational, human part of me knew that would have been a mistake.

He gave me a wry grin. "Trust me, as much as I would love to keep going—and believe me, I *really* would—I think we need to take it slow."

"You're right. I'm glad one of us is thinking clearly," I returned, a shy smile tugging at my lips. I took a deep breath as the riot of emotions and urges in me slowed from boiling to a simmer.

"I wouldn't go that far." He rubbed the back of his neck and chuckled. "Why don't we just take this easy? There's no rush." His eyes slid down my body, his gaze heating. "And I really don't want to rush a damn thing with you."

I bit my lower lip, a nervous laugh bubbling up. "Sounds good. I mean, it's late. Maybe I should head back to my room."

"I'll walk you back," he told me, his tone not offering but telling.

I nodded, waiting as he grabbed his coat off the hook. He glanced back at me and frowned. "Where's your coat?"

I glanced down, realizing I never grabbed it when I left Katy and Larkin earlier. I looked back at him with a shrug. "I guess I forgot it. I was a little distracted."

He laughed, a broad grin on his face. He grabbed a hoodie hanging next to his coat and tossed it to me. "It'll probably be huge on you, but it's better than nothing."

I pulled it over my head, sniffing deeply. My heart

warmed as I was wrapped entirely in Remy's scent.

He was still smirking knowingly at me when I got my arms through the holes, rolling up the sleeves as it hung almost to my knees.

I narrowed my gaze, folding my arms across my chest. "You know you're not getting this back, right?"

He chuckled again, the warm sound rumbling up from his chest as he pulled on his jacket and came over to me. He wrapped an arm around my waist and kissed the top of my head. "It's yours."

I let my head rest against the center of his chest for a long moment, taking comfort and sanctuary in his embrace.

He pressed another kiss into my hair. "Let's get you to bed."

I pulled back and arched a brow.

He rolled his eyes and grabbed my hand, pulling me out the door. "Your own bed," he retorted with a laugh.

His fingers laced through mine as we walked down the stairs and started for the dorms, the lights from the building flickering in the distance like a beacon.

I smiled to myself, wondering if Larkin and Katy would be watching at the window.

"What's that smile for?" he asked, nudging me.

"I was wondering what kind of inquisition I'll get from Katy and Larkin when I get back," I admitted.

His brows raised. "You told them?"

"Was I not supposed to?" I swallowed, wondering if I had done the wrong thing. It's not like an instant mating bond came with an instant manual my brain downloaded.

Wouldn't that have been convenient?

He shook his head. "You can tell them whatever you want. I'm glad you've become such good friends with them. Truthfully, Katy and Larkin have always been on the outs as far as the pack goes. It's why they gravitated towards each other."

I must have looked confused because he went on, "Larkin's always been quiet. Her family joined the pack when she was a kid. And Katy is … Katy."

We both laughed easily because that was the truth; Katy was simply Katy.

"So, I'm just another misfit?" I teased.

He snorted. "It's a little crazy to see how tight you three are. It's like you grew up together. Not like you just got here a couple of weeks ago."

I sighed thoughtfully as he guided us to the path to the dorms, my feet crunching on the ground beneath me. "I never had this at my last pack. Friends, I mean. It's nice."

Nice didn't really begin to cover how I felt about Katy and Larkin. Words weren't adequate to explain how much I was coming to love those two.

He lifted my hand and pressed a kiss to my knuckles. "I'm glad you and your mom got out." He dropped our hands, but still held mine in his. "I meant what I said, you know. Anytime you want to talk about what happened, I'm here. No judgment."

"Thanks," I whispered, my fingers squeezing his briefly. "I'll be ready to talk about it one day, but sometimes I feel like I'm still processing what happened."

"You've only been here a few weeks, Skye. You have to give yourself time," he told me quietly, the warmth of his breath fogging the air in front of us.

"I know. It just feels like I'm always waiting for the monster around the corner or for the other shoe to drop."

He pulled me to a gentle stop, looking down at me seriously. "I won't let anything hurt you." The corner of his mouth hooked up. "Monsters or otherwise."

"Thanks," I whispered. After a second I turned so we

could keep walking. The more his eyes studied me, the more I worried he would see past my flimsy walls to all the dark secrets I had buried.

I cleared my throat and leaned against him as we walked. "I feel safe here. I feel safe … with you. But it's going to take more than a couple weeks to undo a lifetime of feeling scared of everything."

"Is there anything I can do?" he asked as we turned the last bend to the dorm.

I stopped us, turning to face him. "Just be patient?" I requested softly. "I'll probably mess things up at some point or do something stupid. I'm kind of new to the whole relationship thing."

"I can be patient," he said softly, reaching up with his free hand to tuck my hair behind my ear. "Take all the time you want. I'm here whenever you need me. As your friend and … more."

I smiled. "More, huh? I think I like that."

He grinned, his teeth brilliantly white in the darkness. "Good. There's definitely going to be *more*." He dropped his mouth to mine, kissing me softly, but keeping it short and sweet.

I exhaled loudly. "What happens next?"

He glanced up at the windows. "Now you go get some sleep."

I rolled my eyes. "I mean, do we tell people about us? This?"

"That's up to you. Do you want to tell the pack?"

"Please don't do that," I begged, not wanting the responsibility of every decision on my shoulders while Remy gave me room to breathe. "I know you're being sweet and letting me set the pace, but I can't feel like my feelings are the only ones that matter. What do you want?"

Remy ducked his head slightly, making sure I was

looking in his eyes. "Skye, I would be happy to tell everyone about us tonight."

My eyes widened.

"But you might not be ready for that," he added knowingly. "Mate bonds are rare, and I've never heard of one happening to a pair as young as we are. I didn't even know it was possible to bond right now. I think the youngest pair on record were twenty? Twenty-one?"

"Wow," I murmured. "I mean, I knew it wasn't common, but wow."

"That means a lot of questions and a lot of staring," he went on. "I'm used to it. I've had the spotlight on me almost my entire life. But is that what you want?"

I considered it. "Maybe we just tell people we're dating?" I offered hopefully, knowing full well that dating the alpha-to-be of Blackwater would still cause waves.

"We can do that," he agreed. "But we'll probably have to tell the pack before the run next weekend. If we don't, they'll definitely notice it when we shift and are near each other."

"That obvious, huh?" I asked wryly.

He snorted. "I can barely control myself in human form around you. My wolf already has us mated, married, and playing house."

I laughed loudly. "Yeah, mine is pretty much the same." I winked at him. "She's kind of pushy."

"It's easier as wolves," he said, lacing his other hand into mine and raising our hands to his chest. "Wolves are baser creatures. They don't give a shit about human emotions. It's why the bond only happens when you're shifted. There's less emotional baggage and confusion to muddy the waters."

"That makes sense," I agreed, smoothing my thumbs against the backs of his hands.

"So, we tell the pack before the run," he concluded. "That gives us a week to just be us in public, and it doesn't matter when we're with our friends. You already told Katy and Larkin, and I told Rhodes."

"You did?"

He nodded. "He's my best friend. I tell him everything."

"Everything, huh?" I gave him a pointed look.

His gaze smoldered, his eyes dropping to my lips. "Maybe not everything."

I was still laughing as he pressed his lips to mine again, his kiss was lazy and slow. When he tried to pull back, I rolled onto my toes, keeping our lips together. He chuckled against my mouth.

I was still smiling when I broke the kiss. I licked my lips slowly, tasting him there. "I could get used to this," I said softly, almost to myself.

"Me, too." He rested his forehead against mine, and I closed my eyes on a deep, relaxed sigh. "Go get some sleep. I'll see you at breakfast, okay?"

I nodded, my forehead still against his. "Okay."

He lifted his head and kissed my forehead. "Go. I'll wait for you to get inside."

Reluctantly I let him go and turned, heading up the stairs to the dorm. I opened the door and looked back to see Remy still standing there, waiting for me. I smiled to myself and gave him a small wave before ducking inside the building.

I took the stairs again, taking them two at a time, my heart lighter than it had been in years.

I was still smiling when I opened the door to my dorm. I closed the door and looked up to find Katy and Larkin staring at me with matching grins.

"Tell us *everything*," Katy demanded, her eyes sparkling.

## 24

"I'M SERIOUSLY GOING TO THROW UP," KATY DEADPANNED, throwing an arm across my chest to stop us as we walked into the cafeteria the next morning.

"What?" I asked, throwing my arms up in exasperation.

"We're barely in the doors, and you two are already making eyes at each other," she griped, nose wrinkled in disgust.

I wanted to tell her she was wrong, but the second I crossed the threshold, my eyes found Remy's. If my smile matched the energy in his, we definitely looked like a couple of idiots.

He was already seated at our normal table with Rhodes, Dante, Tate, Maren, and Ryder. He stopped mid-conversation with Dante when I came in, his full attention shifting to me.

The grin he gave me almost had me pushing Katy aside so I could run to him.

"Stop," Katy begged, tugging on my arm and pulling my attention back to her. "It's too early for this."

246

I rolled my eyes and glanced back at Larkin, who stood a step behind us. I sighed quietly at her obvious reluctance to enter.

"If you want, we can skip breakfast," I told her. "We can go back to the room."

It was early enough in the morning after the dance that the cafeteria wasn't at full capacity. Trace and his crew were nowhere to be seen yet, but I knew Larkin was afraid of running into him.

I was personally kind of hoping I *would* run into the asshole.

My wolf rumbled in approval.

"I can't avoid the cafeteria forever," Larkin said with a grimace.

"But it's totally okay if you want to avoid it today," Katy assured her, resting a hand on her arm. "I can grab food and meet you guys back in your room. It's Sunday, so we can spend the day watching TV and eating chocolate."

"Or we can hang out at the cabin," I said without thinking.

Katy snorted. "Down girl."

I made a face. "Sorry. I swear, this bond also removed the filter between my human brain and wolf brain."

"I'm going to need you to keep *all* of your brains in check while talking to me about my brother," Katy grumbled, shaking her head.

"I know I know. But seriously, Lark. We'll do whatever you want. We can go back to the room."

Larkin chewed on her lower lip, considering the offer. With a dejected sigh, she nodded and took a step back. Unfortunately, she didn't notice the two girls coming up behind her and she stepped back into them, her heel coming down on the foot of one.

With a gasp, she turned to apologize, but the other girl was already glaring at her.

"Watch where the fuck you're going," Sierra snarled, glaring at Larkin. Her blue eyes were twin chips of ice, hard and glittering. She exchanged a glance with Ainsley who was walking with her.

With a scoff, Sierra looked at Larkin again and leaned in closer, dropping her tone. "And stay the hell away from my boyfriend, skank."

Larkin's face went ashen as she stumbled back into me.

I stepped around Larkin, making Sierra back up a step when I growled. "What did you just say?"

Ainsley flipped her long brown hair over a shoulder, shrugging a bony shoulder. "Trace told us how she basically threw herself at him at the dance. Larkin seems to like spreading problems like she likes spreading her legs."

A low moan came from Larkin. I looked back to see she was white as a sheet and looked ready to throw up.

"You've got to be kidding me," I spat, fury washing over me. I glared at Ainsley and then Sierra. "Your *boyfriend* is an abusive asshole who should be locked up."

Sierra's cheeks turned a brilliant shade of red. "You don't know what you're talking about, new girl."

"Get out of here, Sierra," Katy ordered, stepping up beside me. We formed a barrier between the two girls and Larkin.

Sierra snorted derisively, her lip curling in scorn. "I don't take orders from dykes. Go order your bitch around."

Katy's hand shot out, cracking against Sierra's face, stunning all five of us. Larkin cried out, and a hush fell over the cafeteria. I heard chairs scraping against the tiles and it didn't take a genius to figure out it was likely Remy and Rhodes coming over.

Sierra's face turned bright red as she whirled around

with a growl, her gaze locked on Katy. I caught her around the waist as she lunged at the redhead.

Sierra was about my height, but she had a lot of rage on her side as she tried to fight me off her. My arms were still around her waist as I tried to pull her away from Katy and Larkin. Ainsley was screaming something I couldn't make out behind me, and I briefly wondered if Katy would hit her, too.

Sierra's hands curled around one of my wrists, her nails digging in hard enough that I smelled the scent of my own blood. I shoved her away from me on instinct. She hit the wall across from me and glared, murder in her eyes.

I growled in response, my wolf and I ready for the fight.

Remy was in front of me before Sierra could turn her attack on me.

"What the *fuck* is going on?" he thundered, his voice hard and furious as he leveled a stare at Sierra that had her studying the floor and all but sliding to the floor to submit to his gaze.

"Apparently Sierra and Ainsley are under the completely fucked up delusion that Larkin came onto Trace last night," Katy explained, her voice full of venom.

Remy's dark gaze swung to Ainsley, who also cowered. "Seriously?"

"She hit me!" Sierra shrieked. "As our alpha on campus, I *demand* she be punished for striking another pack mate."

"Are you kidding me?" Katy yelled, hands balling into fists. "After what you said? You're lucky I only slapped you, bitch!"

"Be quiet," Remy ordered his sister.

I could sense his frustration mounting, and I almost reached out to touch his back, wanting to offer comfort.

Sierra pointed a finger at me. "And *she* attacked me when I tried to defend myself!"

Remy breathed hard, his chest heaving as he looked at all of us. Out of the corner of my eye, I saw Rhodes had pulled a shaking Larkin away from the center of the chaos, but we still had every eye in the room on us.

"Cabin, all of you. Now." Remy ordered, his tone clipped.

Sierra and Ainsley glared at Katy and Larkin as they walked by. When Sierra intentionally shoulder checked me, I gritted my teeth and forced myself not to reach out and yank her bleached roots.

"Sierra!" Remy snapped. "That's fucking enough."

Head ducked in contrition, Sierra scurried down the hall with Ainsley.

Rhodes cleared his throat. "I'm going to take Larkin back to the dorm, okay?"

Remy nodded, watching them leave.

"Rem—" Katy started softly.

He whirled on her, eyes blazing. "Not here, Katherine."

Katy swallowed and looked at her feet, hands clasped in front of her. I had never seen her look so small or contrite.

Remy stalked down the hall, Katy and I following behind quietly. I could hear the sudden buzz of chatter swarm as we all walked away from the cafeteria.

So much for laying low.

Pissed off Remy wasn't something I had seen before. I had seen him put some pack members in check before, but nothing like this.

Then again, I had never seen a physical fight break out in the pack like this.

He shoved the door open, holding it for us. He waited until we were out to shut the door and look at his sister.

"Meet me at the cabin. I need to talk to Skye," he said.

Katy nodded wordlessly and headed down the path to the cabin.

"What the hell happened?" he asked me, turning with confusion in his eyes. He raked a hand through his hair.

"What Katy said," I replied. "Sierra and Ainsley started in on Larkin about Trace. Apparently, he told them that she came onto him at the dance."

"Fucking asshole," Remy muttered darkly, eyes flashing. He rubbed the back of his neck with a growl. "I should've made my point a little harder."

"What?" I gaped at him. "You talked to Trace? When?"

He nodded grimly. "After I walked you back. I went looking for him. I told him to stay the hell away from Larkin and any other Blackwater pack member."

Dread pooled in my stomach. "And he just said okay?"

A snort escaped from Remy. "No. He swung at me and missed. I landed a few solid punches. He probably needed a cover story to sell the bruises to Sierra."

"You *hit* him?" I blinked, wishing I had been there to see it.

Remy smirked, reaching up to toy with the ends of my hair. "Only a couple times."

"And then he ran to Sierra and told her Larkin came on to him," I finished grimly. "I really hate this guy."

He sighed and nodded stiffly, letting my hair slide through his fingers. "Me, too. What made Katy hit Sierra?"

"Katy and I were defending Larkin and Sierra ... said something pretty offensive to Katy." I frowned, remembering the slur that flew easily from the blonde's lips. "Katy reacted. I grabbed Sierra when she went to hit Katy back."

"Sierra and Katy hate each other," he replied, shaking

his head. "They always have, but I can't believe Katy hit her."

"But what Sierra said was really cruel," I said quickly, defending my friend.

Remy gave me a hard look. "I don't care what Sierra *said*. What matters is Katy escalated it to a physical level."

My back went stiff. "What does that mean?"

"It means Katy will have to have some sort of consequence," he answered, frustration lacing his tone. "I can't let it slide because Sierra's a bitch or because Katy's my sister. I mean, I'm sure Sierra deserved it, but we don't settle things with fists around here."

"If she deserved it, then what's the issue?" I demanded, not seeing the problem. Hell, if Katy hadn't slapped her, I probably would have.

"I represent the pack here," he told me, his tone final and resigned. "I have to maintain pack integrity and cohesion above all else. Even when I really don't want to."

I nodded and watched him exhale deeply before starting down the path to the cabin. He only made it a few steps when I stopped him.

"Remy?"

He turned and I licked my lips, suddenly nervous. Taking a deep breath and not giving myself time to think it through, I stepped forward and wrapped my arms around his waist to hug him.

His arms closed around me instantly, his head dropping to my neck and inhaling deeply. I felt his muscles relax as I smoothed a hand up and down his back.

"Thanks," he murmured in my hair, nuzzling his nose against my throat. His lips ghosted across the skin there and a shiver tripped down my spine. "I needed that."

His warm eyes were clearer when he pulled back. His hand slid off my back and down to grab my hand in his. I gave him a weak smile and let him lead me down the path to the cabin.

Students were starting to emerge after the late night, and I caught several double takes at watching Remy and me walk by hand-in-hand, but I was too preoccupied wondering what kind of consequence Katy would face.

In Long Mesa, pack punishments were typically public spectacle. I had seen everything from someone being held in a cage in the center of town without food and water for days to whipping. My grandfather wasn't exactly known for his mercy, and as my uncle took more control of the pack, punishments became more frequent and crueler.

I glanced up at Remy. Somehow I couldn't see him making Katy sit in a cage for days without food or water. Or tying her to a post to whip her.

My stomach cramped, remembering a particular punishment from my uncle. A female shifter was found having an affair with another male. Linden had happily told her that since she clearly needed more than her mate could provide, he would oblige her cry for help. My uncle had forced her to strip and walk through the compound naked, before chaining her to a bed at the omega house for anyone to visit.

After several days, she was unchained to shower. She was in the bathroom for all of ninety seconds when she punched the mirror above the sink and used a shard of glass to slit her wrists.

The sounds of her screams gave me nightmares for months.

My steps slowed as the cabin came into view and Remy, noticing I had slowed, stopped and waited for me.

I couldn't meet his gaze. I was too trapped in the past, remembering the way the woman's body was discarded carelessly, like trash, outside the compound. She wasn't even worthy of a burial.

*Fiona*, I remembered suddenly. Her name had been Fiona.

Tears blurred my vision.

"Whoa, hey." Remy's hands framed my face, lifting so he could see me. His eyes went wide. "What's wrong?"

I sniffed and blinked, twin tears falling. "I'm worried about Katy."

Remy gave me a confused look even as his thumbs swept away my tears. "I don't get it."

"I know you said you have to do something," I stammered, unable to meet his gaze, " but I don't want anything bad to happen to her."

His eyes narrowed. "I can't let what she did slide, Skye. You know that."

I nodded miserably. "I just don't want her to get hurt."

"Hurt?" he repeated, incredulous. Suddenly clarity dawned on his face. "You think I'm going to *hurt* Katy?"

"I get it's what you have to do," I whispered. I was trying, and failing, to bury the overwhelming reality that the guy fate had linked to me for the rest of my life wasn't much better than the monsters I had run away from.

"Fucking hell," he muttered. He let my face go and took me by the shoulders. "Skye, look at me."

I couldn't.

I couldn't watch Remy tell me he had to punish Katy. He had to hurt my friend. Not this guy who I was starting to fall for.

"Skye, babe, look at me," he begged, giving me a small shake that snapped me out of my relentless thoughts.

I finally lifted my eyes. My jaw dropped when I saw the pain, the horror, on his face.

"Katy will be fine," he swore, his hands cupping my

cheeks. "I don't know what happened before, but what Katy did? I'll put her on janitorial duty in the girls' dorm for a week. *That* is the standard consequence for striking a pack mate. No one is hurting Katy."

I gulped down a swallow. Relief washed through me, my knees going weak. Remy caught me and held me against his chest.

He swore under his breath, arms going tight around me.

"I'm sorry," I whispered against his chest. My hands went around him, clutching to his back.

"Promise me something?"

I nodded.

"We both know your last pack was seriously fucked up. Can you promise to come to me with questions or anything you're worried about before assuming the worst?"

"Yeah. I can do that," I promised, letting my eyes close as I relaxed against him.

**25**

———

Katy was supremely pissed off to be on janitorial
duty for a week. When she kept complaining, Remy offered
to make it two weeks. I had to hide my giggle, watching as
he treated her like a parent instead of a brother.

Sierra and Ainsley got a strong warning to remember
pack loyalties. Watching Remy put the fear of God into
those two was definitely the highlight of my morning.
Watching them scurry away from the cabin, tails tucked
between their legs, was a close second.

Katy was still sulking on the couch. She glared at Remy
as he shut the door after them.

"What?" he demanded. His eyes narrowed. "You can't
freaking hit people, Kit-Kat."

"I know," she muttered back with a dramatic sigh. "But
this took so long we all missed breakfast."

My stomach growled on cue, and they both turned to
look at me. Remy shook his head with an amused smile.

I shrugged. "Sorry. I'm hungry, too."

"Wow. Bonded less than a day, and he's starving his
mate," Katy chastised with a roll of her eyes.

256

I pressed my lips together, choosing to ignore the way the word 'mate' caused my stomach to flip.

"I'll make breakfast," Remy announced with a chuckle. He looked at his sister. "Why don't you go get Rhodes and Larkin? They're probably hungry, too."

Katy pulled herself off the couch and pointed at Remy. "I want waffles."

He rolled his eyes. "Fine."

"And bacon!" she called, heading for the door. "And eggs!"

"Got it!" he yelled back, exasperated.

"With cheese!" Katy hollered as she slammed the front door shut.

"So demanding," Remy muttered, heading for the kitchen. He glanced back at me. "Help me?"

I followed him into the open space, sliding onto a barstool at the center island and watched him move with purpose to the fridge, pulling items out and setting them on the island.

"You realize I've never cooked before, right?" I asked, resting my chin in my palm as I watched him.

He looked up at me and paused with a frown. "Seriously?"

I nodded, stretching my arms out in front of me, loving the feel of the muscles in my shoulders working out the tension I was carrying from earlier. "No need. Everything we got was microwavable or it was, like, chips or something. I don't think our oven even worked."

His brows rose curiously, but there was an annoyed tick in his jaw I couldn't miss. He reached into one of the cabinets in the island and pulled out a set of pans.

"Come here."

I slipped off the stool and walked around to him.

"Time to learn to cook," he told me, handing me a skillet with a grin.

I smirked, testing the weight of the skillet in my hand before setting it on the counter. "I think I like the idea of you cooking for me. It could be the entire basis of our relationship."

His gaze heated. "And I'm happy to do it for you, but you need to learn to fend for yourself." He went to the fridge and handed me a carton of eggs.

"I'll have you know I can open any kind of bagged snacks in under thirty seconds. Chips, pretzels, even those goldfish things don't stand a chance against me," I joked as I set the eggs on the counter, a little embarrassed I had no clue what to do with the eggs. My limited experience was eating them the last couple of weeks.

Remy laughed loudly, setting my discarded skillet on the stove and flicking a knob. I heard the gas whoosh as the fire caught. Once he had the pan heating, he grabbed a large bowl from an overhead cabinet.

He set the bowl down and opened the carton, pulling out an egg. "Let's start with the basics."

He tapped the egg firmly on the side of the glass bowl. I watched, fascinated, as it cracked. He slipped his thumbs into the crack, dumping the contents into the bowl. He picked out another from the carton and handed it to me.

I took it in my hands, the delicate shell cold against my fingers. I glanced at him dubiously. "I just hit it on the side?"

"Tap it," he corrected, leaning a hip against the countertop and giving me room to work. "Go lightly. You can always tap a couple times to crack it. You don't want to smash it."

Gently, I tapped the egg on the side of the bowl the way he did, but nothing happened.

"Try a little harder," he encouraged.

I added a little force and the egg started to split. I grinned up at him. "I did it!"

He chuckled and nodded, moving his hands over mine. He gently moved my fingers to show me how to pry apart the shell and dump the egg into the bowl.

I smiled down into the bowl, the two yellow lumps bright and sunny against the white of the bowl. I set the shell aside and wiped off the slick residue with a towel.

Still laughing softly, Remy kissed the side of my head. "Can you crack the rest while I start on the waffles and bacon?"

I nodded quickly, already reaching for another egg.

By the time I finished cracking the dozen and a half eggs, Remy had the waffle batter made and bacon halfway done. My stomach kept growling as he added a new scent to the mix. The smell of food cooking was almost better than the actual food.

"Now what?" I asked, turning to watch as he poured a cup of batter into the waffle iron. He closed the lid and came around to me, a weirdly wired contraption in his hand, which he passed to me.

"Now you whisk."

"Whisk?" I repeated, eyeing the instrument carefully.

He took it from me and demonstrated, whipping it around the bowl a few times so the egg yolks started to break apart and mix together.

"Got it," I said, taking over. I concentrated on whisking as the timer on the waffles went off.

I heard Remy moving behind me as he pulled waffles off the griddle and ladled more on. A second later, the smell of warm waffles wafted under my nose.

I glanced down to see Remy holding a piece of the hot dough in front of me. Without thinking, I reached forward and grabbed it with my mouth, my lips grazing his fingers. Remy groaned and pulled his hand away.

"Keep that up and I'm going to burn something," he promised as he moved behind me, shifting my hair to the side to press his lips against the side of my neck.

I damn near dropped the whisk. My head tilted to the side instinctively to give him more access.

How the hell did I crave his touch so much since the bond happened twelve hours earlier?

His mouth lingered for a second, his teeth scraping lightly against the delicate skin of my neck. I pressed back against him with a delicious shiver.

"Shit," he swore, moving back away from me with a laugh.

I glanced over my shoulder at him. "What?"

"My sister is going to walk through the door any minute."

"Ah," I said with a knowing smile as I turned back to the task in front of me. "I've already gotten the 'no PDA with my brother' speech."

"Which is pretty freaking ironic considering she and Maren are the queens of PDA," he retorted, removing the bacon from the pan it was frying in.

"They're cute," I defended, putting down the whisk when I was satisfied the eggs were fully mixed together. I turned and watched Remy move easily around the spacious kitchen.

He jerked a chin towards the fridge. "Can you grab the juice and some cups? Cups are in the cabinet next to the fridge."

I opened the fridge, my eyes going a little wide at how packed full of food it was. Shaking my head in disbelief, I gathered apple juice and orange juice and set them on the counter before reaching for the cups.

Remy pulled another waffle off the griddle, laying it on the thick stack he already had on a plate.

"Okay, come back here." He grabbed the bowl of eggs off the counter and moved back to the stove.

I approached warily, eyeing the empty pan on the stove like it was a snake about the strike.

"Get over here," he said with a laugh, reaching out to snag me around the waist and drag me to him. He moved me so I was in front of the stove, and he was behind me again.

He guided me through dumping the eggs into the pan and told me to let them cook for a minute before starting to use the spatula to scramble them. I watched the eggs starting to cook curiously, but my body was hyper-aware that Remy was still right behind me.

After a few seconds, he slid his arms around my waist and dropped his chin onto my shoulder.

With a sigh, I leaned back into him, resting my free hand on top of his. The only sounds were our breathing and the eggs sizzling. My eyes slid closed as I relaxed against him, once again the warm feeling of safety covering me like a fuzzy blanket. I snuggled deeper against him, a smile ghosting across my face when I felt his lips on the shell of my ear.

"I could get used to this," he admitted quietly, his breath tickling my ear.

"Me, too," I answered honestly. Whatever *this* was, I was definitely on board.

I could practically feel my wolf smirking in satisfaction, as if she knew I would eventually come to that conclusion.

The peace of the moment was completely shattered by the front door flying open and bodies streaming inside.

Remy and I looked over as one to see Katy was back with not only Larkin and Rhodes, but also Maren, Dante,

Tate, and Ryder. The latter four were staring at Remy and me with wide eyes.

Ryder grinned, waving a finger between us. A teasing look started spreading across his face, his eyes bright. "What's this?"

Remy rolled his eyes and let me go reluctantly, taking the spatula to finish the eggs.

Katy groaned again, glaring at me. "Seriously, Skye? We talked about this. I can't see this shit every day."

"Then get out of *my* house," Remy shot back, but there was no heat in the statement.

"You two are together?" Tate asked, looking at me curiously. A small smile tugged at the corners of her mouth. She whirled and held out an expectant hand to Ryder.

"Pay up."

He groaned, shaking his head.

Tate grinned at me over her shoulder. "I bet him you two had a thing after we saw you dancing together last night."

My jaw dropped, and to my surprise Remy chuckled.

Dante clapped a hand on his shoulder. "Sorry, dude, you know I can't control these two."

"Control my ass," Ryder shot back. He gave Tate a firm look. "All I saw was two friends hugging when we came in."

Katy snorted, making her way to the kitchen. "More than that."

"Katy," Remy warned, turning to look at her.

Katy instantly looked guilty. "Wait—are you guys not telling people?"

"Telling people what?" Ryder pressed. He shoved Rhodes' shoulder. "What gives?"

Rhodes ignored him and moved to sit next to Larkin on the couch.

Remy frowned and looked at me. I shrugged. I didn't know the Brooks Ridge group all that well, but it was obvious that Remy, Katy, and even Larkin trusted them. That was enough for me to trust them.

"Last night ..." Remy rubbed the back of his neck with a laugh. His gaze flicked to me. "Skye and I—"

"Got engaged?" Ryder interrupted with a grin. His eyes gleamed as they settled on me. "Are you pregnant?"

Tate reached over and slapped him on the chest a second before Dante cuffed him on the back of the head.

"She's only seventeen," Katy told him in exasperation. Female shifters weren't fertile until they were at least twenty. Fertility usually happened between the ages of twenty and twenty-five. Unlike humans who had monthly cycles, shifters had two a year and apparently, they were hell on wheels.

Yet another thing to look forward to.

"Ow!" Ryder yelped, rubbing the back of his head where Dante had hit him.

"Continue, please," Tate said sweetly. "Ignore this ass."

"You love my ass," Ryder muttered.

Dante reached out to hit him again, but Ryder danced out of the way with a laugh.

Rolling his eyes, Dante looked at us, but his gaze zeroed in on me. "They're bonded."

My eyes went wide. "How did you know?"

"Holy shit," Ryder whispered, looking at us with wide eyes. "For real?"

Dante gave me a small shrug. "You guys ... smell kinda different."

That caught my attention. "Excuse me?"

Dante gave Remy a look. "Your scents. They've

changed. They're kind of … mixed. It's subtle, but it's there."

"Wait, wait," Tate said slowly. "You two have barely known each other for more than a couple weeks. And you're teenagers—that *never* happens."

"True bonds know no time or place," Maren said sagely, leaning against Katy.

"Can we back up to the part where I smell different?" I asked, still stuck on that for some reason. What did he mean I smelled different? Good? Bad?

"You still smell awesome," Rhodes assured me with a wink as he walked to the fridge. He pulled out a bottle of water and twisted off the cap.

"Like peaches and flowers or some shit," Ryder chimed in, catching the water Rhodes tossed him. "But also like Remy. Dante's right; it's not strong, but it's there." He flashed me a shameless smile. "He's marked you, girl."

I rolled my eyes. "Awesome."

Remy plated the eggs, ignoring the current conversation. "Are we all eating?"

"Hell yes," Ryder said, already reaching for the plate of waffles. "It's second breakfast."

"Second breakfast?" I echoed.

Tate groaned and shook her head at me. "Don't get him started."

"Hey!" Ryder pointed at her. "Don't mock the sanctity of second breakfast, Tatum. It's the second most important meal of the day."

☾

AFTER SECOND BREAKFAST, or regular breakfast for some of us, Remy and Dante excused themselves and went into the study to talk about pack business, but not before they ordered Rhodes and Ryder to handle dish duty.

I went out onto the deck with the girls and our drinks, the late morning sun warming us even though the air had a distinct chill.

Tate sank into an Adirondack chair and pulled her legs up. "I love mornings like this."

Katy hummed her approval as Maren sat down, half on the arm of the chair and halfway on Katy's lap. Katy looped an arm around her girlfriend's waist.

I watched Larkin curiously as she sat down slowly in another chair across from them. She had been extremely quiet during breakfast, so much so that Ryder even noticed she seemed off. Thankfully no one pushed the issue with her.

I wrapped my hands around a mug of hot chocolate I had brought with me and sat down on the end of a lounger.

"I'm only going to ask this once," Tate said softly, looking off the deck and towards the woods at the edge of the property. "Are you okay, Lark?"

Larkin sighed. "Yeah."

"Do you want to talk about it?" Maren coaxed, her large brown eyes soft and concerned. She cocked her head, a curtain of shiny black hair falling down around her shoulders.

"No," Larkin whispered, pulling her knees to her chest.

"All right," Tate replied, willing to let Larkin have her privacy. "But we're here if you need anything at all."

"Why are you guys so close?" I asked curiously. "It doesn't seem like a lot of the packs here mix that well."

Maren scoffed and took a drink of her coffee. "They don't. There's definite pack divides."

"But not between Blackwater and Brooks Ridge."

Tate shook her head. "No, our packs have been allies for decades, and it carried over into GPA. Honestly, the original purpose of the school was to unite the packs. In reality, it's exacerbated a big rift between two sides."

"Norwood and Blackwater have always had an antagonistic relationship at best," Katy added. "What happened with my parents just made it more public."

"And uglier," Larkin chimed in.

Katy nodded. "But even still, there's basically two groups in GPA."

"Blackwater and Norwood," I concluded.

Tate nodded. "Some packs are more loyal to one than the other. For example, the way we are with you guys? That's how the Calgary pack is with Norwood."

"Why the divide, though?" I asked. "I mean, I get that what happened with your parents years ago played a part, but you said they were divided before that?"

"It happened decades ago," Maren told me. "It goes back to when the packs started to realize that fertility rates were declining steadily, and females were becoming more scarce."

I wanted to roll my eyes, but the reality was everything in the shifter world seemed dominated by the fact that fertility was an issue and packs were starting to fade into the sunset as birth rates dropped. Males vastly outnumbered females, and it seemed like it wasn't only the southern part of the country that was feeling the strain.

Katy grimaced, her nose wrinkling in disgust. "Half of the packs from GPA, and even several northern packs not attending GPA, believe females should only be mated to upper pack members. Keep the bloodlines strong or some male bullshit. But ultimately the pack Alpha has final say on who mates with who. Some think all mates should be arranged by the Alpha."

"But not Blackwater?"

Tate shook her head. "Or Brooks Ridge, or quite a few other packs. They believe a female should choose her mate."

"Or mates," Maren said, winking at Tate, who grinned back.

"It pretty much boils down to the men telling the women folk how life is going to be," Katy drawled in an exaggerated accent.

"Yeah," I said slowly. "That's how it was in my old pack, too. But worse. Women have no rights in a lot of the southern packs. They're commodities to be traded. Alphas pretty much order all marriages and matings. If a female can't bear a child, she's completely expendable."

Larkin shook her head sadly. "I can't imagine growing up like that. I mean, I know I'm on the bottom, but our Alpha is a good man. He wouldn't ever order us to do something like marry someone we didn't want to be with."

"Elias mentioned something about believing the fertility issue was a direct relation to the Alpha female of the pack," I said, trying to remember what he had told me. "Something like the happier the female, the better the pack moral, which might increase the birth rate?"

"And the likelihood of true mate bonds happening," Tate added. "If you look at the statistics, he's right. When the Alpha female, or Alpha's mate, is the most secure in her role and her mating, there's a trickle-down effect into the pack. Like throwing a rock in a pond. The ripples spread."

"So, all we have to do is convince a group of men that women should be in charge of their own happiness," Katy said with a bitter laugh. "Seems easy enough."

Tate made a face. "The Summit will definitely be interesting this year. A lot of issues are being discussed, but the fertility and mating issues are the top agendas, according to Dante. It sounds like several different factions have ideas for how to control it."

My stomach bottomed out. Control and the Summit. Those two things were all I needed to remind me of what I had left behind. Linden and Cassian would absolutely be at the Summit, likely pressuring packs to convert to their way of thinking.

As my anxiety ratcheted up, my wolf whined inside of me, nudging me to find something to calm us both.

"I'll be back," I murmured, setting my cup on the table beside me and heading for the door before I could over-think what I needed.

I stepped into the kitchen, the sounds of a video game coming from the main room. Rhodes and Ryder were hurling insults at each other, completely absorbed in what-ever was happening on the screen.

I glanced over at the study; the door was partially open now. I walked towards it, feeling better every step of the way as I closed the distance to what I needed.

I never imagined I would be a girl who would need a guy, but something about Remy calmed me and my wolf. Right now, I needed that calm the way a junkie craved a fix.

Remy was visible through the partially open door, hand braced against the desk as he leaned over a paper. A dark expression marred the strong lines of his face, his jaw tight with strain.

"That makes twelve," he said darkly, presumably to Dante. "Twelve shifters that have gone missing this month alone. What the hell is going on?"

**26**

———

*MORE MISSING SHIFTERS?*

Remy looked up as if he heard my silent question, the frown lines in his face smoothing as he met my gaze. The tension seeped from his posture, his shoulders relaxing.

Apparently, I calmed him the same way he calmed me. That knowledge made me smile inwardly.

I took a hesitant step forward, not sure if I should interrupt or not. The pit of anxiety from before was still eating at me. Something in my expression must have given me away, because Remy was suddenly striding forward, his frown back in place.

"What's wrong?" he asked, stopping in front of me, a hand coming up to cradle my jaw. His eyes swept down my body like he was trying to find a physical reason for my stress.

"It's nothing," I mumbled, embarrassed now. He had a lot of shit on his plate and dealing with my panic over stupid thoughts of my old pack was not how he needed to spend his time. "I didn't mean to interrupt."

"You're not," he answered, still concerned. "What's going on?"

"Really," I assured him, forcing my hands to stay by my sides and not reach for him, "I'm good. I just had a stupid thought."

A soft smile curved his lips. "Somehow I don't think any of your thoughts could be classified as stupid."

I arched a brow. "You'd be surprised."

Dante came out of the office, giving me a nod. "Is Tate still outside?"

"Yeah, with the girls," I confirmed, watching as he headed for the back door. I looked back to see Remy still studying me, his expression unreadable.

"What?" I finally asked with a laugh, not sure why he suddenly found me so fascinating.

"Have dinner with me tonight," he requested quietly, his dark eyes practically glowing.

I glanced around. "Don't we all have dinner together?" I reminded him. Ever since I had arrived, I sat with the people in this cabin at every meal.

He rolled his eyes. "No, I mean, we'll go into town and grab dinner. Just us."

"Like a date?" I almost laughed at the breathy way my words came out, but the butterflies currently flight in my stomach had my full attention.

"Yeah, a date," he said with a warm chuckle. He reached up, smoothing my hair away from my face, his eyes tracking the movements of his fingers before coming to rest on my eyes. I let out a breath, feeling my heart rate settle into a steady thrum as the anxious knot in my gut loosened.

Remy was rapidly becoming my harbor in any storm.

"I've never actually been on a date," I admitted, biting my lower lip. Of course, I had never been on a date, and

Remy knew that.. Most girls my age had been on dozens of dates, the male-to-female ratio ensuring there was always a waiting line of potential guys.

But I wasn't most girls.

His brows rose in surprise, but he masked it quickly. "I promise it will be painless."

"Painless?" I echoed, starting to smile.

He shrugged and blew out a breath. "Mostly painless."

"Well if you promise it will only be mostly painless, I guess I'm in."

Shaking his head with a grin, Remy stepped back. "So, it's a date then."

"What's a date?" Katy asked, breezing into the kitchen. She headed for the coffee pot, refilling her mug. She finished pouring and stared at us. "Wait—a date as in you two? You're going on a date?"

"Yes," Remy said with a long-suffering sigh, turning his attention to her.

Katy set the mug down with a loud clack on the counter. "When?" she demanded.

Remy narrowed his eyes. "Maybe now if it gets me away from you and your questions."

Katy glared back at her brother. "No way. She can't go on a date looking like that." She motioned to me.

My eyes went wide. "What's wrong with how I look?" I asked. My hair was down and I guess could be brushed, but I was wearing jeans and a long-sleeved shirt and my sneakers. It wasn't the dress from last night, but was a formal dress a requirement for dating?

"The fact that you don't see what's wrong with your outfit is exactly why you need me," Katy deadpanned, planting a hand on her hip.

"Be nice, Katherine," Remy warned. His tone was light but there was something in his eyes that clearly made the other girl pause. He would allow her to tease me as a friend but making me uncomfortable was a definite no-go.

With a groan, Katy looked at me. "I'm sorry. But am I right in assuming this is your first date, Skye?"

I nodded slowly.

"First dates are a big deal," Katy pushed. "I'm talking hair, nails, makeup—"

"Skye doesn't need that," Remy cut in firmly, shaking his head.

"No girl *needs* it, Remington" Katy whined petulantly. "But it makes us feel pretty and dressing up makes it more special. Less like an everyday thing." She looked pointedly at him. "I *am* assuming you want this date to be special, right? Otherwise we can make pizzas and all hang out here like usual."

Remy shook his head and looked at me, not wanting to admit Katy had a point. "It's completely up to you."

A part of me wanted what Katy was saying—I wanted to get dressed up and let her do my hair, much like I had the night of the dance. Getting ready had been fun.

But I also liked that there was zero pressure with Remy to be anything but me.

What clinched it was Katy's begging puppy eyes. That, and I wanted a night where I felt special and ... pretty. Especially with Remy's full attention on me.

I wanted him to look at me the way he had last night when he asked me to dance, but I wanted that feeling for an entire night.

I rolled my eyes to the ceiling. "Fine," I agreed.

Katy clapped her hands together and looked at Remy. "When is this date commencing?"

"We said dinner, so I guess we'll leave at five?"

Katy's eyes went huge and her jaw dropped. "Five?"

she spluttered. "It's almost noon. That only gives us five hours, Rem."

"What could you possibly need more than five hours to do?" he asked, throwing his hands up as Ryder and Rhodes entered the room.

"Guy Survival Rule Number One, *amigo*," Ryder said as he stopped and took us all in before pointing at Remy, "never, *ever* ask girls why they take so long to get ready."

I raised a slow hand. "Can I ask why it's going to take five hours?"

"No," Katy said quickly. She arched a brow at me. "Go back to the dorms and shower."

My nose wrinkled. "But I already—"

She held up a hand. "Don't argue with my process. Go and shower. I'll get the girls and meet you back in your room." She glanced at the clock on the microwave. She pinched the bridge of her nose. "Shit, less than five hours now. *Hurry*."

"But—"

With a loud grumble, Katy grabbed my wrist and physically pulled me to the door. I managed to give Remy a confused smile. His shoulders were shaking with silent laughter as I stumbled out the door after my friend.

KATY'S worst was assembling an army of people to get me ready that she must have called in when I was taking my second shower of the day.

I had come back from my shower, hair wrapped up in a towel, to find Katy was already waiting with Larkin, Maren, and Tate. They all converged on me as soon as I closed the door.

I was pushed into a chair, my hair pulled from the

towel. I wasn't sure whose hands were where—someone was brushing my hair, someone else was examining my fingernails.

"Where are you going?" Tate asked, the door to my closet open. She was flipping through the hangers.

"Remy said into town?" I winced as the brush caught on a tangle.

Katy clucked her tongue. "Skye, you need a haircut, and I really need to introduce your dead ends to a hair mask."

I arched a brow, looking up at her. "A hair mask?"

Her fingers prodded my cheeks. "And a face mask. Your skin is seriously dry."

I reached up, touching my face. "It doesn't feel dry."

"Trust me," Katy said with certainty. She glanced at Larkin. "Do you still have that—"

Larkin was already pulling a jar of cream from a drawer in her dresser. She passed it to Katy and looked at me, her nose wrinkled. "It actually does make your skin softer."

"Okay, if you're going into town, that means the diner," Tate murmured to herself. She glanced over. "And this is your first date?"

"Yeah."

"First date ever," Katy clarified, slapping cold goop on my face that smelled slightly floral.

"Seriously?" Maren asked, incredulous as she worked some product into the ends of my hair. "How have you never been on a date? You're hot, girl."

"That's what I said!" Katy chirped, rubbing the stuff across my nose and almost making me sneeze.

I hesitated, not sure how to answer. Katy and Larkin knew the details, but I wasn't ready to share with everyone just yet.

"She was kind of sheltered," Larkin said calmly, meeting my gaze. "Her mom kept her close."

"Probably for the best," Tate said, pulling out a deep blue sweater dress. She eyed it critically for a second before putting it back. "Dating can be a clusterfuck."

"Says the girl with *two* boyfriends," Maren added, parting my hair with a comb.

Tate rolled her eyes. "Which means I'm a total expert since I have double the experience."

"How does that work?" I asked, genuinely curious. I knew it wasn't uncommon for males to share a single female but seeing the dynamic up close between the three of them made me inquisitive.

With a sigh, Tate turned and leaned against the wall. "It just kind of ... happened."

Katy snorted, handing the closed jar back to Larkin. "Pimples just happen. Falling into bed with two guys takes a bit more planning and finesse, I would imagine."

Licking her lips, Tate's cheeks warmed. "You'd be surprised. There was some falling and definitely a bed involved."

I choked on my laugh as everyone cracked up.

Waving a hand, Tate turned back to the closet. "Ryder, Dante and I have known each other since we were little. We've always been inseparable. Last year we just sort of transitioned into being more."

"So, it's serious?" I asked.

She gave a firm nod. "It's the three of us for the long haul."

"I do have a question," Katy said slowly, a wicked gleam in her eyes. "I've seriously been dying to ask this."

Tate sighed and waited with raised brows.

"Are Dante and Ryder ... you know? Together, too?"

Katy lowered her voice. "Because something about the way they look at each other sometimes, I could swear—"

Larkin gasped. "Katy! That's none of your business."

"I know it isn't, but I still want to know," the redhead answered with a shrug.

Tate blew out a long breath, looking up at the ceiling. "Dante and Ryder are best friends. More than best friends. All I'm saying is that the three of us share everything with each other."

"*Everything?*" Katy pressed with big eyes.

"Everything," Tate said finally. She pulled a black skirt with silver zippers out of the closet. "This is cute."

"It would show off her legs," Larkin agreed, going to the closet as well. She reached in and pulled out an off-the-shoulder cream sweater. "This would be pretty with it."

"I'm thinking a French braid," Maren said behind me, pulling my hair back from my face.

"Love it," Katy agreed. "Maybe a subtle smokey eye? Something berry-toned to bring out the green in her eyes."

"It's like you're talking a different language," I grumbled, trying not to wince as Maren's fingers started twisting my hair.

"That's how I felt, too," Larkin admitted with a shrug and a smile. She laid the clothes she and Tate had selected on her bed. "Katy will have you speaking the language in no time."

Whatever language it was, by the time they were done —nearly five hours later—I was a believer.

The cream sweater slipped off one shoulder, showing skin that was still kissed by the New Mexico sun I grew up in. My green eyes looked almost otherworldly, ringed with dark kohl and several generous layers of mascara. The black skirt definitely did show off my legs, and coupled with a pair of black ankle boots with a heel, and my legs looked impossibly long.

"Here," Katy said suddenly, reaching behind her neck and unclasping her necklace. She came up behind me in the mirror that hung on the back of our door. Her arms looped around me as she draped the silver chain across my neck before locking the clasp.

My fingers lifted gently, touching the silver crescent moon with a connected diamond chip that hung from the simple chain. "It's beautiful." The diamond chip caught the light, glinting like a star behind the moon.

Katy rested her chin on my bare shoulder, smiling at me in the mirror. "You'll have one of your own soon."

"Remy has this tattooed on his back," I said absently, remembering the flash of the image I saw the night before.

"It's a family thing," she explained. "All the women in my family have this necklace, most of the guys have it tattooed. Kind of a Holt family tradition. It's the symbol of the Blackwater pack." She smiled softly at me, her dimples flashing. "Since you and Remy are bonded ... Odds are you'll be part of that family one day."

I waited for the flash of panic to come at her words, but it never manifested. Instead, there was only a deep settling peace. A sense of rightness that was becoming more and more frequent the longer I stayed here.

I was part of a pack. Part of a family.

Tears, hot and sharp, pricked the backs on my eyes and I blinked quickly. "Thanks, Katy," I said thickly.

Her eyes flared wide. "Don't you dare cry and mess up all our hard work."

I barked out a laugh, shaking my head. I turned and threw my arms around her, hugging her tightly. "Thank you."

Pulling back, I looked at the three girls on Larkin's bed, watching us with smiles.

"Thank you, all of you," I whispered, my heart almost full to bursting because of these girls. My friends.

Tate grinned. "Make sure he treats you right," she said, wagging a finger. "He better get you home on time."

"Maybe they need a chaperone," Maren said. Her tone was serious, but the glimmer in her eyes gave away the tease.

Larkin agreed with a serious nod. "We can sit at the table next to you and make sure he behaves himself."

A slow shiver worked down my spine and I drew in a long, shaky breath.

"He'll behave himself," Katy said quickly, seeing me shiver and mistaking my emotions for fear. Her expression turned fierce. "You know Remy would never hurt you, right? I mean, I've never seen him like this with a girl, but even before you, he would never——"

"I know," I cut her off gently. I bit my lower lip to hide a smile. "Maybe I'm hoping he *won't* behave himself?"

Katy's jaw dropped as the girls on the bed cracked up, their cackling giggles filling the room.

I shrugged at her with a smirk.

I did trust Remy. Implicitly. And not just because of the true mate bond that seemed to be stronger with every minute I spent around him. I trusted the guy who was horrified for what I let slip the first time we talked in his study. The guy who sat next to me in class and teased me. The guy who was the heart and soul of the pack here at GPA.

I had started crushing on Remy when I first met him, but the bond seemed to bring a whole new sort of aware-ness to my feelings.

Even now, as I glanced at the clock and realized he

would be here any minute, my wolf started pacing. She was anxious to be with him again, not liking the distance stretching between us.

My phone chimed from where I had left it on the desk and all our eyes went to it.

With a nervous laugh, I crossed the room and picked it up, my heart pounding so loud everyone in the room had to hear it.

I turned it on to read the message.

**REMY**: *Ready?*

Hell, yes. I was definitely ready.

The truck swerved on the road for the fifth time in as many miles. Remy's hands tightened on the steering wheel and he tried to keep his attention on the road.

"Should I be worried you're going get us killed?" I teased, looking over at him.

He smiled ruefully, shaking his head. "Sorry."

I tried not to smirk as his gaze drifted to me again, his gaze lingering on the exposed skin of my thighs for a second.

The truck jerked again, and I laughed, tipping my head back.

With a low growl, his fingers flexed around the wheel, his knuckles turning white against the black leather. "You're not making this easy."

"Sorry?" I parroted back his apology.

I wasn't sorry at all.

It had been thrilling to have his eyes on me since I met him in front of the girls' dorm, knowing full well that all four of my friends were crowded around a window watching us.

He held my hand as we walked to the SUV in the parking lot, and I barely even noticed the stares we got as we walked across campus. I was too busy focusing on the way his rough hand felt curved around mine, the strength of his fingers as they flexed gently, reassuringly, around my hand.

I walked closely beside him, my shoulder pressed against his arm, stealing some of the heat his body radiated in the late fall night. Inhaling deeply, I was completely surrounded by his scent. I ridiculously missed him for the three seconds it took for him to close my car door and walk around to the driver's side.

Less than twenty-four hours into this bond, and I was falling hard and fast.

I smiled ruefully to myself, thinking of all the books I read where I complained about the couple falling into an all-consuming love super fast. *Insta-love*, I found the internet mockingly called it. Because how was it logical or rational to fall completely in love with someone in the span of a day or a week?

But there were no bonded mates in those stories. No magical shifter fate intervening to determine the course of the couple's lives.

And definitely no Remy Holt in those books.

"What's so funny?" Remy asked curiously, turning onto the road that took us into town.

I looked over at him, letting my head relax against the leather headrest. "I was thinking about how if this was a book, we would get horrible reviews."

His gaze swung to me for a second, surprise in his eyes, before going back to the road. "Oh, really?"

Giggling, I crossed my legs. "We barely know each other. The bond happened less than a day ago. And yet ..."

"And yet?" he prompted, a smile playing on his full lips.

I blushed. "It just seems like this is happening really fast."

"This?" he teased, pushing for me to admit to more. "I'm not sure I know what you're talking about. Care to explain?"

I swung out to slap his shoulder, but he caught my hand in one of his. He brought it to his lips and kissed the back of my hand.

Yeah, I was definitely swooning a little bit at that point.

"We can slow down, you know," he said after a second, our hands still connected but resting on the console between us. "There's no pressure at all. This is whatever we want it to be."

"It's not that," I admitted honestly. "It's more like ... I guess I feel like I should want things to go slower. For us to take it easy. But the truth is, it all feels right. I feel like I've known you forever. Does that make sense?"

"Yeah," he replied softly, turning down the main street of town. "I know exactly what you mean. I know, rationally, that a good part of it is because of the bond, but honestly I liked you before that happened."

"You did?" The note of hope in my voice caught me by surprise.

"Why do you think I asked you to dance?"

"Because you're a nice guy?" I said weakly, my brain short-circuiting.

He gave me a weird look. "I asked you because I *liked* you."

"Seriously?"

He smiled as he pulled into a parking spot in front of the diner, putting the car in park and turning to look at me fully. "Yes, Skye. Why is that so hard to believe?"

"Because you're you," I spluttered stupidly. "And I'm me."

His eyes narrowed. "What the hell does that mean?"

I exhaled a long breath, fighting the urge to lower my eyes from his pressing gaze. "Remy, my whole life I was raised to believe that I was worthless. That there was only ... one thing I was good for." I swallowed hard, noting the way his hand tightened around mine and his jaw clenched. "It's going to take more than two weeks being here to make me feel like I can breathe. My heart is telling me all of this is real. You and I are real. My head is having a hard time catching up."

His eyes lowered for a second, dark lashes fanning across his tan cheeks before lifting and piercing me with a serious gaze. "This is real, Skye. I'm not going anywhere. I know this is fast, and I know on paper it looks completely crazy."

I chuckled softly, nodding.

"But it doesn't change the way I feel when I'm with you," he went on. "I've been raised to be a leader. To be strong and think of the pack first and above all else. When I'm with you ... It's like everything is clearer. You ground me, and not just because of the bond. I liked being with you before last night happened. You make me laugh. Watching you experience things for the first time is absolutely amazing."

"Amazingly pathetic," I deadpanned, wincing as I remembered walking into the grocery store and all of my other firsts I'd had since leaving my old pack.

"Not at all," he corrected, shaking his head. "You see things that I take for granted. I could watch you looking at the mountains every day and never get tired of it. You get this intense look, like you're memorizing the image in front of you."

"They're incredible," I admitted. "The power of the

mountains, the freshness of the air here." I took a deep breath, letting my lungs fill and stretch.

"This is exactly what I mean," he said after a second of silence. "The best part is you don't even know you're doing it. It's completely innocent and pure, Skye."

Innocent and pure.

Two words I never thought would describe me.

We stayed silent for a few minutes as the sun finished setting, darkness settling around us. It was nice not to feel the need to fill the silence. With Remy, I could just be.

I cleared my throat after a minute. "So, I don't think I'm all that impressed."

Blinking, Remy started to laugh. "I'm sorry?"

"I mean, I always thought there was more to dating than sitting in a car quietly," I said seriously, biting my lower lip to keep from smiling.

"Oh, you want more, huh?"

My grin turned wolfish. "I do believe you promised there would be a lot of *more* in the future."

His eyes went molten as his gaze heated. "More is absolutely on the agenda. But that happens after we eat."

"No more," I begged, pushing my plate away with a groan.

Remy reached for my plate, grabbing my fries. He had been picking at them for the last few minutes since finishing his own burger and fries.

I eyed the vanilla milkshake with sad eyes. "I can't finish it."

Remy laughed, popping another fry into his mouth. "Are you going to make it?"

I considered laying on the vinyl bench seat, letting my

forehead rest against the sticky material until all the food in my stomach dispersed to wherever the hell my metabolism moved it to.

"I need a nap," I griped. "I'm so full. I should know better."

He snorted and took a drink of his cookies and cream milkshake. "I didn't peg you for a 'watch what you eat' kind of girl."

"What the hell does that mean?" I said up straighter in mock outrage.

He grinned at me. "You're gorgeous."

Heat flooded my cheeks.

"But I've never seen you shy away from food at school," he went on.

I toyed with the straw in my milkshake. Over the course of the meal, Remy had shared memories of his childhood. Stories of his parents and growing up with Katy, and his younger siblings. I had never met his younger brothers, but they sounded hysterical the way he described the shenanigans the twins got into.

He told me about Blackwater, and how he and Rhodes had become friends when they were little kids. He told me about meeting Dante at his first Summit pack meeting.

The conversation had been almost completely one-sided, but he didn't seem to mind or notice. He answered all of my questions honestly and openly, which made me wish I could be the same with him.

I had added in stories about my mom and I when I could, but I kept it vague. I wanted to share more, but there was still this feeling that as soon as he knew the real me, the damaged me, Remy would run for the mountains.

And I couldn't blame him.

I took a deep breath. "In my old pack, omegas were kept in a separate house inside the compound. You know we didn't get out much, and definitely not to the grocery store."

My stomach churned as I pictured the broken down white house at the end of the dirt lane.

Remy cocked his head, listening calmly.

"We ... We didn't get much food," I admitted, looking at the tabletop and tracing a crack in the quartz. "Mostly it was whatever the pack didn't want or wouldn't use. Usually old food, pre-packaged stuff. Anyway, when my mom and I left, she took me to eat at this truck stop and I ate so much. I had never had food that was hot and made to eat right away. I ate so much that I threw it all up that night." I shrugged, trying to be nonchalant. "So now I try not to get completely full."

"How many omegas were there in the house with you?" he asked, leaning back and resting his arm along the edge of the bench seat.

"Other than my mom and me? Two. Another female and a male." Maisie and Shane. God, I still had no idea what happened to them. If what I had done caused any blowback that they paid the price for.

Mom hadn't involved them in our escape to protect them, but I knew my uncle was vindictive enough to punish them anyway.

Remy's chest moved up and down as he breathed, but that was the only movements he made as he watched me closely. "Did they leave with you?"

I swallowed hard around the lump in the throat. "No," I whispered. "They're still there, as far as I know."

He frowned, choosing his words carefully. "Are they okay there?"

"I have no idea," I replied, sadness and regret lacing my tone. "We left and ... it's safer if we don't make contact with them."

"Safer?" His brows slammed together, his expression fierce.

"We didn't leave under the best of circumstances," I said, my voice pitched low. I sighed deeply. "We—"

"Can I get you anything else?"

The sudden appearance of our waitress made me jump.

Remy gave her a curt nod. "We're good. Just the check, thanks."

She smiled at us both and headed back for the bar, her dark ponytail swishing across her back as she walked away.

I looked around, remembering we were currently in a diner packed with normals. It seemed like this was the place to be on a Saturday night in the town of Granite Peak. Almost every table was full.

Probably not the best venue to pour my heart out.

The waitress came back. She handed the check to Remy with a big smile, barely noticing me. She looked a few years older than us, and she had been blatantly staring at Remy almost every time she came over.

Jealousy had flared in me at first, my wolf ready to rip her throat out when her hand touched Remy's when she passed him a menu. But the more she came over, the more Remy seemed annoyed by her.

When she leaned over to show him the specials, he made a face and slid away from her. The move wasn't subtle at all, and I actually started laughing as the waitress straightened up and hurried away.

She had hid in the kitchen for a solid ten minutes before coming back to take our order, and Remy hadn't ordered the special.

"Thanks," he said, barely glanced at her as he pulled out his wallet.

Uncertainty tugged at me as I tried to see the check. I

reached for my purse, not entirely sure of dating etiquette. I still had most of the cash that Zoe had somehow slipped into my purse before I left. I still planned on returning it when I went back to Blackwater for Thanksgiving, but I could use some of it and figure out a way to repay her later.

Maybe pick up some shifts at the café.

Remy dropped several bills on top of the check and looked at me. "Ready to go?"

I frowned. "How much——"

Rolling his eyes, he slid off the bench and got to his feet. He reached over and pulled me up. "I got it."

"Um, thanks?" I offered hesitantly.

A laugh rumbled in his chest. He rested his forehead to mine for a second. "You really are something else."

I let him lead me out of the diner and back to the SUV. Once again, he opened my door and settled me in the seat before going around the front and getting behind the wheel. He slid the key into the ignition and the vehicle roared to life, the heater blowing lukewarm air across us.

He paused, his hand on the gear stick. "Can we go somewhere and talk?" He rubbed his thumb absently against the steering wheel, his eyes dark as he looked at me. "I'm not ready for this date to be over yet."

I nodded slowly, smiling to myself as he put the SUV in gear and pulled out of the parking spot.

**28**

———

The world was completely silent when Remy turned off the engine. The headlights cut off, plunging us into inky darkness. The dirt road we had been driving down dead ended at a cliff. Remy parked us near the edge, and I watched the sky, absolutely transfixed by the wonder in front of me.

The sky was a riot of lime greens and milky whites. The light dipped and swayed across the sky, touching stars before slipping away. Tinges of pink and purple hugged the outer edges, the colors moving in a seamless, sensual dance through the galaxy.

"Oh, my God," I breathed. I leaned forward in my seat, jaw open as I watched the northern lights play out in front of us.

"Pretty amazing, right?" Remy asked, his tone almost reverent. "You can see them sometimes in Blackwater, but nothing like here. Dante says they're even better in Alaska, though."

"How can this possibly get better?" I murmured, awe

struck by the beauty in front of me. The colors twisted and writhed to the sounds of a song I couldn't hear.

"This is one of my favorite spots," he admitted after a beat of silence. "I come out here when I need to think or process something."

I leaned back in my seat to look at him, the view of Remy's face in the shadows of moonlight was just as breathtaking as the riot of colors dancing in the sky. His jaw was set in a hard line, a weariness around his eyes that I had noticed earlier when he was talking to Dante.

"The missing wolves?" I prompted, wanting to ease his burden.

He exhaled through his nose, rubbing his eyes with the heel of his hand. "Yeah. It started out as lone wolves and drifters going missing a couple weeks ago. Now pack members are starting to turn up missing. All female."

"You think someone is taking them?" I asked quietly, horrified at the idea. "But why?"

He let out a frustrated growl. "Who the hell knows? Especially now. Everyone knows that women are needed now more than ever."

"The declining birth rate," I muttered, knowing all too well the general need of women didn't actually extend far beyond their uterus and reproductive organs.

"It's making the packs testy," he said bitterly. "Some packs are talking about setting up stronger border patrols and not allowing anyone to pass through."

"This is happening all over?" I asked, frowning. Based on what mom had told me and I overheard earlier from Remy, I had assumed it was just Blackwater.

He nodded. "A lot of northern packs are noticing it, especially the more urban populated ones. Twelve missing shifters across the northern packs might not seem like much, but when they're all females ..."

"And there's no clue what happened to them?"

He shook his head again before leaning back and dropping it against the headrest. His Adam's apple worked as he swallowed, the tendons and lines of his throat moving in tandem. "It just doesn't make sense. But we need to figure out what the hell is going on, fast."

I reached out across the cab of the truck, finding his hand with mine. "You will."

He returned a weak smile. "I hope so. I might have to go back home for a little while to help my dad and the pack sort stuff out."

My stomach clenched uncomfortably at the idea of him being miles and miles away. I cleared my throat. "Who would watch out for us at GPA if you're gone?"

"Rhodes," he answered easily. "He's my beta, and despite the fact that he acts like an idiot sometimes, he's the most loyal guy I know. He might act stupid, but he's one of the smartest people I've ever met. He would keep everyone safe."

"How long would you be gone for?"

His eyes cut to me, his expression unreadable. "A week. Maybe more."

Inside my chest, my wolf was pitching a fit. She wasn't happy with this news any more than I was.

"You could come with me," he suggested softly.

I jerked my gaze to his, expecting to see he was teasing, but Remy was completely serious.

He glanced down at where I still held his hand. "I mean, you could come with me if you want to."

I closed my eyes on a sigh, shaking my head slowly with a wry chuckle. "Am I really going to be *that* girl?"

"That girl?" he echoed, confusion lacing his voice.

I looked at him with a grimace. "Yeah. The girl who's clingy and can't let her boyfriend out of her sight—"

"Boyfriend?" he cut in. A small smirk started to pull at the corner of his mouth. His dark eyes warmed considerably, the air in the cab of the SUV heating.

I opened my mouth, moving my lips as no sound came out. Why had I used that word? It just sort of came out, but it felt right leaving my lips.

I cleared my throat. "I didn't mean——"

Remy reached across the darkness and pressed his finger to my lips. "It's fine. I liked it when you said that."

I blushed under his scrutiny, squirming on the seat. This moment felt too intense, too intimate. I was entirely too aware of the way my breathing had become ragged and the way I could feel the pulse in the fingertip pressed against my lips.

His fingertip moved from my lips, tracing down the line of my throat. "I don't like the idea of being away from you, either."

"Really?" I breathed, my voice barely a whisper.

He tucked a loose piece of hair behind my ear. "Really. I know it's only been a day, barely, but the idea of you being so far away is like hell. With all this shit going on, you're the only thing that makes sense right now."

I leaned my palm against his hand, coming up to cover his wrist with my hand. I couldn't even circle my fingers around his arm. Every part of him radiated power, even his wrists, thick with muscles and tendons that I felt flexing under my touch.

"Will it always be like this?" I asked softly, still trying to wrap my head around the multitude of emotions coursing through my body. "This constant need to always be near each other?"

He smiled wryly. "According to my parents, yes."

My eyes rounded. "You told your parents about this? About us?"

He nodded slowly, trying to gauge if that upset me or not. "I had a feeling they might be able to give me some insight into this."

"Oh," I replied, kind of dumbstruck.

"You didn't tell your mom?" He posed the question casually, but there was a note of something else there. Uncertainty, maybe?

"I didn't," I answered. I looked away, back to the riot of colors in the sky. "I don't even know what to say. I mean, I barely understand it. And I know my mom—she'll worry."

Remy hesitated. "Because of me?"

My gaze snapped to him. "No!" I said vehemently. "Not because of you at all. Because of me. Because she risked everything to save me a couple weeks ago. In the span of a month, my life has completely changed. I know she's worried about me. We've never been apart for more than a few hours until I came to Granite Peak. She always tried her best to protect me, and I don't want her to worry."

I hadn't realized I started crying until Remy was wiping a stray tear away with the pad of his thumb.

"You said omegas were kept separate from other pack members," he started slowly. "You had your own house?"

I snorted and pulled away from him. "A house. Yeah, if you could call it that. It was this old building that was basically falling down."

"You lived there your whole life?" he frowned, turning in his seat to full face me. "Why didn't the pack help take care of it?"

"Because the omega house and shifters in it were only worth one thing to the pack," I muttered bitterly.

Remy waited, staying still and quiet as he let me process my emotions. He wouldn't push me to reveal more than I was ready to, but I was getting tired of keeping the Long Mesa pack's dirty secrets.

"The upper pack members would come to the house," I said, my voice low and wooden. I stared straight ahead. I might be able to share part of my life with Remy, but I couldn't do it while I looked at him.

I couldn't see the inevitable looks of pity and disgust.

"I didn't understand what was going on for the longest time. My mom did a good job of shielding me from everything. I didn't understand the noises I heard behind closed doors when I was playing in the hallway. Or the smells when the doors opened. I didn't ... I didn't understand why the omegas were always so afraid when there was a knock on the front door. I didn't understand why the sheets always had blood on them."

I heard Remy suck in a sharp breath.

"I came home from school early one day," I continued, my mind transporting me back to that day when I learned the truth. "I was ten, I think. The heat was so bad, and the air conditioner was broken again, so they let us out at lunch time."

I dropped my head back onto the headrest, letting my eyes slide closed as I relived one of the worst moments of my life.

"I could hear these ... noises as soon as I got to the second floor. The house wasn't that big, only three bedrooms on the top floor. My mom and I shared the room at the back of the house. I had left my book in there and wanted to get it. I figured I could finish my book before I worked on homework."

Hot tears slipped out from under my lids, rolling slowly down my cheeks. My skin felt like ice, the heat from my tears scalding streams down the slope of my face.

I drew in a shaky breath and clenched my hands into fists on my lap. "I didn't knock, I just opened the door. It took a minute. I didn't understand exactly what was going on. My mom was on the bed, on her back. She was crying. And this ... man was on top of her. They were both naked. I still didn't get what was happening until my mom yelled or something. Whatever he was doing was hurting her. I just ... reacted. I threw my backpack at him."

Swallowing, I remembered the absolute fear in my body at that moment. Fear, and rage. "He turned and saw me in the doorway. My mom yelled at me to leave, but he backhanded her and told her to shut up. He got off the bed and grabbed me by the arm. It was so ... *surreal*. I knew my arm hurt, but all I could notice was that this guy was naked and how gross it was."

Squeezing my eyes shut tighter, I tried to control the sudden shaking of my body. "He threw me into the hallway. Literally picked me up by my arm and threw me across the hall. Then he slammed the door and locked it. I could hear my mom crying, sometimes screaming. I kept banging on the door for what felt like hours. Finally, it went quiet. The door opened and the man came out ... and he smiled at me. Fucking *smiled*. Then he walked by me like nothing happened."

"Jesus *fucking* Christ," Remy hissed. I didn't have to look at him to see the waves of fury rolling off of him.

"That's when I knew," I finished, letting my eyes open and coming back to the present. My eyes focused on a particularly vibrant lime green ribbon in the sky. "That's when I knew what being an omega in our pack was. That's when I knew what my future would be."

I heard the door open a second before a frigid gust of wind tore through the interior of the car. My already frigid body barely noticed the extra cold. The door slammed shut as fast as it had opened, violently rocking the entire SUV for several seconds.

My eyes tracked Remy as he stalked around the front of the vehicle and came to my door, ripping it open.

I turned to look at him, surprised and a little wary, but I froze when I saw the look of complete devastation on his pale face. I gasped, undoing my seat buckle and turning to swing my legs over the edge of the seat to reach for him.

He beat me to it, reaching for my face with shaking hands. With exquisite gentleness, he framed my face and leaned his forehead into mine. My hands came up, grabbing part of his shirt behind his biceps. His entire body was trembling.

"I'm so sorry," he whispered, his voice breaking on the apology. "I am so fucking sorry you went through that." His thumbs smoothed across the wet skin under my eyes, ghosting along the angles of my cheeks.

After a beat, Remy moved even closer, banding his strong arms around me in a crushing hug. I wound my arms around his neck, parting my knees to pull him closer to my body.

His lips found the soft stretch of skin where my neck sloped into my shoulder. They pressed there for a second, his arms going impossibly tight around me, anchoring me to his body with everything her had.

"I swear," he whispered fiercely, "you'll never go back there. And they will pay for what they did to you and your mom and any other person they violated."

My entire life I had felt pieces of my heart crack and break off. My heart had become a brittle thing with jagged edges. I had seen things that carved holes in my soul and left me emotionally destroyed.

But that moment, I felt something in my heart knit back together, a small stitch that reattached a discarded piece of my soul. Something I thought I lost, now reclaimed.

## 29

I was completely drained as Remy walked me back to my dorm. He was holding my hand again, and I still leaned against his arm, letting him support part of my weight as we made our way down the path between the main building and some trees.

Despite the chill in the air, students were still loitering on the grounds in groups. One group even had a small fire started and someone with a guitar was strumming chords of a song I didn't recognize, the melody a soft harmony with the sounds of the night. In the distance, a pack of wolves took up a mournful howl.

Remy pulled us to a stop in front of the dorm, to the side of the steps. He linked our free hands together, his chocolate eyes somber as he studied me.

"Thank you for tonight," he said softly. "Thank you for trusting me."

A small smile trembled on my lips. "Thank you for being patient."

"Always," he swore, bending slightly to kiss my forehead.

Before he could pull away, I dropped his hands and wound my arms around his neck, pulling him back down. I pressed my mouth to his, intending to only give him a quick kiss goodnight, but those plans disappeared the second his lips touched mine.

With a low groan, Remy's hands found my waist and pulled me flush against him. His mouth coaxed mine open, his tongue sliding slowly against mine in a sensual rhythm that had nerve endings waking up I never even knew existed.

I gasped into his mouth, pressing my body harder against his. My fingers speared into his soft hair, scrambling for something to hold on to as my knees went weak.

One of his hands moved across my back. His touch blazed a trail of heat through all the layers I had. The sudden idea of his hands on me with no clothes between us had a shiver crawling down my spine and heat pooling low in my belly.

We broke the kiss mutually, struggling for air. Our breaths came out in white puffs as we panted into the cold air, our hearts galloping in a chaotic tandem of beats.

"God, I could get addicted to you," he murmured, his tone reverent as he smoothed loose strands of hair from my face.

I could help the grin that spread across my lips. "Yeah?"

He shut his eyes for a second, a pained expression flashing across his angular features. "Definitely."

His lips captured mine one more time, the kiss short and just as sweet. "Go on. I'll wait for you to get inside."

My wolf whined at me, and I completely understood where she was coming from. I didn't want to leave him any more than she did.

"I'll see you tomorrow?"

He nodded, grinning. "Yeah. I'll see you at breakfast and we can do whatever you want tomorrow."

I cocked my head to the side, a wicked feeling sending a thrill through me. "You mean, we can do more of that?"

With a playful growl, he pulled me back into his chest, his arms going around my back in an iron-clad band. "Hell, yes."

I laughed, the sound muffled against his chest. I rested my head there, reassured by the steady thumping of his heart. "That sounds great," I said softly, my arms coming up around his waist. I let my eyes close for a second, absorbing his warmth and strength.

Stupidly, I wondered what it would be like to wake up like this. With Remy's arms tight around me, knowing I was safe and protected and wanted.

"Seriously," he said a minute later, pulling away. "Go inside before I drag you back to the cabin with me."

My eyes went wide and I caught my lower lip between my teeth. "And that's a bad thing?"

His gaze went dark and hot, the look on his face ravenous as he watched me through thick lashes. "Tonight it would be. But one day it won't."

He was right. If he had said yes, I would have followed him down the path to his cabin and straight up the stairs into his bedroom.

My cheeks heated at the thought of his bedroom. *His bed.*

But tonight wasn't the night for that. Not when things were still so new between us and I had just spent part of the night ripping open old wounds that had never fully healed. Even now, I fought to contain a yawn, losing the battle easily.

His smile was infinitely gentle and patient, the promise of more in his eyes. "Get some sleep, babe. I'll see you in the morning." He kissed my forehead, nuzzling his nose against the crown of my head.

I hummed in agreement, stepping away from him reluctantly. "See you in the morning."

I felt his eyes on me every step I took to the door. I turned at the last minute, stunned breathless at the look on his face when he smiled at me. Pressing my lips together, I ducked inside the door, resisting the urge to turn around again and see him.

My heart was still pounding as I waited for the elevator. I licked my lips, tasting Remy there. I stepped into the elevator, tamping down the reckless urge to run after him. Letting out a sigh when the doors slipped closed, I pressed the button for my floor and waited for the ride up.

The lights were off when I opened the door. I paused, thinking Larkin might be asleep, but I didn't hear her breathing. I flipped on the light, noticing the note on my bed in Larkin's looping script.

*Hanging out with Katy. Be back soon! Don't go to sleep—I want details!*

I laughed quietly to myself, shaking my head. Glancing at the clock, I saw it was a little before eleven. Early by most teen date standards, but exhaustion pulled at my bones.

Setting my purse down, I pulled out my phone. It was an hour earlier in Washington. Biting my lip, I took a chance and pressed the video chat icon for mom's contact. I went to my bed, settling against the pillows as the phone started to ring.

Her face appeared a second later, a brilliant smile on her lips. Her blonde hair was in a messy bun, held up by a pencil.

"Skye!" she chirped, excitement in her tone. "Hey, baby! Everything okay?"

I couldn't help the grin that stretched across my face, making my cheeks ache. "Hey! I'm great. How are things in Blackwater?"

She exhaled loudly but was still smiling. "I'm exhausted, but things are great. The café is going so well, Zoe is thinking about opening up another location in the next town over."

My brows rose. "For normals?"

She nodded, settling back against what I assumed was a couch. "Blackwater has a decent tourist population. The falls in the summer attract a lot of hikers."

"Wow," I murmured.

Mom's eyes narrowed. "Hold on—are you wearing makeup?"

My eyes went wide. "Um ..."

Her jaw dropped. "Is this about the guy you wouldn't tell me about? The one you have a thing for?" she demanded. "As your mother, I demand to know why you look more beautiful than normal."

I groaned, trying to think of an answer when the door swung open and a redheaded ball of crazy was launching herself across the room. I dropped the phone as I pulled my legs clear of her landing zone.

"How was the date? Tell me everything!" Katy cried. Then she held up a hand suddenly. "Okay, not everything because Remy is still my brother, but I want less than detailed details."

Larkin was cracking up as she shut the door and joined us on the bed, sitting at the foot.

"Date?" the tinny voice from my phone asked.

I gave Katy a long glance before picking up the phone to see my mom giving me a stern look.

"Whoops," Katy muttered. Louder, she said, "Hey, Skye's mom!"

"Hello," my mom said with a confused laugh.

I turned the phone so she could see Katy and Larkin. Both waved at her.

Flipping the phone back to my face, Mom was now full on smirking.

"So, a date, huh? And with Katy's brother? Wait—is that *Remington*? Gabe and Mallory's oldest?" Her jaw dropped as she placed who I was talking about. The son of the Alpha. An alpha to be.

"Yeah," I said, fighting a smile. "I've been hanging out with Remy."

"Since when?" she demanded.

I winced. "Last night?"

Katy and Larkin both started laughing.

"Did he take you to the dance? I thought you were going with someone named Andy?"

Oh, shit.

Andy.

In the whirlwind of the last twenty-four hours—*how had it only been twenty-four hours?*—I had completely forgotten about the boy I technically ditched at the dance. He probably hated me, if not because I left him, but then definitely because Remy and I had been seen around campus together. With a student body of less than three hundred, word got around fast.

"I did go with Andy. As friends," I said slowly, not sure how much to explain. "But Remy and I ..."

How did I tell my mother that I was mate bonded to an alpha without her freaking out? From what everyone seemed to say, I would all but be announcing that I was engaged to my mom.

"Remy and Skye have had a thing for each other since she got here," Katy spoke up.

My eyes went to her.

She shrugged and nodded. "Trust me. My brother's been into you since the first day he introduced you to the pack."

"And you like him, too?" my mom pressed, her tone catching a bit with worry.

I hated that she was instantly worried for me. I hadn't told her everything that happened with Cassian and his friends at Long Mesa, but she knew enough. Neither of us pushed the other for details about things we endured, but I knew she wasn't oblivious or ignorant.

But right now I could see my mom trying not to freak out that she had pulled me out of one bad situation and put me in another, only now she was miles away from me. If I said the word, I knew she would be at GPA within hours, dragging me away to protect me.

"I like him," I admitted softly. "I really like him. He's a good guy, Mom. I can't wait for you to meet him."

She sniffled then, wiping at her eyes, relief stark on her features. "Okay, honey. I trust your judgment."

We talked for a few more minutes and by the time I hung up, the tiredness I felt earlier was now turning into excess energy. After the Katy and Larkin inquisition where I had to give them almost every detail, I was wired.

I got off the bed, rolling my shoulders. "I think I'm going to go for a run."

Katy's brows went up. "Now?"

I nodded, my wolf humming her agreement to the idea.

Larkin got off the bed. "I could go for a run, too."

"What the hell," Katy said, getting up as well. "Let's go for a run."

We headed outside, leaving the dorms and heading for the field where I had been working on my shifting. The campus had minimal lighting around the paths. With our heightened vision courtesy of the shifter gene anomaly, seeing in the dark wasn't a big deal. Besides, the moon and stars were bright in the sky, traces of the northern lights on the fringes but mostly blotted out by the mountains and trees around us.

We turned to get off the normal path when a shadow to our right had all of us tensing at the newcomers.

My wolf growled, not liking someone stopping me from letting her out. Then she growled for a whole new reason when the person came closer to the lamp on the path.

"What the fuck do you want?" Katy hissed at Trace. She glared at him and then turned her frigid stare on Sierra, who was walking with him.

Sierra's pretty face curled in disgust. "My boyfriend was walking me home."

Katy and I instinctively closed ranks on Larkin, standing in front of her like a physical shield from their glares. My gaze caught on Trace and my jaw nearly dropped. Half of his face was a swollen bruise, blue and black marks marring his dark skin.

Remy had definitely had a talk with him all right.

Trace scoffed, his gaze cold. "Don't the three of you have something better to do than follow me around?"

I blinked slowly. "Excuse me?"

Trace let go of Sierra and stepped closer to us, his smile all teeth and cruelty as he looked at me. "Every time I turn around, one of you seems to be right there." His gaze flickered across me, lingering on my chest. "I heard you've been seeing Remy, Skye. If you ever want to try a real alpha—"

"I'm good, thanks," I cut him off, my tone dripping icicles. I looked at Sierra, who was staring at the ground, her jaw clenched. Was she seriously going to keep taking up for a guy who was propositioning another female right in front of her?

"Baby, I'm tired," she started with a whine.

Apparently, she was.

"Then fucking leave," Trace snapped, not looking at her. His gaze zeroed in on Larkin. The bastard actually licked his lips.

I clamped a hand down on Katy's arm when I felt her start to lunge for him. The last thing we needed was Katy hitting an alpha, no matter how much the asshole deserved it. Sierra stayed where she was, fuming but silent as Trace fixed his attention on someone else.

"Larkin," he said slowly. "You look ... Wow. What happened to your face?"

Katy growled and I shoved her behind me, stepping closer to Trace.

"Okay, this is over. Get away from us," I demanded, meeting his gaze levelly and not flinching away from his challenging stare.

Staring at another shifter was a dangerous game, but especially when that shifter was an unhinged alpha. What I was doing could be viewed as a challenge, one Trace could accept if he wanted.

My wolf was ready. She wanted that fight, wanted the chance to rip into the monster that hurt our friend.

I kind of wanted it, too.

"You don't get to tell me what to do," he hissed, eyes flashing. "Fucking females thinking they're better. You need to learn your place."

My hands started to shake with the need to shift.

"Stop it, Trace."

Larkin's voice was soft but firm behind me. She stepped out from around us, stopping when her shoulder brushed mine.

"Leave us alone," she ordered quietly. She jutted her chin out, taking a deep breath. "You crossed the line last night. My pack knows what you did, and unless you want me to go public, you're going to leave us alone." She arched a brow, looking at the bruise ringing his eye. "Unless you need me to ask Remy to remind you again that you have no right to touch any Blackwater pack member."

His eyes narrowed, jaw clenched so hard I thought his teeth would shatter. Hate radiated from him as he glared at all of us.

"Sierra," he barked, snapping his fingers like she was a puppy. She hurried to his side, eyes still down. His hand came around her arm like a vice and he dragged her down the path towards the dorms.

Katy let out a low whistle. "Damn, Larkin."

Shoulders squared and head high, Larkin kept an eye on Trace until he was out of sight. The only sign the encounter rattled her was the shaky breath she finally let out.

I touched her shoulder gently. "Are you okay?"

She gave a sharp nod, her eyes bright and alert. "Yeah, I am. I'm just done being his victim."

**30**

___________

THE ENTIRE NEXT WEEK OF SCHOOL WAS STRANGE AS I settled into my new relationship while still trying to play it low-key for the student body. The whole time, I felt a clock hanging over my head as the pack run approached.

After Friday and Saturday, I was more than happy to spend Sunday hanging out at the cabin with my friends. Katy, Maren and Larkin decided to go into town. I opted to hang back, content to read in the corner of the couch, my feet in Remy's lap while he and Rhodes played video games.

The girls came back, and we had another cookout, this time with just the six of us. It was nice and calm; a good way to end the crazy weekend that still had me reeling.

Remy tried to teach me how to grill hamburgers, but when I nearly caught my sleeve on fire, he banished me back into the house before I hurt myself or someone else. Tate came over later on with Dante and Ryder, but everyone seemed content to hang out in the living area of the cabin, sprawled over chairs and couches while they just talked and hung out together.

It felt wonderfully normal.

Monday had been when the weird started. The only thing people were more fascinated by than Trace's sudden bruises was the fact that Remy and I were clearly together.

Sometimes it felt like everything was the same, but then I realized that everything was different now.

When I arrived at breakfast Monday morning, I took the seat next to Remy without thinking. I usually sat across from Rhodes, who usually sat next to Remy.

My butt hit the seat, and Remy hooked a hand around one of the legs of the chair, pulling me close enough for our bodies to touch. He never stopped his conversation with Dante as he did it.

When I stood up to get something and had to walk around him, my hand naturally ran across his broad shoulders as I went.

We were constantly finding small ways to touch each other, but by last period I was tired of the curious looks and whispers we were getting. Remy had pulled our desks closer together in the back row, and I closed my eyes and rested my head on his shoulder to wait for class to start.

Which was, of course, when Andy walked in the room.

He tripped on a backpack in the aisle when he saw me, and the hurt look he flashed my direction made me wince. I definitely owed him an apology and an explanation, but he came into the room seconds before class started and bolted for the door immediately after. Remy tried offering to talk to him for me, but I knew it was something I had to do.

Except Andy was really fast and had managed to avoid me all week.

By the time Friday afternoon came, I was restless and ready for the pack run later that night. I had wondered throughout the week if my wolf would get performance anxiety in front of the whole pack, but thankfully that didn't seem to be the case.

I didn't bother going to my dorm after our last class ended. Instead I went with Remy to the cabin, going immediately to the fridge and pulling things out for us to snack on before the rest of the pack arrived.

As I reached for the cups in the cabinet, I realized how at home I had become in his space. Warmth spread in my chest as I paused.

"What are you thinking?" Remy asked, coming up behind me and wrapping his arms around my waist. He pulled my back against his chest, nipping at my neck.

I shivered in his arms, forgetting why I was standing in front of the cups.

Hell, if his teeth scraped that spot again, I probably wouldn't remember what a cup even was.

"I was thinking about how easy it is to be here," I admitted, giggling when his lips brushed a sensitive spot on my throat he liked to tickle. I reached a hand up behind me, my fingers tangling in his hair.

I felt his lips curved into a smile against my flesh. "Easy, huh?"

One of his hands slipped under the hem of my shirt, his fingers slowly grazing the skin he found there. I shivered once more, my hips canting back to press against him.

He groaned softly, his other hand stealing under my shirt and tracing the line where my jeans met my waist. His lips never stopped moving across my neck, feathering across the curve of my ear and towards my jaw.

A steady throb I was becoming familiar with started pulsing between my legs, and I fought the urge to clamp my thighs together to relieve the insistent pressure.

Remy and I hadn't done anything more than kiss,

really, but every time we did, it seemed to edge a little closer to something more.

I was definitely ready for that elusive more he promised, even if the idea of it was slightly terrifying. My sexual experience was limited to what I had read in books and what I had witnessed or endured in my last pack.

It was a little embarrassing to admit how completely unsure I was about the physical aspect of our relationship. I knew what went where, but only clinically.

The fact that Remy seemed infinitely patient and content to let me set the pace eased a lot of my fear, but I was starting to get a little frustrated by the lack of progression despite my trepidation.

I squirmed against him, my ass rubbing against him and taking note I wasn't the only one affected by what he was doing.

Instead of the flash of pure fear I was used to when it came to teenage males and arousal, I was curious, and it was a curiosity that was becoming more and more insistent.

His hips rocked into me slowly.

*Speaking of insistent.*

With an audible sigh, Remy put some distance between us. He let out a frustrated growl that I damn near mimicked.

"The pack will be here any minute," he muttered, moving away from me.

I caught him adjusting his jeans with a grimace and tried not to smile. I turned away and pulled the cups from the cabinet before shutting the open door.

Clearing my throat, I tried to cool my body down. "What are we going to tell them?"

He frowned, leaning a hip against the counter and studying me. "The truth. We'll leave out the part about

Larkin and why it happened, but they need to know about us bonding."

My shoulders slumped. "I know. I'm just already bracing for the questions and the staring. It's going to be awkward."

Remy snorted. "It would be more awkward if I attacked one of the males for sniffing around you once we shifted."

My eyes went wide, jaw dropping like it was on a hinge. "You wouldn't."

His eyes turned to liquid heat as he stalked closed to me, his long legs eating up the few feet of distance between us in seconds. He braced his hands on either side of me on the counter, caging me in.

"I would. I get jealous anytime any guy checks you out at school. But in wolf form? There's no way my wolf would let another male near you. Period." His gaze flicked to my mouth before coming back to my eyes.

I tried not to smile but failed miserably. "You realize if someone outside of the shifter world heard you talking, you'd probably be arrested, right? Crazed, possessive alpha male?"

He rolled his eyes but hooked a finger in one of my belt-loops, pulling me to him. "I don't care. No one touches you without permission."

Something about that rankled. "Without your permission?"

"Without *yours*," he corrected firmly. "I don't own you, Skye. Despite what my wolf thinks, you get to make your own choices." His lips curled into a smirk. "But that doesn't mean I can't kick someone's ass who touches you if you don't want them to."

I burst out laughing and threw my arms around his neck. "My hero."

His expression sobered. "You don't need a hero, Skye. You're the strongest person I've ever met. The things you survived ... You went through hell, and you're still standing. You didn't let your old pack break you. I've watched the way you are with Larkin and even Katy. The way you protect them."

I dropped my gaze, blushing under his praise and scrutiny. "I'm just me."

With a sigh, he hugged me to his chest. "One of these days, I'm going to make you see just how extraordinary you are, Skye Parker."

I stiffened then, the false name I had adopted a lie between us.

"Markham," I corrected quietly.

Remy pulled back, but still kept his arms around me as he looked down. "What?"

I cleared my throat, meeting his gaze. "My last name. It's not Parker. It's Markham. Your dad suggested we use a different last name in case my uncle was trying to find us."

Understanding cleared his eyes. "Linden Markham is your uncle? You came from the Long Mesa pack?"

I nodded slowly. It wasn't a surprise that he had heard of the Markham name. We were one of the most notorious packs in the south and that was before what happened with my mom. Of course, Remy would have heard of us.

Remy pressed his lips together. "That explains a lot."

"It does?"

"The Long Mesa pack has a bit of a reputation," he admitted ruefully. "I've seen your grandfather and your uncle at the Summit meetings. They're pretty vocal about packs adopting their way of life."

I laughed bitterly. "Of course they are."

"I always thought they were assholes," he went on mildly, "and now I know I was right."

"My grandfather's dead now," I reminded him, knowing he would have heard about the death of an Alpha.

"Can't say that makes me sad to hear." A muscle ticked in his jaw. "As far as everyone here is concerned, you're still Skye Parker. If my dad thinks it's safer, then that's what we'll do. I'm not risking your safety, or your Mom's."

I reached up, cradling his jaw in my hand. "Every time I tell you something about my past, you surprise the hell out of me, Remy Holt. What will it take for me to make you run?"

I hadn't meant to actually voice that question out loud, but I couldn't take it back now.

His eyes cut to mine seriously. "Dressing up like a clown."

It took a second for his comment to register. A stunned giggle escaped me. "What?"

"If you dress up like a clown, I'm out," he said firmly.

I pulled away, bending at the waist as laughter ripped through me. "Are you serious?"

"Hundred percent," he answered. "You show up with a big red nose, giant ass shoes, and some freaky ass giant smile, and I'm reevaluating this whole bond."

My sides ached. "You're afraid of *clowns*? The big, bad alpha is afraid of something that entertains children?" I giggled so hard I snorted, which sent me into a new wave of laughter.

"Coulrophobia is a clinically diagnosable condition," he stated, crossing his arms over his chest.

I slid to my knees, my hands slapping against the floor as I collapsed into a fit of giggles. "Does Katy know?" I wheezed out.

His eyes narrowed. "No. And you better not tell her."

I was still dying of laughter when the front door

opened and Rhodes came in. He paused in the doorway, his eyes flying to Remy.

"Dude, what the hell is with your girl?"

Remy shrugged innocently, barely sparing me a glance. "No clue. Might need to get her checked out."

That only made me laugh harder, tears streaming down my face.

Rhodes looked at us like we were crazy. "Well, get it together. The pack is coming down the path now. I ran ahead to make sure you two were decent." He gave Remy a pointed look. "FYI, bro? It's not a good sign when a girl laughs like that when you're having alone time."

Remy flipped up his middle finger while using the other hand to help pull me into a semi-standing position.

"Are you done?" he asked, arching an eyebrow.

I slapped a hand over my mouth, still giggling even as I noticed pack members starting to come in through the open front door. My sides hurt from laughing.

"It's not that funny," he grumbled with a small smile, turning to go to his pack as they started finding seats. I was still grinning when Katy and Larkin came in, both of them shooting me questioning looks that only made me want to laugh again.

I snagged an apple from the snacks I had pulled out of the fridge and headed for the living room. I moved to sit with Larkin and Katy, but Remy's hand caught my wrist. He gave a subtle nod to the empty armchair directly to his left. Rhodes sat in the one to his right already.

It wasn't butterflies in my stomach, but a flock of birds that took flight. I sank into the chair, waiting until everyone came in. Sierra and Ainsley were the last ones in and kept to the back, looks of complete boredom on their faces.

"Thanks for showing up on time," Remy started, grinning at his pack. "I'll keep this short since I know we're all anxious to get out and run."

A chorus of agreement met his statement and I smiled, looking at the excited faces of my pack mates.

Remy rubbed the back of his neck, glancing back at me for a second. I stiffened, knowing now was the time.

"This is a little ... strange," he began, clearing his throat. The room fell completely silent, everyone's attention on him. "Something happened last week. Most of you know Skye and I are dating—"

One of the wolves gave a sharp whistle of approval that made me blush and had everyone laughing.

Remy gave him a reproachful look, but there was no heat behind the warning. "Thank you, Will. What you don't know is that when Skye and I were out on a run last weekend ... our wolves bonded."

Gasps rose up in the room. There was no need to explain the type of bond he was talking about. There was only one that would warrant this kind of announcement.

"That's impossible," Sierra hissed, her expression livid as she glared at me.

I met her glare, matching it with my own. "I can assure you, it's not. Remy and I are bonded."

"It's true," Rhodes spoke up, his tone firm. Looking at him, I could see the reason he was Remy's beta. He was calm and cool, unfazed. "Once we all shift, you'll notice the way their scents are different. Mixed."

"But that never happens to people this young," another wolf chimed in, his blue eyes big.

"We know," Remy agreed. "It's not the norm."

"So, are you guys, like, engaged?" A younger female asked from the back. She was sitting with two other girls, all of them fourteen or thirteen and part of the freshman class. All three of them looked completely enthralled. I could practically see the hearts and stars in their eyes.

I tried to keep my features neutral even though I wanted to roll my eyes.

Remy laughed. "No. We're still getting to know each other. But we knew that you all needed to be aware before we went out on the run."

"Stay away from Skye," Will piped up, holding up his hands. "Message received."

"Exactly." Remy was smiling, but there was an underlying steel to his tone.

Now I did roll my eyes, catching Rhodes winking at me with a one-shouldered shrug.

"Any other pack business?" Remy asked.

Sierra lifted a hand. "I don't see why we need to be part of Blackwater pack runs when we're planning to leave this pack." She spat the last two words.

My wolf rankled in my chest, growling at the insult to our pack. I rubbed my sternum absently, trying to calm her down.

Remy's expression was unreadable as he stared at her. "You're right, Sierra."

I caught Katy's surprised look out of the corner of my eye, but I was still watching Remy.

"If you don't want to be part of this pack, then you absolutely shouldn't be here." His tone was cold, hard. "Feel free to leave."

With a smug look, Sierra started for the door. She paused when she noticed Ainsley wasn't with her. "Ainsley!" she snapped.

Ainsley sighed and took a step backwards, shaking her head. "I'm not ready to say I'm leaving my pack."

"Fucking bitch," Sierra snarled, whirling and storming out the door. She slammed it loudly behind her.

Remy raised both brows. "Let's go, guys."

He led us outside, the males heading around one side of the house and the females the other. We would all strip and get dressed separately.

There were only eight females in the Blackwater pack that attended Granite Peak. Larkin, Katy, and myself, the three younger girls, and Sierra and Ainsley.

Well, now seven since Sierra was denouncing the pack.

The younger girls scurried over to a dark corner, whispering as they started taking off their clothes.

Katy gave me a knowing look. "Was that as bad as you thought?"

I shook my head, pulling off the flannel shirt I had over my t-shirt and folding it up. There were benches with cubbies under the seats for us to stash our clothes in. I sat on the bench and started pulling off my shoes.

"It wasn't that bad," I admitted. Larkin sat beside me, taking off her boots.

Ainsley stood off to the side, painfully on her own and looking a little lost.

Unashamed, Katy pulled off her shirt in front of all of us before shimmying out of her jeans.

"So, you and Remy are really true mates?" one of the younger girls called over in the dark.

I really needed to try to remember their names.

"Yes, Lea," Katy called over, exasperated. She gave me an annoyed look.

Someone—presumably Lea—giggled. "That's so romantic."

I raised my brows. Romance wasn't the emotion I was feeling that night.

I finished stripping and stood up, rolling my shoulders and neck to loosen my muscles. Closing my eyes, I stepped aside and let my wolf take over.

The snapping of bones took less and less time each time I did it. A second later, I stood with the other girls, a couple feet shorter than them. My wolf eyes picked up everything in the darkness.

A scent carried over on the breeze and I whined, pawing impatiently at the ground.

Remy.

I knew the smell of my mate. The fact that he was so close and I was still here was annoying both my wolf and I.

"Easy, girl," Katy teased, taking off her last layer and shifting herself. A minute later, all of the girls had shifted and were following me to the back of the cabin.

I broke into a loping run when I saw Remy standing with the rest of the pack at the edge of the property. I all but crashed into him, nuzzling his side as he playfully nipped at my mouth.

*There you are.*

My head jerked back as I heard his voice in my head. I blinked, but he sat down as he looked at me inquisitively. I was going crazy.

*You're not crazy.* He huffed out an annoyed breath.

The bond. Zoe had mentioned some sort of telepathy came with it. The first night I had heard him in my head, but it was only for a second and I had a million things going through my mind so I hadn't thought about it.

*We'll get used to it.*

I backed up a few steps, suddenly nervous that he could read my mind. My wolf, however, was pissed that I was letting things like human embarrassment keep her away from her mate. I could feel her tugging at my mind, pushing me to let her take over.

With a huff, I surrendered control to her.

Satisfied, she took us back to Remy's side, nudging him.

With a deep bark, Remy took off into the woods, the

rest of us chasing after him. A chorus of yips and high-pitched barks rang out as the pack ran across the ground, heading up the side of a mountain through the trees.

I felt teeth on my back legs and glanced back to see Katy pressing hot on my heels. I put on an extra burst of speed, darting away from her as she chased me.

She was fast, almost as fast as Remy. She caught up to me in no time, running at my side until Remy brought us all to a clearing after running for several miles.

The pack fanned out, all breathing hard. A few dropped to their bellies, laying down to rest.

Remy sat down off to the side, his dark eyes watching every pack member. He was checking to see who was tired and needed a break, assessing everyone.

*Are we done?* I voiced the questions curiously, watching as his head swung to my direction.

*The younger ones need a break.*

I saw Rhodes lunge at Larkin playfully, flipping her onto her back. Where usually Larkin would have submitted and played along, letting Rhodes have the win, she struggled, snapping her teeth at him until, stunned, he let her up.

Larkin wasn't happy being the pack omega anymore.

Traditionally, omegas could challenge their omega status. I knew logically that Larkin could have easily left the role of omega to one of the younger girls, particularly the one with gray and black fur that hung back and kept whining low in her throat all night. Larkin had simply stayed in the omega role, letting herself be treated as the baby of the group.

Until now.

With a last growl, she walked away from a confused Rhodes.

Remy stood up, sensing his pack wasn't completely in sync.

*It's okay, I assured him. I'll tell you later.*

Somewhat appeased, he sat back down, but his ears were up and alert as he watched the rest of the pack.

I started for him, walking past a group of the younger males. One of them turned, sniffing the air curiously as I moved past.

Remy's low growl was all the warning I had before he was pushing between us, his teeth bared at the younger wolf, who quickly dropped to the ground with a high pitched whine of surrender.

Satisfied he had made his point, Remy relaxed and moved back, his ears flicking.

*Seriously?*

He looked at me with big eyes, not looking apologetic in the least.

**31**

———

SNOWFLAKES STARTED FALLING AS I SHIFTED BACK INTO human form. My muscles quivered as I struggled to get dressed, exhausted from the long run. I had a feeling all the breaks we took weren't just for the younger pack members.

Looking over, I saw Ainsley quickly finished dressing. She had stayed to herself during the run, not joining in or playing with the rest of the pack. She had beat me back here by seconds but was already making herself scarce.

I pulled my hair free of my shirt as Katy and Larkin shifted back beside me. Looking up at the sky, a snowflake landed on my eyelid. I blinked away the sudden cold but couldn't help the smile that spread across my face as I spread my hands wide to catch as many flakes as I could.

"I need to start packing a brush," Katy muttered, finger-combing knots from her hair. She looked at me. "What the hell are you doing?"

"It's snowing," I said reverently, a flake clung to my eyelashes. I almost went cross-eyed tried to study if before it melted.

Larkin smiled indulgently. "Ah, someone's enjoying her first snowfall."

"You've never seen snow?" Lea asked as she and her friends, now changed and dressed, came over to us. She reached up, starting to quickly braid her dark hair.

I shook my head. "I grew up in a southern pack. It didn't snow there." I watched in fascination as the flakes went from small to thicker, their designs more intricate. Within seconds, a thin layer coated the ground.

The blonde beside Lea rubbed her hands together for warmth, her blue eyes sparkling. "I still can't believe you and Remy are bonded. What did it feel like when it happened?"

The other brunette nodded with bright eyes. "Was it magic? Did you instantly fall in love?"

"Of course she did, Megan! Remy is so amazing," the blonde said with a sigh.

"And really cute," Lea added with a giggle. "You're lucky, Skye. All the girls here have a crush on him. Especially Bethany." She nodded to the blushing blonde.

Something tightened in my chest, my wolf growling at them. "I don't share," I said quietly, a tight smile on my face.

All their faces paled and they scrambled back a step.

Katy started to laugh, ducking her face into Larkin's shoulder.

"We didn't mean—" Lea squeaked.

Bethany was shaking her head so fast I was worried she would snap her own neck. "No, no! It's just—"

I winced. I hadn't meant to sound so damn possessive. It just sort of came out. The idea of another female touching Remy made my blood boil and my wolf wanted to rip things apart.

I could see why Remy growled at the younger wolf earlier on our run.

"I'm sorry," I apologized weakly.

Lea grabbed her friends, pulling them away. "It was our fault. We didn't mean to upset you, Skye. We'll see you guys later." They turned as one and darted away.

I sighed. "Well, shit."

Katy was still cackling. "You are a possessive little bitch, Skye."

I turned, throwing my hands up in exasperation. "I don't even know where that came from."

Larkin pointed at my chest. "I'm guessing your wolf doesn't want to share Remy."

*He's ours.*

My wolf was still miffed but starting to calm down. Logically I knew those girls were no threat at all to whatever was happening between us, but my wolf didn't seem to understand logical reasoning. She only knew what was hers and that meant no one else got to touch him.

Or, apparently, talk about him.

Speaking of odd behavior, I looked at my roomie. "What the hell was that with Rhodes?"

"What was what?" Larkin asked innocently, zipping her jacket.

Katy exchanged a look with me before propping a hand on her hip. "You and Rhodes always play around when we run. You almost took his head off."

"I didn't feel like playing," Larkin replied calmly.

Katy's brows rose. "You didn't seem to mind when the McAllister twins wanted to mess around in the woods. You were happy to play with them. I didn't see you snapping and snarling their way."

Larkin folded her arms over her chest with a huff. "Maybe I'm growing up. Maybe I'm realizing that I'm tired of waiting for Rhodes to stop seeing me as a little sister."

Katy let out a low whistle, slow clapping. "It's about damn time."

I wasn't so sure she could turn off her emotions so easily. "Just like that?"

"Yes, just like that," Larkin repeated, but wouldn't meet my gaze as we started for the front of the house.

I gave Katy another look as we rounded the house. Remy and Rhodes were standing on the brightly lit porch, out of the snow currently falling. On the steps were two other males from the pack.

I could make out identical blonde heads, both turned and smiled at Larkin.

The McAllister twins had waited for her.

My gaze flicked to the top of the stairs. Rhodes looked pissed.

"You guys are staying to hang out, right?" Rhodes asked loudly as we approached.

"I told Maren I would meet up with her," Katy said with a shrug.

"Larkin?" Rhodes prompted, his dark gaze focused solely on her.

Larkin barely spared him a glance. "I'm kind of tired. I think I'll head back."

"We can walk you back," one of the twins offered quickly, jumping down the last two stairs. His brother followed close behind. They were cute, with big easy smiles and dark blue eyes.

"Okay," Larkin agreed with a grin. She looked at me. "Are you coming?"

I was already starting up the stairs, my feet taking me to them before my brain processed it. "I'm going to stay here for a bit."

I hit the landing, and Remy pulled me to his side, an arm around my shoulders. I shivered at the sudden heat that wrapped around me. I wound an arm around his narrow waist, pressing against him.

"You can hang out, too, Lark," Rhodes said, his tone slightly desperate. "We can all play a game or something."

"I said I'm tired," she replied evenly, finally looking at him. Her face was cool and unaffected.

"Shit," I mumbled into Remy's side. I felt his chest shake with barely contained laughter.

Rhodes undone was tragically funny.

"Then I'll walk you home," Rhodes said firmly, his brows pulled tight together.

Larkin rolled her eyes. Actually rolled her eyes at him as she gestured to the two boys with her. "I think Kyle and Konnor can get me back down the path safely."

Adding insult to injury, Larkin grabbed a hand of each boy, pulling them away from the cabin.

"What the actual fuck," Rhodes snapped, raking a hand through his long hair. He turned his piercing gaze on me. "What is going on with Larkin?"

"Maybe you should ask Larkin that," I said carefully.

"I've been trying," Rhodes snapped, clearly frustrated as he started to pace on the porch, his heavy boots thumping on the wood planks. "She won't talk to me! And now she's hanging out with Kyle and Konnor? Who the hell names their kids Kyle and Konnor, with a damn K?"

My shoulders shook with silent laughter.

"Kyle and Konnor are decent guys," Remy added, his fingers playing with my hair. "They were just over here last week hanging out after classes. You didn't seem to mind them then."

"That was before they started pawing at Larkin!" Rhodes glared at us.

"Why does it matter?" I asked slowly. "Larkin's free to date whoever——"

"She's *dating* them?" Rhodes roared.

I sighed loudly. "No, but if she wants to, she can. It's not like anyone else is asking her out, are they, Rhodes?" I gave him a pointed glare for emphasis.

He hesitated for a minute, the wind deflating his sails. "I just worry about her. Especially after what Trace did ... Larkin deserves the best."

"I think we all agree on that," Remy told him with a nod.

"Yeah," Rhodes muttered. With a sigh, he turned and opened the front door. "I'm going to bed." He didn't wait for a reply before going inside and closing the door.

I turned and looked at Remy. "That was interesting."

Remy was still staring after his best friend. "He likes her. He just doesn't know how to tell her."

"He better figure it out," I told him, shaking my head. "Larkin's done waiting."

"Part of me wants to tell him to stop being an idiot," Remy said. "But I think he needs to figure this out for himself. Rhodes doesn't usually do well when people explain his own emotions to him."

I wound another arm around his waist, hugging him to me and watching the snowfall. Several inches now coated the ground.

"It's so pretty," I breathed against him, afraid the magic would shatter if I spoke too loudly.

"I forgot you weren't used to snow," he remarked, tightening his hold around me. "If you're cold, we can go inside."

"And miss this? No way."

"It's supposed to be the first big snowfall of the season. Weather reports said eighteen inches. Maybe twenty-four."

"Two feet?" I gasped, looking at him with wide eyes.

He nodded, amused. "Yeah. The school usually closes up for a few days when it happens to let the packs run. Playing in the snow is a blast."

"I can't wait," I admitted. I shivered against the dropping temperatures despite the major body heat Remy gave off.

"Let's go inside," he suggested, pulling me gently to the door. "You can still see the snow from the windows."

I started to nod, but a yawn snuck up on me, almost cracking my jaw with its intensity. "Or maybe I should go back to my room and get some sleep."

"You could stay here," Remy suggested quietly.

My eyes flew to his and suddenly I wasn't tired. "Stay *here*?"

He glanced away, the tops of his cheeks were slightly red. Remy was blushing?

"There's extra rooms here," he said quickly, trying to explain. "You can sleep in one of those. By yourself, I mean. But then you can see the snow. One of the rooms has a great view of the backyard and the mountains."

He cleared his throat, obviously nervous. "But only if you want."

"I think I want to stay," I admitted after a heavy pause.

A small smile started on his lips. "Okay, let's go get you settled."

He led me inside, closing the door behind us. Still holding my hand, he led me to the staircase I had never gone up.

The hallway at the top of the stairs was dimly lit by a single light. Most of the doors were closed or partially open.

Remy pointed to the first door at the landing. "This is Rhodes' room." He moved past it, pointing out a bathroom and three additional guest rooms. Two of the rooms had two sets of bunk beds. He explained that occasionally some of the pack would stay and hang out and crash at the cabin. The last guest room had a queen bed inside it and a stunning view of the snow falling serenely outside, the dusky shapes of the mountains outlining the background.

All the rooms were simply decorated with wood furniture and solid-colored linens. This room seemed the coziest of them all, a small armchair and bookcase against one wall. I saw the door for a closet and a partially open door showed there was a private bathroom attached to the room.

But there was still one door we hadn't gone into.

"Where's your room?" I asked, turning to look at Remy.

"Next door," he replied. He jerked his head for me to follow him into the next room.

The first thing I noticed was the room smelled like home as soon as I crossed the threshold. It smelled like soap and pine. It smelled just like Remy.

It was more effective than any form of aromatherapy. The scent instantly relaxed me.

Remy stood to the side, watching as I walked slowly into the space. The room was the biggest by far. I could see French doors leading onto a balcony and a large en-suite bathroom off to the left. One wall was entirely glass, giving stunning views of the landscape.

But my eyes couldn't stop staring at the massive king bed in the center of the room. The maroon quilt was neatly laid across the bed, the pillows minimal but not messy. Other than a towel in a corner, the room was neat and tidy.

Walking past the bed, I couldn't help but run my hands

over the cotton of the quilt, something low in the belly quivering. His scent was strongest here.

Remy cleared his throat behind me. "I have some clothes you can wear tonight, if you want. Larkin or Katy can bring you a change tomorrow." His voice was rougher than usual.

"Okay," I murmured, walking to the windows and looking out. My breath fogged the windows as I watched the fat flakes dropping from the sky.

I could hear Remy moving behind me as I stared outside.

After a minute, he came up behind me, resting his chin on my shoulder and wrapping his arms around my waist. Sighing, I leaned back against him. The snow looked fresh and peaceful, and in the room, surrounded by everything Remy, I felt completely safe and secure.

The intimacy of the moment struck me, standing in his bedroom, in his arms. My skin started to prickle with awareness.

He cleared his throat again, lifting his chin. "I'm going to change in the bathroom and take a quick shower."

I nodded slowly, turning to watch him with wondering eyes as he stared down at me.

Indecision warred on his face for a second before he swiftly pressed his lips to mine. I barely had time to start to lift my arms before he was retreating to the bathroom.

"Tease," I muttered, sulking as he walked away. My body came alive the second his lips had touched mine.

He gave a nervous chuckle, rubbing the back of his neck. "Let me correct that—I'm taking a *cold* shower."

I laughed as he closed the bathroom door. Sure enough, the shower turned on seconds later. I moved to the bed, lifting up the t-shirt and gym shorts I knew would be massive on me. I quickly shed my clothes and pulled the shirt on. The shorts wouldn't stay up, no matter how tight I tied them. I finally gave up. The shirt was long enough to be a dress, honestly.

I folded my clothes and took them to the guest room, putting them on the edge of the bed. On autopilot, I went back to Remy's room, wanting to say goodnight before I slipped back into the guest room to sleep.

The last thing I remembered was sitting on the bed.

☪

THE SUN WAS weak and warm as it streamed in through the windows.

No, it wasn't the sun that was warm.

I was warm.

Scratch that—I was burning up.

I opened my eyes, blinking against the light as I tried to sit up, but I couldn't move.

There was an arm locked around my waist, pressing me against a furnace that breathed deeply.

*Remy.*

Looking around I realized I was still in his room. I must have fallen asleep waiting for him to get out of the bathroom. At some point, he had tucked us both into his bed.

I stared at him, at the way his lashes fanned against his cheeks. His face was completely relaxed in sleep, his full lips barely parted. His chest moved in a deep rhythm, and I was mildly disappointed to find he had put a shirt on before going to bed. I had wanted to check out the tattoo on his back I had glimpsed the night we bonded.

Okay, and maybe check out a few other things that made my stomach flip and my cheeks heat.

I could see the fine dark hairs on his tanned arms, the curve of his bicep where the sleeve of his shirt had pulled taut. The side of his face was pressed against the pillow, but his head was ducked down, like it had been pressed against my back.

Trying to sit up again, his arm tightened around me. He mumbled something I couldn't make out, pressing his face against my shoulder.

I had slept with Remy.

A stupid giggle slipped out of my mouth unbidden and I winced, hoping I wouldn't wake him up.

Remy was an alpha, and definitely an alert one.

His eyes opened, his gaze unfocused as he looked at me. A slow smile spread across his face. "Hey."

"Hey back," I whispered.

His arm came up, brushing across my chest, his fingers tracing the curve of my jaw. "God, you're gorgeous."

I couldn't help but laugh. "Maybe you need glasses. I'm sure my hair's a mess. And I definitely need a toothbrush."

His eyes narrowed playfully. "Are you questioning my decree, Ms. Markham? You forget I'm the alpha around here."

"Your *decree*?" I echoed, giggling. "At this point I'm questioning your sanity."

With a growl, Remy hauled me against him, his fingers digging into my sides.

I shrieked as I started laughing, trying to wrench away from his fingers. "Stop!" I begged.

He pulled himself up, getting to his knees over me, his hands still tickling. "Not until you admit I'm right!"

I tried to roll away, but he straddled my legs, pinning them in place. After a minute of struggling, he managed to pull my arms over my head, holding my wrists together in one of his massive hands. Which left a whole hand free to attack me.

I yelled and twisted, trying to get him off, laughing the entire time.

He paused, brows raised. "Ready to admit defeat."

"I surrender," I laughed, wishing I could wake up this happy every day.

Grinning at me, Remy let my wrists go and sat back on my thighs. Sitting up, I braced my hands behind me on the bed. Awareness prickled across my body.

Still smiling, Remy leaned forward, bracketing my face with his hands as he kissed me.

"Toothbrush," I murmured against his lips.

He laughed. "I don't care. You taste amazing."

He teased my mouth open with his, nipping lightly at my lower lip. His mouth moved across my jaw and down the column of my neck. He moved off of me to sit on the bed, then reaching out to pull me over to straddle his lap.

The new position put me above him, my chest pressed to his while his fingers stroked across my bare thighs.

"Hi," he murmured, his voice rough and gravelly and his eyes dark as he drank me in.

My heart flipped in my chest. "Hi." I started to raise my mouth to his when a sharp knock at the door startled us both.

Lifting me off of him, Remy got off the bed with a glare. "What?"

Rhodes coughed on the other side of the door. "I take it you two haven't looked outside?"

I had totally forgotten it had snowed.

I scrambled off the bed, coming to a stop by the window. My breath caught.

Everything was white.

I knew, theoretically, where everything was in the yard, but everything was covered in a thick white blanket. The trees glittered in the sunlight, the sun winking off the ice and snow-capped tips of the mountains.

"Oh, my God," I whispered, pressing my hands and nose against the cold glass.

The door opened behind me and turning, I saw Remy blocking Rhodes from entering.

Rhodes grinned at us. "You two are *very* loud, by the way."

Remy growled and shoved his friend back a step.

Holding up his hands innocently, Rhodes still smirked at us. "We need to hurry up and eat. The packs are all going out to run."

Run in the snow. My wolf was waking up, my excitement feeding hers.

After quickly getting dressed back into my clothes from yesterday in the guest room, I shot Larkin a text asking her to bring me new clothes when she came over. I hurried downstairs, eating my bowl of cereal so fast Remy and Rhodes both told me to slow down.

"But I don't want the snow to go away," I whined, taking the time to chew.

Remy laughed. "Babe, it's winter in Montana. This isn't going away until March."

"If we're lucky," Rhodes grumbled. "Sometimes the snow is here until May."

"Really?"

Rhodes shook his head. "It's seriously wrong how excited she is by this."

Remy didn't seem annoyed. He seemed content to watch me with a permanently amused smile on his lips. He took me outside after we ate where I lifted handfuls of powdery snow and tossed it in the air, trying to catch it on my tongue.

Rolling the snow in his hands, Remy lobbed the ball gently at me. It exploded on impact.

With a gasp of mock outrage, I spun around.

Before I could react, a snowball sailed through the air, hitting the side of Remy's face.

"Direct hit!" Katy crowed, throwing her hands up in the air in victory. Larkin was laughing beside her, the three younger females a few steps from them. I could make out the rest of the pack heading towards us.

Rhodes came out the front door, closing it behind him. His boots clomped down the stairs. "Are we ready to go out?"

I nodded quickly. "Yes, please!"

Larkin held up a bag. "Got your clothes here."

Katy gave me a smug look. "I trust you two behaved yourselves last night?"

"Last night, yes," Rhodes replied. "But this morning —*Ooof!*"

Remy tackled him into the snow, holding his beta down with a grin. "You were saying?"

Rhodes got up, brushing the snow off his body. "So touchy."

The rest of the pack joined us and we went to our side of the cabin to change, shedding our clothes and shifting quickly in the frigid air.

The second my paws touched the snow, I felt my wolf's giddiness. I jumped in the snow, testing its depth with a few strides. Seconds later, the other girls, minus a missing Ainsley, were with me. We nipped and yipped at each other, tumbling into the backyard where Remy and the rest of the pack were waiting.

*Are you done yet?*

He stood there patiently, his tail swishing in the snow as he waited.

I barked back in response, still having fun. One of the younger wolves, Lea, I think, nipped at my ear and danced away, her gray coat shining in the sunlight.

*Go,* I told Remy, turning to pounce on my pack mate. *We'll catch up.*

With a chuff, he led the guys off into the woods, their playful snarls and snaps echoing in the woods as they went.

Larkin was chasing Katy and Bethany around the yard, all three of them having a great time. I let Lea go and turned on Megan when she tried sneaking up behind me.

After several more minutes of playing, I rounded up the girls and started into the woods to meet up with the rest of our pack. Ahead, I could hear Remy's howl a second before the others joined in.

We paused at the top of a hill, letting our voices join the pack.

The sense of contentment was a balm to my soul. This was my home. This was my family.

With an excited bark, Katy took the lead, starting to head down the hill to the valley we would cut across to get to the field we played in the night before.

A dark blur out of the corner of my eye, coming from the trees, was all the warning we got.

A massive wolf, dark brown with black markings, came barreling towards us at full speed. His paws had no traction on the snow and he never slowed, his body colliding with a sickening crunch into Katy.

I watched, horrified, as her russet body sailed through the air, landing hard on the ground a few feet away. Her back leg was bent under her body at an unnatural angle and she didn't get up.

**32**

———————

*KATY!*

My mind screamed her name as I scrambled across the slippery earth to get to her side. I could feel Remy's insistent pushing in my head, wondering what was happening.

I could only focus on Katy as I stopped over her. Her chest was moving, her eyes open. A whimper escaped her mouth as she tried to move.

I nudged her with my nose to stay down. She needed to stay still. Larkin laid down at her back, supporting her body.

The three younger wolves came closer, all but crawling on their bellies to us. With a sharp bark I stopped them, swinging my head in the direction of the cabin.

We needed help. Katy couldn't move. She needed medical attention.

With a yelp, Lea leapt up and took off in the direction of the school, Bethany and Megan right behind her.

I turned on the new wolf, not sure if he was hurt.

He stood where he had hit Katy, his head cocked to the side.

337

I sniffed the air, his scent familiar.

I felt my eyes go wide as I dropped into a defensive stance in front of Katy, a deep growl ripping up my throat.

Trace.

As if summoned by him, more than a dozen wolves emerged from the trees behind him. The rest of his pack had followed.

There was no way this was a stupid accident.

*Skye!*

Remy's sharp voice in my head cut through the cloud of rage I was currently in. I blinked, trying to find that tether that linked us together. His confusion and worry was so potent it made me nauseous.

*Trace ran into Katy. Her leg is broken. We're on the hill near the meadow.*

My attention went back to Trace as he stood, slowly approaching us. I gave him a warning snarl, which he didn't bother to heed. He continued to advance on us, his pack following a few steps behind.

Larkin came up beside me, adding her warning growl to mine.

Trace dropped his head, baring his teeth at us.

I tried nudging Larkin to the side. If Trace came at us, I needed someone between us and Katy. Katy was still whimpering behind us, her plaintive cries drowned out by the rumbling growls coming from us.

I had heard her bone snap. I knew she couldn't walk away from this, let alone run.

Stepping forward, I snapped my teeth at Trace with a snarl.

His chest seemed to swell as he widened his stance.

My wolf braced for him to attack.

He didn't disappoint.

Moving faster than I anticipated, Trace launched

himself at me, swiping at me with a large paw, his teeth snapping with a vicious growl.

I jumped back, his paw and claws missing my face. I spun quickly, managing to grab him with my teeth by his back flank.

He yelped and whirled, this time catching me full in the muzzle with his paw.

I blinked against the stars in the vision. I smelled and tasted my own blood as it slid hot and bitter down my throat.

Shaking my head, I missed seeing him round on me, his jaws latching onto my front shoulder.

Yelping, I snarled at him, my teeth snapping near his face until they found purchase. The taste of his blood mixed with mine, and my wolf smiled knowing we had drawn blood.

With a sharp howl, Trace twisted away from me, my teeth ripping through the soft cartilage of his ear.

Panting, I tried to collect myself, unable to put a lot of weight on my front leg.

Trace shook his head, blood splattering the snow nearby.

His pack was in a line behind him, several feet away. They wouldn't insult their alpha by jumping into his fight. But if I beat Trace, there was no way I could hold off an entire pack.

And if Trace won, I didn't know if Larkin could hold him off before Remy and the others arrived.

*Remy.*

I could feel him gain ground, closing in on us. His thoughts were a wild mess of fear and fury. But through our bond, I could also feel his strength. Alpha strength. Strength I needed.

I didn't wait for Trace to make another move. I threw

myself at him, managing to catch him by surprise and knock him to the ground. His jaws closed around the paw of my injured leg, but I managed to close mine around a hunk of skin and fur near his neck, sinking my fangs in.

With a roar of pain, he managed to work his legs between us, pushing me off of him violently.

I slid away on my bad shoulder, the powdery pillow of snow taking some of the brunt of my weight.

Larkin yelped behind me, wanting to help, urging me to get up, but she wouldn't leave Katy unprotected.

With a fierce snarl, Trace got to his feet, looming over me.

I struggled to find my footing, my feet sliding on the ice, unable to gain traction on my injured leg. Trace jumped on me, pressing me into the frozen ground.

I had lost.

Panting hard, I looked up into his golden eyes, cold and cruel. I could practically see the smile in them.

And then the pressure was gone.

I got up, seeing Trace and another wolf tumbled across the white hill, snapping teeth and loud growls echoing through the hillside.

I nearly sagged with relief, seeing Remy nearly on top of Trace.

He was slightly larger than Trace, and he had Trace flipped onto his back, teeth around his neck in what seemed like seconds.

Trace was snarling and snapping uselessly at Remy's legs. He was completely pinned, and my mate wasn't letting him up.

Rhodes came over to me, his dark eyes somber. He nuzzled my side, checking to see if I was okay before going to Katy. As soon as he reached Katy's side, Larkin ran to me, pressing her body against me.

As my adrenaline faded, I sank onto the snow, my shoulder and paw throbbing. My nose still stung from the blow Trace had gotten in when we first went at each other. I let out a soft whimper, keeping my eyes firmly trained on Remy.

The rest of the pack had lined up across from the Norwood wolves, snarling and growling at them, but everyone stayed on their own sides.

I heard a motor in the woods and a second later, several snowmobiles came into view, the girls who had ran for help leading the way to us.

One of the teachers jumped off their vehicle and ran to Katy with a medical kit.

"Leg's broken," he called over. "We need to load her onto one of the stretchers and get her back to the infirmary now."

"Let him go, Remy," another teacher ordered, not trying to get between the alphas.

With a growl and one last shake, he released Trace.

Someone dropped down next to me and I looked up to see Amanda, our English teacher. "Jesus, what the hell happened?"

She touched my paw, and I yelped in pain, pulling away and tucking it under my body.

Remy gave a low growl coming over to push Amanda away.

Eyes wide, Amanda backed off, her gaze swinging from me to Remy and back. Fascinated wonder spread across her face as she gasped. After a second, she stood up and went back to her snowmobile.

Remy licked my muzzle, a low whine in his throat

*What the hell happened?*

He was furious, barely containing his rage.

I tried to look around him to see Katy.

Amanda came back, holding sets of clothes in her arms. She looked at Remy. "We need to know what happened. Change back so we can talk."

She held up a set of clothes and moved around behind a tree, dropping them there before she went to the other teacher who was with Trace, giving him similar instructions.

Remy snarled softly, looking at the tree several yards away from me.

*Go. I'm okay.*

He dropped his head, his breath fanning across my face and he gently nuzzled against me, then he headed for the tree. It took less than a minute for him to shift and get his clothes on, not bothering to lace his boots and put on a jacket.

Trace came from behind his own tree, his ear bleeding and a deep gouge on his neck. I smiled to myself knowing I had caused some damage to him.

"What the fuck?" Remy roared, charging at Trace, his eyes murderous. Amanda stepped in front of him, and he was barely able to keep from running her over. His hands were rock hard fists at his sides.

Trace glared at him from several feet away, the other teacher still near his side to hold him back if needed. "It was an accident. It's fucking slippery, and I didn't see Katy until it was too late, and then your *bitch* attacked me!"

"You're a fucking liar," Remy hissed, chest heaving. "You intentionally ran into Katy, and then you attacked Skye!"

"You weren't even here," Trace spat. "You didn't see a damn thing."

Thanks to our bond, Remy knew exactly what had happened because he got a front row mental play-by-play as I lived it.

But that wasn't something we needed to get into right this second.

"Everyone needs to calm down," Amanda said sternly. "We need to get Katy back to the school, and then we can get everyone's statements to figure out what happened."

The teacher near the Norwood pack looked at Trace. "Shift back and get your pack back to your cabin. I'll be there as soon as Katy gets settled to talk to all of you."

"Remy," Amanda said softly, touching his arm gently, "can you help us get Katy on the stretcher?"

He gave a curt nod, waiting until Trace had shifted back into his wolf and took off with his pack in the opposite direction.

"Skye's hurt, too," he said coldly, jerking his head in my direction.

Amanda frowned. "We only have one stretcher with us, and Katy needs that leg looked at immediately. Let's get Katy back and we can come back for Skye." She looked at me. "Unless you think you can take it easy and make it down?"

I pushed myself to my feet slowly, testing my bad leg. It ached, but I could put weight on it. We were barely a mile out from the cabin. I could make it there.

Remy looked pissed, his jaw tight as he looked at me and then at Katy. She was quiet now, the teacher likely giving her a sedative to help move her.

"Rhodes," he barked, looking at his beta. "Get everyone back to the cabin. Do not let Skye out of your sight. Send one of the others to get me if she needs help getting back."

Rhodes barked in reply.

"All of you follow Rhodes. Get changed and wait for me at the cabin," he ordered the pack. Looking at me, he came over and crouched in front of me. His hand came up, stroking my head.

"Do *not* play the hero, Skye," he said firmly. "If you're in too much pain, stop and we'll send another stretcher. I swear I will lose my damn mind if something else happens to you, too."

I dipped my head in acknowledgment, bumping his chin with my nose.

Letting out a frustrated breath, he pressed a kiss to the star on my forehead and stood up. He went over to Katy, his expression fierce as he gently lifted her into his arms without any help and carried her to the stretcher, helping Amanda and the other teacher strap her down.

They all got onto the snowmobiles, Remy sitting on the stretcher with Katy to watch her. His eyes stayed on me until they turned a corner out of sight.

## 33

THE WALK BACK WAS SLOW, NOT ONLY BECAUSE OF MY LEG, but because more snow started to fall at a rapid pace. Rhodes and Larkin stayed pressed to my sides, checking every few feet to make sure I was still OK.

Mostly I was just tired. I wanted to get back to the cabin and snuggle up in front of the fireplace with Remy.

I could have cried in relief when we finally made it to the cabin. The pack separated, but Rhodes hesitated, clearly taking Remy's order not to let me out of his sight, literally.

Larkin was the one who nudged him away.

Shifting back was the most painful shift of my life, worse even than the first.

My human skin was split open, the wounds pulling as my bones reformed. I was panting and shaking by the time I was done shifting. Thankfully Larkin and the younger girls immediately rallied around me, pulling my clothes as gently over my body as possible before ushering me around the side of the house.

Rhodes was waiting there. His eyes went wide when he

saw me. He crossed the remaining feet to us and swung me up into his arms, carrying me inside the house.

Some of the pack members were in the kitchen, pulling out food and starting pots of coffee and hot water for tea. All conversation ceased as Rhodes carried me in and up the stairs. He went past all the doors until he got to Remy's room, setting me on the bed gently.

Larkin followed him in, closing the door.

"How bad is it?" Rhodes asked, his voice more serious than I had ever heard. His dark eyes glanced at Larkin.

I rolled my shoulder gently, hissing out a breath. "It hurts, but I think I'm okay." I looked down at my hand. There were scratches and a couple of deeper punctures from where Trace's teeth had broken the skin.

"Can you get us a first aid kit? I'm going to get her into the bathroom and see if we need a doctor." Larkin gave Rhodes a gentle shove away from me, taking charge of the situation.

Rhodes hesitated, his eyes still on Larkin. "Are *you* okay?"

Her shoulders drooped, her eyes kind as she tried to reassure him. "I'm fine. But I need to look at Skye."

Rhodes gave her a sharp nod. "There's a first aid kit under the sink in Remy's bathroom."

"All right," Larkin said. "Help me get her into the bathroom and then wait for us downstairs."

I made a small sound of protest. "Guys, I can walk—"

The look on Rhodes' face shut me up. I let him lift me up again, carrying me into the bathroom and setting me on the closed lid of the toilet seat. He hurried out of the bathroom, closing the door.

Larkin turned to me, all business. "Let's get your shirt off and see what the damage is."

I nodded, trying to help her pull the shirt off of me,

but it was already sticky with blood from my shoulder. She was gentle as she peeled it away from my body, but it still hurt like a bitch.

"Shit," she swore, looking at my shoulder. She turned and reached under the sink for the first aid kit, opening it on the counter. She pulled out a small bottle and a thick stack of gauze before turning apologetic eyes to me. "This is going to hurt."

I gritted my teeth as the alcohol made contact with my torn flesh, nearly screaming from the searing pain.

Someone knocked on the door.

"I have the bag of clothes you brought for Skye," Rhodes called through the door. "It's right here."

"Thanks," Larkin called, still cleaning the wound.

I took deep breaths through my nose until she finished.

"Some of this is deep," she muttered. "I think you might need stitches."

"I'll be fine," I replied as she moved to cleaning my hand. I glanced down at my shoulder. The front part I could see was already bruising, and I could see a set of teeth marks in the center of the bruising. The back of my shoulder ached the most. That was where his teeth had really clamped down.

After she cleaned my hand, Larkin looked at my face with narrow eyes. She wiped under my nose. "There's a little bit of blood, but your nose isn't even bruised. I don't think he broke it."

"It doesn't feel broken," I said. It still hurt, but not nearly as bad. I was stupidly glad my face wasn't messed up. The wounds on my arm I could hide under clothes. I didn't want people staring at my face.

Larkin moved to the door and opened it quickly, pulling the bag inside the bathroom before shutting the door again. She started pulling out clothes.

"Maybe I should take a shower first?" I suggested, looking longingly at the large shower in the corner of the bathroom. There was even a bench, so I didn't have to stand for long.

Larkin shook her head. "No. The bleeding has slowed a lot. The water might pull some of it open, and then you would definitely need stitches."

"Ugh," I muttered, just wanting to wash all the mess away.

Larkin rummaged through the drawers and pulled out a washcloth. "This is the best I can do for now."

She wet the cloth and cleaned me up as best and gently as she could. Once she was finished, she helped me into new underwear and my jeans, which might have been humiliating if I wasn't so bone weary. She finished helping me with the clasp on my bra when there was another knock at the door.

"Let him in," I said immediately, my heart slamming against my ribs.

Larkin's eyes went wide, her hands still holding my shirt. "Rhodes can wait until you have a shirt on."

I shook my head, getting up and moving past her. "It isn't Rhodes."

I opened the door with my good arm, barely able to step away from the door before Remy was inside and crushing me to his chest. His hands were shaking as they pressed against my lower back, his lips finding mine in a searing kiss that had my bones turning to jelly for all the right reasons.

"Easy!" Larkin admonished from behind me.

Remy pulled back, his dark eyes wild and angry. His expression darkened, his teeth grinding so hard I heard it, as he looked at my shoulder and then my hand.

"Katy?" I asked.

"Doctor set her leg. She's going to stay in the infirmary for a day or so. Dante sent Ryder to stay with her so I could come back here," he answered, his voice rough and thick with emotion. He smoothed his hands over my face, unable to stop touching me.

His eyes flickered back to Larkin. "How bad is it?"

"The wound in her hand isn't too deep. It should heal in a few days. Her shoulder is a bit more mangled, but I don't think it'll need stitches." She set my shirt down on the counter and gave me a small smile. "I'll leave you guys alone."

Remy waited for her to close the door before he was pulling me close again. "You scared the hell out of me, Skye."

My good arm went around his back, trying to soothe the trembling muscles there. "It wasn't the highlight of my day, either."

He gave me another brief kiss before helping me into my shirt. To his credit, he had barely looked at me beyond my injuries, keeping his movements clinical. I wasn't sure if I was happy or disappointed about that.

Remy led me into his bedroom, setting me on the bed and standing across from me. "Tell me what happened."

I relayed the entire story, trying to keep my tone calm even as he grew more and more agitated.

"Is he out of his fucking mind?" Remy snapped when I finished. He raked a hand through his dark hair.

"I guess there's a chance it was an accident? But it looked deliberate to me," I said. The more I replayed it, the more Trace seemed to shoot out of the tree line like a bullet aimed at Katy.

"It was absolutely deliberate," Remy growled, eyes flashing. "First Larkin, then he hurts Katy and he attacks you?"

"But ultimately it's our word against his," I replied bitterly. "His whole pack was there. You know they're going to back him up."

"He could have killed Katy," Remy whispered. He turned his eyes to me, his expression tortured. "He could have killed *you*. What if he had gone for your throat?"

Telling Remy that Trace actually had tried to go for my throat probably wouldn't help a damn thing. I wasn't entirely sure Trace wouldn't have killed me and then Larkin, maybe even Katy, if Remy and the pack hadn't arrived when they did.

I sighed, pulling my legs up onto the bed. "I should have stayed with the pack. We shouldn't have split up."

"This is not your fault," he replied quickly, folding his arms over his heaving chest.

"Did the doctor say Katy will be okay?"

He nodded. "Yeah. The break was clean and in a good place, whatever that means. Thank God we're shifters. If she was a normal it would take months followed by physical therapy for this to heal. As it is, she'll be in a cast for a few weeks."

"Have you called your dad?" I asked, knowing the Alpha needed to know what had happened, not only as the leader of our pack but as Katy's dad.

"I will after we talk to the faculty. They're putting together a group of teachers to look into this. All the packs will be notified once they finish their investigating. They'll probably issue mandatory boundaries for packs for the rest of the semester." He snorted, his wolf clearly annoyed by having a set area where it could go.

Before I could respond, the bedroom door opened and Rhodes poked his head in. "The council is here to talk to Skye."

It was exactly what I said it would be—Trace's word against ours. Almost his entire pack testified that I attacked him without provocation after he accidentally ran into Katy. Thankfully, the council was saying I acted under duress due to Katy being injured. In shifter terms, not guilty by reason of temporary insanity.

It was bullshit, and Remy was beyond furious.

Katy had woken up later that day and admitted she hadn't seen what happened. She just knew she had been hit and then lots of pain. The doctor gave her another dose of pain medicine, and she went back to sleep.

Remy had the McAllister twins replace Ryder to stay with Katy. The odds of anything happening to her in the infirmary were slim to none, but he wasn't taking any chances. He had assigned rotating shifts of Blackwater pack members to guard Katy.

He had barely let me out of his sight except to go to the bathroom. I had a feeling I would be spending another night in the cabin.

Not that I minded.

I had gone to see Katy a few hours earlier, and the doctor checked me out. I didn't need stitches, but he advised me to get lots of rest and take it easy for the remainder of the weekend. After checking in with Katy, Remy ushered me back to the cabin where I got my wish of curling up in front of the fireplace, cuddled to his side while he talked to Rhodes and Larkin in low voices. I managed to doze off for a little while.

Dinner later that evening in the cafeteria was a strange experience. Hardly anyone spoke, but there was a clear division line between the school to the point where tables and chairs were moved to show a physical line separating the two groups.

Remy kept an eye on Trace and his pack the entire time, his body stiffening anytime one of them got up.

"He won't try anything here," I said softly, resting my hand on his thigh under the table.

"She's right," Dante added, but I noticed he was just as wary of them.

"He should have been kicked out of school," Rhodes said darkly, stabbing his chicken with his fork. "Or had his ass kicked."

"He won't get away with it," Remy replied coldly.

I exchanged a worried look with Larkin. If Remy retaliated in any way now, he would probably be the one kicked out of school. The school council had ordered the Blackwater and Norwood alphas to stay away from each other.

My gaze flicked to Trace and I couldn't help the smug smile from ghosting across my lips. He had several deep scratches on his neck and walked into the cafeteria with a bit of a limp.

He might have beaten me, but I hadn't gone down easy.

Finished with my food, I pushed it away and leaned my head against Remy's shoulder, letting my eyes droop closed.

"Want to go back to the cabin?" he asked.

I shook my head. "No. Just resting."

His lips pressed against my hair for a second, his arm coming around the back of my chair so I could snuggle against his side. The steady thump of his heartbeat helped calm me, and I realized after a minute that my pulse was beating in time with his.

I opened my eyes as someone cleared their throat at the table.

Amanda stood across from me with a grim smile. "How are you feeling, Skye?"

"Okay," I replied, lifting my head.

Her gaze flicked back and forth between Remy and me. "Elias asked me to see if you would be up to talking with him. Both of you, actually."

"Why?" Remy asked.

"I told him what I saw in the woods," she replied softly. "Remy, it's obvious Skye is your mate. This is completely unprecedented for wolves your age, and he has a few questions for you, if you're up for it."

Remy looked down at me. "Your call. We can talk to him tomorrow if you're too tired."

I shook my head, sitting up. "No. Let's go."

## 34

Elias' office was just as crowded and cramped as the other times I had been in there, but things seemed even more disorganized now, if that were possible. The older shifter was still at his desk and gave us a warm, but haggard, smile when we came inside. The loveseat that was usually covered in books and papers had been cleared for us to sit on.

"How are you, my dear?" he asked me, his eyes concerned.

"I'm okay," I replied, pulling one of my legs under my body. The movement made my body lean into Remy, his arm immediately lifting and coming around me.

Elias raised his brows. "So, it is true. You've bonded."

We both nodded, and Elias grinned at us.

"Amazing," he breathed. "When did this happen?"

"Last week," Remy replied, his knuckles dragging absent-minded circles on my shoulder. "We haven't told many people."

Elias waved a hand. "Of course not. It's your own business, but I hope you don't mind an old man asking a few questions?"

Remy shrugged. "It's fine."

"Are you both comfortable with the bond?" Elias leaned forward.

I glanced at Remy. "It's been an adjustment, but yeah. We're both good with it."

"Have you been able to communicate when you shift?"

"Yes," Remy answered.

"Verbally?"

I raised my brows. "Is there another way?"

Elias frowned. "Oftentimes when a new pair bonds, the communication bond is … more impressions than actual thoughts or words. The longer the pair is bonded, the clearer the communication becomes."

I looked at Remy and blinked. "I heard you the night we bonded."

He nodded at me. "Same. Your voice has always been clear. Especially today."

"So, you were able to reach out to Remy when you and Trace had your … altercation?" Elias looked absolutely fascinated, his eyes big as they watched me.

"Yeah. I mean, I was able to tell him what happened and where we were."

A dark look crossed Remy's face and I knew he was blaming himself for not getting to us sooner. I pressed against him harder, trying to reassure him that I was still here and in one piece.

"This is remarkable," Elias murmured. He leaned back in his chair, folding his arms over his stomach. "I watched you earlier, in the cafeteria, before I asked Amanda to get you. I don't think you even are aware of the way you act."

"The way we act?" I repeated skeptically.

"Like you're orbiting one another. One of you moves

and the other moves to counter it, balancing each other. I've seen it before in bonded mates, but usually only ones that have been together for several years." He sighed. "Forgive my frankness, but it's highly unusual for two teenagers to find their true mate, let alone reach the level of harmony you both have. And it's only been a week."

Elias swept a hand over the office. "I've been trying to find any information, but the youngest bonded mates we have on record were both twenty-two."

I glanced at Remy. We knew that it wasn't common, but to be the only teenagers who ever bonded?

*Chalk up another mark in the 'Ways I'm a Freak' column.*

Elias turned his attention to me, his expression guarded. "How are you handling the added ... intimacy?"

I stiffened, not entirely sure what he was implying. "Excuse me?"

Remy bristled beside me but stayed quiet. I didn't have to see his face to know he was glaring at the older man by the way Elias ducked his head.

"I know there were things in your past you preferred not to discuss," Elias explained slowly, looking hesitantly at me.

"Remy knows who I am. He knows about Long Mesa," I replied after a moment.

"So, you trust him?"

"Or course." I didn't hesitate to answer. It was the truth. I had gone from a girl who trusted no one to a girl who had a circle of people she trusted implicitly.

And Remy was at the center of that circle.

He gave me a reassuring squeeze, careful not to touch my hurt shoulder.

"Remy, how are you handling being a mate and an alpha?" Elias turned his focus to Remy, his eyes assessing the boy beside me.

Remy sighed. "It's been an adjustment, but I think I'm handling it all right. Today was definitely the biggest test I've had yet."

"Trace," Elias surmised, rubbing his jaw. "How did you handle the Norwood alpha's incident?"

Remy snarled softly under his breath. "It wasn't an incident. He attacked my sister and then he attacked my mate."

"And yet he is still breathing."

"I should have killed him," Remy muttered.

"No, you shouldn't have," I said sharply. "You got him away from us and immobilized him. You protected us, Rem."

"You didn't let your emotions rule you," Elias agreed. "As an alpha you did the right thing. As a mate you did the right thing. You wouldn't be with Skye right now if you had gravely injured or even killed Trace. You would be held for questioning and possibly banished from Granite Peak. Killing another alpha outside a formal challenge could mean stripping you of your own pack rank or worse."

"Wait," I started, leaning forward. "You mean Remy could be removed as alpha? For beating the shit out of Trace?"

"If Trace or his father, the Norwood Alpha, made a formal complaint with the Shifter Council, yes," Elias replied. He inclined his head to Remy. "You know this is true."

"He's right," Remy told me softly. "There are rules of conduct for Alphas. If we can't keep ourselves in check, how can we lead an entire pack?"

"And no one is asking how Trace can lead a pack? After what he did?" I demanded. "He could have killed Katy."

"The school council ruled it an accident," Elias said simply.

"That's bullshit!" I snapped. "He got his entire pack to lie for him. He was the one who started this whole thing."

"What reason would he have to do that?" The old man quirked a brow up.

I paused then and turned slowly to look at Remy. "He's baiting you."

Remy frowned. "What?"

"Think about it," I said, my words coming out fast. "Larkin, then hurting Katy, attacking me ... Hell, he's dating Sierra, a member of your pack, who conveniently likes to let people think you two had a thing last year."

"But what's the end game then?" Remy's eyes narrowed in thought.

"Maybe his dad put him up to it because of what happened with your parents?"

"That was years ago. It doesn't make sense." He wasn't convinced, doubt evident on his face.

"Norwood and Blackwater have been at odds for years," Elias reminded us. "If Trace can unseat you in the pack, it may cause enough of a disruption prior to the Summit to give Norwood the foothold it needs in the Council to push through their agenda regarding the arranged matings."

"The one where Alphas would set up all mate pairs, right?" I asked.

Elias nodded. "It would explain why Trace is antagonizing you specifically. We both know that Blackwater is held in high esteem with the Council. Smearing the reputation of your pack may help them with their proposal."

"It's working," Remy admitted darkly. "If he goes after another member of my pack, I don't know if I'll stop myself from putting him out of commission for good."

My heart thumped hard in my chest while my blood ran cold at the idea of Remy losing it and being taken away.

"You can't let him win," I replied. "We close ranks—no one goes anywhere alone. When we're out as a pack, we stay together."

"It might not be enough," Remy replied with a frown, his dark brows drawn together. "And if he tries anything else with you ..."

"From what I've seen, your mate can hold her own," Elias remarked casually.

I gave him an incredulous look. "Trace beat me today. If Remy hadn't shown up when he did—"

"One moment in one fight. On your first day, all I heard about was the new girl who stared down the Norwood alpha. If he wanted to come for you, he would have. He likely only turned his attack on you today because he felt he had to." Elias shook his head. "His wolf knows yours could easily challenge his."

Now I laughed. "A female Alpha? Right."

"Why not?" Elias asked, cocking his head to the side.

"Because females can't be Alphas," I said slowly.

His hand settled on the book that was always near him. The leather-bound book with the wolf and the star on the cover. "That was not how it always was, my dear girl."

"Females used to be Alphas?" Even Remy wasn't convinced.

"Females were revered," Elias told us with a smile. "They were worshiped. They led packs, cultivated the population. The role of the male was to protect the female and over time, that evolved into males controlling females."

Elias looked at me. "You remember the story I told you when you first came to see me? About Namina and the Romani?"

The fairy tale? That's what he was talking about?

I nodded slowly.

"Namina was the first Alpha of the first pack, but as the years continued, the packs became more male dominated. As is true with most cultures, not just shifters, the males let themselves be ruled by fear. Instead of elevating females, they sheltered them. And when that didn't fix things, they controlled them. But if you look at the bylaws, the wording states any shifter may challenge an Alpha. There is no distinction on the sex of the challenger."

"So, you're saying I should challenge Trace?"

Remy sucked in a sharp breath, already opening his mouth to shut that idea down.

Elias chuckled. "Not at all. I'm simply saying, females have more power than they know. More than many of us know. One day, I pray the shifter world realizes the truth."

☾

DINNER WAS OVER and the main building cleared of people when we left Elias' office. Remy took my hand in his, leading us down the path to the cabin.

"My dorm is that way," I said, pointing down another path.

He was strangely quiet. "I know," he said after a minute. "Can you just stay with me tonight? So I know you're safe? Please?"

I was only teasing when I mentioned where my room was; I was already planning on staying at the cabin again. It was the *'please'* that fractured a tiny piece of my heart.

He wasn't just worried, he was scared.

First Larkin had been hurt on his watch. Then Katy had been hurt. And finally, I had been hurt.

Remy needed to have eyes on at least one of us tonight to make sure we were safe.

I leaned my head against his shoulder. "I'm not leaving you. But can we swing by my dorm so I can grab some clothes and stuff to take a shower?"

He nodded, guiding me down the other path. After a minute of walking we reached the dorm and I led him up to my room. I opened the door and Larkin was sitting on her bed, her phone in her lap.

She waved the phone at us. "Rhodes keeps checking in. He's really paranoid."

"Skye is coming back to the cabin with me. Why don't you come, too?" Remy suggested, shoving his hands into his pockets as I grabbed an overnight bag from the bottom of my closet. "That way you're not here alone."

I glanced at Larkin, giving her an imploring look. I just needed her to humor Remy right now. He needed to know we were all safe.

Larkin nodded and got off the bed, starting to pack her own things.

Remy sank down on the edge of my bed, dropping his chin to his chest and letting out a long breath.

I finished throwing some toiletries into my bag on top of my clothes and zipped it shut, dropping the bag by the door and walking over to him. I rested my forearms loosely on his shoulders, looking down at him.

"We're going to be fine," I said softly, wishing like hell I could take some of the burden from him.

He nodded slowly before wrapping his arms around me, pulling me between his legs and resting his head on my chest.

"I know," he mumbled, his voice a deep rumble I felt in my bones.

Larkin zipped her bag, giving me a small smile. "Ready."

Remy gave my waist a quick squeeze and stood up, grabbing both of our bags and shouldering them before we could pick them up. We didn't speak as we left the dorms, heading across campus, and to the cabin.

The paths had been cleared of snow, and no one else seemed to be out. The heavy blanket of snow added another layer of silence to the air. Everything was still and quiet, the only sounds were our boots crunching through the snow.

Remy opened the door to the cabin and Rhodes shot off the couch. No one could miss the relieved expression on his face when Larkin came in with us.

"The girls are staying here tonight," Remy said unnecessarily. He glanced at Larkin. "Come on. I'll show you to your room."

We were all quiet heading up the stairs. Even Rhodes was somber, coming up last.

Remy moved down the hall, opening the guest room door with the queen bed. I saw him hesitate, his eyes flickering to me.

I took the decision out of his hands.

"Your room, Larkin." I waved a hand at the next door down. "I'll be with Remy if you need me."

Thankfully, my best friend didn't question me. She just gave me a supportive smile and nodded.

Remy gave me a small smile as he handed Larkin her bag.

"Do you need anything?" Rhodes asked her.

Larkin started to shake her head, but then paused, seeing the lost look in his eyes. He wanted to feel helpful in some way.

"Let me get changed and then we can watch a movie?" she offered.

Rhodes nodded, a smile brightening his face. "I'll go make some popcorn and meet you down there. You two in?" He looked at Remy and me.

"You can," I told Remy. "I'm tired. I just want to sleep."

"We're good," Remy told his best friend, his eyes never leaving mine. We went into Remy's room where he closed the door, setting my bag on the chair by the window.

I sighed, toeing off my shoes. "I just want a shower and sleep," I moaned. My body ached from everything that had happened today. From my feet to the roots of my hair, I was exhausted. I opened my bag and started pulling out stuff I needed for my shower.

"Do you need me to do anything?" he asked.

I pulled out my pjs and hesitated, giving him a nervous look. "Actually? I might need your help getting my top off."

He swallowed visibly, giving me a jerky nod. "Sure. Whatever you need."

He followed me into the bathroom, turning on the light. He opened the linen closet door and pulled out a thick towel, setting it next to my clothes on the countertop.

We stared at each other for a moment before I laughed, nervous by the whole situation.

"This is silly, right? I mean, you literally saw me with my shirt off earlier," I stammered, my cheeks heating.

"Exactly." But his cheeks were slightly red, his pupils dilated. Slowly, his hands reached for the hem of my shirt, helping me lift it over my head. He was careful not to touch any part of me while he did it.

I winced as I pulled my shoulder.

"Sorry," he said quickly, dropping my shirt to the floor.

He frowned as he looked at the bandages on my shoulder. "Do you want—"

I nodded and he slowly started peeling the stained gauze off of me. I tried to stay still and not hiss when he tugged on part of the gauze that had stuck to my shoulder where the blood had dried. After a second, he tossed the used material into the trash in the corner.

"When you get done, I'll wrap your shoulder again," he said softly. "But it's starting to heal."

I nodded and then grimaced. "Um ... I still need your help."

The clasp of my bra was in the back and I couldn't unhook it with my one hand that Trace had bitten.

"Right," he said softly, his voice rough.

I turned slowly, giving him my back. His fingers traced up the line of my spine and I shivered under his touch, goosebumps breaking out across my flesh. He swept my hair to the side.

His fingers deftly undid the clasp, the straps of my bra falling down to my elbows. I held the cups up with my good hand, feeling his breath warm on the back of my neck.

The pure intimacy of the moment struck me dumb for a second.

I wasn't embarrassed at all, but parts of my body were waking up, prickling with newfound awareness under his gaze.

I jumped as his lips touched the base of my neck, and then I relaxed back into him, letting out a sigh of bliss as his lips feathered across my skin.

"Do you need anything else?" he asked, his voice sounding like he dragged it through gravel for a mile.

It took a second for his words to register. I shook my head, unable to formulate actual words to answer with.

"I'm okay," I said after a second, my words coming out in a breathless rush as I struggled to get air into my lungs.

"Yell if you need me," he said softly, backing out of the room and shutting the door.

Taking a shower mostly one handed wasn't great. It took a lot of maneuvering, and I almost screamed when the water droplets hit my shoulder. I adjusted the spray settings on the massive shower head to a gentler speed. It would take forever to rinse my thick hair, but at least my shoulder didn't hurt as bad.

I managed to clean myself up, shutting off the water and awkwardly wrapping the towel around my body. I dried off as best as I could, patting my shoulder gently to absorb the water. I tugged on my underwear and sleep shorts before wrestling myself into my tank top and quickly brushing my teeth.

I was exhausted and breathing hard by the time I finished.

Remy knocked on the door. "You okay?"

"You can come in," I told him, the door opening before I finished speaking.

His eyes swept over me. "Feel better?"

I nodded, checking out my bare shoulder in the mirror. It was already starting to heal in places, the bruising fading around the edges.

Remy took the first aid kit from under the counter and pulled out the last of the supply of gauze. He worked swiftly and efficiently, wrapping me up securely in less than a minute.

"Good as new," I said, smiling at him in the mirror.

A small smile drifted across his lips. "Almost."

I reached for my hairbrush, tugging it one-handed through my hair.

With a laugh, Remy pulled the brush from my hands

and took over the task himself. He gently worked the brush through the knots in my hair. I watched him in the mirror, smiling inwardly at the expression of concentration on his face as he slowly brushed different sections of my hair until it was smooth and wet, the ends dripping against my lower back.

He leaned forward, pressing his nose into my hair and sniffing lightly. "You smell amazing."

I smiled, leaning into his touch. "You ... don't." I wrinkled my nose at him and made a face. It was a lie—he smelled like Remy, incredible and irresistible. But I needed a break from the heaviness of the moment. The simple domesticity of the moment was unnerving me a bit and I needed a second to gather my thoughts.

"Brat," he muttered, pulling away. "I'm going to take a shower."

I scurried out of the bathroom so he could jump in the shower. I closed the door behind me, leaning against the wood and trying not to think about the fact that a very naked, very wet Remy was going to be behind that door in a few seconds.

Licking my lips, I tried to ignore the low pulse starting between my thighs.

I went to the bed, pulling back the covers and sliding into the sheets. Unlike last night when I had accidentally fallen asleep in here, this time it was intentional.

I pressed my nose into the pillow and inhaled deeply. It smelled like pure Remy. The scent wrapped around me, my body melting boneless into the mattress.

I was almost asleep when the door to the bathroom opened. I heard Remy moving around the bedroom and a second later the lights flipped off. I listened to the sound of his feet moving across the floor, getting closer to me.

He slipped into the bed, the mattress dipping under his weight as he laid down beside me.

I started to scoot back towards him as he reached for me at the exact same moment. I settled against his front, feeling the heat of his bare chest pressed to the exposed skin of my back. His arm tightened around my waist and we both sighed deeply, our heart beats finding the same rhythm.

I was asleep in seconds.

**35**

I**T WAS WELL INTO THE LATE MORNING HOURS WHEN** I **WOKE** up. My body ached, stiff and sore, as I slowly stretched. My shoulder didn't hurt quite as bad as the day before, and my hand was mostly healed.

But I was glaringly alone in Remy's massive bed.

I sat up, looking around, but he was nowhere to be seen. The bathroom door was open, but the light was off.

Sitting in the middle of the bed, I listened closely. I could hear voices downstairs, too far away to make out tones or words, but definitely multiple people.

Swinging my legs over the side of the bed, I stood up, getting my bearings before going into the bathroom. After using the toilet, I washed my hands and quickly brushed my teeth and then my hair before inspecting my shoulder.

It throbbed and ached, which was probably to be expected since it was currently four colors of the rainbow. At least my hand was mostly healed.

I headed back into the bedroom, pausing to grab a hoodie Remy had discarded by his dresser. I managed to pull it on and opened the door, heading downstairs.

Larkin and Tate were sitting on barstools at the island chatting quietly, but they were the only ones I could see. As soon as my feet hit the landing, though, the door to the study opened and Remy came out. He quickly closed the door behind himself before meeting me in the middle.

He brushed my hair out my eyes. "You were sleeping so deep, I didn't want to wake you."

"No worries," I replied. I smiled when he leaned down and kissed me quickly.

"I have to get back in there," he told me, jerking his head at the closed door. His brows creased.

"What's going on?" I reached up to smooth away the worry, my fingertips lingering on his skin.

He shook his head, pressing his face into my touch. "Dante showed up this morning. Another shifter went missing. A female from the Brooks Ridge pack."

My eyes went wide. "Seriously? What the hell?"

He shook his head, jaw tight. "I don't know. Dante, Ryder, Rhodes, and I have a conference call with my dad and the Brooks Ridge Alpha in a few minutes."

Worry curdled like old milk in my stomach at the thought of him leaving. "Are you going to have to leave?"

"I won't leave," Remy replied. "Not now. My dad will agree—with everything happening with Trace, we can't leave the pack members here unprotected."

"How's Katy?"

"Good. Maren is with her now. I'm going to stop by later to see her. I might have her move in here while she's recovering."

I rolled my eyes. "She'll love that."

Remy made a face. "She'll deal with it."

"Rem," Dante called, sticking his head out the study door. He flashed me a tight smile. "How're you feeling, Skye?"

"Good," I told him. I gently pushed Remy. "Go talk. Fill me in later."

He quickly kissed me. "Make sure you eat something." He turned and went into the study, closing the door.

I walked into the kitchen, smiling gratefully as Larkin got up to pour me a cup of coffee. In the few short weeks I had been at GPA, I had become addicted to caffeine. I took the mug from her, taking a tentative sip and bit back a moan of bliss.

This was perfection in a cup.

"How achy are you on a scale from one to ten?" Tate asked, a frown on her pretty face. Her dark hair was pulled back into a long ponytail and she looked super comfy in a pair of leggings and a soft sweater.

I took another sip. "A solid eight-point-seven."

She laughed behind her mug. "Did you take anything?"

I shook my head and Larkin slid two pills across the counter to me, giving me a pointed look.

"I knew you wouldn't take anything," she muttered wryly.

I swallowed the pills down without question before sliding onto a barstool beside Tate.

"Another missing girl?"

Tate's expression darkened. "Yeah."

"Did you know her?"

She nodded grimly. "Yeah. Her name is Sage. She's been with the pack for almost a decade. She came to us after her mate died. She's quiet, kept to herself mostly. Our pack has about half the numbers of yours, but we're so isolated in northern Alaska … We all know each other well."

I reached over and covered her hand with mine. "I'm so sorry."

"The guys are really worried. So is my dad."

"Your dad?" I shot her a stunned look over the rim of my mug.

"Her dad is the Brooks Ridge Alpha," Larkin explained. "What do you want to eat?"

I shrugged. "Food?"

Rolling her eyes, Larkin went to the fridge and started pulling things out.

"So, your dad is the Alpha?" I looked back at Tate.

She nodded. "Technically he's my adopted father, but he raised me."

"I had no idea you were adopted," I said, surprised.

She grimaced slightly, her nose wrinkling. "I didn't have the most ... conventional childhood."

"I'm sorry," I said again automatically, knowing all-too-well how unconventional childhoods could royally suck.

"Thanks," she murmured, tracing the bottom of her mug. "My parents ... They actually never wanted kids. They were mostly lone wolves, but oddly enough were mates. Like you and Remy are. They just didn't like being tethered to a pack, conforming to pack laws. I was an accident, but one they realized pretty quick they could cash in on."

A tendril of dread curled low in my stomach.

She flashed me a weak smile. "I don't remember them much, to be honest. From what I gathered, they kind of sucked as parents. And as people. When they had a daughter, they saw me as a winning lottery ticket or something."

"Shit," I murmured, wincing on her behalf.

"They spent the early part of my life trying to arrange a marriage for me. They would get a family on the hook, get the family to send them ... a down payment. Like some twisted dowry or something. Anyway, they would get the money, and then disappear. They did this for years, before they finally got sick of running around the world with a kid." She shrugged one shoulder. "I was six when they decided to just marry me off for good and be done with it."

"They *sold* you?" I whispered, horrified.

"Yeah," she replied simply, then smiled. "But it back-fired. They sold me to my dad. They only told him he would be getting a future mate—they didn't bother telling him I was a little kid. When he went to the meeting, he was so pissed off, he threatened to drag them in front of the Council and have them executed. They took off but let me behind. He adopted me."

"But your dad was still willing to buy a mate," I said after a second.

She shook her head. "He wasn't. My dad was part of a network of shifters trying to eradicate the trafficking of females. The goal was to buy the female and set her free or offer sanctuary. My dad already had a mate who was back in Brooks Ridge."

"And she adopted you, too?"

A sad look crossed Tate's face and she sighed. "She would have. She was actually pregnant when he brought me home. There was a complication in the last month of her pregnancy. She and the baby died. I only knew her for a few weeks. After that it was Dad and me."

"That's unreal," I said, amazed. I glanced up at Larkin, who was making something on the stove. She gave me a terse nod. She knew this story already.

"My dad raised me by himself for the most part. But he did get help from Dante and Ryder's parents. They were all really close, so the three of us grew up together."

"What happened to your biological parents?"

Another shrug. "They're still out there, I guess. Still being miserable excuses for shifters. No way did they bother to come after me once my dad got involved." Her lips curved into a wicked smile. "They literally pissed their pants when he started yelling. I remember the smell of it as they ran away."

"I'm glad," I said with a grin.

"Me, too," Larkin agreed, sliding an omelet in front of me. She pointed at me with the spatula. "Eat the whole thing or I'm telling Remy."

I picked up the fork and took a huge bite, chewing loudly for her benefit. After I swallowed the chunk of egg and cheese down, I pointed my fork at her. "How did the movie go last night?"

Tate's eyes lit up as she looked at Larkin. "Movie night? You and Rhodes?"

Lifting her cup of coffee, Larkin gave a delicate sniff. "There's nothing to tell. All we did was watch a movie."

I arched a brow. "Is that all?"

Larkin set her cup down, bending at the waist suddenly and dropping her forehead to the counter. "No," she whined. "I might have fallen asleep on him and woken up when he carried me to bed."

Tate and I started cracking up.

"Why don't you just tell him you like him?" I asked through my giggles.

Larkin lifted her head, her eyes narrowed into thin slits. "Because I have been pining after Rhodes DeWitt for years, and I'll be damned if I have to spell it out for the idiot."

Tate smirked. "You could always do what I did—just kiss him and see what happens."

I turned to her quickly. "Is that what happened?"

"Something like that," Tate said with a giggle.

Shaking my head, I looked at Larkin. "You know he's like a lost puppy when you're ignoring him, right?"

"Serves him right," she grumbled, but I could see the smile she was hiding.

"I still think you should talk to him," I argued, eating another bite.

Larkin threw her hands up with a sigh. "Not everyone can have an instant bond with their mate, Skye!"

"Oh, so he's your mate now?" I asked innocently.

With a growl, Larkin dropped her head back to the counter. "I hate you," she muttered.

Tate and I were still laughing when the door to the study opened. Four teenage males all paused outside the door looking at us.

"Are you okay, Larkin?" Rhodes asked.

Tate and I exchanged a look and started laughing even harder. My fork fell against the plate with a loud clatter.

Larkin lifted her head, glaring at us. "You guys suck."

**36**

---

The next several days were beyond intense around school. There wasn't a single pack unaffected by what had happened between our pack and the Norwood pack. Tensions on both sides were insanely high and everyone was on edge.

Battle lines had been drawn, but the battle had yet to actually start, which meant a lot of tense shifters in a confined space.

Remy had wanted me to stay with him in the cabin after spending a second night there. Hell, I had wanted me to stay. I fell asleep breathing in his scent, slept deeper when I was in his arms, and I definitely woke up happier seeing him lying next to me.

But I wasn't ready to go from mates to dating to living together in a week. I still needed my space. The fact that I got so comfortable so quickly had my head spinning a bit, so I was glad when Larkin agreed we should go back to the dorms.

Katy's leg was starting to heal, slower than she would have liked, but still faster than it would have had she not been a shifter. She adamantly refused to move in with Remy, raising hell when he mentioned it. Something about letting the terrorists win if she moved out of her room. Instead, Larkin and I checked in on her constantly, and Maren essentially moved into her room at the dorms. Between the three of us and Tate, Katy was covered when Remy couldn't see her, but we were all under orders not to go anywhere alone.

There was a brutal tension that lingered in the air all the time. Like someone playing with a lighter next to a puddle of gasoline. The explosion was inevitable, but no one knew when it would come. Even the teachers seemed more on edge, snapping at us one minute and then babying us the next.

All week there had been scuffles and fights between the packs. I lost count of how many I had seen Remy step into the middle of.

The biggest change that rocked our pack was when Ainsley and Sierra had a massive falling out at the beginning of classes on Monday. Since then Ainsley stuck closer to the pack, and Sierra ignored her at every turn. It got to the point that Ainsley moved out of the room she and Sierra shared, opting to move in with one of the younger girls from our pack on a different floor.

Remy and I barely found time to hang out, and a date with just the two of us wasn't even mentioned. Neither of us were comfortable leaving the pack alone for hours at a time. We mainly hung out in the cabin in the evenings, but there were usually several people with us at any given moment. All of the pack seemed more at ease when we were together, so it wasn't uncommon for a dozen or so shifters to be piled into the living room together.

I loved my pack, but I was getting tired of Remy's lips finding mine for a second before someone walked in on us.

The only saving grace was Thanksgiving break.

I had been looking forward to the week of Thanksgiving for a while. Classes were suspended for a week, giving everyone time to go home and reconnect with their pack before making the final push to the end of the semester.

I was excited to spend a week with my mom, and more excited to be able to have some alone time with Remy. I wanted to run through the Blackwater territory, letting my wolf out on our home turf. We were all a little testy having not shifted more than a handful of times the last couple of weeks, but wolves were more volatile than our human sides, so shifting had been limited and all pack runs canceled.

Most of the pack was heading for the airport in a bus where they would board a plane for the quick two hour trip back to Washington. With Katy's leg, traveling by plane wasn't an option. Remy decided he would drive her back to their house. No one even asked me if I wanted to come—it was a forgone conclusion, but I wasn't surprised when Larkin and Rhodes also got into the SUV with us.

The trip took almost seven hours. We only stopped a few times for breaks, and we were all seriously antsy when we arrived in Blackwater territory. Our wolves hated being confined in the cab of the truck.

Larkin had been listening to music, ignoring us for the last hour. Katy and Rhodes had been bickering for the last hundred miles. I could tell Remy was even getting annoyed with everyone the way his hand kept tightening around the steering wheel, his knuckles turning white as the leather creaked in protest.

He dropped off Rhodes and Larkin at their houses first since they were neighbors, and then headed up the mountain to his home. Gabe and Mallory had invited my mom and I to have dinner at their house, then Mom and I would go back to our apartment.

I was kind of giddy to see the space. Mom had been talking about it every time we spoke the last couple of weeks. I knew she was excited for me to see it, and I was seriously proud of her for making this work. She seemed to really love Blackwater.

Which was good, since I had no plans of ever leaving this pack.

Remy parked the car in front of his parents' house and looked at me with a grin. Katy was already scrambling out of the backseat awkwardly and limping across the yard to climb up the stairs. At this point her leg was mostly healed and she only needed a brace, but I knew standing or walking too long really tired her out.

"Ready to meet the parents?" Remy joked, unbuckling his seatbelt.

I opened my door. "I've already met your parents."

"As a new pack member," he said with a smile. "Not as my girlfriend."

My smile slipped. Shit, he was right.

Remy closed his door and laughed. "Relax, okay? My parents love you."

"They barely know me," I reminded him as we started for the stairs. I winced inwardly. They knew a lot about my former pack and what mom and I had gone through.

In some ways they knew more about me than Remy did.

Anxiety churned in my gut as I wondered how they would react to Remy and me being together. Yes, we were true mates, but that didn't mean his parents would be excited that the future Alpha of Blackwater was bonded to a girl with the history I had.

Katy had left the front door wide open and we could hear shouting and laughing already from inside.

I froze on the top step when my mom appeared in the doorway.

Sudden emotion choked me, my eyes filling with tears as I ran to her. The second her arms closed around me, we both lost it. We both were crying and speaking mostly in squeals and sighs.

I pulled back, sniffling as I touched the ends of her hair. "You cut your hair!"

"You got taller!" she accused, pulling me in for another hug.

After a minute I pulled back, wiping my eyes and remembering we weren't alone. Gabe and Mallory had come to the front door now and were watching our reunion with smiles.

"Mom, this is Remy," I said, turning and reaching for him.

Remy grabbed my hand with one of his, extending the other to my mom. "It's great to finally meet you, Ms. Markham."

"Addie, please," she said with a watery smile. I had told her before we arrived that I told Remy who we were and about the Long Mesa pack. Mom had cried then, glad I had found someone to trust.

I still hadn't told her about bonding with Remy. Something told me that talk needed to be done in person.

Mallory came out onto the porch, and any worries I had about her accepting me were smashed when she pulled me into her arms and squeezed tight. "How have you gotten even prettier?"

"That's what I keep saying," Remy said with a smirk, his dark eyes dancing with laughter as I tried not to blush.

Gabe pointed at him with a grin. "That's because I raised you right."

Mallory turned and gave him a pointed look, eyebrows raised.

"*We* raised you right," Gabe amended quickly. "It was mostly your mother, though." His blue eyes smiled at me. "It's good to see you, Skye."

"Come inside, all of you," Mallory encouraged. She slapped Gabe's chest as she walked by and he chuckled warmly, grabbing for her waist. She danced out of his reach and headed into the house.

A slow smile spread across my face as I realized that could be Remy and me in a few years.

Happy and together.

Mates.

With a swallow, I looked back to see Remy watching me curiously.

I gave him a weak smile, suddenly a little lightheaded by the idea of a future with this guy. I needed a new subject to focus on. "So, where are these brothers of yours?"

"Careful," he warned. "If you say their names enough, it's like *Beetlejuice*."

I frowned. "Like what?"

"Like—" he cut himself off with a laugh. "It's a movie, Skye. Basically, if you say the guy's name three times, he appears."

"And his name is *Beetlejuice*?" The look on my face only made him laugh harder.

"Yeah."

"That's a stupid name," I muttered.

"What's a stupid name?"

I jumped and spun around to see a set of miniature Remys looking up at me. Whoa.

"Skye, this is Dax and Sam," Remy said, coming up behind me. He pointed them out as he said their names. The one with the shorter hair and black shirt was Dax, the one with the longer hair and button up was Sam. Both had Remy's dark brown hair and similar bone structure, but they had their father's bright blue eyes.

"The girlfriend, right?" Dax asked, his eyes lighting up as he looked at me.

"Be nice," Remy warned.

"We're always nice," Sam added.

"Nice to meet you," I said with a laugh. Remy had said they were thirteen and would be starting GPA next year. They must have hit a growth spurt this year, because they were only a few inches shorter than Remy and a couple inches taller than me. In the family picture he had framed in the cabin, they were a solid foot shorter. They weren't as muscular as Remy, but the frame was there. In a few years they would likely be as big as their brother, and just as good looking.

Dax grinned, sidling up beside me and slinging an arm over my shoulders. I blinked in surprise.

"So, Skye," he started.

Remy ripped his arm off of me with a warning growl that vibrated low in his chest.

I turned, expecting to see Dax and Sam laughing at Remy's possessive streak, but they both looked stunned, eyes downcast.

"Sorry," Dax said, his tone genuinely apologetic. "I was just playing, dude."

Remy huffed out a breath, his eyes rolling to the ceiling as he reigned his wolf in. "It's fine. I'm sorry, too. It was a reaction."

"You're mates," Sam said simply, shrugging.

Dax and Remy turned and stared at him.

"Dad told you?" Remy demanded, his wide eyes looking at me.

Sam shook his head, waving a hand between us. "It's pretty freaking obvious. I've never seen you get all growly over anyone else."

"Dude, you're mated? Like *bonded*?" Dax made a face. "But you're not even out of high school. Isn't that a little soon to sign up for a lifetime commitment?" He gave me a sheepish look. "No offense."

"None taken?" I wasn't sure if I should be offended or not.

Sam slapped Dax's shoulder. "That's not how it works, numb nuts."

Dax glared at his twin. "Call me that one more time and I'll give *you* numb nuts."

"Daxton!" Mallory's sharp voice cut like a whip through the foyer.

Cringing, Dax turned to his mom.

"We have guests," she snapped, jaw set firmly as she gave him the stare every mother had perfected. "Do I need to remind you to act appropriately?"

"No, ma'am," Dax said softly, the picture of innocence. The hard line of Mallory's mouth softened slightly.

These boys were definitely hell on wheels.

"Finish setting the table, please," Mallory instructed the twins before turning back down the hallway.

As the twins headed for the formal dining room, Remy and I went down the hall into the kitchen where more people waited.

"Skye!" Zoe immediately grabbed me in a big hug.

"Hey!" My arms quickly went around her, squeezing tight. "I didn't know you were going to be here. Hi, Michael."

He lifted his wine glass at me and smiled. "Hey, Skye. Remy."

"Michael." Remy did that universal nod thing back at him that they must teach guys in a special elective class or something.

Zoe grinned at me, taking a sip from her glass of water. "When your mom said you were coming home, I begged Mallory to let us come, too. How do you like school?"

"It's been ... great," I said, not entirely sure how to answer. As a whole, it had been. The last week or so, not so much.

Zoe frowned, lines cutting deep into her pretty face. She dropped her voice. "We've all heard about what's happening at the school. How are you doing? I'm sure it's probably triggered some old memories."

I shrugged. "It has, but I'm dealing with it. It's nice having actual friends now. Larkin and Katy are the best." Katy was currently chatting up my mom while they cut up vegetables for a salad. She picked up a carrot from the cutting board and popped it into her mouth.

Her brows raised suggestively, her eyes flickering to where Remy stood talking with his father and Michael. "Just Larkin and Katy?"

I couldn't help the smile that started to pull at my lips, my eyes following her gaze. "Okay, maybe not just them."

Zoe hummed under her breath, green eyes gleaming. She nudged her shoulder into mine. "You seem happier than when you left here."

"I do?"

"There was such a sadness in your eyes," she said, a sad smile on her face. "You always looked like you were waiting for something bad to happen. You are too young to have that look in your eyes, to look so exhausted. Now ...

you look lighter. Like maybe you found someone to help shoulder the burden a bit?"

Suddenly emotion clogged my throat. I coughed, trying to clear the lump as I blinked away tears. "I never knew that being in a pack could feel this way. That I could feel safe."

Sniffing, Zoe pressed her hands to my cheeks. "You are incredible, Skye. And you're going to do great things, I know it."

"Now you're clairvoyant?" I teased, trying to lighten the mood.

Her hand settled over her stomach. "Call it mother's intuition."

"I'm so happy for you and Michael. You're going to be great parents." Whoever that kid was, he or she was going to have an amazing life full of love and support.

"Time to eat!" Mallory called, lifting the serving platter of pot roast. Gabe snatched the heavy plate from her hands with a wry grin, stealing a kiss on the way as he carried it into the dining room.

Dax and Sam were already in their seats, and I noticed that the table had been extended out from the first time I was there to accommodate more people.

Everyone found a seat and, without thinking, I slipped into the seat next to Remy.

My mom glanced up at me across the table, surprise flitting across her face when she noticed I wasn't in the vacant seat to her left. Katy claimed it immediately, flashing me a knowing smile.

Under the table, Remy's hand found my thigh and rested there. I could feel the heat of his hand through the denim of my skinny jeans.

During the meal, we talked about everything except Granite Peak and the pack tensions. It was like the adults all had an unspoken agreement not to bring it up in front of us.

But I saw Gabe's jaw tighten when Katy struggled to get up from her chair, the way Mallory caught herself from asking us about our upcoming finals.

By the time dinner was over, I was exhausted. The week of stress at GPA, the long drive, and a belly full of hot food made me ready to sleep for a week.

Across from me, Katy barely stifled a yawn behind her hand.

"It's getting late," Mallory said, smiling softly at her daughter, but there were small worry lines around her dark eyes as she noticed Katy was getting more and more tired.

It was barely seven o'clock.

My mom stood and started to gather the plates around her when Mallory waved her off.

"Don't worry about that, Addie," she said. "We'll take care of it. Why don't you and Skye head for home? I'm sure she's exhausted, too."

"I can help," I protested.

Remy turned teasing eyes to me. "Are you questioning my mother?"

"She gave you a get out of dishes free card," Dax said, taking a bite of his fifth dinner roll. Everyone had finished eating almost fifteen minutes earlier, except the twins. "Use it while you can. Odds are she'll be treating you like one of us soon enough since you're basically part of the family."

There was a scuffling noise and Dax hissed, glaring at his twin. "Why did you kick me? It's true. She and Remy are practically married since they're bonded and all."

"Dax!" Gabe snapped sharply. I wasn't sure if that was a dad tone or an Alpha tone, but it had Dax blanching.

"Dammit, Dax," Remy muttered, shooting his brother an exasperated look.

Dax held up his hands innocently. "What? It's not like it's a secret. Besides, Skye seems cool. She can be part of the family."

Katy groaned, dropping her head into her open palm. "Shut *up*, Dax."

The table was completely silent and I was having a hard time looking anywhere except my plate.

"What do you mean bonded?" my mom asked calmly, setting her glass down.

My eyes lifted to hers, and I flinched.

She might have sounded calm when she spoke, but her emerald eyes were a turbulent riot of emotions right now.

*Shit.*

**37**

---

"Skye? What's going on?" my mom demanded, her eyes narrowed across the table from me.

How did I even start to answer that question?

I had a whole speech planned out to tell her about Remy and me and the bond. A speech that was best delivered after she was on cloud nine having shown off our new apartment, and we curled up on the couch together.

It definitely wasn't a speech I planned to tell a room full of people, and even if I had wanted to, the words I planned to say vanished like smoke in the wind when I felt all eyes turn to me.

"Addie, maybe we should—" Zoe started softly.

"I need to know what's going on, Zoe," my mom said, her tone quiet but firm. Her eyes never left mine. She arched a single brow. "Skye?"

Remy leaned his shoulder against mine, silently offering support.

I took a deep breath. "Remy and I are mates. Bonded mates."

She blinked once. Twice. Three times.

And then laughed.

Not just a little chuckle, but a full-blown belly laugh that had her gasping and everyone glancing around at each other.

"Very funny," Mom said, wiping her eyes. "You almost had me, kiddo."

"I'm not kidding," I said carefully.

She snorted. "Of course you are. I mean … you're only seventeen. You can't have a mate."

"Adalynne," Gabe said softly. "I know it's hard to believe since they're so young, but they *are* bonded."

Mom's gaze swung down the table to the Alpha. His words seemed to slowly be penetrating her brain. "Bonded?" Her gaze jerked back to me.

I shrugged, helpless. "The bond snapped into place the first time we were shifted together."

Her eyes narrowed as confusion set in. "Are you sure?"

I felt my eyebrows raise. "Do you honestly think I would make up something like this?"

"When exactly did this happen?" she demanded, her eyes flickering to Remy.

"A couple weeks ago," I admitted.

Her face went ashen. "A couple of *weeks* ago? And you're just now mentioning this?" She looked so sad in that moment it broke my heart. She was sad because I kept this from her.

Because I didn't trust her with this.

Without thinking, my hand found Remy's under the table. I needed some sort of physical anchor to him right now.

"I was going to tell you tonight," I said gently, needing her to understand. "I wanted to wait until we were alone so I could explain in person."

Her wide eyes swung back to Gabe and then Mallory. "You knew about this? You all knew?"

"Remy told me when it happened," Gabe admitted, "and I told Mallory."

"We only figured it out right before dinner," Dax added softly, his head ducked. "I'm sorry—I didn't mean to mess anything up." He looked imploringly at me and then Remy, trying to convey how sorry he was.

I gave him a small smile. It wasn't his fault. This was all on me.

Closing her eyes, my mom dropped her chin to the chest, taking several deep breaths. After a heavy pause, she lifted her eyes to me. "Thank you all for dinner. If you don't mind, I need to be excused."

I swallowed, my heart sinking. "We're going home?"

Her jaw tensed and she looked down the table at me, her expression sad. "I need a minute, Skye."

Zoe sighed softly, her hand covering her mouth. "Addie—"

My mom's gaze stayed glued to the table as she stood. She slowly got to her feet, the move fluid and graceful even as her hands shook visibly. "Zo, I need some time to process this. Alone, please."

My hand covered Remy's under the table, my nails digging into the back of his hand as I swallowed my emotions. Katy's eyes were huge across from me.

"Adalynne," Gabe said quietly, his voice patient, "they didn't have a choice in this."

"Believe me, I understand that better than most," my mom whispered, stepping around her chair.

"Mom." I looked at her desperately. No matter what had ever happened, it was always Mom and me. Her leaving me behind, even for a minute, felt like I was being abandoned.

Her gaze snapped to me. "I need a few minutes, honey. It's going to be fine."

Panic swelled up in me. I had made the wrong choice. I had chosen Remy, and it was going to cost me my mother.

I slowly stood up, hearing Remy's low growl as I got to my feet.

"I can come with you."

Her chest heaved as she breathed, nostrils flaring. "Skye—"

"Mom," I cut her off, trying to be as kind as possible despite the storm of emotions brewing in me. "Mom, you need to understand. I'm okay with this. I *want* to be with Remy."

"You're my child," she said, her eyes starting to fill with tears. "All I want is for you to be happy. But this is ... a lot for me to take in right now."

"Let me come with you." I threw my napkin on my plate. "We need to talk about this!"

"Skye ..." Her voice shook as she tried to stay calm for both of us. "Baby, you have to know this isn't the life I wanted for you."

My hand landed on Remy's shoulder, touching the rock-hard muscles tensed there. "Mom, please listen to me. No one is making me do anything. This is my choice. I'm so sorry I didn't tell you before—that's on me. But I was going to tell you tonight that I choose Remy." I sucked in a shaky breath, biting my lower lip. "Please don't be upset I didn't tell you. I wasn't trying to hide anything from you, I swear."

I drew in a ragged breath. "Can't you be happy for me?"

With an anguished cry, the dam broke in my mom and she started crying. With a sob, she shoved away from the table and all but ran from the room. The front door slammed a second later.

Zoe immediately got to her feet. "I'll go after her."

"No, I will," I said, shaking my head, feeling completely gutted.

Remy lifted his eyes to mine. He knew how much I was hurting, and I could see it was killing him that there was nothing he could do. "Babe."

I raised the hand on his shoulder to his face, cradling his jaw and smiling when he leaned into my touch. "I know. I'll be back in a minute."

He turned his head, kissing the palm of my hand.

I turned to Gabe. "I'm sorry—"

Mallory sighed. "Honey, you don't have to explain anything to us. We all knew this would be an adjustment. I think something else is going on here. Give her time to sort out her emotions, love."

I nodded and hurried out of the house to catch up to Mom.

I didn't have to go far—she was sitting on the bench in the far corner of the porch. One hand was resting on her neck, absently rubbing across the scar that had been there as long as I could remember.

She always rubbed that same spot whenever she was nervous, anxious, or a combination of the two.

Silently I walked over to her, sitting down and pulling my knees up to my chest before leaning my body against hers. Her arm came around me immediately.

"I mean it," she said softly. "I'll be all right. I need some time to ... adjust to this."

"Mom, talk to me," I replied, begging her to understand. "I'm sorry I didn't tell you. I know you probably feel like I was lying to you the whole time I was with Remy."

She stiffened beside me as I confirmed her worst fears.

I plowed ahead. "Trust me, I know how crazy this sounds. A couple months ago we were still in Long Mesa and ... Jesus, we both know how messed up *that* was. Then we run away, find a new pack, and I leave for school? Then I bond with my mate after only knowing him for less than two weeks? Trust me—I was seriously losing it."

She turned to me. "Then why didn't you come to me? Why am I just now hearing about this, Skye?"

I squeezed her fingers in mine. "Because I knew you would think this was somehow your fault. I knew you would think the same thing I did at first—that, once again, my life is being controlled by something other than me."

She sighed. "Honey—"

"But then I talked to Remy," I continued, making sure I had her eyes on mine. "Mom, he's amazing. I mean, I knew he was a great guy before we bonded, but now? He lets me set the pace. He knows Long Mesa was a bad situation."

"You told him?"

I hesitated. "Not everything." Looking down I picked at the toe of my shoe. "He knows about being an omega in the pack and what it meant. I didn't tell him ... the other stuff."

"Are you going to?" she pressed gently.

I shrugged. "I know I will eventually. It's just... embarrassing."

A pained noise escaped her. "Baby, you have done nothing to be ashamed of. And if he's truly your mate, it won't matter to him what happened to you before."

"I know that in my head," I agreed. "But it's hard to get my heart on the same page, you know?"

With a snort, she rolled her eyes. "Oh, I absolutely get that."

My throat worked around the lump of emotion lodged there. "Mom, I'm falling in love with him."

Her eyes flared wide.

"And I'm scared, Mom. I'm scared that for the first time in my life because I'm happy, and I'm so afraid I'm going to mess it up."

I choked on a sob as she pulled me into her arms fiercely. "Oh, my girl," she whispered, rocking us.

After a second, she pulled back and framed my wet cheeks with her hands, meeting my gaze.

"Skye, look at me. I need you to hear this, honey." She sniffled and shook her hair out of her eyes. "You are *not* going to mess this up. You are worthy of love, and you are destined for great things."

A strangled laugh escaped me. "Great things, huh?"

"The best," she swore, pulling me against her side and cuddling me close the way she had when I was little.

"You've been through so much," she whispered, stroking my hair. "If Remy makes you even a little happy, then I'm okay with this. It just ... caught me by surprise. All I will ever want is for you to be safe and happy."

"He does make me happy," I told her. "He also makes me feel safe. I know he won't let anything happen to me."

"Yeah?"

I rolled my eyes and smiled. "I can't explain it. He's the person that calms me down when I feel like I'm going crazy. When I'm on the verge of a panic attack, everything in me knows I'll be okay if he's with me."

I realized what I was saying and stopped, blushing. "Probably sounds ridiculous, huh?"

"No," she replied softly, touching my hand supportively, "it sounds like you ... found your mate."

I ignored all the hurt in her voice when she whispered that last word.

"He's going to be Alpha one day," she reminded me, her tone brighter. "Are you ready to be Mrs. Alpha?"

I wrinkled my nose. "Seriously?"

With a chuckle, she shrugged. "Hey, I'm just pointing out the obvious."

I looked out into the darkness, peace settling on me and something else that felt a lot like pride. "Remy's going to be an amazing Alpha. I'll do whatever it takes to support him."

Mom looked down at me with a soft smile. "Who are you, and what have you done with my baby girl?"

I smirked. "Ha ha."

"I guess we should get inside so I can apologize to Gabe and Mallory for running out like that," she said, then winced. "And I need to apologize to Remy."

"Mom." I hesitated but then pushed on. "Is something else going on here I need to know about? Something you aren't telling me?"

A dark look shuttered her eyes. "Of course not, honey. It's just been a long, exciting day. I'm tired. Why don't we go say goodnight, and I can show you the new apartment?" She stood up and held a hand out to me.

Grabbing her hand, I pulled her into a fierce hug as I rose to my feet.

"I love you, Mom," I whispered into her neck, locking my arms tight around her.

Her hands came up around me just as hard. "I love you more."

Laughing, I shook my head as I pulled away and looked at her. "I love you most."

She smoothed a hand across my cheek. "Not even possible." Smiling, she dropped her forehead to rest against mine.

The peace of the moment was shattered a second later

when a car came careening around the bend, the engine revving as the tires caught on gravel and started to spin.

My mom shoved me behind her as the front door flew open. Gabe and Remy stormed through the door. Remy's eyes went to me, checking quickly to make sure I was okay. His eyes narrowed when he saw I had been crying, but the car sliding to a stop in front of the stairs had everyone's attention.

Mallory and Michael came outside, flanking Gabe and Remy as they watched with wide eyes.

The driver's side door opened, and a tall figure tumbled out, landing hard on their hands and knees. Sniffing, I caught the scent of blood in the air.

Gabe came down two stairs, Remy at his back. Both were tense and poised for a fight.

I gasped as the person literally crawled around the front of the car, into the beam of the headlights.

"Oh, God," mom whispered, her voice breaking as she stumbled forward.

Gabe and Remy were already thundering down the last of the stairs as the person at the foot of them collapsed.

Gabe managed to drop to his knees and catch Zara's head right before she hit the ground.

**38**

———

Chaos exploded around us.

Mallory and Michael raced down the front steps, followed closely by Mom and I. Mallory dropped down to her mate's side, taking over assessing Zara while Remy and Michael immediately took up defensive positions, checking for any threats.

Mom fell to her hands and knees beside Mallory, checking Zara's pulse and trying to wake her up.

A strangled cry behind us had me spinning and stepping aside as Zoe ran to her sister. Katy and the twins stood stunned in the doorway.

"Katy, get the twins back in the house!" Remy ordered, not turning to look back at his sister. "Skye—"

I growled in warning. No way in hell was I being ordered back into the house until I knew what was happening.

Sighing, Remy shook his head in frustration.

"See anyone else?" Gabe asked, his blue eyes piercing the darkness as he looked out for movement.

Michael shook his head, backing towards the house. "I think it's just Zara."

My eyes tracked to the car as the headlights died suddenly, plunging us into an inky darkness. The only lights were from the front porch and interior of the house.

Movement in the front seat caught my eye.

"Someone else is in there," I murmured, trying to make out the figure. I took a step towards the car and Remy grabbed my arm, physically hauling me behind him as Gabe got up and went around the passenger side.

Michael knelt beside Zoe, who was sobbing over Zara, pulling her to his side to let my mom and Mallory work.

As Gabe opened the door, the interior light flickered on and I gaped at the person sitting there.

"Bella?" I stepped around Remy.

Now Remy growled at me. "Skye—"

I put a hand on his shoulder. "That's Bella. She's my cousin. Zara's daughter."

Reluctantly, Remy let me by him but stayed close on my heels. I could feel his breath on the back of my neck, felt his hands brush against me as if he couldn't help himself but to touch me to make sure I was within grabbing distance if he needed to pull me away.

Gabe reached out and gently touched Bella's shoulder. She looked like she was asleep, her face relaxed and soft. The second Gabe touched her, her body came alive. Her eyes flew open and she shrieked, scrambling away from him in complete terror. The seat belt around her kept her pinned to the seat, which only seemed to make her even more agitated. She thrashed uselessly in the seat with a screech.

Gabe recoiled back, trying to calm her, but Bella was completely out of it.

"Let me try," I urged, moving around Gabe's massive body. The Alpha shifted back a step and let me in.

I lowered myself in front of the open passenger door, kneeling beside Bella. "Hey, Bella? It's Skye."

Her screams had started to quiet into pitiful whimpers as she curled her body into herself, muttering broken words I couldn't understand.

"Hey," I tried again softly, wanting to reach out to touch her, but afraid I would only scare her more.

Bella wrapped her arms around her head, eyes squeezed shut. "Please. Please. Please. Please. Please."

"Please what?" I asked gently, trying to understand her frenzied pleas. I tried to see if she was hurt, but it was too dark outside.

"Please no more. *Please no more.*" Her voice caught on a sob that turned into a keening cry of pain.

Zara was still unconscious in front of the car, and Bella was hysterical inside the car. Something had happened. Something awful.

My stomach twisted painfully. I turned back and gave Remy a helpless look.

His jaw was set in a hard line as he exchanged a look with his father.

"Let's get them inside," Gabe decided, looking around in the darkness once again.

With Gabe's order, Michael lifted Zara and carried her into the house. I turned back to Bella, extending a hand that she shied away from.

"Bella, let's go inside where it's warm, okay?" I tried to coax her from the car calmly despite the serious wave of anxiety cresting in my chest.

Her gaze flickered up and caught Remy and Gabe in the open door. She cringed and cried harder.

With a frustrated sigh, I turned back to them. "I'll get her inside, guys. Give us a minute?"

Gabe nodded and stepped back, heading for the house. Remy wasn't as easily swayed. His gaze stayed focused on Bella, like he was worried she would turn and attack me.

"Rem," I started softly, reaching out to touch his leg. I waited for his dark gaze to meet mine.

"Let me get her out of here, okay?"

He rubbed the back of his neck roughly, breathing hard through his nose. "Fine. But I'm waiting for you on the porch."

I smiled up at him, happy for the concession. I turned my attention back to Bella. After several minutes I managed to ease her out of the car. Her legs shook like a newborn baby deer trying to find its footing. I wrapped an arm around her waist, guiding as much as supporting her body weight.

She froze when she saw Remy standing at the top of the stairs. He had to go into the house before Bella would lift a foot onto the bottom step.

Mallory met us at the door, her expression troubled but kind as she reached out and took Bella from me.

"Zara is awake. Your mother and the others are in the sitting room with her," Mallory told me in a soft voice, her dark eyes full of compassion. "I'll take Bella upstairs and have Katy help me clean her up. I think your mother needs you."

I nodded, watching as Mallory led Bella up the stairs. Bella had gone from full blown hysterics in the car to practically catatonic now. She simply stared vacantly at the floor, letting us pass her back and forth.

Squeezing my eyes shut, I rubbed my hands over my face. None of this made any sense.

I sensed Remy seconds before he reached for me and pulled me against his strong chest.

Resting my head on the soft material of his shirt, I listened to the steady beats of his heart, letting the rhythm settle my nerves. I wound my arms around his waist, hugging him as tight as I could.

His lips pressed to the top of my head, and I pulled back so I could look up at him. My eyes flickered to his lips, my body voicing what I needed before I could form the words.

His mouth found mine in a slow kiss. My stomach flipped in all the right ways as one of his hands came up to cradle my face, his touch exquisitely gentle as his lips moved against mine.

The kiss wasn't about passion; it was a kiss of comfort. A kiss to remind us both that we were whole and safe and together.

He pulled away, breaking the kiss and resting his forehead on mine as we took a second to catch our breath.

"You good?" he murmured, his thumb sweeping the curve of my cheek.

I nodded, my nose bumping his.

Remy took my smaller hand in his and led me into the sitting room.

Zara was on the couch and in the light, I could see the dark purple and black bruises on her skin and the jagged cut under her right eye. She was somehow sitting up between my mother and Zoe. Michael and Gabe sat across from them. Zoe was crying, Zara kept hissing in pain, and the other three adults equally looked furious. Everyone's eyes swung to us when we came into the room.

"What happened?" I asked, dread coiling in my stomach. I dropped Remy's hand and kneeled in front of Zara, resting a hand on her knee and trying not to react when I felt her violently shudder.

Mom got off the couch and stalked to the window, looking out into the darkness as if the answers lay somewhere out there.

"Zara, can you start at the beginning?" Gabe asked softly.

My eyes went wide. "Shouldn't we get a doctor?"

"No," Zara said, her voice rough. "I need to tell you all what happened."

"Katy already called our physician," Gabe informed her. "He'll be here shortly to examine you and Bella."

Zara closed her eyes, grief etched across her face. "Oh, Bella. My baby."

"Linden did this?" Mom asked, her voice frigid and her spine stiff.

Zara started to nod and then hissed in pain, raising a hand to her temple. "He knew I helped you two escape. He was ... furious. We argued. He hit me."

"That bastard," Zoe growled, swiping furiously at her eyes.

Zara sighed sadly, leaning back slowly into the cushions. "He locked me in the basement. In the cells."

There were a series of cells set up in the basement of the Alpha house. A prison of sorts that was rarely used. Long Mesa pack members who violated a pack law were usually dealt with too swiftly for the cells to be needed.

"I could hear him arguing with his council in the evenings," Zara continued. Her eyes went to mine. "Things got so much worse after you and your mother left. Worse than I think even Linden expected. His council started pushing for more things, more rights. They argued he couldn't control two omegas, so he shouldn't be Alpha.

At one point, I thought Allan would challenge Linden for the pack."

My eyes slid shut and I sank back onto the floor, my butt hitting the ground and absorbing all my weight as I ducked my head to my chest.

Quite possibly the only wolf more volatile and cruel than my uncle would be Allan Loomis. He would drive Long Mesa into the ground in a spectacular ball of fire.

"Instead," Zara went on, dropping her eyes as her voice shook, "Linden decided to make an example. Of me. To show the pack he still controlled his mate, and that no one was beyond his wrath."

Nausea churned in my gut.

Mom turned sharply from the window, her eyes wide with fear. "Zara—"

Zara shook her head firmly. "What's done is done, Addie. We can't go back."

"How did you get away?" Michael asked softly, his hand smoothing across Zoe's shoulders.

Zara grimaced. "Something happened to Bella. Linden brought me to her room and told me to care for her. He left us alone to meet with his council. She was bleeding and crying, and wouldn't tell me what happened." She looked up in terror and tried to push herself up. "I need to see my daughter."

"Mallory and Katy are taking care of her," I assured her even as Zoe tried to get her to lay back down. "She's safe with them."

"How did you get away?" Gabe asked, rubbing his jaw.

"Linden didn't lock the door. I got Bella downstairs and managed to get her into one of the cars. I never stopped. The guard at the gate tried to stop us ... I ran him over and opened the gate."

"Oh, God," Mom whispered, horrified.

"I had to get my girl out," Zara said forcefully, grabbing Mom's hand. "You understand."

"Of course I do," Mom replied, her eyes going to me.

Gabe cleared his throat. "Blackwater will stand behind you. You have our support and our protection."

She gave him a weak, tenuous smile. "Thank you, Gabriel." She looked at me and her eyes filled with sudden tears. "I need to see Bella."

"I can go check on her," I offered, getting up off the floor. "I'll let her know you're awake and will be up soon."

Zoe covered her sister's hand. "You two are coming home with us."

"Actually," Gabe started, his mouth set in a grim line, "I think it best they stay here. At least for tonight. Neither Zara nor Bella are in any shape to travel." His eyes went to Zoe, his expression soft. "But you and Michael are welcome to stay here. We have more than enough room. Addie, you and Skye are welcome as well. It's been a long night for everyone."

I watched my mom for her reaction. Relief shot through me when she nodded in agreement.

She looked across the room to me. "We'll stay. I want to be close in case Zara needs anything."

"I'll go check on Bella. It's going to be okay, Aunt Zara." I left the room and started for the stairs.

I realized I wasn't sure where to go beyond upstairs when Remy came up behind me and wordlessly took my hand. He led me up the main staircase. The twins were sitting on the top step, identical expressions of worry on their faces. I was struck by how young they looked.

"Everything okay?" Dax asked seriously.

Remy nodded and motioned for his brothers to move. "Everyone's staying here for the night. Can you start getting the guest rooms ready?"

They both nodded in tandem and stood, heading off to get the rooms prepared.

Remy led us down the other end of the hall to the last door on the right, next to the back staircase that led to the kitchen. The door was open, and I stepped inside to see Bella laying on a double bed, Katy and Mallory standing at the foot of it with matching frowns.

"How is she?" I asked, coming into the room.

Bella's eyes opened slowly and settled on me, but then I noticed the change when they settled on Remy hulking behind me.

She started shaking, her chin wobbling as she started to cry.

Stunned, Mallory and Katy turned and looked at Remy, who looked completely confused by Bella's reaction.

"Can I have a minute alone with Bella?" I requested. I had a feeling Bella might relax a smidge if she wasn't surrounded.

"Of course," Mallory said, ushering both of her children out the door and closing it behind us.

I moved slowly to Bella's side, not sure if I should stand over her or sit down on the bed next to her. It's not like I had a normal relationship with my cousin. We had lived very separate lives. Truthfully, I didn't think Bella had ever spoken to me aside from passing on a message from her father the day I left. With her being a year and a half younger than me, we didn't have classes together.

"You used to make me so angry," she whispered, not looking at me, but I knew her words were meant for me.

I swallowed. "Um—"

Now she lifted her green eyes to me. Eyes like mine. "He was supposed to be *my* mate, but he was always around you."

Oh, hell. I wasn't ready for a conversation about Cassian.

I ground my teeth together, trying to remember Bella was currently a refugee in the Blackwater pack. "Bella—"

"I'm so sorry, Skye."

I froze, my jaw dropping open as her soft apology registered on my ears.

She was sorry?

Sniffling, Bella lifted a trembling hand from beneath the sheets and wiped her eyes. "I didn't understand. I didn't know what a monster he was."

My legs gave out, and I dropped onto the edge of the mattress.

Bella's eyes closed, tears leaking out from the corners. "I didn't know about ... about omegas. I didn't understand what was happening to you."

I tasted bile in my mouth.

Bella went on, and I wasn't even sure if she knew what she was saying. "But he said ... he said one Markham was as good as another. And since the omega house was gone—"

I choked on a cry. "What do you mean, gone?"

Her eyes opened. She blinked, finally focusing on me. "They killed them. And then burned the house down."

The world tilted around me. I fisted the plush comforter in my fingers, scrambling to stay upright.

"Maisie and Shane—"

"Maisie and Shane are dead. They helped cover up Dane's murder. They helped you escape. They had to pay." Her wooden voice was barely above a whisper, but it was like someone had set off an explosion in the room. My ears were ringing, my vision blurring.

"There were no more omegas," she kept going. "Just ... the council and not the council. My father didn't even try to stop it. Why didn't he try to stop it? Even after what they did … he said it didn't matter. I was going to marry Cassian anyway one day."

I was still struggling to pull my scattered thoughts into one coherent stream.

I tried to blink away the confusion and figure out what Bella wasn't saying.

Bella was sadly shaking her head. "He said … It was my duty. Since Cassian was my mate and would be our Alpha one day."

My stomach roiled. I was going to throw up.

"He raped you?" I whispered, horrified. I raised my hands to cover my mouth, wanting to scream. Wanting to cry.

Blinking, Bella didn't seem to register my question. "Maybe it was my duty. But … but I was only Cassian's mate. Not theirs."

*Theirs.*

Preston and Marc.

Jesus Christ.

"Bella—"

She looked at me, her expression almost serene. She blinked slowly. "It wasn't about me. I know that. It's because he didn't get what he wanted."

I stood up slowly, shaking my head. What the hell did-

"Cassian said to tell you he'll see you soon."

## 39

I THREW OPEN THE BEDROOM DOOR IN A BLIND PANIC, barely registering Remy leaning on the wall across the hall and the way he straightened when he saw me.

"Skye—"

I turned and headed for the stairs next to Bella's room. I ran down them, nearly tumbling down the last few steps. I managed to trip on air as I ran across the kitchen, slamming painfully into the back door before wrenching it open and running out into the night.

I could hear Remy behind me, but I didn't slow down as I ran across the deck and down the stairs towards the woods. I picked a direction and simply ran. I considered shifting and letting my wolf carry us farther and faster than my human legs could manage, but that's what started this whole mess.

Me losing control of my wolf and killing Dane.

It was the catalyst that set us all on this collision course.

I crashed through the underbrush, barely feeling the biting cold of the night air on the mountain nipping at my skin.

Remy was following me, his footsteps getting closer.

"Skye, slow down!"

I couldn't. I wouldn't.

I had no idea where I was going, but I couldn't stay there. I ran through the trees, into the dark of the cold night as fast as I could.

*Cassian said he'll see you soon.*

I was so stupid. So fucking stupid.

How had I let myself think that this would ever be over?

*Maisie and Shane are dead.*

I had done this. Maisie, Shane, Bella ... All of this was on me because of one night.

"Dammit, Skye!"

Remy was gaining on me, but I barely processed it. I was so blinded by my own fear and self-loathing that I never saw the root of the tree curled up.

My foot caught in it, my ankle wrenching painfully to the side as I fell to my hands and knees with a sob.

"Skye!" Remy closed the last few feet between us, dropping to his knees beside me. His hands touched my back. "Babe—"

"Don't *touch* me!" I shrieked, twisting away from him as hard as I could.

Stunned, he fell back, hands held open in front of him. His eyes were huge as he looked at me like a wounded animal ready to bolt.

I couldn't stand the look of confused pain on his face— yet another person I managed to hurt.

It was too much. Everything inside of me was ripping apart at the seams. Pressure built in my chest, in my veins, until I needed to find a way to release it all before I exploded.

I squeezed my eyes shut, covering my face with my hands as I screamed.

I screamed and screamed.

I screamed so loud I heard nearby animals scatter and run.

I screamed until my throat went raw, and I could only choke on my tears.

I knew I sounded—and probably looked—completely crazy. And maybe I was. Maybe I had finally snapped.

Cassian didn't even need to touch me to finally break me.

A low whine caught my attention, something cold and wet pressing against the side of my neck.

I jolted and snapped my head up, stunned silent to see Remy in front of me. He had fully shifted, his dark eyes luminous in the scattered moonlight. He touched me again with his nose, and when I didn't flinch away, he curled his massive body around me.

When I couldn't handle the touch of human hands, he knew the only other way to comfort me.

My wolf pulled at my chest, reacting to her mate.

*Our* mate.

With a shuddering sob, I wound my arms around his neck, burying my face in the thick black fur. His body absorbed my sobs as I kept crying, keeping me warm against the frigid night air.

It seemed to take ages before I finally started to settle. I pulled back to look into his eyes, knowing I probably looked like a hysterical mess. How he wasn't running for the hills, I would never know.

I stroked his head, my fingers tracing the outline of his massive muzzle. "Thank you."

He gently butted his head against my shoulder.

"You can change back now," I whispered, letting

him go.

His dark eyes studied me for a moment, then he got up and went behind a tree. I heard his bones snap and pop as he shifted, emerging from behind the tree a moment later, fully dressed. He dropped to his knees in front of me.

"I'm sorry," I mumbled, shaking my head and unable to meet his gaze. "I'm so, so sorry."

"Skye, I don't give a shit if you lose it," he said, still not touching me. "But I can't help you if I don't know what's going on."

A new wave of tears started, these quieter. "You can't. You won't. Not when you know."

"Skye, look at me."

He waited until I met his gaze. I could barely see him through the blurry wash of tears flooding my eyes.

His expression was fierce, determined. "There isn't a thing you could ever say to make me turn my back on you. Ever. It's you and me now."

My vision cleared for a second as the tears I was holding in fell free. "You don't understand."

"Then make me understand." He was practically begging. This amazing guy who would one day be an Alpha of one the biggest packs in the country was begging.

"I killed a member of my last pack."

The confession slipped past my lips on a whisper, and I waited for the fallout. But Remy's gaze never wavered, never dropped from mine. He didn't even blink.

"Did you hear me? I *killed* a member of my own pack." I spat the words at him like venom from my lips. I braced for the explosion.

Killing a member of your own pack was one of the worst offenses a wolf could commit, no matter the circumstances.

"I love you."

I froze, not sure what I had heard, but Remy wasn't smiling. Or laughing.

"What?" I whispered the word.

He leaned forward, finally reaching out to touch me, taking my face in his hands with infinite gentleness. "I love you, Skye."

My heart tripped in my chest, the muscle spasming as I realized what he said.

"You can't."

We had only known each other for a few weeks. And yeah, the mate bond was definitely a major factor here, but he was ... Remington Holt. And I was a murderer.

Now he smiled, a slow curve of his lips that always made my pulse race. "I can. And I do. I love you."

I sucked in a shaking breath, my hands coming up to curve around his wrists. I wasn't sure if I wanted to pull him close or push him away.

"You love me?" I could barely get the words out through the lump in my throat.

"Completely."

I gasped around a sob, staring into his beautiful eyes. Eyes that didn't judge or condemn me but were begging me to accept what he was saying.

"I love you, too."

No four words had ever been easier for me to say.

His mouth covered mine, heat searing across my skin, flames licking my blood. I was going to die in a fiery explosion of sparks and smoke, dust on the wind. My entire world narrowed into only Remy, into this perfect moment.

I had never known love like this. Acceptance like this.

He pulled away then pressed one more gentle kiss to my lips. "Tell me everything. Tell me nothing. It doesn't change how much I love you."

I shuddered, the cold from the ground starting to seep

into my body.

Frowning, Remy pulled us both to our feet.

"Let's go." He took my hand in his, pulling me forward.

I planted my feet in the ground. "I can't. Not yet. I can't go back there right now."

"Okay," he said slowly. "There's a cabin nearby. We let people who pass through or are visiting stay there. It's small, but it's dry and clean. I can start a fire to help you warm up."

I nodded, letting him tug me deeper into the woods.

It only took a few minutes of walking in the darkness to make it to the cabin. It was a small structure tucked into a corner of the property, probably a mile or so from the main house. It looked beautifully rustic.

Remy opened the door, guiding me inside before turning on a light switch.

Warm light suffused the room, giving everything a warm glow. The floor and walls were all a light-colored wood with dark knots peppered into the planks. There was a simple sitting room in the middle by the fireplace Remy was already kneeling in front of.

There was a galley kitchen off to the left, and I could see an open door leading to a bathroom to my right. I headed into the small powder room, turning on the light and shutting the door.

I flinched at my reflection in the mirror. My hair had been in a ponytail earlier, but now it was practically falling out, chunks of hair hanging in my face.

I removed the elastic band and finger-combed my hair for a second to work out most of the tangles before quickly braiding it to the side. I hurried and used the toilet.

As I washed my hands, I couldn't help staring at the pale girl looking back at me. My eyes were ringed with red, and I looked exhausted. I splashed water onto my face before drying my hands with the hand towel hung by the side of the sink. I turned off the light and opened the door.

Remy was still kneeling by the fireplace, but he pivoted on the balls of his feet to smile back at me. The fire in the stone hearth looked cozy and inviting. Remy had pulled pillows and a blanket off one of the couches, tossing them onto the rug in front of the fireplace.

I started to walk towards him but stopped to turn the main lights off.

The room fell into a soft golden dimness, shadows pushed to the corners as flames danced in the fireplace.

I toed off my shoes and crossed the room to him, waiting for him to rest his back against the base of one couch before I sat down, settling between his open legs and leaning back against his chest.

The ice that had seeped into my bones was slowly thawing, chased away as his heat enveloped me. His arms came around my waist, anchoring me to him. Pulling my knees up to my chest, I snuggled back into his chest.

Both of us stared at the crackling fire for several minutes, not speaking. We simply sat in silence, letting the stress of the evening—hell, of the last week—slip away.

Remy's fingers found mine, his index finger tracing the edges of my fingers.

"I don't know where to start," I admitted quietly, my voice barely audible over the fire roaring before us.

"Start wherever you want." His voice rumbled out of his chest, and I felt the soft vibrations on my back.

"Things in Long Mesa have been seriously messed up for a long time," I started slowly, my mind already picturing the dusty compound and skittish shifters inside it. "My grandfather ruled the pack like a dictator, and when he died, we knew my uncle would be ten times worse."

"Bella's dad," Remy murmured.

I nodded in affirmation. "Mom and I left the night my grandfather died." I glanced down at where I had twisted my fingers in his, focusing on this way his hand dwarfed my own.

"Because of your uncle."

Another nod. "My uncle called us to the Alpha house that evening. He had already picked his new council members and they were discussing ... a change to pack law." A shudder rippled down my spine, and Remy's arm around my waist tightened in response.

It was hard to swallow around the lump in my throat. "I knew I would be declared an omega as soon as I turned eighteen. It wasn't a secret. But my uncle decided ... Well, he and his council decided why wait?"

All the air left Remy in a rush. His body locked down, frozen in place.

"They decided to change the age of majority and make me an omega starting the next day." That old tendril of shame started working its way through my stomach, into my chest, strangling my neck.

"Why?" The single word was a low growl.

I snorted. "He gave some bullshit reason about the younger wolves needing an outlet for their ... baser instincts. I think it was really just one final 'screw you' to my mom."

"What. The. *Fuck*." Fury radiated off of Remy in palpable waves.

I touched his thigh with my hand, gently stroking the denim as I tried to calm him down.

"My mom tried to fight it, but Linden almost killed her for even speaking," I added, wincing when I remembered the way my uncle pinned her mercilessly to the floor. "He let her go and we left."

"And you escaped?"

I sighed loudly, shaking my head. "We went back to the house. I think we were both still in shock. When we went inside the house ... one of the omegas, Maisie, was on the floor. She was being attacked by a wolf. She was crying and bleeding and ... I lost it, Remy. I didn't even know I had shifted, and next thing I know, I had ripped his throat out. I killed him."

He dropped his head into the curve of my neck, his chest heaving behind me. "Good. Fucking good for you."

"I didn't realize I had killed the son of my uncle's new beta and best friend until after it happened," I went on, remembering how stunned I had been to know I had taken down a Loomis. Dane was just as psychotic as the rest of his family.

"Anyway, Mom and Zara got me out of there before ... you know."

He let go of my hand, bringing both arms up around my chest and hugging my hard, his nose was still nuzzled against my neck.

My hands came up, grabbing onto his forearms as I tucked my head against his shoulder.

"They're dead."

His head snapped up.

"Bella told me. Maisie and Shane, the other omega that was with us ...They're dead. They were killed for helping me." I choked out the last word on a sob.

"Shit," he swore softly, his arms going impossibly tight around me. And yet, I still wanted to be closer to him. "That is not your fault."

"They were killed because of what I did. Bella was ... Dammit." I swiped a hand furiously over my eyes.

"Bella is *fifteen*, Rem. She's a kid. And what Cassian did to her ..."

"Cassian?" The scorn in Remy's voice was undeniable. "That prick I've seen at Summit meetings?"

"He's next in line to be Alpha after my uncle. He and Bella were engaged. Bella said that Cassian and his friends ..." I couldn't finish the sentence. My body had started shaking, remembering all the times Cassian, Preston, and Marc had pinned me against a wall or backed me into a corner.

"That is *not* your fault," Remy snapped, his voice firm. "What they did had nothing to do with you."

"You don't understand."

*It was supposed to be me.*

"Skye, babe, come on——"

I pulled myself out of his arms, getting enough distance between us so I could spin and look at him. "No, Remy, this was my fault."

His brown eyes were blazing, flames from the fire reflected in them. He leaned forward, jaw clenched. Clearly, he was going to fight me on this point.

"My whole life I grew up knowing people hated me, but Cassian and his friends were different."

Something in my tone shifted his expression from fury to worry. His hands clenched into fists at his sides.

"The older I got, the worse it got. He loved to remind me that he would be one of the first in line when I became an omega. He was there the night my uncle passed the new law. He was so ... excited."

Remy's face went pale and then flushed a vibrant, violent shade of red. I could hear his teeth grinding together. He breathed hard through his nose, blinking slowly as he tried to control his anger.

"They would make comments when they saw me, shove me ... your basic bully behavior." I flinched at the memories but reached out to touch Remy's fists. They opened on reflex, curling around my hands.

"I learned how to avoid them. How to survive," I whispered. "For the most part, it worked. They hated me, made my life hell, but there was always a line that never quite got crossed. But it did with Bella. Cassian, Preston and Marc ... all three of them." I squeezed my eyes shut, my heart shattered for Bella. "Cassian told her it was supposed to be me. He told Bella he would see me soon."

The tightening of his hands on mine was the only warning I got before Remy hauled me to him. I scrambled onto his lap, straddling him as he tucked me against his chest.

"No one is ever touching you again," he swore after several long minutes of silence. His whole body was vibrating with rage. Rage for *me* and what I had endured.

"*You're* touching me," I offered weakly, needing to break the heaviness of the moment before I started crying again.

With a snort, Remy pulled back to look at me, a hand sliding down the length of my spine. "Fine. Only I get to touch you."

I rested my hands on the hard planes of his chest, loving the feel of hard muscles under my fingertips, feeling the steady beat of his heart. My lips quirked into a small smile. "What about my mom?"

His shoulders relaxed a fraction and a begrudging smile hitched up one corner of his mouth. "Fine. Only me and you mom."

I lifted my brows. "Katy and Larkin are huggers. So is Rhodes, for that matter."

His dark eyes narrowed. "Anyone else?"

I rolled my eyes to the ceiling, thinking. "I mean, we haven't even mentioned Tate or Maren. What about Dante and Ryder? Those two—"

With a growl, Remy flipped us. I landed on my back on the rug with Remy looming over me, bracing his weight on his hands, his hips between my legs.

My arms went up around his neck, my fingers lacing together behind his head.

"Are you done?" He raised an eyebrow.

"With you?" I asked softly, biting my lower lip. "Never."

His eyes heated, darting down to look at my mouth when I seized my lip between my teeth. He lowered his head, pressing his lips to mine gently at first, and then more insistently. I immediately opened my mouth to his, groaning as I tasted him.

His tongue slid into my mouth, stroking slowly against my own as he explored me. One hand came up to caress my face, his forearm resting in the valley between my breasts. My arms tightened around him, tugging him down to pull him closer.

Remy gently eased more of his weight onto my body, my thighs falling open a little more to cradle him and pressing us together in a way that had me gasping into his mouth.

He pulled back on a ragged breath. "Too much?"

I hooked a leg around his and pulled him flush against me, rolling my hips up experimentally. Another strangled gasp clawed out of my throat, my eyes flaring wide as nerve endings came alive.

His hips flexed, pressing the hard ridge in his jeans against my center.

"God," I gasped, my eyes sliding shut against the exquisite torture.

Remy's head dipped again, his mouth trailing lazy, open mouthed kisses along the column of my throat. The hand that had been holding my jaw slid slowly down the side of my body, coming to rest on my hip for a brief second before slipping under the hem of my shirt.

The touch of his warm, calloused fingers on the soft skin of my belly triggered a throbbing tug between my legs that matched the racing thump of my heart. His fingers slowly moved up my ribcage, tickling the flesh there.

With a small giggle, I tried to twist away.

His lips curved into a heart-stopping grin as his hand kept moving north. "I'll keep that spot in mind for another time."

My shirt bunched up under my breasts and Remy hesitated for a moment, his eyes flicking to mine. "Can I—"

I pushed myself up pulling my plain black t-shirt over my head with his help. Laying back, I bit back a hesitant smile as his expression went almost feral for a second. I glanced down, trying to see what he saw, but all I could notice was I had opted to wear my plainest white cotton bra today. It wasn't even the one that had a little satin bow in the middle for decoration.

*Way to be sexy, Skye.*

He didn't speak for the longest time, and I almost lifted my arms to cover myself from his intense scrutiny.

"You're incredible," he whispered reverently, using a single finger to trace the outline of my bra.

I flushed under his praise, and then groaned as his dark head dipped down, his mouth closing over a nipple through the cotton of my bra. With a hoarse cry, my hands came up around his head, fisting in his hair as he switched attention to the other breast.

The throb between my thighs became an insistent pulsing that couldn't be ignored. I lifted my hips again, rubbing against him recklessly as I tried to ease the ache with some sort of friction. His hips met mine in a punishing thrust as he ground against me so hard stars danced behind my eyes.

"Shit," I swore, gasping as my head fell back against the rug. My hands slid to his shoulders, clinging to his shirt as he rocked into me again, a hand lifting to tease the nipple he wasn't currently sucking on. His fingers teased it into a tight peak, pinching lightly on the sensitive skin as his teeth gently closed down on its twin. At the same time, he pressed himself harder against my center, and that feeling I was chasing exploded like fireworks.

The blood rushed from my head in a dizzying wave that left me spinning, clinging to Remy's shoulders to ride out the wave as it crested and crashed over me.

He rested his forehead in the center of my chest as I struggled to catch my breath. My entire body felt absolutely boneless and sated. A gentle nudge of his hips between my legs sent off a cascade of aftershocks that made my heart stutter for a second.

I could still feel the evidence of his arousal pressed against the inside of my thigh.

A log snapped and popped in the fireplace. Lifting my head, I tried to push myself up to see his face. "Remy—"

His head came up slowly, his dark eyes molten pools of brown. Shifting up on his forearms, he moved his mouth across mine lazily.

I pulled back. "But you didn't—"

He smirked ruefully. "No, I didn't. But this wasn't about me."

"But—"

He silenced me with another searing kiss. "You can make it up to me later if you want."

Oh, I wanted.

"Promise?" I teased him with a smile.

"Promise," Remy echoed, kissing me again.

# 40

When I woke up I could feel the sun warming my face, slanting across the bed. The arm wrapped around my torso and breaths on my neck were a familiar reminder that I was safe. Everyone I loved was safe.

For a second, I let myself lay there, relaxed and happy and content despite the crazy events of the night before.

"I know you're awake," the voice behind me grumbled, the arm awkwardly tightening in a lopsided hug.

Smiling, I flipped over onto my back and smiled at my mom.

Her green eyes opened, a mocking glare on her face. "Why can't you be like every other normal teenager and want to sleep in?"

I arched a brow. "Are you saying I'm not normal?"

Her nose wrinkled and she turned away with a delicate sniff. "No. But I am saying you need to brush your teeth."

My jaw dropped with a stunned laugh.

She was still making a face at me, but there was a smile in her eyes. "You kiss Remy with that mouth?"

"I've had no complaints," I retorted, happy that we were able to joke about this.

When Remy and I returned back to the main house, we realized no one noticed we had left. The adults were too busy dealing with the fallout of Zara and Bella leaving Linden and having them both examined by the doctor. We had snuck back into the house as their conversation was ending and everyone was going to bed.

The Alpha house was big, but there were only so many guest rooms. I considered rooming with Remy or Katy, but quickly vetoed it in favor of sharing a room—and a bed— with my mom once again. Besides, I could probably get away with staying in Katy's room. Remy's room ... not so much.

We had stayed up until the early hours of the morning talking quietly. I told her more about Remy, about what was happening at GPA. She told me all about the café and her job, how she was making friends in the pack. It was the reunion I had craved despite all of the drama.

I even told her about what Bella shared and my subsequent freak out. How Remy calmed me down.

How Remy *always* calmed me down.

She agreed none of it was my fault and blaming myself wasn't helping anyone. Cassian and his friends were completely to blame. I wasn't responsible for their actions, which I understood logically.

But emotionally, my heart still ached knowing I played a part in all of this.

Mom rolled away from me, standing up and stretching her arms languidly over her head. "Want to use the bathroom before I take a shower?"

I nodded and got up, walking to the bathroom that joined our room and Katy's bedroom. The door to her room was shut, but I wasn't surprised. Katy was definitely a teenager who could sleep in.

I used the bathroom, quickly brushing my teeth and then brushing my hair into a quick ponytail before opening the door for Mom.

She leaned forward, sniffing at my face, and then nodded. "So much better."

I playfully pushed her into the bathroom with a laugh. "Shut up."

"I'm just looking out for you, baby girl," she called, closing the door.

I hurried up and made the bed before changing into a pair of leggings and a long-sleeved shirt Katy had loaned me the night before. Heading out into the hallway, I checked and noted the door to Bella and Zara's was slightly cracked. Silently padding over, I nudged the door open and checked on them.

Both were still asleep in the king-sized bed they shared, mother and daughter curled together in the center.

I slowly eased the door shut before heading down the staircase to the kitchen where I could smell food cooking.

Mallory was standing at the stove in a pair of flannel pajama pants and a black t-shirt, her dark hair thrown up in a messy bun. She glanced over her shoulder as I came down, smiling warmly at me.

"Hey, honey. Sleep okay?" Her brown eyes, identical to Remy's and Katy's, held warmth and kindness.

I nodded, moving to the large center island. "Can I help?"

She pressed her lips together. "I think I'm okay right now."

I slid onto one of the barstools at the island countertop, watching as she moved easily around the kitchen. It was obvious where Remy got his culinary skills from.

She reached into the fridge, pulling out a container of orange juice and setting it in front of me, followed by a glass.

"Would you rather have coffee?" she asked suddenly, looking at the pot that was currently brewing the dark liquid.

I grinned like a little kid and quickly poured myself a cup, inhaling the steam a second before letting the liquid past my lips with a groan of appreciation.

That was amazing.

Mallory laughed, the sound smooth as water over river rocks. "Gabe and Katy are the main coffee drinkers in the family. We just started letting the twins drink it, but they aren't full on addicts yet. Well, Sam might be. I think Dax just doesn't want Sam to do anything he doesn't do, too."

"Katy got me hooked on it," I confessed, taking another drink.

Mallory set a spatula aside, turning down the heat on the burner she was working on, before turning to me. She rested her forearms on the marble countertop across from me.

I shifted in my seat after a second, nervous. "Is everything okay?"

"That's actually what I wanted to ask you," she said softly. "How are you handling everything?"

"School is good," I answered honestly. I was doing well in all of my classes and completely caught up.

She smiled gently. "I mean with the mating bond. I know how I felt when Gabe and I bonded. It was amazing and absolutely terrifying at the same time. Then again, we had been together for years at that point. You and Remy didn't have much of a chance to get to know each other."

I ducked my head, not sure I was ready to have the

relationship talk with my boyfriend's mother. "Remy's great."

Mallory shrugged a shoulder, her dark eyes glittering. "Eh. He's all right, I guess. Definitely not the worst kid I have."

Surprised laughter bubbled out of me. "Oh, my God."

She grinned at me. "Remy's a great guy. He's going to be a wonderful Alpha, and, whether you believe it or not, the Remy that left for school in September is not the same boy that came back to me."

I frowned, not sure what she meant.

"To be fair," she continued, "you're not the same girl who left here a few weeks ago either. It's absolutely fascinating to watch the two of you together."

"How so?" I asked carefully.

"You both act like you've known each other for years, not weeks."

"It's probably because of the bond," I guessed. Elias had pretty much said the same thing to us, too.

She hummed in agreement. "It is to an extent. But I've seen a few couples who bonded and knew each other for years beforehand who didn't seem as comfortable with one another as you two are."

I had no idea how to answer that.

Mallory came around the island, taking my hands in hers. "Please don't think I'm making any kind of judgment here, Skye. Every parent hopes their child finds love and happiness, and I truly believe you and Remy are meant to be together."

"Because of the bond."

She shook her head. "No, because of who you both are. I know we haven't really talked, but you're a survivor, Skye. You're a fighter. You have spirit and passion, but you haven't forgotten to see how wonderful the world can be.

Remy needs someone like you to balance him out. Sometimes he can get a little serious—"

I rolled my eyes. "You don't say."

Mallory laughed. "But there's a lightness around him with you. He acts like the little boy who used to pick me flowers from the meadow. As he's gotten older, I sometimes worried he was taking on too much responsibility too soon. I still want him to be young and have fun. And I see him doing that with you."

I blushed, biting my lower lip.

"So, thank you," she finished, touching my cheek. "Thank you for being you and sharing that with my son."

Blinking furiously, I leaned back. "Are you trying to make me cry?"

She chuckled and pulled me into a quick hug that I was all too happy to return.

The sound of footsteps entering the kitchen had us both turning and looking up to see Remy and his father coming in.

"Are we interrupting?" Gabe asked, brows raised.

"Just girl talk," Mallory replied with a wink, moving back to the stove.

Remy came up behind me, his hand wrapping around my ponytail until he could arch my head back to kiss me.

Part of me was a little embarrassed that he was kissing me in front of his parents, but when I looked over, Gabe was currently kissing Mallory.

I wasn't sure if it was adorable or icky.

Remy sighed and climbed onto the stool next to me, taking a drink of my coffee and gesturing to his parents with the mug. "You'll get used to it."

"Yes, you will," Gabe mumbled against his mate's lips.

Mallory twisted away with a laugh. "Why don't you go see if everyone will be ready for breakfast soon?"

The words were barely out of her mouth when the twins tumbled into the kitchen, identical expressions of sleepiness on their boyish faces.

One twin looked around and glowered. "Why did we have to wake up early if Skye and Remy are already up?"

I figured it was Dax by the sullen tone, but it was confirmed when Sam went to the coffee pot.

"Because we have a house full of guests, and I need both of you and Remy to help me with breakfast for everyone," Mallory replied sharply. "And Skye is our guest."

Dax opened his mouth to speak, but Sam, who I was quickly beginning to see was the filter for Dax, spoke up first.

"What do you need us to do?" Sam asked, sipping his coffee.

"See? One of them isn't a total heathen," Gabe chimed in, leaning his hip against the counter near where Mallory was working. He pointed at Sam. "You're my favorite, you know."

Remy leaned in next to me. "His favorite kid is whoever is sucking up the most, which means it's usually Sam or Katy." His hand settled on my thigh, a comforting touch that made me lean a shoulder against him.

Gabe's head snapped around. "And I heard that, least favorite kid."

I couldn't help but laugh.

Mallory sighed. "Remy can help me cook. Dax, set the table. Sam, go check on everyone upstairs."

Gabe reached around Mallory and snagged a piece of bacon from the massive pile. "What can I do?"

"Absolutely nothing," Mallory said emphatically, turning pleading eyes to her husband.

Remy cracked up next to me, throwing his head back

in a full belly laugh that had me smiling. Even Dax laughed as he started pulling plates from a cabinet.

Gabe gave me a helpless look. "I burn water."

I nodded in understanding. "Remy banned me from the grill after I almost burned the cabin down at school."

Gabe grinned broadly at me. "Same! Except it was a smoker, and how was I supposed to know it was a bad kind of smoke?"

I frowned. "Shouldn't a smoker smoke?"

"Thank you!" Gabe slapped a hand on the counter. "Skye is in the running for new favorite kid, by the way," he informed Remy.

Remy just shook his head, but I could see the pleased smile toying across his lips that I knew matched mine.

His parents accepted me. They even seemed to like me.

"I can make eggs," I offered to Mallory, who was pulling two cartons out of the fridge.

She set them down in front of me. "You're hired."

I was halfway through cracking the eggs when my mom came downstairs. She froze at the landing, her eyes going wide when she saw me.

"What are you doing?" she asked, slowly coming to my side.

"Making eggs," I replied, focused on not getting a single shell in the bowl of already cracked eggs.

"You can make eggs?"

Was it seriously so surprising I learned one life skill at school?

"Yes, *Mother*," I said in exasperation, throwing her a look. "I can make eggs. Scrambled, anyway. Remy taught me."

The guy in question closed the oven door and turned to give me a soft, intimate smile that made my stomach quiver.

Mom gave him a genuine smile. "That's great."

Remy came around the island on his way back to the stove, pausing to swoop in for a quick kiss that made me laugh. Then he pulled out the chair next to me for my mom to sit down, flashing her a grin.

Mom sat down beside me and leaned in close to whisper, "Okay, he might be a keeper."

I smirked back at her. "Told you so."

"Yeah, yeah." She reached over, moving the eggs and bowl between us to help me finish cracking everything.

Sam, Katy, Zoe, and Michael all came downstairs while we were making breakfast. Right before everyone was finished, Zara came downstairs.

"Is Bella coming down?" I asked softly, setting the serving platter of bacon on the center of the table in the dining room and looking at Zara.

Zara sat down in a chair with a sigh, her face grim and exhaustion weighing on her shoulders. "I don't think so."

Zoe slipped into the seat beside her, wrapping an arm around her sister's shoulders.

I hesitated behind my chair. "Do you want me to go check on her?"

Zara gave me a sad smile. "No, honey. I think Bella needs sleep right now. She's trying to process ... everything."

I flinched and felt Remy's hand at the small of my back as he came up behind me. I leaned back into his touch, grateful for the support.

Katy eased into her own chair. "I pulled out some extra clothes in case Bella needs them. She's welcome to use them."

Zara gave her a tight smile. "Thank you, Katy. We didn't have a chance to grab much before ..."

I dropped heavily into my chair, the food in front of me suddenly looking as appetizing as sawdust.

Just like last night, Remy sat next to me, but he hooked a hand on the leg of my chair and tugged me flush against him.

As much as I didn't want to be that girlfriend, I couldn't help but crave the comfort he offered. I shifted in my seat, my right side was touching him from shoulder to knee. His hand came down on the inside of my thigh above my knee. The intimate, familiar touch soothed a jagged edge of my heart.

I met Mom's eyes across the table, stunned to see the tears pricking her eyes as she watched us. When she noticed me looking, she flashed me a quick smile and blinked away the emotion, reaching for a biscuit.

Conversation at breakfast was quiet and subdued. Only hushed conversations and the scrape of silverware against plates filled the room for the longest time. I forced myself to choke down some of the food, not wanting to be rude, but my appetite was nonexistent.

After he finished, Gabe pushed back his plate and surveyed the table with solemn eyes. "I know the last few days have been hard on everyone. I'm calling a pack run tonight. I think it will help all of us."

I blinked up, noting the surprise on everyone's face.

"Zara, you and Bella are welcome to join us, but we understand if you need more space," Gabe added. "With everything happening, we need to make sure the pack is as united as possible."

Michael sighed, but nodded. "I agree. Between what's been happening at the school and at home, the pack needs this."

Mallory reached over to grab her mate's hand, giving him a firm nod. "It's a good decision, my love."

A nervous flutter took root in my chest. I had only run with the pack at my school. The pack here was massive. My wolf loved the idea of interacting with her pack mates and exploring our home.

Katy speared a bite of potato and waved it at Remy and me. "Then you can see what those two look like when they shift. It's crazy."

"What do you mean?" Mom asked, shooting me a curious look.

Katy smirked and leaned back in her seat. "You'll see."

☾

"THIS IS INSANE," Gabe whispered, his human nose almost touching my canine one as he studied me.

The pack had been notified of the run at sundown hours earlier, but after Katy told everyone about the way Remy and I matched, the adults asked to see it firsthand before the rest of the pack showed up. Twenty minutes before wolves were scheduled to start showing up in the meadow at the base of the mountain, Remy and I had shifted for our parents.

It was kind of comical to watch all the adult's jaws drop simultaneously.

Mallory knelt next to her husband, her wide eyes swinging from one of us to the other. "Have you ever heard of anything like this?"

"Definitely not," he replied.

Mom hadn't said anything, but I noticed the tightness that always lined her mouth whenever I shifted around her was even more pronounced now. She stood at my side, stroking my head.

*So we're still freaks? I asked Remy.*

He snorted, shaking out his fur as he looked at me. *Obviously*.

"Wait—are you two communicating?" Mallory demanded, eyes wide as she looked back and forth between us.

Remy gave a small yip in reply, his tail thumping on the hard ground.

Gabe's jaw fell open again. "It took us almost a year to do that."

Mom's lower lip caught between her teeth. "So, this isn't normal?"

Gabe and Mallory looked up at her, their expressions smoothing as they noted her worry.

"It's unusual," Gabe said, standing up. "But it's fascinating. The connection between them must be really strong." After a second, he flashed Mallory a wolfish smile. "He gets that from me."

With a sigh and a roll of her eyes, Mallory slapped his shoulder. "We need to shift. The others will be here soon."

I was surprised when they went in different directions to shift, ducking out of sight to remove their clothes. Mom followed Mallory to a cluster of trees to the right and Gabe headed left. The others would show up already shifted.

In Long Mesa, it was just assumed the pack would shift together. Strip and shift.

I always hated those nights. I was one of the last ones to shift since my wolf and I were so distant, which gave everyone plenty of time to stare at me with leering eyes.

I always took insanely long showers when we got back, trying to scrub away the feeling of eyes crawling over my naked body.

Sensing my unease, Remy nudged my shoulder with his nose and a low whine. I could feel the unasked question pressing against my mind.

*The pack doesn't shift together?* I posed the thought as a question, trying not to focus on the past.

*He seemed confused but answered me quickly. No. The mated pairs tend to get territorial over others seeing their mate naked.*

That made complete sense. Even at Long Mesa, some of the pack had gotten into fights during a pack run. Usually it was a mated pair that instigated the incident.

I sat down, lifting my nose to sniff the cool mountain air. It was somewhat warmer here than in Montana, the scents of mossy earth and pine trees were fresh and cozy.

Pawing at the ground, I felt the playfulness of my wolf rising to the surface. Like I had been doing the last few weeks, I let her impulses control our actions.

I reached over, nipping Remy's shoulder with my teeth and jumping away, tail swishing happily.

His dark eyes glittered as he lunged at me, giving chase as I spun away and took off at an all-out run, zigzagging my way through the meadow and heading for the far tree line.

Remy was faster than me, and I knew it wouldn't take long before he caught me, but I was stunned when sharp teeth bit down on my tail, hard enough to make me yelp and my tail sting.

I immediately stopped, dropping to my side and trying to roll away from the hold Remy had on me.

*Ouch!* I shouted at him, whimpering as he let me go.

He dropped to his belly, crawling forward in apology. His dark eyes swung over several feet away from me.

... Where a giant ass bear trap lay open.

I would have run straight into it.

*I just reacted. I didn't know how to make you stop.*

He gently licked at the part of my tail he had bitten, trying to soothe the sting.

*I'm fine. I nudged him. Thank you.*

Remy still looked upset he had hurt me, his eyes sadly looking at my tail.

I thumped it against the ground, lifting my head to nuzzle against his and inhaling deeply.

Remy in wolf form was more potent than Remy in human form, and I loved the smell of Remy in human form. He smelled like the woods and fresh air and something that was completely and totally just Remy.

He smelled like Blackwater.

He smelled like home.

I jumped as he got to his feet suddenly, his body towering over mine, blocking me from whatever was coming.

I slowly got to my feet, not wanting to be laying down for whatever had him alert and looking around.

A plaintive howl sounded, followed by a cavernous echo of replying howls that sent shivers across my body. Remy instantly responded, adding his voice to the crescendo.

Their bodies moved silently into the meadow, lithe forms peeling from the shadows and stepping into the fading twilight of the meadow.

The pack was here.

# 41

The drive back to school the following Sunday was peaceful.

Again, the five of us decided to road trip back. Remy had to drive the SUV back anyway and there was no way I wasn't going with him. It was only natural that Rhodes, Larkin, and Katy, who's leg was completely healed now, came with us.

The rest of the week at Blackwater had been incredible. Remy and I had managed to carve time out of almost every day to just be together. Even if it was only sitting on the porch swing at his house or having dinner at the café while my mom worked. I loved watching her run the restaurant and the way customers responded to her.

Spending time with Mom was great. I absolutely loved our apartment and my room, which she left intentionally bare bones so I could paint and decorate however I wanted when we were home for winter break in a month.

We spent Thanksgiving at the Alpha house with Remy's family, and after dinner, Katy and the twins spent several hours explaining the meaning of Brown Thursday,

Black Friday, and online shopping. Apparently, there was also a Cyber Monday, but we would all be in classes for the bulk of that.

I wasn't entirely sure what they bought or why, but they all seemed excited as they sat in the family room on their laptops. Even Remy seemed to be scrolling websites on his phone with one hand, the other wrapped around my shoulders and tucking me to his side on the couch.

The campus was quiet when we finally made it back in the late afternoon, the sun already setting against the mountains to the west.

Remy parked the truck and the five of us all went to the alpha cabin after making a quick stop to deposit our bags in our dorm rooms.

Once we got inside, Katy and Larkin collapsed on the couch, looking exhausted even though we had basically sat on our asses all day.

Rhodes immediately went to the fridge, pulled the door open and then closed it with a frown. "There's nothing to eat."

I knew for a fact that wasn't true—there's a pantry full of canned soups and nonperishables, and that wasn't counting stuff in the freezer—but they did clear out the fridge the weekend before so nothing would spoil and start to smell.

"We can make a run out to the store," Remy said, rubbing the back of his neck.

I frowned at that, seeing the weariness around his eyes. He had done most of the driving and was tired. We had all managed to take naps during the trip, but Remy stayed awake and alert the whole time.

"Bring me back chocolate," Katy said loudly, lifting a magazine from her tote bag and settling into the couch.

Larkin tucked her legs up, too, reading the same article over Katy's shoulder.

Remy looked back at me and opened his mouth to speak, but Rhodes quickly cut him off.

"Why don't the girls hang here?" He flashed wide eyes at me.

Katy snorted, thumbing to the next page. "I told you, Rem."

Remy started to laugh as Rhodes spun on her. "Told him what?"

She barely looked at him as she kept reading. "That you were getting jealous."

Rhodes sputtered incoherently for a second, making Larkin duck her head into Katy's shoulder to hide her laughter.

"Jealous?" I repeated, arching a brow.

Rhodes gave me a weak smile. "I just mean, I could use some guy time."

"Remy having a mate is really cutting into their bromance time," Katy quipped with a smirk.

Remy was still laughing as his arms came around me from behind. He rested his chin on my shoulder, his thumbs hooked in the belt loops of my jeans.

"I never said that, Katherine!" Rhodes retorted.

Katy's head snapped up, her eyes narrowed into tiny slits. "Call me Katherine again."

Remy's ear brushed my cheek, and I reached an arm up behind me, tangling my fingers in his hair. He turned his face into my neck, and I shivered in delicious anticipation as his lips teased my skin.

"Okay, *enough*," Rhodes said suddenly.

Remy raised his eyebrows and looked at his best friend, his fingers teasing along the waistline of my jeans as he made no move to stop touching me. I wasn't sure if I wanted to pull away or press myself against him.

Rhodes pointed a finger at us, slapping his other hand over his eyes. "Katy's right—you two are the worst."

"Told you," Katy piped up from the sofa, barely glancing up from her magazine.

"Rem, bro, come on," Rhodes pleaded, his brown eyes wide and begging as he raked his fingers through his long hair. "Skye got to have you all week—"

"Not *all* week," I muttered, leaning my head against Remy's shoulder and feeling it shake under me as he tried not to laugh. We had spent a lot of time together, but I also had been with my mom and the girls. I made it a point to check in on Bella and Zara. Remy and I weren't glued together or anything.

"Can we please have a guys' afternoon? No estrogen required?" The beta was full on begging now. It was kind of adorable to see him like this.

"Technically men have estrogen, too," Katy added with a shrug.

"Seriously?" Rhodes looked decidedly grossed out by that newfound info.

Larkin nodded, glancing up at him. "Weren't you paying attention in biology?"

Rhodes grinned wolfishly. "Not to that."

Larkin blinked slowly before she pressed her lips together, turning back to the magazine so she wouldn't give him a response. I mentally high-fived her for not blushing at the innuendo.

"Go," I told Remy, looking up at him.

"You sure?" he asked, smoothing my hair away from my face.

"Yeah. Go get stuff for the week, especially since you

want to have the pack over next weekend. We need supplies. And Rhodes needs a date with you."

"Exactly!" Rhodes cried, punching a fist in the air.

"Told you he always wanted to date you, Remy," Katy called.

"That's not what—"

"Let's go," Remy said, cutting him off before it could turn into a full-on squabble between the two of them. I wondered if Remy had played peacemaker for them their whole lives.

Talk about exhausting.

Remy's head dipped, his lips pressing to mine. It was supposed to be a quick kiss, but I stood up on my tip-toes, chasing his mouth as he started to pull away.

He chuckled against my mouth, the hand on my hip tightening for a second as Rhodes groaned behind us.

"I'll be back soon," he promised when I finally let him go.

"Good," I said, smirking. My gaze went over his shoulder to Rhodes. I made a show of sighing loudly and taking a step away from him. "He's all yours, Rhodes."

"Finally!" Rhodes grabbed Remy's wrist, physically hauling him away from me.

"Let go, man," Remy said, laughing as he pulled free from Rhodes. He shot me a grin that did funny things to my heart. "Any requests?"

"Apple pie?" My stomach growled in response to my answer. Since discovering the magic of apple pie on Thanksgiving, I had become obsessed.

Remy nodded. "You got it."

"Lark, you want anything?" Rhodes called.

She barely spared him a look, taking Katy's magazine from her hands and settling back against the cushions. "I'm good."

A frown passed over Rhodes' face for a second before it cleared. He glanced at Remy. "Okay, one apple pie for Skye, chocolate for Kit-Kat, and whatever else we'll need for the week." He snapped his fingers. "We should do a taco bar for dinner tonight."

Remy grabbed the keys from the counter he tossed them on when we came inside. "Sounds good."

There was something about watching Remy walk away from me and a door closing between us that set me on edge. Even my wolf seemed pissed off when he left us.

I thought I was doing a good job of hiding it until I turned back to Larkin and Katy, and they were both staring at me.

"What?" I demanded, planting my hands on my hips.

Katy gave me a slow once-over. "You're aware he'll be back in a couple hours."

"I know," I said with a huff, dropping into the armchair across from them. I glanced back at the fireplace wishing it was lit. The heat in the cabin had been turned down while we were away and a chill still lingered in the air.

"You look like he just left for war and you're not going to see him for a year."

I winced. "That bad?"

Larkin smiled sweetly. "I think it's cute."

Katy rolled her eyes. "You would."

Jaw dropped in mock outrage, Larkin pushed Katy with her foot. "What the heck does that mean?"

"It means, I'm waiting for your new lady balls to drop so you can tell Rhodes you want to jump him," Katy returned with a grin.

I couldn't help the giggle that escaped me. I slapped my hands over my mouth, but Larkin was already glaring at me.

"I told you—Rhodes and I are a no-go," Larkin informed us stiffly, sniffing lightly as she turned her nose up. "I'm moving on."

Katy cracked up. "Where exactly are you moving to that you think that boy won't chase you down?"

"If you really want to know," Larkin said slowly, a blush creeping up her cheeks, "the twins asked me out."

My jaw dropped open like it was on a hinge. A barely intelligible squeak coming out of my mouth. How the hell was I just finding out about this?

"What?" Katy shouted, getting to her knees on the couch and leaning towards our friend. "Way to bury the lead, Lark! When did this happen?"

"Wait—both of them?" I asked quickly. "At the same time?"

Larkin nodded, biting her lower lip. "Crazy, right?"

"Can I please be there when you tell Rhodes? He's going to lose his shit." Katy clapped her hands together, her dark eyes filled with joy.

I sucked in a sharp breath through my teeth. "I actually want to be far away from him when he finds out."

"You guys are wrong," Larkin muttered, running a hand through the dark curtain of her hair. "Rhodes sees me like a sister. Besides, I can't spend my life waiting for him to maybe notice me one day in a future that probably doesn't exist."

Katy's expression softened as she glanced at me and then reached for Larkin's hand. "Honey, I don't think you see what we see."

Larkin stubbornly pulled her hand away. "Either way, I'm tired of waiting. I want to go out on a date. I want to get dressed up and kiss a boy—"

"Boys," Katy corrected, her dimples deepening as she smirked. "As in multiple sets of lips and hands and—"

"Okay!" Larkin laughed, waving a hand. "I get it."

"You're living the hetero-girl dream life, Lark," Katy replied with a shrug. "Two hot guys at your beck and call?"

"It's just a date," Larkin said in exasperation, trying to downplay it.

"Back me up, Skye." Katy looked at me expectantly. "What straight female wouldn't want two gorgeous guys worshiping at her altar?"

The idea of picturing a third person in my relationship with Remy had me simultaneously sick and angry. My wolf was furious at the idea of anyone except Remy touching me. Touching *us*.

Katy arched a brow as she read my look. "Okay, maybe not *every* girl's dream."

"It's weird," I admitted, "but as soon as you said it ... there was like this gut reaction that made me want to throw up. The idea of being with anyone else makes me really pissed off."

"That bond is no joke," Larkin murmured.

I absently rubbed my chest. "You're telling me."

A chime filled the air, and Larkin pulled out her phone, glancing at the screen. "Oh good! I can pick up my extra credit assignment from Mrs. Carver. She's back."

Katy made a face, her nose scrunching up. "You're picking up *more* extra credit?"

Larkin got up, tucking her phone back into the pockets of her jeans. "If I want to graduate with you guys, I need a couple more credits."

"We can come with you," I offered, getting up. I gave Katy a look and she reluctantly got to her feet.

"Fine. Group trip to go into school before we physically have to," the redhead said with a sarcastic smile.

We pulled on our coats and headed out into the cold

night air. A new layer of snow had fallen while we were gone, and I could almost smell more snow in the air.

"When does Maren get back?" I asked Katy as we started down the path.

Katy sighed loudly, her feet crunching on the gravel of the pathway leading to the main building. "Not until tomorrow evening. Flights from their part of Alaska are sketchy and they had a big storm this morning. The plane can't leave until tomorrow."

Larkin hummed under her breath. "Have you guys thought about what you'll do after graduation?"

Katy shook her head, catching her lower lip between her teeth. "No. I think we're both trying not to think about it."

"Do you think you'll leave Blackwater?" I asked hesitantly, hating the idea of Katy being hundreds of miles away.

"I don't see me ever leaving home," Katy admitted. "That's kind of the problem. Maren's entire family is in Brooks Ridge. Her parents, grandparents ... She doesn't want to leave them anymore than I want to leave mine."

I hooked an arm through Katy's as we approached the steps to the doors. "I'm sorry. That really sucks."

She shot me a wry smile. "Wouldn't it be easier if we were mates?"

Larkin frowned. "You still would have to figure out whose family to leave and which pack to be part of."

Katy stuck her tongue out at Larkin.

I couldn't help but be relieved that deciding what pack to be part of wasn't an issue Remy and I had to face. Thank God we were both heading back to Blackwater once we graduated.

Katy made a face, her eyes narrowing as we walked by the girls' dorm. "Is that Ainsley?"

I turned and looked. "I think so."

"Hey, Ainsley!" Larkin called.

The brunette looked up from where she was messing with her phone on the front steps.

Katy turned and gave her a wide-eyed look. "What the hell, Lark?"

Larkin narrowed her eyes. "Oh, come on. She has, like, no friends. I saw her over break and she even apologized to me."

"An apology is the *least* she could do," Katy shot back, grimacing as Ainsley stood up and started walking over to us. "She's the devil's best friend!"

"You know Sierra blew her off after Remy made her pick between us and Trace," Larkin reminded her.

Katy rolled her eyes and threw her hands in the air. "Oh, for fu—"

"Hey, guys," Ainsley said as she slowly approached. She stopped several feet away.

"When did you get back?" Larkin asked, ignoring the way Katy was glaring at her.

Ainsley gave a small smile. "A few hours ago. I took an earlier flight than the rest of the pack."

"That's great," Katy said sharply. "We have to go." She grabbed our arms to turn us back towards the main building.

"Katy!" Larkin hissed, jerking her arm away.

"No, it's cool," Ainsley said stiffly. Her gaze flicked to Katy. "For what it's worth? I'm sorry, Katy. What Sierra and I said wasn't cool. She deserved the slap you gave her. I probably deserved it, too."

Katy folded her arms over her chest. "Oh, you definitely did."

"Katy," I muttered, giving her a look.

She exhaled loudly. "Thank you for the apology."

Ainsley nodded. "Yeah, of course."

"We should probably go. I have to pick up something," Larkin said, knowing that this encounter should end on a good note.

I turned to follow her, but Ainsley stopped me.

"Actually, Skye? Can I talk to you for a minute?"

Katy gave her a suspicious look. "Why?"

A hint of the old Ainsley flared to life. "Is your name Skye?"

Katy snorted. "You know what? You can go—"

"Stop," I ordered, stepping between Katy and Ainsley. I looked at Katy. "Give me a second. I'll meet you guys at the doors, okay?"

"Sounds good," Larkin agreed, linking arms with Katy and pulling her away.

"Sorry," Ainsley apologized again with a grimace. "I made that worse, didn't I?"

"What do you need, Ainsley?" I was tired and not in the mood for games.

She looked suddenly nervous and took a step towards me. "Listen, Sierra was over my house for Thanksgiving."

"My condolences," I deadpanned.

Ainsley smirked. "Yeah, well, our parents have been friends for years. We always spend the holidays together. Anyway, I overheard her on the phone after dinner talking to Trace."

That caught my attention. "Okay."

Her lips pressed together in a thin line. "Look, I didn't hear much, but I think you need to watch your back, okay? You and Remy."

I sucked in a sharp breath.

"It's stupid, but Sierra always had it in her head that she would be with Remy, and it really messed her up when he rejected her last year," Ainsley explained quickly.

"That's why she's with Trace, but I think she's in over her head. I only heard her say something about you and Remy not seeing whatever they have planned coming."

Panic started building in me, swelling and brimming over the edge.

"I was going to tell Remy, but I saw you first." Ainsley shrugged. "Just, be careful, okay?"

"Yeah, okay," I mumbled.

She gave me a tight smile and walked back to the dorms. After a second I headed to meet Katy and Larkin at the doors.

"Everything okay?" Katy demanded.

"Um, yeah," I muttered, still wrapping my head around it.

"Are you sure?" Larkin pressed, touching my arm.

"Yeah, I'm good." Part of me wanted to tell them, but I needed to talk to Remy first.

Larkin pulled open the heavy door for us, and we stepped into the hallway. "She left the assignment at the front office."

With a nod, we started down the hallway, our shoes echoing off the walls of the silent hall. I could hear faint noises coming from the direction of the cafeteria as the staff started setting up for dinner. The bulk of students still seemed to be missing from campus, milking every last drop of our week off before classes started in the morning.

We turned the corner for the office and I came up short, nearly slamming into a body.

"Sorry—" The apology died on my lips when I realized it was Trace. He was leaning against the wall in front of the office. If I didn't know better, I would have sworn he was waiting for us.

"Ladies," he said with a leering smile, his eyes slowly raking down all of us.

"Douchebag," Katy returned with a cold smirk.

Trace's eyes narrowed.

"What are you doing here?" I demanded, not in the mood for his shit. Especially not after what Ainsley had told me.

His lips turned up, revealing a row of even, white teeth. "Pack duty, sweetheart. Caleb's cousin is visiting. His pack is thinking about enrolling in GPA, so we're giving him the tour for a few days."

Larkin was still quiet behind me, but I felt her shifting restlessly on her feet. We needed to move this along.

"Good for you," I said with a grimace. "My sincerest apologies to the guy who has to hang out with you and your pack for a few days."

Trace straightened, his smile grew even wider as he watched me, his dark eyes glittering with some unspoken promise that made my stomach clench. "I don't know that *apologies* are what he would like from you."

I was about to tell him I didn't give a damn what his beta's cousin wanted when the door opened, and Caleb came out of the office. I hadn't talked to him since the bonfire when I first came to GPA, only seeing him mostly in passing. He held the door for his cousin to come out.

My knees buckled and I almost went down, all the blood rushing from my body in a tsunami that left me seeing spots. I blindly reached out, my icy fingers clamping onto Katy's arm with bruising strength.

Trace was still grinning as Caleb and his cousin stopped beside him. "You've met Caleb's cousin before, right? Rumor has it you and Cassian go way back, Skye."

## 42

I HAD NEVER HYPERVENTILATED BEFORE, BUT I WAS PRETTY sure that was what was currently happening to me.

My lungs struggled to pull in any sort of oxygen as I stared at the face of the boy who made my life a living hell for all but a couple months. The hallway was tilting, the whole world's axis tipping precariously. Fear clawed at my throat, rendering me silent.

"Skye." Larkin's hand gently touched the small of my back as she and Katy closed ranks around me.

That only made Cassian smile even bigger, an amused chuckle coming from his mouth. "Skye, Skye, Skye. Did you get my message?"

*"Cassian said to tell you he'll see you soon."*

Bella's words swam up in my muddled thoughts, giving me something to focus on. Something to anchor to.

Cassian's bright blue eyes swept down my body, his grin deepening. "You look amazing."

An all-too familiar rage started to swell in me as I remembered Bella's broken spirit, her used and discarded body. I could feel ice settling into my veins as I watched this boy who tried to break me.

Tried and *failed*.

I took a step forward, refusing to cower to him again.

This wasn't Long Mesa. This wasn't his home. And I definitely wasn't the girl who was just trying to survive day by day now.

I was the girl who was *living*.

I had friends and family. I had a *mate*.

Calm settled on me as I took a cleansing breath before letting my lips twist into a smile I directed at Cassian.

"Cassian," I said coolly, ignoring the gasps of my friends behind me.

"How's Preston?" I continued, my tone conversational like I was asking about the weather.

The sound of my voice startled him, making him blink in surprise. He had probably expected me to run away, tail tucked between my legs and crying.

I made a soft clicking sound, flicking my tongue against my teeth as I shook my head. "Sorry I missed his brother's funeral. But I guess it would have been kind of mean to show up at the funeral of the guy I killed, right?"

His teeth ground together so hard I was sure they would shatter, his hands balling into fists. "You stupid bitch," he spat, taking a step forward only to be retrained by his cousin.

"Careful, man," Caleb warned, looking around.

I wasn't sure why Caleb was calling him off until I heard footsteps behind me. I didn't bother looking away from Cassian, my eyes locked onto his in a battle of wills that had me shaking, but not from fear.

"What's going on?"

I was flanked on either side by a McAllister twin. I wasn't sure if it was Kyle or Konnor that asked the question, but both looked lethal, and they weren't alone. At least seven other pack members were with them.

My pack.

The other twin glared at Trace. "You know the rules. You're supposed to stay away from us, especially the girls."

Trace held up his hands innocently. "I was simply waiting for our friend to come out of the office so we could go to dinner. Your bitches were the ones who came up to us."

Several low growls started behind me. As touched as I was by their anger on our behalf, I needed to diffuse this situation fast so I could get out of here and figure out what the hell to do next.

I needed Remy.

"We're good," I said, my voice clear and even. I lifted my chin, still not breaking eye contact with Cassian. "We were just leaving." I took a step back, slowly retreating.

"So soon?" Cassian hissed, his hands curling and unfurling as he struggled to contain his hate.

As soon as I stepped back, a wall of McAllister muscle blocked me from Cassian's view. Several other pack members stepped forward until Katy, Larkin, and I were at the back of the Blackwater pack.

"We'll walk you back to the cabin," one of the twins announced. "Is Remy there?"

I saw the spark of interest flare in Cassian's eyes at the mention of Remy. My wolf roared inside of me, and it was all I could do not to hurl myself at him as I sensed the unspoken threat to my mate. My teeth clicked as I clenched my jaw.

"Yeah," Katy lied easily. "He and Rhodes are waiting for us, so we better get back."

As a unit, like we were in some kind of shifter militia, we backed around the corner of the hallway and headed back the way we came. I held my breath the entire time, only breathing once we made it outside.

"What the hell was that?" one of the twins demanded, touching Larkin's arm with concern.

I didn't stop for her answer, instead lengthening my strides to stalk down the path. The crunching behind me let me know that the others were behind me.

I jerked when I felt a hand touch my arm.

"Sorry," Katy apologized before reached down to hold my hand. "Are you okay?"

I gave a stiff nod, but I wasn't. My adrenaline rush was crashing, and the stark reality that Cassian was here was sinking in. It didn't matter that I had a pack of wolves around me for protection. Granite Peak was supposed to be safe. Blackwater was supposed to be safe.

Nothing felt safe now.

Ainsley's warning had come too late.

I broke into a run, my stomach cramping as the cabin came into view. I thundered up the stairs, throwing open the door, barely registering Rhodes and Remy were standing in the kitchen unpacking groceries. Both of them looked shocked to see us bursting through the door.

Remy stepped forward. "Skye—"

I ran across the room to the bathroom, barely making it to the powder room and hitting my knees before I started throwing up in the toilet. All the anxiety and fear, along with my rapidly dropping adrenaline levels was a recipe for vomit soup.

"What the fuck happened?" Remy demanded, his tone dangerous even as his hand gently stroked my back.

"She ran into Trace and Caleb in the hallway," I could hear one of the twins start to explain. I really needed to learn how to tell them apart.

I blindly reached up, flushing the toilet and swallowing

back another gag. I braced my forearm across the back of the seat, resting my forehead on them.

"They had a new guy with them—"

"Cassian," I muttered. I grabbed a handful of toilet paper, wiping my mouth and throwing it in the toilet, flushing again.

"What?"

I lifted my head enough to see Remy's eyes. "Cassian is *here*."

Remy went still. It looked like he was frozen in time, but I could see the tick of a muscle in his jaw and felt the way his hand shook against my back. It was a small tremor, but I felt it.

A dark look passed between Remy and Rhodes, and I glanced back to see Katy, Larkin, and the twins crowding in the doorway. The rest of the pack that escorted us was talking in the main room, their voices pitching higher and higher as their agitation grew.

"Everyone out!" The sudden booming voice from Rhodes made me jump. He pulled the bathroom door shut, closing us off from everyone else. I could still hear him herding everyone away from the bathroom.

Bracing my hands on the toilet, I pushed myself up, closing the lid. Remy's hand was still on my back as if he couldn't stand to not touch me in some way.

Silently I washed my hands and rinsed my mouth, not caring how unladylike it may be when I spit into the sink basin.

Remy opened a drawer next to me and pulled out a travel size bottle of mouthwash.

I grabbed it from him, twisting the cap to break the seal before I poured a mouthful past my lips. The alcohol in it burned as I swished it in my mouth. I rinsed the sink out when I was done and turned around, my eyes on the wall behind Remy.

"Skye," he started softly.

"I'm sorry," I said abruptly. "I'm so sorry."

A frown pulled at his mouth as a wrinkle formed between his brows. "You don't have to apologize, baby."

His words barely registered in my brain. I was already thinking ahead, trying to plan this whole mess out. "If I leave, he'll probably follow me."

His entire back went ramrod stiff, his dark eyes narrowed. "What are you talking about?"

"If I leave, Cassian will follow me. I never wanted any of this to blow back on the pack—"

With a growl, Remy's hands found my waist and lifted me up until I was sitting on the counter. He stepped between my legs before I could think to close them and braced his hands on the counter on either side of my legs. The move put him at eye level with me.

"You're not going *anywhere*," he said emphatically. "Not now, not ever."

"Remy—"

"No, Skye!" he snapped, eyes flashing. "I don't give a shit if your entire old pack shows up here. No way would I ever let you go. Would any of us let you go. You're part of our pack now." He reached over, grabbing my hand and pressing it to his chest. "You're part of *me* now."

"I can't ask you to put yourselves in danger because of me," I whispered back, feeling the steady thump of his heart under my fingers.

"You didn't ask," he countered, lifting a brow.

"If something happens to you ..." I trailed off, my heart seizing in my chest at the thought of something happening to him.

"Exactly," he retorted, nearly brushing my nose with his. "If I left you to protect you, how would that feel?"

It felt like a physical punch to the stomach. The air rushed out of me leaving me dizzy.

Remy gave me a knowing look, his expression softening. "We're in this together, babe."

I nodded slowly, accepting that I had dragged him into this mess and now we were all stuck. But at least we were stuck together.

Sliding off the countertop, I held his hand in mine, waiting until he opened the bathroom door and we walked out.

Rhodes had cleared the pack away from the bathroom, but they all still lingered. I flinched as almost a dozen sets of eyes landed on me, trying to figure out exactly what was going on. They had to know this was about more than Trace.

"Are you okay?" Larkin asked softly, her doe brown eyes huge and somber. She stepped around Rhodes but stopped short of touching me.

I gave her a short nod, not trusting my voice to say anything quite yet. I leaned against Remy, needing his strength. My body felt like an overcooked noodle, weak and limp, now that my adrenaline rush had fully crashed.

"I'm going to keep this short," Remy started, giving my hand a squeeze as he addressed the pack. "Stay away from the Norwood pack. The ... guest they brought here is someone from Skye's former pack. He is not to be trusted. None of them are. From here on out, no one is to be alone. Until all this is sorted out, stay alert. Everyone moves in pairs, even to the damn bathroom."

Several nods and murmured agreements met his mandate.

Remy's hand went tight around mine again, a small

tremor rippling down his arm. "Thank you for protecting my mate tonight. For protecting your pack."

My head drooped, resting on his shoulder as I watched the male chests in the room puff up a bit at his praise. Out of the corner of my eye, I saw Katy roll her eyes to the ceiling, clearly not happy to need any male protection or the testosterone wave currently invading the room.

One of the twins cleared his throat and stepped forward, his somber gaze going to Larkin where she stood by Rhodes. "We can walk you back to the dorms, Larkin." His gaze moved to Katy. "Both of you."

Rhodes bristled, his lips pressed into a thin line and his nostrils flared.

"We're going to stay here for now," Larkin said softly, giving him a kind smile. "Thanks, Kyle."

Her answer seemed to make Rhodes relax. That, or the hand I noticed she placed against the small of his back.

Kyle gave her a nod in return, and I mentally tried to find a way to tell him apart from Konnor. Konnor had a small scar on his chin. That was something.

"Thank you," I echoed, my voice raspy. I cleared my throat. "You guys—"

"We're your pack," Will cut me off, catching my attention. "Whatever you need, we're here for you."

I was stunned silent as something warm crept into my chest. The pack all cleared out until I was left with Remy, Katy, Rhodes, and Larkin.

Remy blew out a long breath, wrapping an arm around me. He glanced at the others. "Why don't the three of you head to the dorms and get a change of clothes? I'd feel better if you guys were here tonight."

Larkin and Katy both nodded, not fighting him, which made me feel relieved. I needed to know they were both safe tonight, too. The idea of me going back to the dorms tonight never even crossed my mind. No surprise that Remy was on the same page.

"Want me to bring the other girls back here?" Rhodes offered, shrugging on his jacket.

Remy shook his head. "They all room together. Just make sure they know to stay together. If they want to come back, they're welcome to."

Katy had her own room, and with me here, Larkin would be on her own. They could technically room together, but I wanted them close by. Larkin and Katy had both already been hurt by Trace. Now with Cassian wandering around…

A deep shudder tripped down my spine, my fingers fisting in Remy's shirt.

Rhodes nodded at us and escorted Larkin and Katy back out into the night. Glancing at the clock in the kitchen, I saw it was barely past six.

"Are you hungry?" Remy asked, my cheek feeling the vibrations from his rumbling timbre.

I shook my head. "I'm just tired. And really cold. Why am I so cold?"

He wrapped both arms around me, his heat a comforting blanket. "It's the adrenaline rush. You're crashing."

Lifting my head, I slowly blinked up at him. I hated seeing the tension around his mouth and eyes as he studied me. I could feel the way his muscles were locked, braced for whatever came at us next.

"Can I just please go to sleep?" I asked softly, wanting nothing more than to crawl into a soft bed—preferably with Remy—and forgot the world for a few hours.

He gave me a reluctant nod. "Why don't you go on up? I'll make you some hot chocolate. The heat and sugar should help."

I slowly disentangled myself from him, cold air rushing between us like a physical thing I instantly resented. Slowly I climbed the stairs, completely ignoring the spare room I had previously been offered and heading for Remy's.

I started taking off my clothes, almost on autopilot. My mind was numb as I opened a dresser drawer, remembering Remy stashed his t-shirts there. I grabbed the first one off the top of the pile, pulling it over my head quickly. The soft material brushed the middle of my thighs as I robotically moved to my next task.

Opening the door to the en-suite bathroom, I quickly used the bathroom before washing my hands. I opened the tube of Remy's toothpaste, brushing my teeth with my finger quickly. Hopefully Larkin or Katy would remember a toothbrush.

I glanced at my reflection in the mirror and frowned.

And hopefully they would remember a hairbrush, too.

I quickly finger combed my hair, scraping it into a simple braid and securing it with the elastic around my wrist. I was nearly finished washing my face when I sensed Remy behind me.

Drying my face on the hand towel beside the sink, I met his eyes in the mirror.

He extended the mug to me as I approached, and I smiled seeing he used mini marshmallows and whipped cream. I brushed by him, parts of me I thought were numb suddenly firing to life.

I focused on the heat of the mug seeping into my fingers and I moved to what I considered my side of the bed and sat down, folding my legs up.

Remy stood on the opposite side of the bed, still watching me. Like he was waiting for me to crack.

"I'm okay," I finally said, taking a sip of the sinfully

decadent drink. The steam wafted across my face, as I hummed in appreciation.

According to Larkin, most people used some powder concoction with hot water to make hot chocolate. Remy melted thick bars of chocolate and stirred in heavy cream slowly. The result was something like liquid heaven.

"It's okay if you're not," he told me quietly.

Sighing, I shifted on the bed. "I think I'm ... numb right now. I'm angry and frustrated and ... sad," I finally admitted, ducking my head until my chin touched my chest. I set the mug on the nightstand as my hands started to shake. "I just wanted this to all be over, and it feels like it never will be."

I heard Remy move across the floor and then he was climbing into the bed behind me, arranging me between his legs and wrapping his arms around me much like he had the night I spilled everything a week earlier.

"This will get better, Skye. You're not alone anymore. I've got you. We've all got you." He rested his chin on my shoulder, his arms strong bands around my waist and chest. "We're going to get through this, and Cassian is going to pay for what he's done."

I nodded, believing him but not sure how any of this was going to be okay. How any of this would be right.

"Ainsley tried to warn me," I mumbled.

I felt his surprise. "Ainsley?"

I jerked my head. "Yeah. She overheard Sierra talking to Trace. She didn't know much, but said it was about us."

Remy sighed deeply.

"Trace said Cassian is here to check out the school because Long Mesa might start sending students here," I said suddenly, a sick pit forming in my stomach. "Does that mean he'll be sitting in on classes? Wandering around campus?"

"I don't know," Remy answered honestly. "I'm going to call my dad and see if he knows what's going on. Regardless, Cassian is here as an extension of Norwood, and after what happened on the run, Norwood and Blackwater are being kept separate. While he's here, you won't have to see him, and if you do, I'll be with you."

That made me feel slightly better.

Remy cocked his head, listening. "Rhodes and the girls are back. I need to fill him in on ... a few things," he said hesitantly.

"Everything," I said firmly. "Tell Rhodes everything. I trust him. And he needs to know exactly what Cassian is."

Remy pressed his lips to my jaw, moving to kiss the corner of my mouth when I turned, pressing my mouth to his. Sighing, I opened to him, taking comfort in the taste and smell of him. The kiss was as charged as every other one we had, but there was a softness in the way his mouth coaxed mine into a slow dance with his. This wasn't just about love or passion, it was about comfort and reassurance.

My hand came up to cradle his jaw as he started to pull away. His dark eyes glittered as he looked at me.

"I love you," I whispered, needing to say the words.

A slow smile curved across his lips. "I love you, too." He kissed me once again and then climbed off the bed. "Want me to send Katy and Larkin up?"

I nodded, reaching for the mug to take a sip, watching as he walked out of the door, leaving it open. I took another drink before setting the cup down and sliding under the covers, still craving warmth.

I was asleep before Katy and Larkin ever made it upstairs.

**43**

I woke in Remy's bed, warm but glaringly alone. I knew Remy had come to bed at some point. I had woken up to him sliding into bed beside me, tucking me against his chest. My sleep was shockingly dreamless in his arms.

I reached for the spot where he slept. The bed was still slightly warm, but it was obvious he was up.

Glancing at the clock, I was shocked to see it was past eight o'clock in the morning. Classes started at nine.

I threw back the covers, grateful when I spotted a duffel bag on the armchair in the corner. Rifling through it, I pulled out a set of clothes and toiletries. I rushed through a shower, brushing my teeth and again opting to braid my hair. It was freezing outside, but I didn't have time to dry it.

I was hurrying down the stairs when I saw Remy and Rhodes leaning on the counter in the kitchen drinking from mugs of coffee. They both looked at me wordlessly as I slid into the kitchen on socked feet.

"Why didn't you wake me up?" I demanded, trying to remember where the hell my shoes were. "We're going to be late."

Both of them were dressed in jeans and Henley's, dark boots already on their feet.

Rhodes gave Remy a strange look before clearing his throat and taking a step back.

"What?" I asked, my attention swinging from one to the other. "What aren't you saying?"

Remy cleared his throat, taking a sip of his coffee. "Skye, I talked to my dad."

"And?" I found my shoes by the door and started to pull them on.

"We think it would be best if you go back to Blackwater," Remy said quietly. "There's a flight leaving in five hours. I'll drive you to the airport."

I blinked slowly, trying to process what he was saying. All I could manage was a strangled, "*What?*"

He set his cup down, his expression pained. "Babe, it's the best way to protect you. You'll go back to Blackwater for now where you'll be safe."

"For how long?" I demanded, folding my arms under my chest as I tried not to freak out.

He sighed, not meeting my gaze. "I don't know. A few weeks at least."

"A few weeks?" My heart thumped painfully in my chest. "What if I don't want to?"

His eyes hardened a bit, his jaw going tight. "It's what the Alpha thinks is best for you and the pack right now."

My eyes narrowed. "And what do you think?"

Remy kept his gaze steady on me. "I agree with him."

I couldn't help but feel sucker punched. "You want me to ... leave?"

He growled, raking a hand through his dark hair. "It's not what I want, but it's what needs to happen."

"You said we were in this together," I snapped, stepping back when he moved to reach for me. "You said we were stronger together. How is me being hundreds of miles away from you equal to us being *together*?"

Something flashed in his eyes a second before his expression went carefully neutral. His Alpha expression. The one he used when he was trying to separate emotion from logic.

"We're still together. This just keeps you safe." Remy ground the words out.

Anger burned in my chest. I clenched my hands into fists. "Cassian shows up, and I'm the one who gets sent away? How the hell is that fair or right?"

"I didn't say it was fair—"

I threw up my hands. "Can you stop being so damn neutral?"

"Neutral?" he echoed, eyes narrowed. "What does that mean?"

"It means maybe I expected you to fight for me instead of doing whatever your father wants," I retorted coldly.

His jaw dropped open. "Are you serious right now? All I've been doing is trying to keep you safe. I've been fighting for you since day one, Skye. I want you to go because I know Blackwater is the safest place for you."

"*You* are the safest place for me!" I finally yelled.

His chest heaved as he took a step away. "Not now I'm not."

"What does that mean?"

"Larkin got hurt on my watch. Katy got hurt on my watch." Pain and regret filled his dark eyes. "I'll be damned if I let you get hurt again, too."

"Skye," Rhodes started gently, holding up his hands, "Trace brought Cassian here to mess with Remy as much as you. He's been trying to provoke him all year. You know that. Hell, *you* figured it out. Removing you from the equation is the easiest way to stop him right now."

I opened my mouth to speak, but he beat me to it.

"I'm not saying it's fair or right," Rhodes continued sadly, "but it's where we're at."

I knew what he was saying made sense, but I still felt like my heart was being ripped out of my chest. I had come so far, and now I was back to square one.

I glanced down at the floor, gathering my thoughts. "I understand what you're saying, but I'm sick of running away."

"Skye—"

"No, Remy," I interrupted, my head snapping up. "I have been running from Cassian my entire life. I'm done running from him. I'm done hiding and being afraid of everything. You taught me I was strong, that I could handle *anything*. And now you're telling me I'm ... not strong enough?"

He flinched, my words hitting their intended mark. "You're the strongest person I know."

"Then why are we arguing about this?" I asked, my tone pleading.

He took a deep breath and squared his shoulders. "We aren't arguing about this."

I exhaled loudly, relief coursing through me.

"I'm telling you how it is," he said, his tone firm and final. "You're leaving. I'll take you to grab whatever you need from the dorms before I drive you to the airport."

I couldn't have been more stunned than if he'd slapped me. Even Rhodes sucked in a sharp breath.

"Remy," he warned softly, only for Remy to shake his head.

"Go pack, Skye," Remy ordered quietly.

I glared at him. "You want me gone so bad, *you* can pack my damn bags." I stormed past him to head to the front porch.

Remy reached out for me, his hand barely closing on my bicep before I wrenched away.

"Do *not* touch me," I hissed, not sure how I could love him so much and want to beat the crap out of him at the same time.

"You can't go out there alone," Remy reminded me coolly, folding his arms over his chest.

"So now I'm a prisoner?" I demanded, laughing bitterly. "Wow. It's like I never left Long Mesa."

Remy recoiled, finally his seemingly unbreakable calm composure cracking. Hurt flashed in his eyes, and I instantly regretted what I said.

Using his confusion as my out, I stormed outside, slamming the door violently behind me. My feet thundered down the steps. I considered going to the dorms or going to class, but I could feel my wolf stirring, her anxiety ramping up my own.

I needed to shift and run.

I turned to go around the house, hearing the door slam a second time.

I whirled at the footsteps hurrying up behind me, but the retort on my lips died when I saw it was Rhodes who decided to chase after me—not Remy.

Rhodes stopped in front of me, holding out my jacket as a peace offering.

I took it slowly, shrugging into it, grateful for the warmth. My rage fire wasn't going to keep me warm for long out here.

"Thanks," I told him, zipping it closed. I gave him a wary look. "I take it you're my babysitter?"

Rhodes grinned, dimples flashing. "Nah. You're *my* babysitter."

I couldn't help the chuckle that escaped me. "Right. I'll protect *you*."

He clutched a hand to his chest. "I promised Remy my virtue would be safe with you. Don't make me a liar."

I laughed again, shaking my head. Typical Rhodes breaking the tension.

"Walk with me?" He asked, starting off towards the lake without waiting for an answer.

I fell into step with him. "Is this the part where you tell me Remy's only doing what's best for the pack? It's his job?"

"He *is* doing what's best for the pack," Rhodes replied.

I stopped suddenly. "How is—"

"He's scared, Skye," Rhodes said softly, pressing his lips together.

"Scared?" I scoffed. Remy was … *Remy*. He was solid and strong and confident. Definitely not scared.

"The idea that something could happen to you scares the shit out of him," Rhodes explained gently, touching my arm. "He's so focused on you that he's worried he can't protect the pack the way he should. He's fucked either way, Skye. He's either going to let you down or the pack. At least this way he knows you'll be safe."

That sucked some of the anger out of me.

"This mate bond is no joke," Rhodes said with a forced smile. "I've seen Remy with other girls—"

I couldn't help the low growl that rumbled in my chest.

Rhodes smirked. "You're not like any of the others. Even before you two bonded, he looked at you different. Treated you different."

I shifted on my feet, spurring us into walking again. "He knew I came from a shitty pack. He felt sorry for me."

He shook his head. "No, never. He never felt sorry for you. Pissed off for you, yes. But he never pitied you. He respects you." He nudged my shoulder. "So do I, for what it's worth. Remy told me what happened with you and your pack and that walking bag of dicks. The fact that you're still standing is incredible. Most people would have folded. A lot of people have for a lot less."

I snorted, brushing a low branch away. A dusting of snow fell around us and the branch trembled. "I survived. Barely. Most people can do that."

"Did Remy or Larkin tell you about my parents?" Rhodes asked, glancing at me.

I shook my head. "No."

"I don't really remember my mom," he admitted, shoving his hands into the pockets of his coat. "She left when I was little. It messed up my dad. He still loves her even though she hasn't spoken to us in a decade. So my dad drinks. A lot."

I looped my arm through his, leaning against him to offer silent support.

"My dad loved her since they were little. I don't know the whole story, but I don't think my mom was ever happy. She settled for my dad. And one day she decided not to settle anymore."

He blew out a long breath. "Sometimes when he's drunk, I can hear him crying in his room, talking to this framed picture he has of her by his bed." Rhodes's cheeks tinged pink, and I didn't think it was entirely from the cold. "He tells her that they were supposed to be mates forever."

My heart ached for Rhodes and his father. As shitty as my childhood was, at least I had my mom. It sounded like Rhodes lost both his parents when his mom left.

"I think he really believes that if she had stayed, they would have eventually bonded," Rhodes mused.

"What do you think?" I asked slowly.

"I think it scares the shit out of me to love someone so much that I would completely break if they left," he murmured, running a hand through his long hair.

I was still trying to figure out what to say when he rendered me speechless.

"I love her, you know?" he said softly, coming to a slow stop in front of the lake. "Larkin, I mean. I've always loved her. First like a little sister when we were growing up, but the last couple of years ..."

I gaped at him. "Why haven't you told her?"

Rhodes gave me a slow shrug. "Because I don't know if I'll ever be able to completely give her every part of me. Losing my mom wrecked my dad. Who knows what would have happened to me if Remy's parents and Larkin's parents didn't step in when I was younger. I can't imagine losing her and ... God, leaving our kid to fend for himself? I think that would hang over me every day."

"It's not the same thing. You're not your dad anymore than I'm my uncle, Rhodes."

"I know," he replied. "But right now, that's all I can see, and Larkin deserves someone who won't shut her out. She deserves someone who can love her without any extra baggage."

"We all have baggage, Rhodes," I replied, shaking my head. "I don't think you give Larkin enough credit."

"Maybe not," he agreed. "But if it means she'll have a happy life with someone who loves her, someone who can share everything with her, then I think I'm okay with that."

"You think?" I repeated, not convinced at all.

He smiled ruefully. "Larkin deserves everything. I don't want to be the guy who only gives her pieces of his heart."

I shook my head sadly, frustrated Rhodes couldn't see what was right there. "You'll never know if you don't try. Do you think it was easy letting Remy in? He told you what happened to me. I don't just have baggage—I have an entire cargo plane of shit."

He chuckled, licking his bottom lip. "Fair enough."

"If I can let someone in," I said, poking his chest, "then so can you."

"I'll think about it."

"Think fast," I said, arching a brow. "The twins asked her out, and she said yes."

The smile slid off his face, taken over by shock and then jealous anger. "What?"

"Larkin's done waiting for you to wake up. If you don't want to make a move, there's a line of guys who happily will," I told him. "Time for you to go get your girl."

He started to smile when several cracking branches made us spin around. I barely blinked before Rhodes had me behind him, putting himself between us and whatever was crashing through the brush a few feet away.

A tiny figure tumbled out, blond hair tangled with twigs and leaves. Her huge blue eyes looked up at us. Blood was smeared across a swollen, bruised cheek.

"Help me," Sierra begged, dropping to her knees with a shudder. "Please—he's coming."

"Jesus," Rhodes hissed, running to her side.

We both dropped down, to our knees on either side of her.

"Sierra, what happened?" I asked, checking for injuries. I resisted touching the side of her face. "Did someone hit you?"

Rhodes gently started to lift her up, turning her over. I was still searching for where she was hurt when I heard Rhodes give a soft grunt.

I moved her hair from the side of her face. "Where are you hurt?" I asked.

Rhodes let Sierra go and fell backwards with a groan, sprawling out on the snow.

"Rhodes, what—" The words died on my throat when I saw the needle sticking out of his leg.

Sierra pulled away from me, slowly standing and moving back. I dropped forward, reaching for Rhodes as his eyes rolled back in his head.

"What the hell did you do?" I demanded, glaring up at her as I felt for a pulse.

She didn't speak, but her eyes lifted to something or someone behind me. She smiled.

"I told you I could help," she chirped happily.

I started to turn, but I felt the sharp prick of a needle piercing my skin. The drug was something thick and viscous, burning as the plunger was pressed down.

Everything shifted and blurred, tilting disturbingly.

And then it was dark.

**44**

---

SOMETHING'S WRONG.

That was the only thought I had when I started to wake. It was cold, and I could feel the heat of the sun behind my closed lids, the weak winter light somehow too bright. Pain pierced the fog of my mind like an icepick.

I flinched, the movement causing my head to throb. A low moan escaped me, and I tried to think back and figure out what had happened.

*Something is wrong.*

I remembered waking up in Remy's bed. My stomach rolled as I remembered our fight. Leaving the cabin. Talking to Rhodes. And then …

I struggled to focus my thoughts.

My eyes flew open with a gasp as everything crashed back into me. I immediately regretted the action. The sunlight was like daggers to my sensitive eyes. I squeezed them shut quickly, not catching more than a canopy of skeleton trees above me.

*Something is very wrong.*

"Rhodes," I mumbled, blindly reaching out for where I

remembered him falling. My hand only met cold rock and ice.

"Now *that* is not the name of your mate," a familiar voice chided. "But I guess we can't be surprised if a slut like you would be happy with only one guy."

*Something is seriously wrong.*

Alarm was starting to set in, and I tried opening my eyes again, this time slowly letting myself adjust to the brightness. My head still felt like a marching band had taken up residence inside, but at least I could see.

My stomach twisted so violently I was sure I would vomit.

Cassian smiled down at me, his all-American good looks a cruel facade for what lurked beneath. His cheeks were rosy from the cold, and he was bundled up in a winter coat. He was kneeling at my side, his body looming over mine.

I looked around, realizing we were on a part of the mountains I didn't know. How long had I been out? How far had he taken me? There was a fire crackling beside us, so clearly Cassian had time to stop and build a fire.

"Rhodes—"

He pressed a gloved finger to my lips. "Rhodes is ... detained. He won't be coming to your rescue."

He pushed hair out of my eyes with a grin. "Hey, question—who do you think Remy will try to save first? The bitch he got stuck with a few weeks ago? Or the guy who's been his best friend since they were kids?" He traced the curve of my cheek. "Does he save his best friend's ass, or his piece of ass?"

"Shut up," I hissed, jerking away from him so hard I hit my head on the rock under me and saw stars. "Where the hell is he?"

He rolled his eyes. "I said he's busy." He spoke slowly, like maybe I had sustained several blows to the head.

"How the hell did you get Sierra to help you?" I asked, remembering the very convincing role the blond had played.

His full lips curved into a wicked smirk. "That girl is seriously unhinged, you know that? Although, the shit Trace has her doing, it's no wonder. You think I'm fucked up? That guy takes the cake. She was all too happy to help her *mate* out." He laughed at the word. "She doesn't even know he's setting her ass up."

"What are talking about?" I asked slowly, the world still spinning.

He waved a dismissive hand. "I'm not sure of all the details, but Trace said she'll be on the next van to the facility. I'm just now starting to understand all the shit your uncle and grandfather were into, but apparently this alliance with the Norwood pack includes providing females —willing or otherwise—to a facility that's working on a cure or some shit to this fertility thing."

The missing shifters.

"Where is the facility?" I asked.

He gave me an indifferent look. "Not sure. We're supposed to go there in the next few weeks so we can see the progress they've made."

"And you have no idea where it is?" I pressed.

Cassian sighed, shaking his head. "Why the sudden inquisition? I thought we were having a nice conversation, but now you're interrogating me. I'm not sure I appreciate it when I'm trying to help us establish common ground."

A strangled laugh escaped me. "Conversation? Common ground? Are you *kidding* me?"

He gave me a confused look. "I thought we should catch up first. I'm trying to be polite."

"Polite would be *not* kidnapping me, Cassian!" I snapped, pushing myself into a sitting position. The world around me tilted a bit, the edges going fuzzy for a second.

Cassian rolled his eyes, standing up and wiping his gloves on his jeans. "You're part of my pack. We own you. I'm simply taking back what's ours."

I started to scramble to my feet and back away when I stumbled and nearly went sprawling. Glancing down, I saw the metal cuff around my ankle, chained around a boulder a few yards away.

I gave it another jerk, praying it would miraculously come loose.

It didn't.

"Sorry about that," he said, motioning to the chain. "I didn't want to have to spend all of our time together chasing you around when you woke up. As much fun as it would be, we're on a timetable."

Fear settled like a concrete block in my stomach. "Timetable?"

He glanced over the edge of the cliff we were on. "The road down there. Our ride will be here in about an hour. Not as much time as I would have liked, but we'll make do, right?" He turned, grinning at me. "Besides, once we're back at the Compound, we'll have as much time as we want."

"I'm not going anywhere with you," I spat vehemently. Every muscle in my body went tight, ready to fight and claw our way out of this.

He moved away from the edge, slowly walking towards me, every bit the predator. "Skye, I didn't come all this way just to see how you've been. I came here for *you*." He frowned. "Didn't Bella give you my message?"

I sucked in a sharp breath. "You're a fucking monster. How could you?"

Cassian rolled his eyes. "She was going to be my mate eventually. She should have known what to expect."

"You *raped* her!" I hissed, balling my hands into fists. "She's a kid!"

He sighed, shaking his head. "She's old enough."

"You let your friends take turns!" I jerked at the chains again, wishing I could wrap my hands around his throat.

He paused thinking. "She belongs to me, and sharing is caring."

"She's a person! She doesn't belong to you!" I yelled.

"Not anymore," he agreed. He made a face. "She seriously just wasn't cut out to be my mate. I'm just glad Linden finally sees that. She never stopped crying the whole damn time. I had to gag her to shut her up before we even got started."

"You're insane," I whispered, shaking my head. "You've completely lost it."

"Did you know most omegas only live about four years?" The sudden change of topic left me reeling.

"I mean, in our pack," he amended. "I'm sure in other packs omegas ... limp along like fucking dead weight for decades unless an Alpha is smart enough to get rid of them. Not every pack embraces what an omega is meant to be."

I was barely breathing, watching him like he was a snake about to strike.

"Your mom lasted seventeen *years*. That's incredible!" Cassian clapped his hands together, smiling like he had won a prize. His eyes slid over me. "Which made me think, as much of a fighter as you are? I'm sure you've got seventeen years in you, easy."

My eyes went wide, bile rising in my throat.

Cassian shrugged. "I mean, you won't technically be an omega since you'll be my mate. But you know I like to share with my friends. Besides, you killed Preston's brother. You definitely owe *him*."

The blood that had been roaring in my ears since I woke up went blessedly silent, the world going into high definition focus.

"I have a mate," I growled.

He snapped his fingers. "So, another question: rumor has it that this bond thing can be broken if you cheat." He grinned at me, his eyes glittering with something maniacal. "If we're holding you down, does that count as cheating? Or maybe it'll just be having me inside of you day after day? Or my child growing inside you one day?"

Horror crept over me.

He winked and tapped my nose. "Gotta admit, it would be a gorgeous kid." He glanced at his watch. "They should be here soon."

I looked down at the chain and realized I had zero hope of freeing myself.

My wolf growled, snarling and ready to attack in my head.

I dropped my head and took a slow breath, letting the mountain air fill my lungs as I let my shoulders relax, as I let my body release the tension coiled tight in me. I forced myself to clear my mind.

"What are you doing?" Cassian seemed amused.

"Accepting my fate," I said softly, opening my eyes and looking at him. I smiled slowly, feeling my wolf ripple under my skin.

He smirked at me. "Might be the smartest thing you've ever done." He took another step towards me. He reached out, grabbing the ends of my braid in his fingers and studying the texture.

I smiled at him, showing my teeth. "You don't get it," I said slowly, shaking my head.

"Oh?"

"I didn't mean I accept my fate as going with you to be your whore for the rest of my life. I have a mate that I love, and I'm not interested in downgrading," I explained, feeling my wolf stir in my chest. "I meant, I'm okay with dying today as long as I take you with me."

I didn't stop to think or gloat over the brief flash of worry in his eyes. I let my wolf take over, shifting suddenly. My smaller joint easily slipped through the cuff as I lunged at him.

I had the element of surprise, but it only got me the chance to clamp my teeth into Cassian's arm for a second before he shifted himself with a roar.

I immediately let go, dancing away from him and staying alert, but he was close to the edge. Leaping at him had caught him off guard, pushing him closer to the edge of the cliff.

I waited for my in, knowing I couldn't outright attack Cassian and win. I had barely survived a fight with Trace, and I knew Cassian was bigger and faster than Trace was when I fought him. I had seen Cassian take down several pack members over the years.

I hated to admit it, but the psycho was really good at being a psycho.

Cassian snarled at me, baring his teeth a second before he lunged, his tawny coat gleaming in the light. I moved as fast as I could, barely avoiding his teeth sinking into my back leg. I managed to put the fire he had built between us.

His blue eyes glittered in the firelight, his hackles raised and lips pulled back as he growled again at me.

Flames be damned, he launched himself through the fire, managing to knock me to the ground. His teeth caught my shoulder and I yelped in pain, blindly snapping my teeth until I felt them bite down on some part of him.

Instead of letting me go, he bit down harder, his teeth shredding the muscles of my shoulder. Trying not to scream in pain, I forced my jaws to clamp harder until I felt the delicate bones of his foreleg start to grind together.

With a growl he let me go and limped back, giving me enough of an opening to scramble backwards.

But it wasn't enough.

I couldn't put any weight on my front leg, which meant I was fighting with a serious disadvantage.

Growling, Cassian advanced on me, backing me against the mountain. I had no place left to go, and there was no way I could take him down.

I looked past him to the cliff, wondering if I had time to jump over the edge before he caught me.

I had no clue what was on the other side. No idea if it was a sheer drop off or a slope or some mixture of the two. Maybe I would be able to survive the fall ... but maybe not.

I looked back at Cassian, my decision made. If I had to go back to Long Mesa, I would. I would fight and survive as long as it took to get back to my pack. To my mate.

Remy.

I growled back, my back arching as I braced myself for him to attack.

*Skye.*

I could hear his voice in my head, clear as day, and it almost brought me to my knees.

I hated the way I had left things.

I was an idiot. A stupid, emotional idiot who acted like a brat storming out earlier.

*Skye. Hold on.*

My ear perked up as I realized I wasn't just thinking of Remy's voice, but I was actually hearing his voice.

He was coming.

I looked up to see Cassian hurl himself at me. I barely

scrambled forward, the back half of my body taking the brunt of the hit. My hips twisted as my legs slid out from under me, the air knocked from my lungs.

Wolves couldn't smile, but I could have sworn Cassian grinned at me, his teeth bared and chest heaving as he stood over me, victorious.

I tried to get up, but Cassian pressed one massive paw to my injured shoulder and pressed down. I collapsed with an inhuman scream. The pain lanced through me, spots dancing in my vision.

Cassian's jaws snapped, a roaring growl vibrating through his chest as he pinned me down.

I whimpered and stopped fighting, submitting the fight to him as wolf instinct kicked in.

Still, he kept adding his weight onto my shoulder. The shoulder was going numb as my body started going into shock.

And then it was simply gone.

I heard snarling and snapping, yelps and growls. It took several seconds, maybe minutes, for me to focus on the wolves fighting in front of me.

Remy and Cassian were slowly circling each other. Their wolves looked evenly matched, but I knew Remy was the better wolf. He was bigger, faster, and stronger.

I tried pushing myself up to my feet, but I could barely keep my balance on three legs.

Cassian went for Remy's face, but Remy dropped at the last second, his jaws closing around Cassian's throat and giving him a vicious shake that sent Cassian tumbling across the rock and ice. He stopped a foot from the edge, struggling to get to his feet.

Remy put himself between us, protecting me.

I wanted to reach out through the bond and tell Remy

all the things I never said earlier, but I was scared of breaking his concentration.

A rock skittered down the side of the mountain beside us, and I turned my head to see Trace coming down the side of the mountain. The dark brown wolf was snarling as he ran at us.

Remy noticed him, repositioning himself so he was between both of them, still keeping me behind him, as Cassian finally got up.

I knew Remy was a strong fighter. I had watched him throw Trace around like a rag doll. But taking on two alphas at the same time?

*Remy.*

His ears flicked back, the only sign he heard me.

*I'm sorry.*

He growled as Trace and Cassian started to advance.

*I love you.*

I only had to run five steps. Five agonizing steps that had my shoulder screaming and my leg nearly giving out.

But those five steps gave me enough momentum to barrel into Cassian with enough force to pitch him over the edge of the cliff.

The only problem was my leg had finally given out completely, and I had no way of stopping myself from going over with him.

There wasn't a slope on the other side.

It was a sheer eighty-foot drop to another rocky shelf below.

I was vaguely aware of my body soaring through the air.

I heard more than felt my body crash into the ground, the snapping of bones and tearing of flesh. Pain seared across me, a raging inferno that finally engulfed me into nothing.

I was swimming in a mud pit.

My limbs were tired and sluggish, nothing made sense, and everything was suffocating as it pressed in around me. It was dark and lonely, and I wanted to give up and sink back down, but I could hear muted voices pulling me up.

Pulling me out.

After trying for several minutes, I finally managed to blink my eyes open. The room looked vaguely familiar, white and sterile with a few beds separated by white curtains. I turned my head to the side and could make out people standing in the doorway, their voices quiet as they talked.

Talked about *me*.

I tried to open my mouth, tried to let them know I was here, but the words got stuck in my throat. My tongue had turned into a thick wad of cotton in my mouth. Frustration started to bubble up in me.

Then a dark head snapped up, a hand flying up to stop someone from talking a second before he shoved past several adults.

"Skye." Remy's voice was more soothing than all the cool water in the world could be on my desert dry throat. "Hey, babe. There you are."

His hand grabbed mine, infinitely gentle as he lifted it and pressed his mouth to it. Blinking, I realized there were actual tears in his eyes. A sensation of panic fluttered in my chest.

I swallowed roughly, flinching at the rough sensation. A straw appeared in front of my mouth and I greedily sucked in mouthfuls, taking the time to realize the other people in the room were the campus doctor who treated Katy, Elias, Gabe, and my mother.

Mom smoothed my hair away from my face, her voice catching on a sob. "Jesus, baby." She pressed her forehead to mine.

I let the straw go and cleared my throat, still wincing at the pain. "What ... What happened?"

Gabe pulled my mom back gently, giving the doctor space to move in. He flashed a light in my eyes, softly prodding at different parts of me.

"Skye, do you know where you are?" he asked, his blue eyes intelligent and keen as he waited for my answer.

My eyes went to the nametag at his chest. Dr. Lupin.

A snort escaped me before I could stop it. How appropriate.

His brows went up. "Skye?"

Remy smirked at me, his hand squeezing around mine. He knew exactly what I was thinking. "She's laughing at your name."

Dr. Lupin rolled his eyes. Clearly this wasn't the first time someone commented on his name. Probably wouldn't be the last either.

"Right," he said with a sigh. "Do you know where you are?"

"The school infirmary," I murmured, my eyes moving around the room slowly.

"And do you remember what happened before?" he asked carefully, making a note on the chart in his hand.

I frowned, the thoughts jumbled.

But then everything snapped into picture perfect place.

"Rhodes!" I gasped, my eyes going frantically to Remy.

He settled a hand on my shoulder, easing me back against the bed. "He's fine, babe. Whatever Sierra drugged him with just knocked him out, but he's fine. He's back at the cabin."

My breathing went ragged as I kept flipping through the memories. I looked at him again and felt as my chin started to tremble. "Cassian?"

"Dead," Remy replied softly, no remorse in his eyes.

"Dead?" I echoed.

"You tackled him and you both went over the cliff. The fall ... broke his spine," Remy told me quietly. "He died instantly."

Dr. Lupin cleared his throat, catching my attention. He passed the clipboard to Elias, who offered me a small, encouraging smile. "How do you feel right now, Skye? How's your pain?"

"Everything hurts, but considering I fell off a mountain, that's to be expected, right?" I still could only whisper my words, anything more made my head pound.

He moved to the foot of my bed, lifting the covers off my bare feet. "Can you flex your right foot?"

Not sure what he was getting at, I pushed down with my right foot.

"Excellent. And now your left?"

I repeated the motion with the opposite foot, arching a brow.

He straightened and looked at me, folding the covers back over my toes. "Can you raise each of your arms?"

By the time I got to the second arm, I felt like I was a puppet. "Anything else?"

Dr. Lupin was frowning when he looked at me, but then his gaze went to Mom and Gabe. "I can't explain it, but it appears all motor functions are working. She's alert and talking. There doesn't seem to be any cognitive impairment."

With a cry of relief, my mom hugged Gabe and then Elias.

I looked at Remy, confused as hell, but he looked as relieved as the adults.

"What's going on?" I asked, my voice tiny.

"Skye," Dr. Lupin started as Mom grabbed my other hand, "you've been unconscious for almost three weeks."

"What?" I whispered, stunned. That couldn't be right. It felt like I had just been fighting with Cassian on the mountain.

"You and Cassian both went over the side of the mountain," Remy said slowly, his voice rough with emotion. Regret and anguish filled his gorgeous eyes, making my heart wrench painfully in my chest. "You were barely breathing when I got to you."

"You broke all four of your legs," Dr. Lupin added. "You had a skull fracture, dislocated your jaw, and that's not counting the bite on your shoulder that went down to the bone. For what you went through ... I honestly didn't think you would make it out of the first surgery."

"I had surgery?"

"Five," Dr. Lupin told me. "The only reason you're still here is you've been too unstable to move."

"That," Elias added, finally joining the conversation,

"and we weren't sure how to explain transporting an overly large wolf across state lines if stopped."

I looked down at my hand wrapped in Remy's and frowned. I had been a wolf when I went over. I didn't remember shifting back.

Elias sat down in a small rolling chair and wheeled it to my side. "You didn't shift back into human form until a few days ago."

"When I was unconscious?" I asked, still confused as hell.

"The best explanation is that your wolf sustained the injuries, letting you heal that way because, well, had you been human, you absolutely would have died," Dr. Lupin said bluntly.

I flinched, and Remy sucked in a sharp breath.

"Doctor," Gabe murmured gently, clearly trying to steer him away from that topic.

"It's true," Elias said, his eyes bright and kind. He pulled off his spectacles, folding them and dropping them into the front pocket of his button down. "Our human bodies are infinitely more fragile than our wolf's. Usually once a shifter body is unconscious, the wolf recedes and the dominant human form takes over. The human mind must cognitively allow the wolf to exist. It's why you were able to suppress your wolf for so long. And then you had to learn to summon her all over."

"So, why didn't I shift back?" I asked slowly.

Elias smiled. "I can only think your wolf knew shifting back would be disastrous. The bite severed what would have been your human subclavian artery. You would have bled out before we even got you back to the school to treat you."

Mom moaned low in her throat, burying her face against my hand.

"But I didn't shift back. My wolf ... didn't go away?" First, I couldn't get her to come out and now she wanted equal body time?

"I truly believe it had more to do with the fact that Remy stayed in wolf form with you the entire time," Elias said breathlessly, his eyes bright.

My gaze shot to Remy. "You what?"

He shrugged, clearly as confused as I was. "I don't know. But I could still ... feel you when I was a wolf. So, I stayed shifted. I didn't shift back until you did."

"We have barely begun to tap the surface of what a bonded wolf can do. We know it increases their years of living amongst other things. Why can't it help the healing process, too?" Elias murmured.

"There's no science to prove that," Dr. Lupin added, clearly only willing to give Elias so much latitude with his theory.

"Why else would Remington feel the compulsion to stay in wolf form and stay at her side?" Elias countered, spinning in the chair to face him.

"We can debate this later," Gabe interrupted. "Skye probably needs rest now."

"Apparently I've been resting for three weeks," I muttered, not wanting to admit I was already getting sleepy.

"He's right, honey," Mom said, smoothing my hair back again. "Get some sleep."

Dr. Lupin and Elias moved to the door.

"I'm glad to see you're awake and doing well, Ms. Markham," Elias said, smiling once again at me.

"Thanks, Elias."

Dr. Lupin cleared his throat. "Don't visit too long. Skye does need rest." His gaze moved to Remy, growing serious. "You need rest, too. Now that Skye has started to recover, it might be time to return to your cabin where you can get a good night's sleep."

Remy nodded, but I could see from the set of his jaw he didn't plan on going anywhere.

As they left, I looked back at my mom, taking in her messy ponytail and simple jeans and flannel shirt.

"How long have you been here?" I asked her, still amazed she was here.

Mom glanced back at Gabe. "We flew out within hours of finding out what happened. Mallory came, too. She left last week to be with the twins."

"They definitely need adult supervision," Remy cracked, winking at me.

I wheezed out a small laugh, but my ribs ached with the movement.

"Easy," he admonished, settling a hand against my stomach. "Take it easy."

"You came, too?" I asked Gabe, amazed he would come out here.

Gabe nodded. "Of course. You're family, Skye. And with everything that happened, I needed to have a few meetings. Things are going to change around GPA now."

A tendril of worry wound its way inside me. "Like what?"

Gabe smiled. "Nothing that matters now. Get some rest. We can talk about everything soon. As soon as you're cleared for travel, you'll fly back to Blackwater with us."

"But school—"

"We basically missed the last part of the semester, babe," Remy said wryly. "Winter break starts in five days anyway and we would be going home then anyway."

That shut me up.

"If you two wanted to skip finals so badly, next time ask

for a note or fake the flu," Gabe said lightly, his eyes sparkling. "No need to literally jump off a cliff."

Remy rolled his eyes as I tried to hold in a laugh. "Ha, ha, Dad."

Mom squeezed my hand once more and let me go. "I'll be back in the morning, okay? But if you need anything—"

"You'll come running," I finished.

"I love you."

I grinned. "I love you more."

Her eyes narrowed. "I love you most." She looked at Remy. "Make sure she rests?"

"I promise," he swore, his eyes warm as he looked at me.

Gabe and Mom headed out, closing the door behind them. And then it was just Remy and me.

Finally.

"Rem—"

"Me first?" he begged, his eyes pleading.

I nodded slowly. "One condition."

He raised his brows, waiting.

With a grunt and a grimace, I pushed back a few inches.

Remy shot to his feet. "Skye—"

I patted the now empty space. "If we're doing this, I want you right next to me."

His eyes slid shut for a second before he moved, gently easing into the bed beside me. He worked an arm under me until I was resting my head on his shoulder, his other arm wrapped loosely around my waist.

"Better," I murmured, inhaling his scent.

I stiffened.

"What? Did I hurt you?" he asked quickly.

"How bad do I smell?" I demanded. Three weeks in a

bed with no shower didn't sound like I wanted him this close.

He chuckled, the sound soothing. "You smell amazing."

"Liar," I muttered.

Dipping his head, he sniffed my hair. "You smell like you. I love that smell."

Okay, as far as compliments went, that was pretty solid.

"I'm sorry," he started after a second. "I'm so sorry for what I said. I was scared and worried ... I should have handled things differently."

"Maybe if I hadn't acted like a brat," I countered, fully ready to admit my role in this mess, "you wouldn't have said what you said. Jesus, and when I said this was like Long Mesa—I did not mean that. You, Blackwater ... it's nothing like that place."

"I know you didn't mean it," he replied with a sigh.

I pulled back to look him in the eye. "I still shouldn't have said it."

"And I shouldn't have ordered you to do something."

"So, next time," I said slowly, "you ask my opinion and I think before I speak? And maybe then I won't end up in a coma?"

He winced. "Not funny, Skye. Seeing you go over that cliff ... I thought I lost you. I've never been that scared in my life."

"Sorry," I murmured, wrapping my arm around his torso and squeezing as much as my muscles would allow.

"Never do that again," he demanded. "Please."

"I promise I will never shove Cassian off a cliff again," I vowed, but then sobered. "He's really dead?"

"He's really dead," Remy answered. "I'm a little pissed I didn't get to beat the shit out of him first, but the end result was what I wanted."

"I've killed two people," I said softly as the realization slammed into me.

"Yeah," Remy said, his arms going tight around me. "Both times to protect someone in your pack. You're not a killer, Skye."

"You sound pretty sure about that."

"I've never been more sure." He never wavered once, conviction strong in his tone. His confidence gave me confidence.

"What happened to Trace?" I had almost forgotten about his appearance at the end.

"He's gone."

I reared back. "He's dead?"

"No," Remy said with a dark chuckle. "But he probably wishes he was. He took off. The entire Norwood pack did, actually. A couple of other packs, too. They cleared out before you even made it into surgery."

"Wow," I whispered. "What does that mean for the school?"

"That next semester we won't have as many people here?" he guessed with a halfhearted shrug. "I don't know. Odds of them coming back are slim."

Something was flashing in the back of my mind, a memory I couldn't quite grasp.

"Rhodes is really okay?" I pressed, snuggling into his side. The heat radiating from his body was sinking into my bones, making me lethargic and drowsy.

His fingers played with the ends of my hair. "He's really okay. He feels like shit, but he's fine."

"It wasn't his fault!" I protested.

"He still blamed himself for buying Sierra's act."

"Sierra! Where is that bitch?"

"She took off with the Norwood pack as best as we can tell. Her parents are a wreck about it. They came out last week to collect the rest of her things, but she's gone."

Gone.

*Gone.*

"Rem," I said slowly, a memory starting to form. "When I was on the cliff, Cassian said something. Something about the missing shifters."

Remy went still beneath me before pushing himself up partially to look down at me. "What do you mean?"

I swallowed, trying to focus. "He said ... My uncle and grandfather had some kind of alliance with the Norwood pack. He mentioned something about a facility?" I frowned, my head throbbing as I forced myself to remember.

"A facility?"

"Yeah. Some place where they were working on a cure for the fertility issue? He said they were going to visit it in a couple weeks." I gasped. "You need to get someone to follow my uncle. If he goes, then you can follow him and see where they are!"

"I'll tell my dad," Remy said, then hesitated, "but if they were planning a visit a couple weeks ago, then odds are it already happened. That's if it even happened after Cassian died."

"Has ... has my uncle made contact?" I asked, kind of terrified to know the answer.

Remy gave a small nod. "Yeah. He contacted my dad. Made some big production about Blackwater stealing females from the Long Mesa pack. Apparently, he's going to bring it to the Council at the Summit for a formal inquisition."

My fingers curled around the fabric of his shirt, fisting it. "What does that mean?"

"I don't know," he whispered. "Technically you all left

on your own free will and we offered sanctuary, but it wasn't done through the proper channels."

I bit my lip. He was right; pack law had specific ways of requesting a pack transfer. Mom and I had completely disregarded them all. There were sanctum laws in place, but those were difficult to enforce.

"The Council could start asking questions. Want to interview you and your mom to make sure we didn't kidnap you or something."

"I'll happily tell anyone who will listen what those assholes did to me, to my mom. To Bella. Cassian didn't even care, you know? He was practically joking about it when we were alone on the mountain." I shuddered in revulsion, remembering how he taunted me.

Remy went oddly silent beside me. So much so that I finally looked to make sure he wasn't sleeping. He wasn't. He was wide awake, his expression fierce and wary at the same time.

"What?" I asked, lifting my head.

He visibly swallowed, glancing down for a second. "This changes nothing, okay?"

That didn't sound good.

"Okay," I replied, dragging out the word.

"When I got to where you two were, I saw ..." He trailed off, his eyes glittering with something dark. "Your clothes were shredded. Skye, if he——"

I quickly covered his lips with my fingers. "Because I shifted suddenly. He didn't—nothing like that happened."

"It wouldn't matter to me if it did," he emphasized gently, his fingers trailing across the curve of my jaw.

"But it didn't," I promised, leaning into his touch. "He said some crazy shit, I shifted, he shifted, and ... you know the rest."

"What did he say?"

"Nothing that matters," I answered honestly. "Nothing that was true."

His eyes drifted to my lips, and I read his intention and closed my mouth.

"No toothbrush in three weeks," I reminded him through tight lips.

He laughed, a deep belly laugh that made his eyes crinkle at the corners. "I don't care. I haven't kissed you in three weeks."

"Three weeks is a long time," I admitted, my eyes falling to his full mouth.

"Okay, maybe not exactly three weeks," he relented. "I might have tried kissing you once to see if you would wake up."

"Like *Sleeping Beauty*?" I giggled.

"Yes," he grumbled. "And if you tell Katy ..."

"You'll what?" I challenged, still smiling.

"Nothing," he replied softly, his eyes sweeping across my face. "I'd do nothing. You own me, Skye Markham. I'm yours."

"One condition," I countered with a whisper.

"Okay." He smirked at me.

"You can be mine if I can be yours." My heart flipped in my chest as his brown eyes melted.

He pressed his mouth to mine, slowly moving his lips against mine for a long moment, before barely pulling back an inch. "Deal."

**46**

———

The hot chocolate I held in my hands wasn't nearly as good as Remy's, but the one from the café was pretty good, too, and definitely warmed my body as the bitter December night air whipped around. I sipped at the drink and leaned back against Remy's chest. His hands rested on my hips casually as he kept talking to Rhodes.

The center of town was packed with shifters waiting for the annual Christmas tree lighting to commence. Town tradition had the Alpha family turn on the lights three days before Christmas.

The towering pine in the town square was dark, but the white lights strung between the downtown buildings gave a soft glow. Almost every storefront was decked out with some holiday theme, and all businesses were open to capitalize on the fact that so many shifters were milling around.

Mom had made my hot chocolate between customers at the diner. I could still see her in the big windows of the restaurant as she moved easily, smiling and talking with customers. She really seemed to love her job.

Zara had started working there as well, but Bella still kept to herself. She was supposed to return to GPA with us in a few weeks, but I wouldn't be surprised if she took the rest of the year off. She was doing better, but she was still fragile. Hearing about Cassian's death definitely seemed to help with the healing process, but she was still shaky. She and Zara had stayed in tonight. Crowds seemed to unnerve Bella.

Remy, Rhodes, Katy, and I had staked out a spot a few yards away from the tree, opting to stand instead of using the folding chairs set out in front of where the tree would be lit.

I craned my neck, looking at the top of the dark tree. I had only seen a couple of Christmas trees, but they were quickly becoming something I loved. I had even taken to reading in front of the small Christmas tree Mom and I had in our apartment.

Katy's phone started to ring and she pulled it from her jacket pocket, fumbling with the buttons through her gloves. Turning on the screen, Maren's face appeared.

"Hi, love!" Katy greeted.

I leaned over her shoulder and gave Maren a wave of my own that she returned with a bright smile.

"I'll be back," Katy told us, walking away to video chat with Maren. Katy was planning to go to Brooks Ridge the day after Christmas and visit with Maren and her family for the rest of winter break.

I was going to miss her, not that I would have seen her much if she stayed.

Remy and I had come back to Blackwater a few days after I had woken up, which was the start of winter break. Thanks to missing the last three weeks of school, GPA had allowed us to bring all our assignments home to catch up over the break. We had to take, and pass, our finals before we went back to school for the spring semester.

Holding my cup in one hand, I slowly rotated my left wrist. I had mostly healed from the fall, but some of my joints were still stiff and recovering. The cold didn't seem to help.

"Are you okay?" Rhodes demanded, his eyes watching me carefully.

If it were possible, Rhodes was more protective of me than Remy was.

Rhodes had come into my room the day after I woke up and repeatedly apologized for what happened even though it definitely wasn't his fault. I also learned that while Remy and I were shifted during my recovery, Rhodes set up a rotating series of pack members to guard our room, with him taking the bulk of the shifts.

Even though the Norwood pack was gone and Cassian was dead, Rhodes wouldn't relent.

While Remy and his dad had meetings about what I learned about the facility, Rhodes was often in my room playing cards or introducing me to all the Star Wars movies. He hung out with me just as much as Katy and Larkin did, sometimes more.

"I'm fine," I assured him, feeling Remy chuckle at my back.

He thought his best friend's sudden devotion to me was adorable.

I thought Rhodes needed to devote more attention to another female.

Rhodes didn't look convinced. "Are you still taking the pain meds?"

"She's fine," Remy told him, still laughing. "She just needs to stretch her muscles sometimes or they get stiff."

Rhodes huffed under his breath. "Fine."

I reached out and touched his arm. "I'm good, really. Thanks, Rhodey." I adopted the nickname for him after an *Avengers* marathon he had me sit through.

He smirked. "Anytime, Skywalker."

He had finally got me to watch the original three *Stars Wars* movies.

Remy shook his head with another sigh. "You two are a mess."

I tilted my head up to look at him. "But you love us."

His eyes went soft a second before his lips descended on mine. "Yeah, I do." His arms wrapped tighter around my waist, and I snuggled back into him.

I heard Rhodes suck in a sharp breath and my head turned in his direction. "What?"

He didn't say anything, but I followed his gaze to where Larkin was across the town square with Konnor and Kyle, laughing about something.

I sighed, feeling Remy's chest rise and fall as he mirrored my sigh with one of his own.

"Rhodes—"

I cut myself off when one of the twins pointed to something above Larkin's head, hanging from the awning of a store.

Mistletoe.

I winced and checked Rhodes, who looked like he was ready to grind his teeth to dust. He still hadn't talked to Larkin, and Larkin had definitely decided she was done waiting for Rhodes to wake up.

I hadn't told Larkin about what Rhodes confessed to me. Larkin was my best friend, but Rhodes was also my friend, and I knew he wasn't ready to take that step.

But watching one twin and then the other kiss her as

several adults smiled and cheered might be the kick in the ass he needed.

"I'm leaving," Rhodes announced quietly.

Or maybe not.

"Rhodes, come on, man," Remy tried.

"Hang out with us," I added, giving him my best puppy eyes.

Rhodes shrugged, ducking his head as he shoved his hands into the pockets of his coat. "I just can't deal with that right now. Besides, I should check on my dad. This time of year always sucks for him."

"You can always stay with us," Remy offered sincerely. I knew it bugged him that Rhodes was basically on his own all the time.

"I know," Rhodes told him with a small smile. He took several steps backwards. "I'll see you guys tomorrow?"

"Yeah," I said sadly, watching as he left. I took another sip of my drink and offered Remy some. "Do you think he'll ever tell her how he feels?"

"I don't know," he answered, passing the drink back to me. "Rhodes is complicated. He really thinks he's doing the right thing."

My gaze drifted to where Larkin was still joking with the twins, her cheeks flushed and eyes sparkling as she giggled. She looked happy.

"Our best friends are idiots," I muttered.

He barked out a laugh, pressing his forehead to the top of my head. "They really are."

"Should make next semester interesting," I commented.

"Speaking of next semester," he started slowly, "what would you think of moving into the cabin?"

I turned in his arms, surprised. "With you?"

He rolled his eyes. "Yes, with me."

I gave him an incredulous look. "We can't."

"Why can't we?" he countered.

"Because the school has rules," I reminded him. Rules we definitely had broken, but sleeping over once or twice in the midst of trouble was one thing. Teenage shifters shacking up on school grounds was a whole different thing.

"They do," he agreed, "but we're mates. That makes things a little different."

I went quiet for a moment, thinking it over. Part of me was all in. I loved Remy, and I loved spending time with him.

But part of me was a little scared. Since Thanksgiving, we had done barely more than kiss since I was recovering and now, we were trying to cram a months' work of school into two weeks. What kind of expectations went along with moving in?

"Hey." His hand came up to cradle my jaw, his warm breath smelled like peppermint and chocolate as it fanned my face. "There's no wrong answer here. It's just an option we can consider. And you moving in doesn't mean you have to sleep in my room. You can have your own room."

"What about Rhodes?" I asked. I finished my drink and tossed it in the trash can a few feet away.

Remy shrugged. "He can stay or go to the dorms. If you're more comfortable without him there—"

I shook my head. "No. I don't want to kick Rhodes out. He needs his friends around."

He nodded, his expression slightly relieved. We both knew Rhodes got zero support at home, so at school Remy tried to compensate for that.

"Can I think about it?" I gave him a small, hopeful smile.

He grinned in response, kissing the tip of my cold nose and then my lips. He coaxed my mouth open, his tongue sliding languidly against mine. After several seconds, he lifted his head. "Of course you can."

Smiling, I pressed my head against his chest, wrapping my arms around his narrow waist. The feel of his arms banding around me made me sigh, completely content in that moment.

"How did I get so lucky?" I asked softly.

"It helps that you're gorgeous," he replied seriously.

I jerked back to see him grinning down at me. A second later he kissed me, his touch and taste engulfing my senses.

I pulled away with a laugh as Mallory moved to the edge of the platform. After a second of searching, her eyes found Remy and me, and she waved him over.

"Time to go do your thing," I told him with a grin, pulling away.

He gave me a funny look. "You're coming with me."

I blinked. "I thought this was an Alpha family thing."

"And you're family," he reminded me, taking my hand and pulling me to the stage with him.

Dax and Sam were already there with their parents as we climbed up the stairs. Katy joined them a second later.

"Everyone ready?" Gabe asked, looking over his family with bright eyes.

Mallory slipped between Katy and me, wrapping an arm around each of us. "We're all ready."

My heart warmed at that. Looking up, I saw Mom and Zoe come out of the café, joined by Michael. The crowd slowly quieted, drawing closer as Gabe went to the center and lifted a microphone.

"Good evening, friends," he greeted warmly, looking out at his pack.

Our pack.

Mallory let me go and went to join him. I smiled when

Gabe reached out and tucked her into his side as Remy did the same to me.

"This has been a year of change for our pack, and for my family," Gabe went on, his voice rich and smooth as he spoke. "Next year will likely prove challenging, but I know that as a pack, we can face anything together."

A cheer rose up in the crowd.

"Happy holidays, friends. Here's to another incredible year." Gabe put the microphone back in its stand and stepped back. Mallory handed him a small box with a switch.

Seconds later, the Christmas tree lit up in a brilliant explosion of color that had the crowd gasping and then clapping loudly.

My eyes were riveted to the tree until I felt something cool against my throat.

My hand flew to the base of my neck and I felt something there. I pulled it away from my chest, blinking back tears when I saw a necklace that was identical to the ones Katy and Mallory had. The moon with a diamond chip for a star nestled into the crescent.

The Blackwater symbol.

Remy finished closing the clasp at the nape of my neck. "I thought you needed one of these, too."

I turned, throwing my arms around his neck. "Thank you. I love it."

His arms went around my waist, lifting my feet from the stage as fat snowflakes started falling from the night sky. "I love you."

Moving my head back, I looked at his eyes. Those warm brown eyes that looked like melted chocolate. "I love you, too."

The kiss he gave me had my toes curling and my mind

spinning until I realized the clapping and cheering was no longer about the Christmas tree, but about us.

With a laugh, I broke our kiss, ducking my head into his chest as the pack kept going, adding whistles and shouts to the cheers. Apparently, the pack approved.

*My* pack approved.

# EPILOGUE

Another female was dead.

Sighing, the doctor removed his glasses, setting them on the workspace beside the bed. Looking over the female's body, the doctor bowed his head. This was the thirteenth dead female in a row.

They only had a few females left, but all signs pointed to the same outcome.

They would all die, and all of this would be for nothing.

"Doctor?"

Turning, the doctor saw the orderly standing in the doorway to the operating room, likely coming to dispose of the body.

He was so tired of the bodies. Of the failures.

"I was sent to get her," the young man stammered, looking entirely too young for the task of lifting the female into the basement incinerator. "Get the body."

Always the body.

He had quickly drilled into the heads of his staff that these women were not females or persons. They were subjects, vessels to be used in the name of science. It was the only way to stomach the work that needed to be done.

It was easy to explain in theory. Infinitely harder to implement in practice.

Stepping aside, the doctor picked up his glasses, waving the boy forward. "Go ahead. We've extracted all the samples we need from this one."

He left the room, heading for his office a few doors down. He wasn't surprised to find the man waiting for him inside.

He wasn't happy, but then, the benefactor was never happy.

"Another dead?" His deep voice rang with disappointment.

Nodding, the doctor moved to his seat. He reached for the stack of charts on the glass desk, flipping open the top one. Taking a stamp out of his desk, he slapped the 'DECEASED' mark across her image before closing the file.

The man stood by the window, looking down at the world beneath his feet. "I expected better results."

"Then get me better candidates!" the doctor finally snapped. The sudden surge of frustration ebbed as quickly as it rose, leaving him pale when he realized the tone he had used with the man before him.

"You're saying I'm not providing adequate samples?" The benefactor never turned or showed his displeasure, but his tone was arctic. He rarely showed any sort of emotion aside from annoyed indifference.

"We've exhausted every human option to solving the problem. We need to start exploring the wolf aspect," the doctor explained, his voice small and tired. "Lone wolves and unmated pack members are not giving us the results we expected. The results we *need*. Age may also play a part in the degradation of the cells for the procedure, but I think it's their pack connection."

The man turned, his eyes hard. "What do you need?"

The doctor leaned forward. "Find me younger females, preferably those who have an established mate."

"How young? Thirties? Twenties?" The man looked intrigued by this new prospect. A new option.

"The younger the better," the doctor sighed, rubbing his forehead. "But they need to have an established mate or potential mate. No more single, lone wolves."

"You're asking me to have my men remove a young female ... from her mate?" The benefactor snorted at the audacity of the suggestion.

With a sigh, the doctor rubbed his temples. "Unless you're prepared to witness the extinction of our species, yes. The time for quietly stealing inconsequential, uncommitted females is over. I understand it will bring a new level of scrutiny and outrage in the community, but we need this. We need something to turn the tide. We need a proverbial white whale."

The benefactor smirked, looking back at the window. "I think you mean a white wolf, doctor."

# ACKNOWLEDGEMENTS

First and foremost, thank you to God from whom all things are possible. This book is literally proof of that. Thank You for gifting me with a love of words and writing, and a lifetime of hearing voices in my head with stories to be told.

Considering I never, ever expected this book to ever see the light of day, there are a few people who made this book possible, and to who I owe all the things:

Krista Davis - my bestie and my sister in every way but blood. Thank you for listening to me bounce ideas off of you, for reading the very beginnings of this book (and countless others), and for pushing me to be the best version of myself. I love you more than all my makeup. And glitter. And … everything. Thank you for holding my hand when I need it, kicking my butt when I need it, and always loving me.

Jessica Baker - the smallest girl with the biggest personality and heart. Thank you for your friendship and support and for all of the horror movie recs. I am so insanely blessed to have you in my life. #HellHouse4Eva

Valerie Fink - the woman who pushed me to follow my gut and be true to my characters. Every time I think about a scene or get stuck, I hear you reminding me to "always be true to your character." Your feedback and support and love made this book what it is. I owe you a peanut butter and jelly sandwich.

Vonetta Young - the person who has championed this book the hardest. Without you, this book would be buried in a well where not even Uncle No-Neck could pull it out. Your passion and beauty are awe-inspiring. Also, you totally owe Alyna (my girl!!!) a trip to Disney or a trip to the well. Depends on the day.

Jen Fisher - Thank you for all the Panera dates and insanely long conversations; the brain-storming sessions and for also never making me walk home (seriously, *thank you*). There's a permanent spot being held on my shelf for your book.

Massive thanks to my family, who has dealt with all my crazy; the years of me hoarding books and daydreaming about characters that existed in my head.

My amazing Mom and Dad, who have stood by me way more than 70x7. Thank you for always being there for me and for being such an amazing example of the very best a person can be.

Shoutout and hugs to my sister, Sherry, for being my movie watching co-pilot.

My not-so-little-brother, Micah … There aren't words for how much I love you, and how insanely proud I am of you. Plus, you gave me another amazing sister when you married Lauren (who is my go-to girl when I need a meme to laugh over or a partner in prayer).

Thank you to my incredible nieces, Aria and Nora, for showing me that every day has smiles and giggles tucked in them. Thank you for every single time you burst into my room when I was writing to show me a card you created (Aria) or a pebble you found (Nora).

Nicole Sanchez - there's no one else in the world I would rather marry, and I'm holding a spot on my shelf for you, too.

For my friends who read super early versions of this book: Lisa Carina Gaibler, Asis Gonzalez, Geri Novak, Brigid Kemmerer, Kelly Wilmer, Jennifer Edwards Whiteoak, ChrisAnn Simek, and Alex Grayson - thank you so freaking much for taking the time to read this book, giving me feedback, and encouraging me to keep going. You guys are amazeballs.

This book would not be possible without the amazing support of Elle Christensen who helped walk me through a lot of publishing steps. Thank goodness I found a friend like you. Or, I guess I should say thanks, Rochelle Paige for introducing us. And thanks for lending me your sister to talk to (Roni is the best).

Shout out to some other friends who have supported and inspired me through this journey: Diana Chetelat, Jennifer Armentrout, Stephanie Brown, and Christina La Forest.

Thank you to every single blogger, publicist, author, agent, and editor I've ever met. In some way you helped shape me into the writer I am today.

Finally, thank you to every single reader who picked up this book. If you're holding this in your hands right now, reading this line: Thank You. There truly are not enough ways to describe the surreal joy of letting me tell you a story.

# ABOUT THE AUTHOR

Hannah McBride has been many things in her life: a restaurant manager, a clinical research coordinator, a dreamer, a makeup brand ambassador, an event coordinator, a blogger, and more. But at heart, she's always been a writer, and in 2020 she decided to make it official. Good luck stopping her now.

# ALSO BY HANNAH MCBRIDE

Blackwater Pack Series:

SANCTUM

BROKEN

PREY

LEGACY

SCARS (coming Winter 2022)

For giveaways, teasers, and overall fangirling about books, join
the Facebook Group:

BLACKWATER PACK

Mad World Series:

MAD WORLD (coming Fall 2021)